ECLIPSE THE MOON

ALSO BY JESSIE MIHALIK

Hunt the Stars

Polaris Rising

Aurora Blazing

Chaos Reigning

The Queen's Gambit

The Queen's Advantage

The Queen's Triumph

ECLIPSE THE MOON

A NOVEL

JESSIE MIHALIK

This is a work of fiction. Names, characters, places, and incidents are products of the author's imagination or are used fictitiously and are not to be construed as real. Any resemblance to actual events, locales, organizations, or persons, living or dead, is entirely coincidental.

HarperCollins books may be purchased for educational, business, or sales promotional use. For information, please email the Special Markets Department at SPsales@harpercollins.com.

FIRST EDITION

Designed by Paula Russell Szafranski
Fox art © Alexdarfox / Shutterstock.com

Library of Congress Cataloging-in-Publication Data has been applied for.

ISBN 978-0-06-305106-5

22 23 24 25 26 LSC 10 9 8 7 6 5 4 3 2 1

To my favorite brother.
Even if you weren't my only brother,
you'd still be my favorite.
Love you!

And to Dustin, my heart.

ACKNOWLEDGMENTS

While I can write a story on my own, it takes a team to turn it into a book, and I'd like to thank the following people for their help and support:

Thanks to Sarah E Younger, my fabulous agent. I'm so glad we get to work together!

Thanks to Tessa Woodward, my awesome editor. Your uncanny ability to see exactly how to get to the story I meant to tell always astounds and delights me. And thanks to the entire team at Harper Voyager who work their magic every day to get my books into readers' hands.

Thanks to Tracy Smith and Patrick Ferguson for listening to me complain, reading early drafts, and being generally awesome people!

Thanks to Ilona, Gordon, Bree, and Donna for all of the help, support, encouragement, and cheerleading. I really, really appreciate it!

And finally, thanks to Dustin, who puts up with me while I'm on deadline and is always my first and most supportive reader. I love you!

ECLIPSE THE MOON

CHAPTER ONE

I settled into my usual spot at the galley table with a gently steaming cup of hot chocolate. The rare treat wasn't enough to break me out of the slump I was in, so I set a timer on my comm and gave myself five solid minutes to brood.

It was often difficult to find time alone in the common areas on a smaller ship like *Starlight's Shadow,* especially with eight people aboard now, but it was mid-morning, and the galley was blessedly empty. The large space had seating for twenty around two big tables, and a long bar separated the dining area from the food prep area.

I had just worked up a really terrific moody stare when Tavi swept into the room. The captain's golden-tan skin was flushed with color, and she'd pulled her long, curly hair up into a messy bun on top of her head. I didn't know how Octavia Zarola managed to be effortlessly beautiful even when she looked like she'd just rolled out of her bunk far later than usual, but her satisfied smile and glowing joy certainly helped.

At least one of us had had a fun night.

In truth, I was delighted that Tavi had found happiness with Torran Fletcher, the former Valovian general who'd lured us into Valovian space with the promise of a lucrative job. Tavi's hard shell hid a soft heart, and if Torran had broken it, I would've broken *him*. Everyone underestimated me because I was petite and delicate-looking, with my rainbow hair and sunny smile, but I hadn't survived the war without learning a few tricks.

Not that they would've done me much good against a Valovian telekinetic, but I would've tried it anyway.

Luna chirruped a greeting from her place on Tavi's shoulder. The small, fluffy white burbu was part pet, part mascot, and all imperiousness. She rode around on our shoulders often enough that Tavi had fashioned padded shoulder guards for everyone in the crew to keep the burbu's sharp claws out of our skin.

Luna jumped down and headed straight for her food bowl. A wave of longing pierced me when she found the bowl empty. The small animal, native to Valovian space, was mildly telepathic, much like the Valoffs themselves.

Tavi ignored Luna's theatrics and stopped to peer at me. "Kee, why are you scowling at the table?"

"I'm brooding," I explained. Unfortunately, brooding was a lot more difficult with an audience, especially one as cute as Luna. I didn't know how the Valoffs constantly managed it. Must be genetic—Resting Brooding Face.

Tavi's lips twitched. She managed to keep her expression serious as she asked, "Is it helping?"

"I don't know." I checked my comm. "I have two minutes left."

This time, Tavi couldn't quite suppress her grin. "Is there anything *I* can do to help?"

I gave up on the useless brooding with a sigh. Tavi was one of my closest friends, the sister of my heart if not my blood. "Not really," I said. "I just had a long night, and I still haven't found anything useful."

I did not tell her that during the short amount of sleep I'd gotten, my dreams had been filled with a certain Valovian weapons expert. Varro Runkow had ignored all of my subtle attempts at flirting—and the not-so-subtle attempts, too. After weeks of trying, I'd taken the hint and settled into a teasing friendship with him, but my subconscious still hadn't gotten the memo.

Neither had my neglected libido. I'd wanted Varro from the moment I'd laid eyes on him, and that instant, fierce attraction had only grown into deeper affection the more I'd gotten to know him. Getting over it was proving harder than I'd like.

Tavi rarely missed anything. Her assessing gaze flickered over me and the hot chocolate that I usually hoarded like a dragon. She waited, expression open, but when I didn't take her silent offer to talk, she nodded once and changed the subject. "Still no sign of Morten?"

I shook my head. A little over a month ago, Commodore Frank Morten had kidnapped the young heir to the Valovian Empire. We'd rescued the kid—*just*—but we still didn't know what Morten's endgame was. A representative for the Federated Human Planets, commonly called the FHP or Fed, had denied that Morten was still part of the military, but the Valovian Empire wasn't buying it.

And neither was I.

If Morten wasn't stopped, he'd push the FHP and the Valovian Empire back into war, but none of us knew *why*.

What did he gain from a war that would kill thousands, if not millions?

The question had plagued me for weeks. I'd chased down lead after lead, only to run into nothing but dead ends and more questions. The team counted on me for information, and right now there was precious little. Eventually, Morten would slip up, and I would catch him, but I wished the whole process were faster.

Luna had no time for the problems of people. She chirruped demandingly and sent us a telepathic picture of a little Valovian creature that looked something like a rabbit—her idea of food. Tavi *tsked* at Luna's impatience, but she still went to feed her.

I grinned at the two of them. Tavi liked to pretend that her heart wasn't made of marshmallow fluff, but anyone who watched her around Luna would figure out the truth in no time flat.

After the burbu was fed, Tavi poured herself a cup of coffee. She took a sip, then leaned against the bar and returned to the conversation with a sigh. "Do you think Morten's still on Valovia? Should we head back to Valovian space?"

"No," a hard male voice answered from the doorway. My eyes were drawn to the sound despite the fact that I knew exactly who I'd find. Varro stepped into the room in dark pants and a deep blue shirt that emphasized his tan skin and short, curly, dark blond hair. It also emphasized the hard expanse of his chest and his muscular arms.

Not that I noticed.

Varro had been in the gym when I'd checked on him earlier. I wasn't *avoiding* him, but after my tumultuous dreams, I'd decided to keep my distance for a bit until I could be a good friend again—and nothing else.

But Varro had a habit of silently appearing wherever I was, even when I expected him to be elsewhere.

I dipped my head in greeting and his gaze swept over my face. His mouth turned down in apparent distaste as he caught sight of the deep shadows marring the pale skin under my eyes. Unlike Tavi, my skin tended toward pasty when I spent too much time in space. I looked washed out on the best of days, and today wasn't exactly that.

I *knew* he wasn't for me, but that look still stung. It wasn't my fault that I hadn't slept well. He should go grump at someone else.

Except I liked it when he was around, even if he spent the time scowling at me.

I was hopeless.

I redirected my thoughts to the question at hand and asked, "Why shouldn't we head into Valovian space?" I wasn't eager to return to Valovia, but it was looking more and more likely that we'd have to.

We'd spent the last month patrolling between Bastion, the last space station in Fed territory, and the wormhole that would spit us out in the Valovian Empire. Staying close to Bastion meant that our information connection stayed fast, but the station itself was too expensive to dock on for longer than the time needed to restock food and supplies.

"The empress has a long memory," Varro said. He looked at Tavi. "You rescued her grandson, but you also embarrassed her. She will not appreciate your return, and it's possible she rescinded your bounty because she hopes you will try it."

"Torran said the same thing," Tavi agreed with a sigh. "We should save returning to Valovia as a last resort." She glanced between the two of us, then lifted her coffee cup in farewell. "Keep me posted," she said as she slid from the room.

Traitor.

I sipped my hot chocolate and waited for the questioning to begin. But Varro wasn't so easily understood. He moved toward the food prep area. "I'm going to make a snack. May I make you something, too?"

The simple question shouldn't have made me feel like crying, but my emotions were all over the place today. I summoned a smile and tried my best to make it real. "That depends . . . is it going to be full of protein powder?"

He shot me a dark look. "Protein is good for you."

"Maybe, but it's not good for my tastebuds."

He muttered something in Valovan too low for me to catch. The ache in my chest deepened as he moved around the food prep area with ease. He always took care of the people around him, both human and Valoff. At first, I'd foolishly thought he was singling me out for special treatment, but I'd seen it time and again, the quiet, steady way he helped everyone on board.

He might scowl and grumble, but he wasn't fooling me.

And it wasn't his fault that I wished for more. No, that was entirely on me. Perhaps I needed some time away. The thought hurt, for a myriad of reasons, but after our last job, I had enough money saved up for a stay on Bastion, and I needed a better source of information anyway.

The FHP base on the space station would be an excellent place to start. I could track down Morten, take some time to get my head on right, and then rejoin the team for the final hunt.

The longer I thought about it, the more it made sense.

Tavi wouldn't like it, but she would understand. She wanted Morten found just as badly as I did. The asshole had paraded her around as the Hero of Rodeni for months, despite the fact that he'd left our squad to die on the battlefield. She'd done it, because it was the only way the FHP would let us go.

I knew she still had nightmares about it.

We were due to restock at Bastion in a few days. I could stay on the station until *Starlight* came back for the next resupply stop in three weeks. While I was there, I would have direct access to the encrypted FHP communication links. If I *happened* to stumble across the keys, well, no one would blame me for poking around a bit.

The tentative decision lifted some of the restless turmoil I'd been feeling. When Varro set a vibrant blue smoothie in front of me, my smile was easy and real. "Thank you."

He nodded, then watched me from the corner of his eye until I took a sip.

The fruit—mostly frozen blueberries—masked the taste of the protein powder he'd added. I didn't eat meat, and despite the fact that there were plenty of vegetarian options for protein, Varro grumbled that I didn't get enough. I didn't take it personally because Tavi had worried, too, until she'd gotten used to cooking vegetarian.

"It's delicious," I said. "Thank you."

Varro dipped his head in acknowledgment. He poured the rest of the mixture into a glass for himself, then joined me at the table. My traitorous heart quivered.

Varro Runkow looked like he was built for battle. He was the most muscular of the Valoffs who had joined us, and while he wasn't objectively handsome—his face was too broad, his features too rough—he was everything I'd ever wanted.

Next to him, I felt dainty and delicate and protected. Storms would break upon his back without ever touching whoever was lucky enough to be sheltered in his arms.

But Varro's eyes were my favorite feature. Deep, tawny brown with streaks of brown-black, they seemed to change with his emotions. The darker streaks widened, and Varro frowned at me.

I dropped my gaze to the table. Usually by now, I'd be chattering at him about my latest obsession, whether it was the newest vid drama I'd pulled from the network or the data I had uncovered while digging for Morten, but with my dreams still haunting me, I was having trouble finding normal.

Eli sauntered in, saving me from having to explain my unusual behavior. His deep brown skin still glistened from his workout, and when he caught sight of Varro sitting across from me, his grin turned teasing. "Ah, there you are. I wondered where you'd vanished to."

Elias Bruck was the older brother I'd never had. He, Lexi, and I had survived the war thanks to Tavi. Afterward, we'd started hunting bounties as a group. Lexi had since moved on to do her own thing, but Eli, Tavi, and I had stuck together. Eli was our muscle, though most people were so entranced by his gorgeous face that they failed to notice said muscle until it was too late.

Behind Varro's back, Eli tilted his head in question. "Are you okay?" he asked me over our subvocal comm connection.

I rubbed my cheek self-consciously. *How bad did I look?* "Rough night," I responded in the same manner.

Varro had to know that Eli and I were communicating, but he didn't interrupt. Valoffs tended to be tolerant of simultaneous private conversations because they could all communicate telepathically—one of the skills that had given them a lethal edge during the war.

Luna chirped a greeting at Eli, and his attention transferred to her. "I'm not feeding you more, you little monster," he said, his voice soft with affection. "You still have food in your bowl."

We all spoiled the adorable burbu, and Eli was just as susceptible to her big violet eyes as the rest of us. With the extra Valoffs on board, Tavi had finally had to set up a treat schedule just so we didn't overfeed her.

I finished my smoothie, then rose and snagged Varro's empty glass before he could stop me. Everyone had duties on the ship, and generally, if you cooked, you didn't have to clean. Varro often tried to do both.

I washed the glasses while Eli puttered around behind me, making himself an early lunch. The familiar routine settled my nerves. Tavi and Eli had been my anchors for nearly a decade, and I would miss them terribly.

But staying on Bastion for a few weeks would give me more time to devote to finding Morten as well as giving me space to sort out my feelings for Varro. It was exactly what I needed.

Decision made, I just had to figure out how to break the news to Tavi in a way that would prevent her from worrying about me. I shook my head with a grin. It was an impossible task.

I TOOK THE COWARD'S WAY OUT AND DECIDED THAT I SHOULD GET my work done for the day before I talked to Tavi, so after breakfast, I returned to the engineering control room, a fancy name for the utility closet I'd converted into my personal workspace. Before Anja, our new mechanic, had joined our team, I'd been responsible for keeping the ship running.

I was no mechanic, but I did know my way around the ship's electronics. Finding my way into the networked components, figuring out how they worked, and optimizing them for greatest efficiency was something that brought me an immense amount of satisfaction. *Starlight's Shadow* was Tavi's ship, but she'd given me complete control over the systems that kept us alive and moving.

I checked the quartet of monitoring screens as I slid into my chair. The ship would send an immediate alert if anything went wrong, but seeing it on the screen was a comfort that I refused to give up. With a single glance, I could confirm that every element was within spec.

And that the searches I'd left running for news of Morten had not returned any new results overnight.

Tavi and the rest of the crew depended on my ability to unearth information about our targets, and I was letting everyone down. My main job was to find the data Tavi needed in order to plan, and right now, I couldn't even do that right.

I'd been breaking my way into restricted networks since I was old enough to know what a network *was*. Both of my parents were engineers, and they'd encouraged my interest in technology and skepticism of authority. They'd also helped me cover my tracks more than once when my ambition had gotten ahead of my skill.

I'd joined the military straight out of school because my family couldn't afford the fee to avoid mandatory service, and I'd fudged my aptitude scores so none of the conglomerates would be interested enough to offer an indentureship.

Unfortunately, my dismal aptitude scores meant I was put in a front-line unit rather than a tech unit. I wasn't wired to be a good soldier—or even a mediocre soldier—but the FHP had tried their best to grind me into submission. They might have succeeded had Tavi not accepted my transfer into her squad. I owed her everything, and the least I could do in return was find the Lady-damned information she needed.

In my years of tracking people down, I'd never had someone elude me for so long. I was starting to suspect that Morten had people high up in the FHP covering his tracks. Or maybe someone in the Valovian Empire.

The fact that I didn't know *which* was its own annoyance.

But it wasn't all bad news. The rumors of a big event on Bastion that I'd been seeing for the past couple of weeks had finally solidified. There must've been a news embargo date, because now there was a flood of information from a variety of reputable sources.

The reports indicated that the space station would be hosting a high-end fashion exhibition at the end of the week—a first-of-its-kind collaboration between human and Valovian designers that merged fashion and technology. Several very important people, both human and Valoff, had either arrived early or indicated they were on their way.

Bastion wasn't exactly the epicenter of haute couture, so the exhibition was likely a cover for a more interesting meeting. Perhaps the FHP and the Valovian Empire were renegotiating the peace treaty. Or maybe they were trading threats. Whatever the reason, I wanted to be there to see what sort of data I could dig up, especially with so many Valoffs on the station.

The timing firmed up my intent to stay on Bastion after we docked for supplies. I'd still have to explain my reasons to Tavi—all of them—or she'd send Varro with me as backup. But information recon was something I needed no help for. If I planned it right, I could sift through the data from the safety of my bunk.

I started looking for a room that had the best network access but also wouldn't break the bank. I lost myself in the data until my comm buzzed to remind me that I was scheduled to help Anja down in maintenance this afternoon. It took two more alarms to pull my attention away, which was why I always set multiple. It was a pain, but it kept me on track.

Mostly.

I stood up before shutting off the third alarm. If I didn't, I would get sucked back into the search. I headed down to the maintenance level before that happened.

The deeper I delved into the narrow access corridors, the higher the temperature rose. When I found Anja, her short, black curls were matted to her head and sweat beaded on her light brown skin. She'd removed her shirt and worked only in her sports bra and pants, both of which were soaked through.

She'd warned me the temperature would be high today, but I'd forgotten. At least my short-sleeve shirt and long pants were lightweight and breathable.

Anja Harbon had joined our team a little over a month ago, but she'd slid into place so seamlessly that it felt like she'd been with us much longer. She was tall and fit, with defined muscles in her stomach that I would dearly love, but not enough to actually work for them.

She was gorgeous, and if I hadn't laid eyes on Varro and immediately thought *Mine!*, I would've flirted with her as boldly as Eli did.

Anja swiped an arm across her brow and gave me a tired grin. "Sorry about the temperature. I had to close this section off to work on the scrubber and it's miserable."

I waved her off. "I made you spend hours wedged under a terminal that was apparently built for teeny tiny children in order to upgrade the processing unit. We'll call it even."

She grimaced. "It's going to be that bad again, unfortunately. The part that needs replacing is a flow control valve at the very edge of the access hatch and it needs two sets of hands. But this is the last one, so hopefully we won't have to do this for another decade or so."

I peered in the open panel and spotted the flow valve marked with orange chalk. Thanks to my slighter frame, there was just enough space for me to crawl in and brace it while Anja worked. "You're lucky I'm not any taller," I grumbled good-naturedly. "And that I like you."

"I'll make you a dozen of your favorite cookies," she promised.

I grinned at her. "You should've led with that. Pull me out if I get stuck."

ANJA HAD THE KIND OF CALM STEADINESS THAT SOOTHED MY CONstant need to *go* and *do* and *perform*. She reminded me a lot of Tavi in that way. Even when the flow valve slipped and smashed her finger, she just cursed once, *emphatically,* and kept working.

By the time we got the new valve installed and tested, I'd been crammed in the crawl space for nearly three hours. I was made of sweat and sore muscles, but we'd upgraded an integral piece of the ship's life support system, so the pain was worth it. And now I could spend the evening sitting on the couch, binging my newest vid series without any guilt.

Assuming I could get out of this damned hole.

My legs were asleep from where Anja had leaned against them, and my spine felt welded to the deck at an awkward angle. When I didn't move after Anja had worked herself out of the uncomfortably close space, she poked her head back in. "You okay?"

I waved a tired arm. "I live here now. I've become one with the crawl space. You can just deliver my cookies here."

She grinned. "I'm pretty sure the crew wouldn't appreciate me letting you slowly roast to death, so out you come. Give me your hand and I'll help you."

With Anja's assistance, I managed to wiggle my way out. We tidied up the work area, then both headed up to the main deck to clean up before dinner.

After a shower and a change of clothes, I felt more like a human, albeit a tired one. By the time I made it to the galley, Tavi was just finishing cooking and the rest of the crew had gathered.

We'd found early on that the ship ran better if Tavi cooked dinner while Eli and I took turns cleaning up. Eli and I *could* cook, but neither of us had the same passion for it that Tavi did. That tradition had carried over after the Valoffs had joined us, though these days Torran often either helped or cooked the evening meal himself.

Communal dinners built camaraderie, something we'd needed a lot of as the two crews had gotten used to each other, but now it was just a nice excuse to get everyone together once a day to hang out and chat.

My thoughts drifted, as they often did, to Varro. I sat across from him at dinner, and I adored being the center of his focus, right up until I remembered that he was just being friendly, and he treated everyone the same. Then I felt guilty for wanting more.

It was a vicious spiral, and it only firmed my resolve that I needed some time away. Pining for someone who wasn't interested was not a productive use of my time, but I couldn't seem to stop. Tavi would understand, just as soon as I gathered the courage to tell her—not that I held much hope that she hadn't already figured it out.

But pride was a funny thing, and I had more than my fair share.

As if summoned by my thoughts, Varro appeared at my side and handed me a tall glass of icy water with an irritated grunt.

"Thank you," I said, then greedily gulped down the cold liquid. I was parched after spending the afternoon in maintenance, but I had no idea how he always knew what I needed. It was impressive and infuriating in turns.

Varro had impeccable manners, so I wasn't surprised when he grumbled, "You're welcome."

We lapsed into a silence that I was too tired to fill. A glance around proved that Anja had gotten ready faster than me, and she was deep in conversation with Eli, Havil, and Chira.

Chira Pelek, the Valovian first officer, had pale skin and natural silvery-white hair that made her the most distinctive looking of the Valoffs who had joined our crew. She was beautiful, with a sharp mind and a backbone of steel. Next to her, Havil Wutra, the Valovian medic, had deep brown skin and a kind face framed by straight black hair.

The four of them—Eli, Anja, Chira, and Havil—flirted shamelessly with each other. Well, Eli flirted shamelessly, and the other three were a little more discreet. I was pretty sure that it had recently moved past flirting, at least for Eli, but I was doing my best not to pry, especially in the delicate early stages of a relationship.

Looking around, I kept expecting to see Lexi's pale blond hair. She was the fourth member of our military squad—the fourth *surviving* member, at least. Before she'd joined us for the job on Valovia, it'd been nearly a year since we'd seen her.

And as soon as the job was finished, she'd had to return to her own contracts.

I still felt the hole she'd left behind. I hoped it wouldn't be another year before we saw her again, but her jobs took her all over the galaxy and our paths rarely crossed.

When we'd let Lexi off at Bastion, Nilo—Torran's second officer—had disembarked as well, heading back to Valovia to be Torran's eyes and ears on the ground. Without the two of them, the room felt a little emptier, even when filled with people.

I pushed away the sadness. They both knew what they were doing, and just because I preferred to stick close to the people I loved didn't mean everyone was the same.

But it would certainly make my life easier.

Torran helped Tavi move food to the table. The former Valovian general was tall, lean, and muscular, with short black hair and lightly tanned skin. As a telekinetic, he was the most dangerous person on the ship by an order of magnitude—or ten.

But tonight his face was soft with affection as he gently teased Tavi about her cooking. She glared at him, but a smile kept trying to break through her stern expression.

"They are so happy together," I murmured.

"They are," Varro confirmed, startling me. I'd almost forgotten that he was beside me.

"I would like to be that happy." The wistful words slipped out before I thought about who I was talking to. I winced internally, but there was nothing to do but brazen it out.

I could feel Varro's gaze, but I resolutely kept my eyes on Tavi. "Are you unhappy?" he asked, his voice surprisingly soft.

Yes. The certainty of that answer surprised me. I could usually find the upside in any situation, but the cycle of guilt and longing had worn me down. I *wanted* to be a good friend, but my feelings refused to cooperate.

I turned to him. He was close, and I had to tip my head back to meet his eyes. His dark gaze swept over my face, his eyes oddly intense.

"I'm happy," I lied with a smile. I vowed I'd make it true, just as soon as I had some time to get my head on straight.

Varro's expression didn't change, and I worried that he'd seen through me. But before he could call me on it, Tavi announced that dinner was ready.

I thanked the Blessed Lady for the lucky break and headed for my seat. My resolve firmed. After dinner, I would tell the captain that I planned to stay on Bastion, and why. She would be loath to send me off on my own, as would Eli, but as much as they wanted to protect me, they knew I could take care of myself, at least for a little while.

But I wasn't so sure about the silent Valoff sitting across from me. He tended to hover, as if overprotectiveness was built into his DNA. If I told him that I was going to stay on Bastion, he would insist on accompanying me, which was exactly the opposite of what I needed.

So I wouldn't tell him.

He was going to be so mad.

CHAPTER TWO

After dinner, I found the captain on the bridge, sitting in her usual place with her feet up on her terminal. Luna was curled in her lap, basking in Tavi's gentle attention.

I settled into the navigation terminal, but gave the screen only a cursory glance before swiveling my chair toward Tavi. "When we stop at Bastion, I'm going to stay on the station until the next supply run," I blurted.

Tavi's posture didn't change, but her eyebrows rose. "Why?"

I'd had all day to mentally craft my message, so I didn't falter. "Because my research on the ship is limited, and I can't find Morten. I need better access and Bastion provides that." I paused and swallowed. "And because I need some time away from Varro."

Tavi's relaxed form tensed into alert readiness. "Did something happen?"

"No, not at all. I just have feelings that aren't reciprocated, and I need some space to clear my head."

Tavi's expression turned speculative, but she nodded once. "I'll send Chira with you."

"No," I bit out, surprising us both with my vehemence. I took a deep breath. "She's needed on the ship, and I don't require a babysitter," I said, my voice steady despite my internal nerves. "I will be fine on the station, you know I will."

Tavi sighed and slumped back in her seat, her gaze on the ceiling. "I know you will, but I still worry." She paused, then murmured, "I wish Lexi were here."

Longing tugged at my heart. "Me, too," I agreed, then shook my head with a grin. "I'm going to sit in my room on Bastion and poke at the FHP network, but think of how much trouble I could get in if I had Lexi to open doors for me."

Tavi chuckled, then shot me a knowing look. "Why don't you tell me why *else* you're going to Bastion? It wouldn't have anything to do with a certain fashion and technology show, would it?"

Busted.

I didn't even try to deflect, because Tavi would see straight through it. "I think the exhibition might be a front for a more important meeting. Even if it's not, a lot of important people will be there, and I might be able to glean some information from them."

"Two conditions," Tavi said. She raised a finger. "You will send me daily reports on everything you find." A second finger joined the first. "And if the fashion exhibition looks like it's a front, you will notify me immediately and promise not to get involved."

I opened my mouth to respond, but she cut me off. "Oh, and if you feel unsafe or want to come back early, you have to tell me that, too."

I rolled my eyes in exasperation. "Anything else? Should I sign over my firstborn?"

"Kee, we're poking our noses into matters that could lead to war between the galaxy's two superpowers. It's dangerous, we both know that, but I won't let anyone on my team get hurt if I can prevent it."

"I'll be careful."

Tavi nodded. "You planning to tell the rest of the crew?"

"No."

Tavi's eyes sparkled. "Good luck with that."

TAVI HAD AGREED TO KEEP MY PLAN TO HERSELF AFTER OUR CHAT last night, but trying to keep a secret on a ship as tightly knit as *Starlight's Shadow* was a nearly impossible task, which was proven true as soon as Eli saw me at lunch.

"Just tell me," he wheedled after we finished eating. "You know I'm going to find out."

I appreciated his finely honed intuition a lot more when it wasn't directed at me. I summoned my sternest glare, which, based on his grin, wasn't very stern at all. "No."

He held up his hands in surrender, but I knew it wouldn't last too long, especially if he couldn't get the information from Tavi. His gaze lingered on my face and his expression softened. "I'm glad you got some sleep last night."

"Me, too." Thanks to the hours spent helping Anja, I'd been so tired that I'd all but collapsed into my bunk after my talk with Tavi. A solid eight hours of sleep had done wonders for both my appearance and my mental health.

That plus having a plan meant that I was feeling particularly happy today.

Maybe that's why Eli had immediately known something was up, and wasn't that a depressing thought.

I gathered my dishes and put them in the sanitizer. "What's your plan for the afternoon?"

Eli followed my lead and dropped his dishes beside mine. "It's my week for bathroom duty," he grumbled.

I grimaced in sympathy. Everyone on the ship, including Tavi, had cleaning duties assigned. The tasks rotated and bathrooms were no one's favorite. They weren't ever that dirty—we were all adults who generally tried to keep the ship in good shape—but deep cleaning still took a while.

"What about you?" he asked.

"I've got the garden this week."

"Oooh, lucky." His smile was quick and sly. "Want to swap?"

I laughed at him. "Not even a little bit." I didn't mind most of the shipboard duties, but gardening was easily my favorite.

He shook his head in mock sadness. "Your loss."

"I'll survive, somehow." I raised my hand in farewell. "You know where to find me if the fumes get to be too much for you."

He waved me off. "Happy gardening."

I left the galley and headed toward the garden. Tavi was once again on the bridge, staring at the main screen that displayed the vastness of space, her feet propped up on her terminal. I poked my head in the door. "Everything okay?"

She nodded without turning around. "Just thinking."

"I'll be in the garden if you want to chat."

She gave me a silent thumbs-up, so I left her to it. Tavi

enjoyed sitting on the bridge, monitoring the ship and our surroundings. She was always looking out for us, even if we didn't see her doing it.

The door to the garden slid open at my approach. The room was filled with tall racks of plants growing in shallow trays, and if you squinted just right, the grow lights resembled sunlight.

Sort of.

In the back corner, Tavi had installed a small arbor with a few chairs and a hanging drape of honeysuckle that sectioned the space into a tiny green oasis. Luna could often be found napping on her perch in the vines, and I'd fallen asleep in one of the chairs more than once.

I loved being in space, but there was something magical about green growing things, no matter where one was. The arbor was one of my favorite places on the ship.

As I approached, low voices caught my attention. "Hello," I called before I could overhear something I shouldn't.

"Hello, Kee," Havil called back. The soft-spoken medic spent a lot of time in the garden. Whoever was with him remained silent, and the curtain of honeysuckle remained closed.

I hesitated. "I'm on garden duty this week," I said slowly, "but I can come back later if you'd like to have some more time alone."

Havil ducked through the honeysuckle, a small smile on his face. "We won't disturb your schedule," he said.

"Oh, I don't mind—"

Varro stepped out of the arbor looking flushed and guilty, and I froze. Had I interrupted them in an intimate moment?

If he and Havil were together, then I was happy for them, truly, but if my heart cracked, just a little, no one would know but me. I hoped Eli and Anja knew or I wouldn't be the only one with a bruised heart.

I snapped my jaw closed, but Havil must've caught my stunned expression because I felt the lightest brush of a mind against mine. The medic tilted his head in question.

I nodded my permission, and his voice whispered into my head. "It's not what you're thinking," he said. "Varro has been dodging his regular checkups for weeks, even though he's in pain. This is one of the few places I can corner him successfully."

Before the embarrassment at making the wrong assumption could rear its head, I processed what he'd said. "Varro's in pain?" I thought as loudly as I could. Telepathic communication was slightly different than our subvocal comms, but I muddled through with the Valoffs' help. My mental shields were so bad that they could usually pick up my thoughts without any trouble.

Havil nodded. "Talk to him about it. Maybe he'll listen to you." With that, he slipped past me, leaving me alone with Varro.

If I didn't know better, I'd think the whole ship had it out for me.

Varro moved to stalk past me without a word, but I stopped him with a light hand on his forearm. "Are you okay?" I asked softly.

Varro grunted, then his eyes narrowed on my face. "He told you."

"He just told me you're in pain and skipping your checkups. What's up with that?"

"It's not something you need to worry about."

My own eyes narrowed. "If you think I don't worry about my friends, then you don't know me very well at all."

His expression flickered, then he ran a tired hand down his face. "I apologize. I know you care about your friends."

Was there the slightest emphasis on the word *friends* or was I imagining things?

I shook my head. A couple of weeks ago, I'd sliced my arm on a sharp piece of metal while digging around under my terminal, and Havil had fixed it with just a touch and a few minutes. I knew healing was Havil's innate ability, but it still seemed like magic to me. I didn't know why anyone would turn down his help.

Before I could ask, Varro said, "Nothing is physically wrong, so there's nothing Havil can do except lecture me. That's why I've been avoiding him."

His tone and entire posture screamed his discomfort, so I let it go, even though curiosity gnawed at me. "Well, if you want to keep avoiding him, you can hang out in here with me. If he comes back, I'll protect you."

Some of Varro's tension drained away. "Thank you. I would not mind a few more minutes of rest."

I waved at the arbor. "Knock yourself out. I have to check on the plants anyway. You want me to wake you when I leave or let you sleep?"

"Please let me know before you leave." I nodded and he retreated to the arbor, but he left the curtain of honeysuckle open so that he could see into the main part of the garden.

At first, I could feel his eyes on me and it made me self-conscious. But as I got more involved in my work, the feeling faded. I hoped that he was getting the rest he needed.

I checked on the hydroponics system and slightly adjusted the nutrient levels in the water. The system was mostly self-sufficient, but Tavi liked for us to keep an eye on it. We bought most of our food, but the garden helped us stretch our time between supply stops, so it was important to keep it in tip-top shape.

The last trays of salad greens had been planted a couple of days ago, so I planted three more trays and carefully labeled them with the date and time. With the additional people on board, we were planting more trays, more often, especially the quick-growing greens.

I checked on the other plants, making sure they were healthy and strong. I talked to them as I worked, telling them how nice it was that they were growing food for us, and how pretty they looked with their green leaves and strong roots. It was mostly happy nonsense, but I'd read an ancient study that said plants did better when they were spoken to, and I tended to anthropomorphize them anyway, so talking to them came naturally.

I noted the tomatoes and other veggies that were ready for harvest and put them into the log so Tavi would know what was available for dinner. If she didn't harvest them tonight, I would pick them tomorrow and put them in the galley for everyone to enjoy.

By the time I was done, several hours had passed. I hadn't heard a peep from Varro, so I hoped he had fallen asleep. With nothing else to do, I approached the arbor on soft feet.

Varro's head was tipped back, his breathing deep and even. I hesitated for a moment, then slipped into the arbor and sank into the chair beside his. I stared at the leafy vines overhead and enjoyed a moment of peace as the sweet smell of honeysuckle drifted around me.

"You talked to the plants," Varro said, his voice low and

rough. I bet he sounded just like that in the morning, sleepy and rumpled after a night in bed.

Heat crept into my cheeks at the imagined visual, and I redirected my thoughts to a safer subject. I peeked at him, but his eyes remained closed, so I went back to staring at the ceiling. “I thought you were asleep.”

“It’s harder to sneak up on me than you might imagine. Your approach was quiet but not *that* quiet.” After a pause, he added, “But the talking was nice.”

“It’s supposed to help the plants grow better, and it gives me something to do.”

“I enjoyed listening to you. It was soothing.”

I laughed quietly. “Most people would disagree.” I rolled my head toward him with a grin. “Have you considered that you may be part plant?”

“Mmm,” he murmured without opening his eyes, “perhaps that is why I’m drawn to sunshine.”

I glanced at his sun-kissed skin before reminding myself that he wasn’t for me. I purposefully kept my tone light. “Well, it’s hard to get sunshine in a spaceship, but you’re welcome to hang out in here with me for the rest of the week and pretend. If you want, I’ll even babble at you like you’re a plant.”

He slanted a glance at me, his eyes dark and fathomless. “I would enjoy that. Thank you.”

AFTER DINNER, WE ALL HEADED DOWN TO THE REC ROOM ON THE ship’s middle level to watch the latest episode of the vid drama I’d gotten everyone addicted to—and with time travel, alternate universes, and romance, what wasn’t to love?

Tavi and Torran sank into their usual loveseat at the back of the room. The rest of us didn't really stick to the same seats every night, but I preferred the couch that was front and center. Tonight it was empty, so I flopped onto one side and put my feet up on the middle cushion. There was plenty of seating, so I didn't feel *too* bad about taking up more than my fair share.

Eli sat at the other end of the couch and gave me the classic *I'm watching you* gesture, swiveling two fingers in the air between his eyes and mine. I guess he hadn't forgotten about our conversation at lunch.

Havil, Chira, and Anja sat together on the last sofa, which left Varro on his own. I started to move my legs so he could join us—and help block Eli's inquisition—but Varro merely waved at me and settled into a nearby chair.

I swallowed my disappointment and started the vid.

Luckily, I lost myself in the unfolding plot and two hours passed in a happy blur. Havil climbed to his feet before I could start a third episode, and without the distraction of a show, tiredness slammed into me.

I yawned and stretched. My bunk was so far away, and this couch was so comfy.

Eli stood and asked, "You want me to carry you up?"

I widened my eyes and pressed my hands together over my heart. "Would you?"

Eli's grin was light and teasing. "Nope. Not unless you'd like to answer a question or two on the way."

"You're the worst," I grumbled as I sat up.

He sent me a disbelieving look. "I let you skip out on the gym this morning."

"Okay, you're marginally acceptable."

"In that case, I'll see you bright and early tomorrow.

I expect you to be warmed up and ready to spar by oh six hundred."

I dramatically flopped back on the couch and clutched at my chest. "I take it all back—you really *are* the worst! What kind of monster feels like exercising that early?"

Eli's mouth tipped into a wry grin as one eyebrow rose. "Pretty much the whole rest of the ship?"

"Monsters, every one of you." I lifted my arm and he pulled me to my feet. "Some of us need our beauty sleep."

Eli's eyes lingered on my face and his expression turned serious. "Are you okay, really?" he asked softly.

I hugged his side with one arm. "I am. I'm just working through a couple of things. But for all I complain, I appreciate you looking out for me." Even if it sometimes bordered on smothering.

Despite being one of the most gorgeous people I'd ever laid eyes on, I'd never been attracted to Eli. When I'd first been assigned to Tavi's squad, Eli and I had fallen into friendship like we'd known each other for ages, but there had never been any kind of spark between us. I loved him like I loved my family, but that's all it was.

At thirty, I was four years younger than him and Tavi, so they both tended to hover. I appreciated their concern because it made me feel loved in return.

But I still wasn't going to tell him that I was leaving until I absolutely had to.

THE NEXT MORNING FOUND ME ON A TREADMILL, PLODDING ALONG at a slow jog well before any smart person would've left their cozy bed. Tavi and Eli both enjoyed the gym. I did *not*.

I avoided it whenever possible and only tolerated it when forced to participate.

I *knew* being able to defend myself and outrun bounties was useful, but my strengths lay elsewhere, and I'd made peace with that. I could find all of the information about someone from birth until now, but if I had to chase someone down, they were as good as gone. Tavi and Eli couldn't hack their way into an open server, but they could run for kilometers without breaking a sweat. We each played to the others' strengths.

Next to me, Chira ran at a brisk pace, her silvery hair pulled up in a high ponytail. Her long legs made her look like she was floating over the treadmill and I kind of hated her.

Okay, not really, but I wouldn't mind half of her ease. She caught my look and grinned in encouragement at me. "I heard you're sparring with Eli this morning."

I couldn't help the grimace. "You mean I'm getting flattened by Eli. Again."

"If you want help, I'd be happy to train with you."

"Thank you, but I'm a hopeless case. Tavi and Eli have been working with me for years. I know what I should do, but half the time I just . . . don't do it."

"You should get Varro to help you. He helped Havil."

I shook my head. The very last thing I needed was to get up close and personal with Varro. "That's okay. Eli will ensure I haven't forgotten *everything* I've learned, then I can go back to hiding in my control room."

I kept up my slow jog while Eli finished his full workout. His muscles weren't just for show, and he worked hard to keep himself in top form. By the time he was done, I was dripping sweat.

Blergh.

I wiped down the treadmill and joined Eli on the sparring mats after toeing off my shoes. "Are you sure you're not too tired?" I tried. "We could reschedule."

He tossed me the cloth wraps for my hands with an exasperated sigh. "If you put as much effort into training as you did into *avoiding* training, you'd be undefeatable."

I didn't even try to hide my eye roll. "We both know that's not true."

He grinned. "I did lay it on a little thick, didn't I?"

"Don't you always?" I asked as I wrapped my hands and then bounced on my toes. My leg muscles protested, proving that I probably *should* spend more time in the gym, not that I would ever admit it.

His grin took on an evil edge. "Just for that, let's work on your defense."

That was all the warning I got before he lunged at me. I was supposed to step in, to use his momentum against him and get under his guard. I *knew* that. But instead, my thoughts scattered, I tried to do six things at once, and I ended up stumbling back and falling on my butt without Eli ever touching me.

Frustration rose and with it the useless tears that I'd fought all my life. I blinked them back. Any strong emotion and I became a watering pot. It was infuriating, which only made the tears worse. I took a deep breath and let it out slowly.

Eli offered me a hand up, his expression soft but not pitying. When I was on my feet, he said, "Let's try again, slower."

Prepared and focused, I slid past his slow strike and drove my fist toward his chin. He let me connect, knowing I would pull the punch. I barely tapped him.

He stepped back. "Better. What was different that time?"

"I was prepared."

"*That's* why we train," he said patiently. "If someone comes at you, I want you to be prepared."

"Tell that to my brain," I grumbled.

His smile was part sympathy, part steel. "I plan to."

Eli drilled me on offense and defense until I could barely lift my arms before he called it quits.

"You've killed me," I groaned, bending until I could touch the floor, stretching out my arms, back, and thighs.

His chuckle drifted down from somewhere over my head. "You know, if you're energetic enough to complain, we can keep going."

I huffed at him. "That wasn't a complaint; that was a fact."

As much as I hated training, I did appreciate that he was trying to help me. I would never be a great hand-to-hand fighter, but with focus, I could hold my own long enough for help to arrive.

Give me a weapon, however, and the odds changed. My hand-eye coordination was second to none. As long as I had distance and a ranged weapon, I was untouchable.

"Well, if you're done stating facts, then let's clear out so Torran and Varro can use the mats."

I straightened and found both Valoffs wrapping their knuckles. Varro had more muscle, but Torran was telekinetic. I didn't know if he used his ability while he trained, but I was going to find out.

I wasn't the only one planning to watch. Tavi had given up all pretense of rowing, and Chira lingered at the edge of the mats barely pretending to stretch.

Eli and I joined her, then Tavi joined the three of us.

Torran raised his eyebrows and tipped his head at Tavi. "Care to join us?"

"Nope," she said, her eyes sparkling. "I'm just here for the show."

She wasn't wrong. Any time two of the Valoffs sparred, it was worth watching. They were fast and fluid and obviously very well trained. It was like watching ballet, just with a lot more punches thrown in.

"They are well matched," Chira said softly as the two men circled each other. "Torran is faster, but Varro is stronger."

"Couldn't Torran just telelock him and be done?" I asked.

Chira shook her head. "Varro isn't just physically strong. Torran can lock him, but not for long. He's the only one of us who can really make Torran work for victory."

As if to prove her point, Varro froze in place as Torran's fist flashed toward his side. At the last moment, Varro twisted away from the strike, and I let out the breath I'd been holding.

He'd broken Torran's lock in less than a second.

I kept my eyes glued to Varro. When I paid close attention, I could see all the little stops and stutters that happened when Torran locked him, but Varro never stayed still for long.

Varro was so quiet that it was easy to forget that he was a trained soldier, and he was far more powerful than I'd given him credit for. Not too many people could take on a telekinetic and remain on equal footing.

After twenty minutes, both men were sweating and breathing hard. At some unknown signal, they stopped and tapped their knuckles together, ending the fight.

Varro's eyes found mine, and something hot and feral lurked in his expression. My heart tripped over itself, but I blinked and the look was gone, smoothed away into his usual neutrality. I had *not* imagined that look, but I had no idea what it meant. I refused to get my hopes up. I'd done that before and nothing came of it but an aching heart.

"Good fight," Torran said, drawing Varro's attention away. "You're getting faster."

Varro dipped his head. "You, too. Your locks are getting stronger. You almost had me there at the end."

Torran grimaced and his gaze slid to Tavi before flashing away. "It wasn't good enough."

Torran still blamed himself for Tavi's injuries during our last fight. We'd fought another telekinetic, and Torran was the only reason Tavi had survived at all, but he didn't see it that way. Ever since, he'd been relentlessly training.

Torran's contacts were quietly searching for the telekinetic's name and location, but he thought she was one of Empress Nepru's Fiazefferia—Sun Guardians—which meant her identity was protected by the empress herself. We had about as much information on the Sun Guardian as we did Morten—far too little.

A problem I planned to fix just as soon as I was on Bastion and my searches couldn't be traced back to *Starlight's Shadow.*

CHAPTER THREE

The next couple of days passed in a blur, and before I knew it, *Starlight's Shadow* had docked on Bastion for a resupply. Tavi put everyone to work on restocking so that I could slip out unnoticed.

She met me in the cargo bay and gave me a tight hug and a firm look. "Contact me at the first sign of trouble. If the fashion exhibition is a front, do *not* attempt to go to the real meeting without backup, no matter what the reason. And stay vigilant."

"I'll let you know as soon as I find something, and I'll be on my best behavior," I told her with a grin. "You won't even notice I'm gone."

Her smile was gentle and kind. "We'll notice," she said quietly. "Take the time you need, but be careful. You're the one who warned me that Bastion had gotten rougher lately. A certain Valoff is going to murder me when he finds out what you've done."

Varro wouldn't resort to violence, no matter how angry he was. But selfishly, I hoped that he *was* furious. I secretly feared that he was going to be happy that I was gone and fury beat that any day. I shook off the negative thoughts and responded to Tavi. "Thank you. And I will be careful. I'm going to sit in my room and let the improved access speed up my search for the commodore we both hate."

And maybe do a little bit of in-person digging around the exhibition that Tavi definitely wouldn't approve of—so I wouldn't tell her. She had enough to worry about without me adding to it.

Tavi nodded. "We can afford to dock for a bit longer now, so if you find something that looks promising, I want to know before you start digging into it. If Morten is still tied to the FHP, then they'll be willing to go to some length to keep his involvement in the kidnapping secret."

Half of Bastion was still held by the FHP military, so I wouldn't poke the beast without good reason. I didn't need to disappear into a deep, dark holding cell without notice. "I'll be careful," I confirmed again.

Tavi touched my shoulder one last time—touch was her talisman against bad luck—and reluctantly dropped her hand. "See you in three weeks."

I waved farewell and slipped from the ship. I'd worn my oldest clothes and tucked my distinctive, colorful hair carefully under a knit cap. My pack looked like it might fall apart at any moment. The ruse was designed to deflect attention. Based on my appearance, no one would suspect that I carried thousands of credits worth of tech equipment carefully wrapped in a pack that was far sturdier than it looked.

Tavi had landed in a slightly nicer part of the station,

despite my protests. I *might* have led her to believe that I was staying in this section so she wouldn't worry about me. But in truth, the room I'd rented was in a much cheaper—and more dangerous—sector, so I had a plas blade strapped to my leg and a plas pistol tucked under my jacket. I knew how to use both, but fighting would never be my first choice.

It was hard to tell from the landing bay that this was a nicer part of the space station. Perhaps the paint was a little less worn and the ships a little newer, but the air reeked of hot metal, grease, and ozone. Bastion had become a massive trading hub, and even the nicer landing bays were packed with as many ships as they could squeeze in.

I joined the stream of people heading deeper into the station. Once I was safely lost in the crowd, I blew out a slow breath. I might've turned thirty this year, but I'd rarely spent time on my own. I'd moved straight from living with my parents to living in FHP barracks to living on *Starlight's Shadow*.

I'd taken a few solo vacations over the past three years, but I hadn't enjoyed them as much as I'd hoped. I thrived best when I was surrounded by the people I loved. Case in point, I wasn't even a hundred meters from the ship, and I already missed Tavi's gentle smile and Eli's good-natured teasing.

I refused to think of the quiet Valoff whose rare smiles lit up my world. The whole point of this time was to get my head right.

I didn't know how Lexi did it. She'd been on her own for a couple of years, and as far as I could tell, she enjoyed it. Or, at least, she enjoyed the money she made from taking jobs Tavi would refuse on principle.

I crossed the airlock into the main part of the station.

This section had been designed for civilian use from the beginning, so it was bigger and brighter than the sections that had been converted from a military base. The crowd thinned as people peeled off in different directions. Most of the people in the crowd were human, but I saw a few Valoffs as well.

It was hard to spot Valoffs at a distance because their multicolored eyes—their most distinctive feature—were best viewed up close. But they moved slightly differently, and they tended to have a wider variety of skin and hair colors, though with the hair dye options available, that wasn't always a good indicator.

I'd tried to get Chira to let me dye her silver hair into a rainbow like mine, but she had smiled and told me that rainbow wasn't really her style.

Too bad, because it would've looked *amazing*.

And it would've been less work than doing my own hair, since my natural blond had to be lightened to get the most vibrant color. I hadn't touched my hair up in a while, so the bold colors had faded into soft pastels. Eli called it my fairy princess look. He had a surprisingly whimsical side for someone who was so often pragmatic and pessimistic.

I suppressed the wave of homesickness by closely observing the station. The farther I delved, the smaller and dingier the hallways became. By the time I made it to the room I'd rented for the next three weeks, the hallway was narrow enough that I could touch both walls—and at a meter sixty-five, I wasn't particularly tall.

At least there weren't a lot of places for people to hide. If someone was going to ambush me, I'd see them coming.

I'd already loaded the electronic key on my comm, so

once I waved the device over the lock, the door slid open. I stepped into the tiny room. The lights came on automatically, and the door closed behind me.

"Welcome, Sarah Martin," a computerized voice said. "You have twenty-one days left on your reservation. Damages will be billed to the reservation account. Have a pleasant stay."

"Thanks," I said, though I knew the automated system wouldn't hear me without the trigger words. Though I'd purposefully booked the room with a false ID, just in case, it still felt weird to be called a different name.

I dropped my pack on the narrow bunk. Every square meter of a station was at a premium, and this space was even smaller than my room on *Starlight*—mostly because I had an officer's cabin on the ship.

I stretched out my arms and couldn't quite touch the walls, but it was close. The room was deeper than it was wide, barely two meters by three. A minuscule bathroom was tucked against the back wall. I'd paid more for a private bath, but having to leave during the night to trek to a communal bath was a risk I'd decided not to take.

By now, *Starlight* would be heading back out into space. Had anyone noticed that I wasn't on board?

I refused to let melancholy take root, so instead of dwelling on it, I unpacked my bag. The room contained a slender wardrobe that doubled as a clothes refresher—another upgrade. The wardrobe just fit the trio of extra outfits I'd brought. Without the refresher, I would've had to bring more clothes, which would've taken up space in my pack that I needed for meal bars and tech equipment.

Food on Bastion was as expensive as everything else, and without the ability to cook in this tiny coffin of a room,

I would have to live on meal bars or pay for meals in one of the large mess halls or at individual restaurants.

I'd made decent money on our last job, but I'd also sent a lot of it home to my family. I didn't need to put too much stress on my remaining account balance, so meal bars were going to be the bulk of my food for the next three weeks. I was one of the rare people who didn't mind the taste too much, so it wouldn't be a hardship. And Tavi had been kind enough to let me raid the ship's supply before I'd left.

Food and clothes sorted, I opened the main part of my pack by placing my palm on the biometric lock and then entering a twelve-digit passcode. My new slate was nestled in the padded interior. The powerful tablet computer had shown up outside my door while we were at Torran's house on Valovia.

Valoffs had a custom of *vosdodite*—an apology gift—but no one had claimed responsibility for the gift, so I hadn't been sure it was meant for me. When I'd tried to give it to Torran, since I'd found it in the hallway of his house, he'd grinned and told me to keep it. When I'd asked him point-blank if he'd left it for me—he'd given Tavi a new comm, after all—he'd denied it.

But he also wouldn't tell me who *had*.

In fact, all of the Valoffs had been cagey about their answers, which didn't help me narrow it down. I'd gone so far as to check the security footage, but whoever had left the slate had expected that, and the crucial five-minute drop-off window had been looped. On the video, it looked like the slate had appeared out of thin air.

Still, I strongly suspected a certain Valovian weapons specialist was behind the gift, despite his denial. I just didn't know *why*. Varro and I had gotten off to a rocky start when he'd mistaken my perkiness for foolishness. But he'd made me my favorite cookies and sincerely apologized, so I'd forgiven him long before we ever made it to Valovia. An additional apology gift didn't make sense, and it was far too nice to be a gift between friends.

But whoever had given it to me knew me well. It was the exact model I would've bought myself, if money hadn't been a consideration. Once I had it, I was far too selfish to give it up if no one else was going to claim it, so I'd kept it. Now it would be my window out of this tiny room.

And a way into the secured FHP communication links.

The *other* reason I'd chosen this particular room was because one of the station's backbone network connections ran directly behind the bathroom wall.

I pulled the slate out. Hidden underneath it was a small device a little larger than my palm. The innocuous-looking little black box was designed to splice into fiber-optic cables. When used properly, there were just a few dropped packets and no other network interruption. But getting it right was tricky, and if I fucked it up, the Feds would trace the break directly to my door.

I didn't want to have to move rooms quite yet, so I'd try less risky options first. I pulled out another little black box, this one filled with highly illegal specialty chips designed to crack encryption. I connected it to the slate.

The slate would direct the effort, but the security cracker would do all of the heavy computational lifting required to break into the wireless communication network. FHP security was usually pretty good, as long as the station commander made it a priority, so it would likely take a while to break in even with the illegal help.

I locked the pack, slate, and security cracker in the storage bin under the bed. There wasn't anything I could really do here until I broke into the FHP's network, so I checked my weapons, tucked my comm in an inside pocket, and then let myself out of the room.

Time to do a little reconnaissance.

I MET ONLY TWO PEOPLE ON MY WAY OUT OF THE RESIDENTIAL SECtion and neither of them bothered me. As I emerged into the more crowded areas, I let the current of foot traffic carry me along. The station was huge, one of the largest in the system, and every level was packed with shopping, entertainment, and food, at least on the civilian side.

Getting into the military side would be a little more work, especially with the way I'd gotten *out* of the military. To say I wasn't their favorite person might be a bit of an understatement.

But that was a problem for another day. Today I would scope out what I could of the accessible areas, then head back to my room and get down to work. If I kept myself busy enough, I might forget how much I missed everyone on *Starlight*.

It was a vain hope, but I tried it anyway. I wandered around taking in the sights for a few hours until my stomach growled. I found one of the smaller, cheaper mess halls and bought a plate of food. Most of the people around me were shift workers on break. I sat next to a group in dirty coveralls. After a few minutes, the woman beside me pulled me into the conversation, a kindness that I appreciated.

We chatted about nothing in particular, but I left the meal with contact information for a half-dozen people who promised to help me find work if I needed it thanks to a slightly fudged story about how I'd left my last ship without much of a plan.

As I exited the mess hall, the back of my neck prickled, and a shiver worked its way down my spine. I glanced around, sure that someone was watching me, but other than a few glances from passersby, not a soul paid any attention to me.

I picked a direction and wandered at random. The feeling faded somewhat but didn't go away. After an hour, I shook my head at myself. I hadn't caught a single person following me, despite darting down long, mostly empty corridors where it would've been impossible for someone to hide.

It was possible, though unlikely, that someone was monitoring my movements via camera, but I'd never felt the same shiver while under electronic surveillance.

Deciding that my ghostly friend could tag along as long as they kept their distance, I headed up to the fanciest level in this section. As I stepped off the lift, I tried my best to look like I belonged in the wide halls lined with high-end shops. A single night in one of the hotels on this level would cost more than the whole three-week stay I'd booked.

Most of the people who were arriving for the fashion exhibition would be staying here. Indeed, the exhibition itself would be held in the Eminence, one of the large, opulent hotels that catered to the most elite clientele. Hotel staff didn't take kindly to riffraff like me hanging around. Getting close enough to peek at the guest's data would take a little planning.

For now, I didn't *need* to be on this level, but I enjoyed looking around at how the other half lived. If nothing came of the meeting rumors, then once the security cracker broke into the network, I'd be spending my days staring at the four walls of my tiny room, so it was nice to be able to stretch my legs for a bit now.

I walked until the hour grew late enough to pass the overnight shift change. A station never really slept, so the only indications of the time were the glowing numbers on my comm screen and the heavy feeling of my eyes.

I was nearly back to my room when two men—one dark-haired and one blond—straightened away from the corridor walls in front of me with identical leering grins. I stopped, cursing myself. I'd gotten used to the weird feeling of eyes on me, and I'd been so lost in my head that I'd forgotten to watch my surroundings. I should've been smarter than that, but it was too late for regret.

A quick glance behind me revealed that a man and woman had stepped out of a nearby room. The four of them had neatly hemmed me in.

The blond in front of me said, "If you want to travel through here, you need a pass." He must be the leader of this little band of thugs. He continued, "And I haven't seen you around before, love. A thousand credits and we'll let you go on your way."

There was no way he'd missed the plas blade strapped to my leg. Either he thought I wouldn't use it, or he wasn't worried about it, which meant he had a way to neutralize the threat. None of the goons were overly large, but they all had the lean, wiry strength that came from hard work. Running would be my best bet, but they'd taken that option away.

I also had a plas pistol, but killing someone on a station—even in self-defense—would bring far more scrutiny down on me than I needed.

I drew myself up to my full height and channeled my best impression of Tavi. "And if I refuse?"

The blond smiled, but it didn't reach his eyes. "Don't refuse."

I had a thousand credits. I *could* pay them. The financial hit was survivable. But then they'd keep on targeting others. I sighed. I was about to do something very stupid, but what if the person they caught after me was even less prepared than I was? I couldn't have that on my conscience.

I wrapped my fingers around the plas blade's grip and pulled it from the clip on my thigh. I flicked the setting to nonlethal and activated it. A twenty-five-centimeter blue energy blade flashed into existence. If I changed the setting to lethal, the blade would turn red and cut through flesh like butter.

The blond sneered at my blade then swept his coat back, revealing the plas pistol on his hip. "Last chance to be smart, love."

If I'd been smart, I wouldn't be here in the first place. Smart had vacated this hallway long ago. Now I just had to survive.

A thick arm wrapped around my waist and a hand clamped over my mouth. I didn't have time to do more than freeze in alarm before I heard a deep, familiar voice whisper directly in my mind, "Don't move or speak."

"What the fuck?" the blond yelled. "Where'd she go?"

The pair behind us muttered curses under their breath. I didn't know what was happening, but I trusted Varro. I nodded and he let me go, then he plucked the energy blade from my nerveless fingers. He herded me to the edge of the hallway, then telepathically warned again, "Do not move."

He stepped away from me and the dark-haired man

down the hall gasped in surprise. "Is she some sort of fucking *shapeshifter*? I'm out." He broke and ran.

The blond sneered and drew his pistol. "It's not a shapeshifter, it's a Valoff fucking with our heads. Kill it."

Varro didn't respond, but the three assailants staggered, horror on their faces. Either they hadn't been shielding or they weren't strong enough to withstand Varro's telepathic assault.

The blond leader recovered fastest, but Varro was already in motion. He lashed out with the plas blade and caught the blond in the chest. The man went down with a scream. The shock wouldn't kill him, but I knew from experience that it felt like it should.

Behind us, the man had sunk to the floor, his head in his hands. "Get out, get out, get out," he moaned, rocking. The woman leaned against the wall, squinting and trying to bring up a plas pistol.

Varro hit them both, his movements spare and fast.

When he turned back to me, the fury in his gaze caused me to take an involuntary step back. The darker streaks in his tawny brown irises had spread, making his eyes look pitch black.

"How far is your room?" he bit out.

I pointed down the hall with a hand that shook. "In the next section."

He snapped the deactivated plas blade into the clip on my thigh, then wrapped a hand around my arm, his grip surprisingly gentle. "Let's move."

Varro marched me down the hall like I was a wayward child. When he noticed that I was trotting to keep up with his long strides, he slowed, but his body remained a tense line from his jaw down.

Now that the danger had passed, the adrenaline had nowhere to go. I took a shaky breath, and when that didn't help, I held my breath entirely. I was fine. I would not cry.

Traitorous tears gathered in my eyes.

I clenched my teeth. I was so busy trying not to cry that I nearly passed right by my room. "Wait," I said, pulling against Varro's hold. "I'm here."

He reluctantly let me go while I opened the door, then he crowded in behind me as if he were afraid I would lock him out.

And now that I thought about it, that would've been a fantastic idea.

My eyes narrowed. The haze of the fight was wearing off, and my brain started working again. What was he doing here anyway? He should've been on the ship.

I pulled out my comm and fired off a message to Tavi. *Anything you'd like to tell me?*

Her response was nearly instant, which meant that they were still nearby and she was up late. A series of messages rolled in, one after the other. *He threatened to go out the airlock if I wouldn't dock. Torran said he would do it, too. So I ordered him a transport and gave him the fake address you gave me rather than your real location. Thanks for that, by the way.*

I turned shocked eyes to Varro. "Did you seriously threaten to go out the airlock?"

"I *promised* to go out the airlock," he corrected, his voice a low growl.

"That's . . ." I spluttered as words failed me. Jettisoning into open space near a station was a very good way to end up impaled on a ship's hull or knocked off course and lost forever. "*Why?*"

He took a step closer, his eyes burning and his muscles clenched tight. "It's not safe for you to be here alone. The captain should not have allowed it."

His anger stoked mine. I drew myself up, though the top of my head barely cleared his chin. "You are not the boss of me."

"Someone needs to be," he muttered darkly in Valovan. Either he didn't know I spoke the language or he'd forgotten.

I shivered before remembering that he was not for me. Frustration mixed with the fear and anger and adrenaline of the last few minutes until only white-hot rage remained. "Get out." His spine stiffened, but I just pointed at the door. "Now."

He looked like he was getting ready to argue, but my damn tears came back and the world went watery. I swiped at them angrily, but more just ran down my face.

Varro made a low sound and held up his hands. "Don't cry, *hisi las,*" he murmured. "I'm going."

The door slid open and then he was gone. And I was alone. The realization brought more damn tears, so I flopped on my bed and let the pillow soak up all of the emotion that bled out of me. I'd learned that it was best to get it over with because the longer I fought, the more upset I got and the more I cried.

It wasn't until much later, when I was wrung out and exhausted, that I realized what he'd said on his way out.

He'd called me "bright star" in Valovan.

CHAPTER FOUR

After a short, fitful night of sleep, I got ready to go find Varro. I'd cooled off enough that I felt bad about kicking him out without giving him a chance to explain himself. He didn't know that part of the reason I'd left the ship had been to get away from him. He was just trying to help a crewmate stay safe.

I'd done a cursory search of room registrations but hadn't been able to find him. Either he wasn't using his real name or he was staying in a hotel. It would take too long to search every hotel on the station, so I planned to go out and wander around until he found me again.

But when I stepped out of my door, I immediately felt the weight of eyes on me. A glance left and right revealed an empty hallway, as shown on the control panel, but I remembered the surprised gasps from the thugs yesterday.

"Come out, Varro."

I waited long enough that I started to feel stupid, but just before I decided it was all in my head, Varro blinked into view against the wall in front of me, wearing the same clothes he'd had on last night.

He tilted his head. "How did you know I was here?"

"How *are* you here?" I demanded. "And more importantly, why didn't you tell me that you can turn invisible?"

The corner of his mouth quirked up. "I was not invisible; you just couldn't see me."

"The camera by the door couldn't see you, either. If that's not invisible, then I don't know what is." I frowned as I looked closer at him. He had dark smudges under his eyes and his face was set into the lines of steely determination that meant he was silently suffering but not going to do anything about it. "Did you stand out here all night?"

He stared at me and didn't say anything.

"Do you have a room?"

More silence.

"Did you at least pack a bag before vaulting off the ship in a fit of temper?"

He grunted and turned slightly to show me the thin pack he carried. "Do not worry about me."

I sighed, then turned and waved my comm over the door. "Come on."

Varro frowned at me. "You were going out."

"To find you. Which was easier than I thought. Now you're going to take a nap while I do some research."

He tensed. "I am fine. I will accompany you."

I snagged his wrist and pulled him into the tiny room with me. The door slid closed, and my pulse spiked at his nearness—and the feel of his skin under my fingers. I dropped his wrist and stepped back, but there wasn't much space for retreat.

"Lucky for you, I'm going to do electronic research this morning, and I promise I won't leave without letting you know." I smoothed and straightened the blankets on the bed. I hadn't expected company, so I hadn't bothered making it, but now it gave me something to do with my hands.

Varro stopped my nervous fluttering with a light touch on my shoulder. When I froze and glanced up at him, he said, "I am here to help you, not to make more work for you. I am fine. One night awake does not bother me."

"But you used your ability all night, didn't you? So no one would see you? Isn't that draining?"

His mouth tightened, but he didn't deny it.

I darted into the bathroom and quickly washed the only cup I'd brought. I filled it with water, then dug under the bed for my pack. I pulled out a couple of meal bars, looked at Varro, and then added two more. I also pulled out my slate and the security cracker. I wasn't into the encrypted network yet, but I could at least poke around on the open net while Varro slept.

I handed him the cup of water and three meal bars. "If you want to shower first, there's one in the attached bath."

He watched me with a patient stare, and I huffed out a breath. "I promise I'm not going to run off while you're in the shower. Get cleaned up, eat, and take a nap. You'll be more helpful if you're not dead on your feet."

He dipped his head. "Thank you."

Once he was safely hidden behind the flimsy bathroom door, I blew out a slow breath and tried to get my hammering pulse under control. To keep myself from thinking about him naked in the shower, I perched on the edge of the bed and unlocked my slate.

Tavi and I had exchanged a few more messages last night. She'd told me that she was sticking close by and could pick me up in a matter of hours, but I'd already paid for the room. The fashion exhibition was in a couple of days and digging into FHP's network while I was on the station wouldn't implicate the ship, so I would stay for the three weeks I'd planned.

And with his ability to move unseen, Varro could be a huge help, especially if I wanted to take a peek at the exhibition attendees and the FHP-controlled part of the station—both of which I did.

Maybe I could make this work.

Maybe.

NONE OF MY SEARCHES HAD TURNED UP ANYTHING NEW ON MORTEN, so I was in the middle of tweaking them when the bathroom door slid open and Varro reappeared. He looked much the same, except his curly hair was damp against his head and his shirt had changed from black to dark gray.

After a brief pause, he sat next to me. I nudged the meal bars his way, only half paying attention.

He ate while I worked. It took me a while to notice that he'd finished his meal and had leaned back against the wall at the head of the bed. It was the feeling of his gaze that eventually pulled me from the data on-screen.

I glanced at him. "You should lie down and sleep. I'm going to be a while." At his steady look, I rolled my eyes. "I didn't sneak away while you were in the shower, did I?" I tilted my head as I considered him. "How did you find me in the first place?"

He lifted one shoulder. "Your mind glows. It took me some time to find the right level, but you are not hard to track."

The last was relayed as a warning, but I was too stuck on the glowing mind thing. "Is that something any Valoff can do?"

He shook his head, and a dark look passed over his features. "My telepathy is much stronger than most."

"That's why you can disappear. You're not really gone; you're just tricking my mind into not seeing you. But how does it work with video?"

"It doesn't. If you go back and look at the recordings from last night, you will see me. But when you are looking at a live video, my telepathy still works if I am close enough."

"That's incredible," I breathed. "What if I'm shielding?"

"Depends on the shield. Most humans don't have mental shields strong enough, but it's harder to trick other Valoffs."

I built the shield around my mind that I'd learned during the war. I wasn't very good at shielding—too many other thoughts liked to get in the way—but when it was as stable as I could make it, I said, "Try it now."

Varro disappeared.

I reached out with a gasp, and my hand met the cloth covering his calf. But even *feeling* that he was there wasn't enough for my mind to believe it. I poked him again, then squinted at where his leg should be. It looked like an empty part of the bed. "How strong *are* you?"

He blinked back into view, displeasure clear on his face. "Your shield needs work."

I grimaced and let the ineffective shield go. "Tell me about it," I muttered. "Try fighting a war like this."

His fists clenched on his thighs, but I didn't know if it was from the reminder of the war or because my shields were trash. He frowned at me. "Why didn't you practice with Tavi and the others before we reached Valovia?"

"I did. It's not lack of practice; it's lack of ability." I slanted a glance at him. "You didn't help much with the shielding practice, either. Why is that?"

"I'm too strong," he said matter-of-factly. "I can break through other Valoffs' shields, so it would be demoralizing for a human to try to keep me out. And because of how my ability works, I shield differently."

"Differently how?" Standard shielding didn't work well for me. If he did it differently, maybe he could teach me how to improve my shield.

"My mental shield is more fluid than most because I can detect and deter intrusions easier than others. It lets me sense more of what's around me."

The tiny kernel of hope died. I needed Shielding 101, not advanced shielding. I would just have to keep using what I already knew. I squinted at him. "Can you read my thoughts?"

"I could, but I won't. My own shields are very good at filtering out other people's thoughts."

"Could you read my thoughts even through my shield?" When he warily dipped his head, I wrinkled my nose. Now that was an unpleasant thought. But I trusted him when he said he wouldn't, so I let it go and moved on to the next thing I wanted to know. "How long can you remain unseen?"

"Around humans? Indefinitely. For Valoffs, it depends on their strength and specialty, but it can be anywhere from seconds to hours."

"So if I wanted to sneak into the FHP part of the station, you could keep us hidden?"

He immediately shook his head. "The cameras would see us."

"Good thing you know someone good with technology, then," I said with a grin. When he looked like he would protest, I waved a hand. "We're not going *today*. It's just something to consider. For now, lie down and sleep. I promise I'll wake you before I leave."

Varro slid down into the narrow bed. His body took up most of the space until he shifted on his side and leaned back against the wall, giving me enough space to sit on the edge of the mattress with my legs crossed. I dimmed the lights, then stared unseeing at my slate's screen while his breathing deepened into sleep. Despite his protests, he had been exhausted.

A quick glance confirmed that the tense lines of his body had softened into relaxation. Without the tension, he looked younger. I didn't know exactly how old he was, but he couldn't be more than a few years older than me, which put him in his early to mid thirties.

A dark blond curl had fallen over his forehead and my fingers twitched with the desire to smooth it back. I ruthlessly suppressed it. The only way I was going to get through the next three weeks unscathed was with iron-willed control, something I wasn't exactly known for.

I reluctantly turned back to my slate and checked on

the security cracker's progress. It was halfway through processing. Unless it found a pattern, it would take another twelve hours or so to find the key. I let the little box continue doing its job and returned to the data I could find from the public network.

I set up a heavily encrypted tunnel to a secure endpoint that I paid way too much to maintain and started poking around on the public part of Bastion's network. My searches for information relating to the fashion exhibition turned up a lot of fluff and not much else.

As far as I could tell, both publicly and privately, it really *was* just a fashion show in a strange locale.

Hopefully I could snag some interesting data from the people attending so the whole thing wasn't a complete bust, but for now, I turned my attention to hunting Morten. If he had returned from Valovian space, then it was a near certainty that he'd passed through the station.

The FHP didn't have authority to send random ships into Valovian space, so Morten had likely escaped Valovia on a diplomatic ship or one of the few human ships allowed through the wormhole. Otherwise, he'd caught a ride with a sympathetic—or mercenary—Valovian crew. If we hadn't been able to escape on *Starlight's Shadow,* Torran had planned to get us back to human space via a smuggler friend of his.

Smuggling was big business, even though both the Valovian Empire and the Feds imposed steep penalties on anyone who was caught.

Fewer than a hundred ships had standing authorization to traverse the wormhole between the two territories. Most were large cargo haulers, designed to transport goods. A dozen or so were diplomatic vessels, and the rest were various smaller ships that ranged from the personal ships of wealthy contractors to specialty shippers to passenger transport.

The smugglers would very likely fall into that last category of smaller ships. It was *possible* to smuggle people on a cargo ship, but they weren't designed to carry more than the minimum number of crew, and they were monitored closely. But the ships belonging to the wealthy contractors? Much less closely scrutinized, thanks to a combination of greased palms and aggressive lawyers.

We had video evidence of Morten on Valovia, so I started pulling a list of docking tickets going back to the day after he'd been spotted. He had most likely stuck around on Valovia for longer than a single day, but I liked to have all of the possible data. I could narrow it down later.

Hundreds of ships docked on Bastion every day, and the vast majority of them never went near Valovian space. Matching docking tickets to flight plans would take *forever*, but this was what I did. I might not be the strongest or fastest member of our team, but I could find data like nobody's business, and I had a persistence all my own.

I started digging.

After an hour, I had a huge list of every ship that had registered with Bastion's docking department. The civilian department didn't handle military traffic, so there would be even more ships on the military side, but that information would have to wait until I'd cracked the encrypted network.

I wrote a little script to pull all of the relevant information into a datastore and let it run. I was going to have to do a lot of cross-referencing. Having all of the data readily available and easily sortable was worth a little up-front effort.

While the script chewed through the data, I set another one to keep pulling down the docking tickets. If Morten was coming to Bastion, then he was likely already here, but the pattern of regular shipments would let me know if a ship had deviated from its normal schedule.

Also, the possibility remained that the fashion exhibition wasn't a secret meeting so much as a quiet way for Morten to sneak back into FHP territory aboard one of the ships inbound from Valovia.

Only ships traveling through the wormhole to Valovian space were required to file flight plans with the FHP, but many ships filed them even when it wasn't required. If something happened in deep space, the flight plan was a helpful way for rescuers to know where to start looking.

Because flight plans contained more potentially sensitive data than docking tickets, it was a little more work to get access to them—but not enough to make me feel good about Bastion's security.

The gentle rasp of Varro's slow, deep breaths lulled me while I worked. A yawn cracked my jaw. Last night had been too short. The nights before hadn't been much better. I had trouble sleeping when I was worried, and planning to go off on my own had made me one big ball of worry.

My eyes drifted closed for a second while my scripts worked, but I jerked awake as the slate nearly slipped from my fingers. I blinked at the screen, disoriented, but the scrips were still running, so not much time had passed.

I covered another yawn. I should get up and fold out the top bunk, but then I'd have to make sure it had sheets on it and then climb up there, all for a ten-minute power nap. Just thinking about it made me more tired.

Instead, I set the slate safely on the floor and curled

up against the wall at the foot of the bed. I'd nap for a few minutes while my scripts finished so that I didn't miss important information because of exhaustion. Morten *would* slip up, and I *would* catch him, but not if I was too tired to think straight.

Plan set, I closed my eyes and let Varro's breathing guide me into sleep.

WARMTH RADIATED FROM MY FRONT AND A HEAVY WEIGHT OVER my waist held me securely in place. I snuggled deeper into the gentle heat. My bed hadn't been this comfortable last night, but I wasn't complaining.

Consciousness arose slowly and with it, memory.

I'd closed my eyes for a minute to catch a power nap, but I'd been leaning against the wall at the foot of the bed. I *could not* be where I thought I was.

Without opening my eyes, I traced my fingers over the wall in front of me. Fabric covered flesh met my fingertips and my breath caught. *Oh shit.*

I was on my side, pressed up against Varro's front, and one of his arms was wrapped around my waist. I froze as my thoughts scattered. Half of me wanted to go back to sleep, to enjoy the rare treat of someone to snuggle.

The other half was running around in a blind panic.

"Are you awake?" Varro asked quietly. His voice came from somewhere over my head and vibrated through his chest and into my cheek.

I wondered if I could count on a hull breach to suck me into the vastness of space before I had to answer that question.

When the room remained dreadfully intact, I opened

my eyes. My head was pillowed on Varro's arm, and I was pressed up against him like I'd melted into him. Mortification rushed through me and I jerked back.

It was only thanks to the arm around my waist that I didn't end up on the floor.

I flailed for a second before he hauled me back, and I ended up exactly where I'd started. "Careful," he admonished with a grunt before slowly removing his arm.

I sat up so fast my head spun. "I'm so sorry," I said, scorching heat in my cheeks. "I don't know what happened. I didn't sleep well last night, and it was so quiet in here. I was just going to close my eyes for a second. I didn't mean—"

"Kee," he said, interrupting my babbling, "it's fine. You were leaning against the wall, but you nearly fell off the bed. When I asked if you wanted to lie down, you curled up next to me. I put an arm around you to prevent you from rolling over onto the floor. I apologize if I overstepped."

A vague memory assaulted me of a sleepy-eyed Varro inviting me to bed. I'd thought it was a dream.

Then his words sank in. He was worried *he'd* overstepped? I'd wrapped myself around him like a clinging vine. I pressed my lips together. I could still feel the phantom heat of his body. "I'm so sorry," I said again. "I should not have invaded your personal space."

"We're crewmates, Kee. You did not invade; I invited. And you needed the rest."

I nodded even as guilt wormed its way through me. He didn't know I wanted to be more than crewmates, and I vowed to keep it that way. I would not make things uncomfortable.

I checked my comm. I'd been asleep for a couple of hours. No wonder I felt so fuzzy-headed.

"Are you rested?" I asked, hoping the burning in my cheeks would decide to subside sometime this century. When he nodded, I continued, "In that case, let's go out. I still have a few areas I want to check."

And I really, really needed more space between us than this tiny room could provide.

CHAPTER FIVE

I hadn't felt unsafe while out yesterday—well, not until the end—but Varro's shadow at my back gave me an immense feeling of security. Before, I'd had to slide through the crowds while trying not to get trampled or elbowed.

Today, the crowds parted around *me,* and I couldn't stop grinning. If it wouldn't draw too much attention, I'd wave my arms and pretend I was parting the sea.

Varro noticed my quiet amusement and loomed closer, so the crowd parted even earlier. I flashed a smile at him over my shoulder. "I'd ask you to teach me how you do that, but I feel like I'd need to grow twenty centimeters and gain a few dozen kilos of muscle for it to be effective."

His eyes slid down my body, and I stopped mid-step as he tipped his head in consideration. "It's not all physical, but your petite stature would put you at a disadvantage to start."

I turned the rest of the way around and leaned in. "Are you mojoing them?" I whispered.

He frowned at the unfamiliar term but figured it out when I wiggled my fingers and made an "ooOOOoOooo" noise. He shook his head. "I'm not using my ability. Also, I believe you are imitating a ghost, not a Valoff."

I grinned at him. "Why not both?"

Varro didn't even crack a smile. The taciturn Valoff tolerated my jokes, but he rarely joined in. When he did, his humor was so dry, and his delivery so deadpan, that I sometimes thought he was serious when he was joking. I was slowly learning to read his tiny tells—the glint in his eye, the subtle quirk of his lips—but I was still far from accurate.

Someone bumped into me, causing me to stumble forward a step, and Varro's glare turned ferocious. The poor woman nearly tripped over her own feet in her haste to get away. Varro gently clasped my elbow and scowled at the rest of the crowd. The gap around us widened, and he returned his attention to me. "Do you have a destination in mind or are we wandering around aimlessly?"

"I mean, I wouldn't call it *aimless,*" I hedged. "We're exploring."

He sighed. "You don't have a plan."

"I don't have a plan," I confirmed with a smile. Technically, I *did* have a plan, but nothing was happening with the fashion exhibition and searching for Morten had to wait until I cracked into the secured network, so today was more about killing time than doing any real work.

"Would you like help?" Varro asked quietly.

"Help with what?"

"With whatever you're here to do. I'm happy to keep

following you around, but if you'd like me to help you with a plan, I can do that, too."

"You would help me even though you don't know what I'm doing?" I asked in surprise. "What if it's illegal?"

One corner of his mouth pulled up in a tiny, devastating grin. "I would be surprised if it wasn't."

I pressed a hand to my chest and widened my eyes. "How dare you besmirch my honor like that." When he just raised an eyebrow, my serious expression cracked into laughter, and I leaned in closer. "You're not wrong, but I have to get into the system before I can really start causing trouble. Today we're just getting the lay of the station."

"Have you been here before?"

"I've spent some time on the military side, but it was years ago, so I don't expect the knowledge to be worth much. I've visited the civilian side more recently, but never for very long. Most of our stops are as quick as possible to avoid docking fees. So I'm getting familiar with the station's layout as well as looking for places to get lost in the crowd and lesser-known routes between levels, things like that." I considered him. "Have *you* been here before?"

His eyes glinted. "Not officially."

When he didn't say anything else, I bounced on my toes and gave him my best pleading look. "You can't say something like that and then not elaborate!"

His shoulders lifted in a careless shrug, like it wasn't a big deal. "I did some recon."

"During the war?" The question popped out before I could stop it. Curiosity remained a bane even for things I didn't really want to know the answers to. If he'd been here, it'd been while he was the enemy. My heart twisted.

It was hard to tell that Varro wasn't human when he

was standing still and wearing casual clothes instead of his distinctive Valovian armor—only his eyes gave him away. But not that long ago we had been on opposite sides of a brutal war.

I locked down the memories before they could rise and turned around, facing the way we'd been walking before. "Never mind. Let's see what's this way, yeah?"

Varro did not comment on my abrupt change of topic, thank the Blessed Lady and all of her handmaids. He fell in next to me without a word, and I breathed a quiet sigh of relief. There were some things I didn't want to talk about—*ever*—and the war was high on the list.

We walked for a while in comfortable silence. Bastion kept expanding, so some of the areas were less tightly integrated with the rest of the station, including the section we were in now. It was newer, a massive, circular, self-contained module that connected back to the main station only on the top three levels.

As far as I knew, there was no military presence in this module. Docks ringed the outside of the lower levels and the rest was mostly used by higher-end traders and corporate drones looking to make new connections and strengthen existing ones.

Varro and I didn't quite stand out, but our sturdy utility pants and T-shirts weren't the norm, either. If we needed to escape through this module, running would draw far more attention than on other parts of the station.

We worked our way down to the docks on the bottom level. Shiny, expensive ships were crammed together in landing bays that were filled to capacity. Bastion was known for its docking delays, and it seemed that even the rich were not immune.

If we needed to leave in a hurry, our best bet would be to take a transport rather than waiting for Tavi to get clearance to pick us up. The station transports had permanent berths, so they were always available to tender passengers from larger ships and ships that didn't want to dock. Booking one if we were tagged hostile might be a little troublesome, but it shouldn't be too hard as long as I had access to the system.

Varro slanted a glance at me. "What are you plotting?"

"Who says I'm plotting anything?" I asked with my most innocent smile. Unfortunately, it didn't seem to work on him.

He stared me down until I grinned and said, "I'm just doing a little contingency planning in case we wear out our welcome. I need to look up the location of all the transport hubs."

"There are four hubs in this module, ten in the main station, and a dozen more spread throughout the other modules. The military has their own transports in at least five separate hubs."

I blinked at him in surprise. "You just had that information floating around in your head?"

"I've researched the station, and I have an excellent memory."

"What else do you know?"

"The station's civilian population fluctuates between fifteen and twenty thousand, depending on trading levels. The FHP keeps twenty thousand soldiers based here, but most are deployed on ships, and Command can comfortably increase that number to forty thousand in times of need. In the event of another war, the FHP has the right to take over the entire station."

"How do you know all of that?"

Varro's expression remained flat. "Bastion was a priority target."

A shiver slid down my spine. If we'd lost control of the wormhole that linked FHP space to Valovian space, then of course the Valoffs would've taken out Bastion. The station's proximity to the wormhole had been one of the few advantages we'd had during the war.

I swallowed. "Right. That makes sense. Do you know how to get us out in a hurry if we need it?"

He paused in thought, then shook his head. "The transports are the best option."

Before I could question him further, his stomach growled loudly enough that I could hear it, and I frowned at him. "Why didn't you tell me that you're hungry?"

"It's not important."

I rolled my eyes. "You're constantly trying to feed me, so don't expect me to believe that shit. Let's go get some food—my treat."

When he tried to argue with me, I wrapped a hand around his wrist and marched back toward the main part of the station.

He didn't try to free his arm.

WE FOUND A CHEAP MESS HALL—THE SAME ONE I'D EATEN IN yesterday—and grabbed dinner. I bought Varro's food despite his sneaky attempts to pay for his own meal.

I was heading for an empty table in the corner when I noticed the growing ring of silence around us. In a rookie mistake, I'd stopped paying attention to my surroundings, lulled into a sense of security by Varro's presence.

But not everyone felt the same.

While I felt safer with Varro around, that was not an opinion shared by a large swath of the human population, especially those who had fought in the war. Three years of peace was not enough time to mend a rift decades in the making.

Cold eyes and hostile looks tracked our progress. I debated the merits of continuing to the table versus turning and exiting the mess hall. It was unlikely that the spectators would do more than whisper, but if it looked like we were fleeing, would that tip the balance?

"Ignore them," Varro murmured. "Let's sit and eat. If it becomes a problem, I will handle it."

I summoned a grim smile. "Are you *sure* you're not reading my mind?"

"I don't need to read your mind when I can read your expression far more easily."

My smile turned real. "It's not my fault that some of us have more expressions than scowling, frowning, and glaring. You should give it a try sometime."

A slow, wicked smile curved across his mouth, and I tripped on nothing. Varro's hand flashed out, steadying me, and the heat of his fingers burned against the delicate skin of my inner arm.

I'd kept my plate of food by sheer luck, and I used fussing with it as an excuse to drop my eyes and focus on breathing. *Blessed Lady,* that smile was dangerous. If I'd fallen and given myself a concussion, it would've been worth it.

I made it to the table without any further incidents. Varro waited for me to take a seat and then sat across from me. I hadn't taken more than a few bites of my food before a woman approached. She was a handful of years older than me, with ebony skin, dark hair, and the kind of musculature that meant she had a physically demanding job.

She stopped beside me and waited until I turned my face up to hers. Once I did, she leaned down and whispered in my ear, her voice lightly accented, "Do you need help?"

"No, I'm fine," I assured her.

Under the table, out of Varro's sight, she slid a thin composite card into my hand. "I will help you escape if you are not with him voluntarily. You don't owe him anything, no matter what he says, and you wouldn't be the first I've helped."

"Thank you for looking out for me, but *he's* with *me*. I am perfectly happy in his company."

She leaned back until she could peer into my eyes, then her gaze slid to Varro, who watched her with careful attention. After a moment, she looked back to me and said, "You mean that, don't you?"

"I do."

"Why?"

I lifted one shoulder and gave her the simplest answer. "He makes me feel safe."

If my answer surprised Varro, he didn't show it.

The woman flicked a glance around us. "He may make *you* feel safe, but that's not true for everyone. I suggest you eat on the upper decks in the future."

I rolled my eyes. "Not all of us are posh pleasure yacht captains with too much money and not enough sense. The food here is reasonably priced. We're not here to cause trouble. We just want to eat."

The woman gave me a hard stare, and when I held it calmly, she nodded once. "Very well. I'll spread the word that you're welcome to eat here. And if you change your mind about the other thing, you know where to find me."

My fingers curled around the hidden card. "Thank you. I'm glad someone is looking out."

After one last searching glance, she returned to her seat. Conversation slowly restarted, and the mood shifted to be marginally less hostile. Whoever the woman was, she had serious clout with this group.

Her card didn't have a name, just a contact address. I slipped it into my pocket. I'd never met a piece of information I didn't want to hoard, and this one might come in handy someday.

"She thought I was holding you against your will," Varro said, an odd note in his voice.

I shrugged lightly. "It's happened before."

He stilled and his gaze sharpened. "To you?"

"No, thankfully, but I've heard stories. Bastion probably isn't as bad as some of the remote stations, but border stations can be iffy. It's good that someone cares enough to pay attention."

Varro muttered something in Valovan too fast and low for me to catch.

We finished our food without anyone bothering us. No one joined us, either, but I'd take what I could get.

WE WERE HALFWAY BACK TO MY ROOM WHEN I STOPPED AND looked at Varro. "Where are you staying?"

He watched me with quiet resolve and said nothing.

"No. No, no, no," I said, waving a finger at him. "You are not staying with me."

"That was not my intention."

I squinted at him in suspicion. "Did you book a room near mine?"

"I tried. There were no rooms available in your section."

"So where did you end up?" When he didn't say anything, the suspicion turned to certainty. "You *cannot* mean to guard my door every night. I am perfectly safe in my room."

His expression hardened, and his eyes turned flinty. "And when you start poking in the encrypted network you're trying to crack, will you be safe then? I can't protect you if I'm halfway across the station. I will be fine. Do not worry about me."

I pulled out my comm and checked the available rooms. Varro was right—there weren't any available anywhere near my section. Longer-term rooms were snapped up as soon as they became available. I'd gotten my room only thanks to a script that checked availability every ninety seconds. I would have to tweak the script to narrow down the search area in order to find Varro a room close to mine.

"The security cracker is still running, so tonight you can stay in a hotel or a short-term unit. I'll find you a room closer tomorrow." My fingers flew across the screen. "I assume you want something cheap. Let's see, there's a short-term room available down on Level Twenty." My nose wrinkled. "But it's a shared bathroom. Let's keep looking."

"Kee," Varro interrupted, and by the emphasis, I assumed it wasn't the first time he'd said my name. "I don't need a room."

I glanced up at him. "Then tell me you're not planning to spend the night in the hallway outside my door."

His lips pressed into a hard, flat line.

I should leave him to it. I hadn't invited him along—and had, in fact, left the ship to escape his presence. He was a grown adult who was perfectly capable of making his own decisions, no matter how stupid those decisions might be.

But he was also my friend.

And I couldn't let him suffer, not even to spare myself. I sighed and rubbed my forehead. How had my plan to spend time alone gone quite so wrong?

"My room has two bunks," I said quietly. "You can stay with me until we find you a room close to mine."

"No."

The rejection was harsh and instantaneous, and the pain of it slammed through me from head to toe. I ducked my head so I could blink away the shimmery film of tears. Damned tear ducts.

Once I had myself under control, I met Varro's eyes, my expression as firm as I could make it. "You can either stay in a room of your choosing or you can stay in the extra bunk in my room, but you can*not* stand outside my door all night. If you try it, I will join you until I drop of exhaustion."

Varro must've read the truth in my gaze because a muscle ticked in his jaw.

I waved my comm with its list of available rooms. "What's it going to be?"

"I will stay with you," he growled, each word seemingly pulled from him against his will.

Well, this would be delightful for both of us.

CHAPTER SIX

I hesitated before unlocking the door, steeling my nerves and trying to shake off the awkwardness that had plagued our steps for the past ten minutes. It didn't help, so I swiped my comm over the lock.

After the door opened, I stepped inside and gestured Varro in after me. He took one look at my face and said, "I will book another room."

I waved a tired hand at him. "Tomorrow. It's already late. Before I go to bed, I'll set up a script to find you something close, and then you won't have to worry about me."

I reached for the blanket covering the bottom bunk. "I'll take the top bunk. Help me strip the sheets and I'll swap them."

"Leave them," Varro said. "I don't mind."

I ignored him. "It'll just take me a second and then you'll have clean sheets."

Varro's hand closed around my wrist, halting my progress. "Kee, I don't mind. I've slept in the dirt. I was prepared to stand watch all night. Your barely used sheets are a luxury that I don't deserve."

"But—"

He stroked his thumb over my wrist and my thoughts derailed.

"I appreciate your care," he said, his voice velvet soft, "but I've already caused you enough trouble today. Leave it."

I glanced up at him. He was so close and so solid and so warm that I swayed toward him before I remembered exactly why that was a terrible, terrible idea.

Friends. We were *friends,* and unfortunately not the kind that came with benefits.

I whirled around before my mind could conjure up an image of what exactly those benefits might look like. I reached for the top bunk's release but before my fingers could do more than graze the bottom of it, Varro was there, reaching over my head, his warmth a taut line against my back.

"Allow me," he murmured into my ear.

I was so busy trying to ignore the way his voice made my body light up that I didn't notice the bunk snapping down until it was millimeters from my nose. Clearly, the man was trying to kill me.

By the time I'd herded my thoughts into some semblance of usefulness, Varro had already secured the bunk and extended the ladder. A quick peek showed that the mattress was bare. I pulled the extra sheets from the drawer below the wardrobe and made the bed with Varro's help. His height meant that he could reach the mattress without the aid of the ladder, so it made the whole process faster.

Thankfully the bunks each had a privacy curtain, which was good because I hadn't exactly packed any roommate-appropriate pajamas. I usually slept in an oversize T-shirt and nothing else.

Leaving that as a problem for future me, I unlocked the storage compartment and pulled out my slate and the security cracker. A tap on the screen revealed that the cracker had found the password.

I grinned at the screen. I was *in*.

I stored the password, then detached the cracker. I would probably need it again later to get deeper into their systems, but for now, its job was done. I pulled up all of my security scripts and ensured that no one on the FHP network would be able to trace the device back to me, or worse, Tavi and *Starlight*.

With the device secure, I connected to the encrypted network. I was familiar with FHP systems, so it didn't take me too long to find the server where they posted announcements and hosted forums that no one actually used for anything important. The public announcements probably wouldn't reveal anything, but I started pulling them down anyway. Better to have too much data than not enough.

I found a few more servers. On the surface, none of them contained what I was looking for, so I made notes for later and kept going. I had just started easing my way toward what I hoped was the docking ticket server when a cup of water appeared between my face and the screen. I blinked at it, stupidly, before I remembered where I was—and who I was with.

I took the cup from Varro, surprised to find that I was parched. I drained the cup and stretched my back with a groan. I'd been perched on the edge of the lower bunk, hunched over the slate as I worked.

A check of the time indicated that I'd lost three hours.

"Thank you and sorry," I muttered, heat climbing my cheeks. "You should've kicked me out a long time ago so that you could sleep."

He lifted one muscled shoulder, and I finally noticed that he'd changed into a tank top and soft black pants. "I enjoy watching you work," he said. "You are absolutely focused."

"Sometimes too much. If I forget to set a timer, then Tavi has to remind me to eat."

"Have you found anything?"

"Not yet. I have to be careful so they don't realize someone is poking around. It's slow going." Energy hummed under my skin. It was late and I should sleep, but patience had never been a virtue I'd been very good at.

I forced myself to stand and get ready for bed. Just because I was going to be up all night didn't mean that I had to keep Varro up, too. I retreated to the bathroom to brush my teeth and wash my face. The mirror revealed that the dark circles under my eyes were back. With my fading hair, they gave me a sort of despairing fairy princess look that I kind of dug.

Too bad I wouldn't be able to pull it off. I couldn't go more than five minutes without smiling. Life was too short to be cynical and gloomy all of the time.

Back in the main room, I found Varro sitting on the edge of his bunk with his elbows on his knees, staring at the floor. He sat up so I could move past him, but his mind was clearly far away.

I pulled off my shoes and socks, then moved my slate

to the upper bunk. I'd have to wait to shimmy out of my pants and bra until I was hidden behind the privacy curtain. Then I could get back to tracking down the military docking tickets.

I was two steps up the ladder before I remembered Varro. "Good night," I said.

He glanced up in surprise. "Are you sleeping?"

I mentally crossed my fingers. "Yes. I'll see you in the morning." I'd have to sleep eventually, so technically, it wasn't even a lie. Well, the morning part might be, depending on how late I stayed up.

He stood, but thanks to the ladder, he had to look up at me. I enjoyed my new vantage point for a few seconds before he said, "You're planning to keep working, aren't you?"

Busted. A smile tugged on the corners of my mouth, even as I fought to keep my expression serious. "I have no idea what you mean."

"Do you always lie so poorly?"

"No," I said with a grin, "usually, I lie much worse." I leaned toward him and told the truth. "Until I don't. That's when you have to watch out."

His dark gaze roamed over my face, expression unreadable. "I'll keep it in mind," he murmured. His voice curled around me, tempting me to lean just a little farther, to reach for a little more.

But he wasn't for me.

I straightened abruptly, nodded at him, and then started to climb up to the next step. Varro's hand on my arm froze me in place. "Don't stay up too late."

"I'll sleep before I get careless," I told him. "Wake me up for lunch."

I WOKE TO VARRO'S VOICE CALLING MY NAME, WHICH WAS ONE of the better ways to leave my tumultuous dreams behind. My bunk's privacy curtain remained closed, cocooning me in comfortable dimness.

"What time is it?" I asked, swiping a hand over my gritty eyes.

"Nearly one. I brought lunch. And hot chocolate."

Trust Varro to know the one thing that would tempt me from my warm, cozy nest of blankets. I frowned at the pants and bra I'd folded at the end of the bed last night. I didn't relish wiggling back into them only to have to change again in five minutes when I made it to the bathroom with clean clothes. "Would you mind closing your eyes while I climb down?"

"Let me put the tray down." I heard the soft sounds of movement, then Varro said, "My eyes are closed."

I pulled the privacy curtain back and found Varro leaning against the entrance door, his head tilted back and his eyes closed. The rich smell of spices and hot chocolate filled the air, and my stomach growled.

I climbed down, clumsy and awkward as the last dregs of sleep slipped away. "I need to get in the wardrobe," I warned Varro. "You're okay where you are, but I'm going to move close to you. Don't freak out."

A tiny smile played over Varro's lips, there and gone so fast that if I hadn't been looking at him, I would've missed it. "I will try to keep my freaking out to a minimum," he said, his tone as dry as dust.

I grinned, delighted. "When my elbow ends up in your ribs, I'm going to swear I tripped."

Varro shook his head in mock disappointment. "You lose a lot of tactical advantage when you announce your plan in advance."

"Maybe I'm just trying to throw you off, so you won't figure out my *real* plan."

His eyebrows rose in inquiry, even though his eyes remained closed. "Which is?"

"To drink all of the hot chocolate, of course," I said as I opened the wardrobe. I was close enough that I could feel the heat of his body, but I carefully kept my arms and legs to myself.

"Hmm. Considering that I brought it for you, that plan lacks the nefarious flair you were hoping for."

I pulled out my clothes for the day and hung my dirty clothes in the refresher. When a peek revealed Varro's eyes were still closed, I pulled my shirt over my head and added it to the unit. "Who said anything about being nefarious?" I asked lightly. "I'm the hero of this story. Rescuing the hot chocolate from the fierce dragon guarding it is part of my quest line."

The tiny smile was back. "And I suppose I'm the dragon?"

"I don't know. Do you have a pile of gold stashed in a mountain somewhere?"

"No."

"Too bad. I suppose you can be my trusty sidekick, then." I closed the wardrobe with a click. "We'll go defeat the dragon just as soon as I shower. Thank you for bringing lunch."

He nodded at me with his face tilted in my direction. His eyes were closed, but I had the uncanny sense that he could still see me. I shivered in the cool air and retreated to the bathroom before I did something that would break our friendship forever.

It was only after the bathroom door closed behind me

that I let out the breath I'd been holding. I'd been attracted to Varro from the moment I'd laid eyes on him. It was a problem, and I was working on it. But when he smiled and joked and played with me, then he became nearly irresistible.

I was in so much trouble.

AFTER A QUICK SHOWER, I JOINED VARRO ON HIS BUNK FOR A LATE lunch. The hot chocolate had cooled, but it was still delicious. The dish he'd brought for me was a spicy veggie combo over fluffy rice, and I devoured it like I hadn't eaten in a week.

Once we finished with the meal, he looked at me. The circles under my eyes had only gotten worse, so it didn't surprise me when he asked, "How much sleep did you get?"

I did the mental math. "Four hours, give or take."

He grunted in disappointment. "You need more rest."

"Yeah, but I can sleep once I've found Morten. I made some decent progress last night, but it's slow going. Fed security is better than most, and it's been a while since I've tried to pry information from them. It's frustrating, but it can't be rushed."

"What can I do to help?"

I held up my hot chocolate with a smile. "You already did it. But if you want, you can look around and see what kind of information you can find about the upcoming fashion exhibition."

Varro's brow furrowed. "I've seen the signs. Why do you care about it?"

"Because it's a collaboration between a Valovian designer and an extremely famous human designer. Lots of important people are on the station for it. I was thinking about trying to crash the party, but I'm a little concerned that I won't be the only one with that idea."

He effortlessly followed my train of thought. "You think Morten will show?"

"I doubt it. But Bastion is a weird place for a fashion unveiling. I think *something* is going on, but I haven't found any evidence, and I looked. Hard."

"So what is your plan for the day?"

"I need to send Tavi an update, then I'm going to keep digging on the FHP servers. You don't have to babysit me today. I'm stuck in here, but you don't have to be. Go enjoy the rest of the station. Look around and see what you can find. I promise that I'll contact you before I leave the room."

I frowned in thought. Something about that sentence jogged my memory, but it took me a second to figure out why. "Shit, I forgot to find you a room of your own. I'm so sorry. I was going to update my script to search last night, but then I got distracted with the FHP network. But I'll do it right now."

I was already halfway off the bed before Varro raised a hand to stop me. "I don't need a room. If you're going to be working, I can guard at night and nap here during the day. That way I'll always be available in case something happens."

"Last night when I offered to let you stay here, you turned me down, *emphatically*. Why the sudden change of heart?"

"I didn't want to impose. This way, your nights will still be your own. You'll only have to deal with me during the day, and you'll be busy, so hopefully I won't bother you."

"And you think I'm going to be able to sleep at night knowing that you're standing outside my door suffering instead of sleeping?"

Frustration bled through his expression. "I was a soldier for over a decade. Standing guard for a few weeks isn't going to hurt me."

His frustration fed mine. "Why are you so adamant about this?" I demanded. "What's wrong with having a room of your own?"

His eyes flashed. "Because I know how the FHP operates. If they determine you're a threat, you won't have time to call for help before it's too late. Even if I'm *right next door,* they'll snatch you out from under my nose. I'm not risking your safety just to be a little more comfortable."

I threw my hands up. "Then why not just stay *with* me? Am I so horrible to be around?"

His jaw clenched, and I thought he wouldn't answer. I was about to give up and get my slate when he said, "I know why you left the ship."

Every cell froze.

I might've stayed trapped in that frozen limbo forever, but Varro plowed on. "You've been avoiding me lately. You hide it well," he said when I tried to interrupt, "but I make you uncomfortable. I know you don't like being around me, but your safety is more important than your comfort right now. I tried to get Chira to come in my place, but she refused."

Before I had time to absorb that bombshell, he continued, "I will protect you, but I don't want you to be miserable while I'm doing it. That's why I hadn't planned to let you know that I was here at all and why I won't stay with you."

He finally ran out of words, and I tried to get my brain to focus on a reasonable argument, but instead, I blurted, "You think I don't like you?"

His chin dipped a bare centimeter.

I laughed. I couldn't help it. The sound had a slightly hysterical edge that I couldn't seem to control. "I'm sorry," I said at last, wiping tears from the corners of my eyes, "but you could not be more wrong."

His expression had flattened into nothingness. "What do you mean?"

"I haven't been avoiding you because I don't like you or because I'm upset with you." My throat closed. I would rather eat glass than admit to my one-sided feelings, but I couldn't let him think I was avoiding him because of something he did. This was my problem, not his.

His skeptical expression didn't change, so I gathered all of my courage and told him the truth. "I've been avoiding you because I'm trying to be a good friend," I said, pushing each word past the wall of anxiety that tried to freeze me solid.

I paused for a steadying breath, then finished in a rush of words that I half hoped he wouldn't understand. "But the truth is that I'm wildly attracted to you, and you've made it clear that you are not interested, so I'm keeping my distance. I'm avoiding you because I like you *too much*."

CHAPTER SEVEN

Varro's eyes narrowed a tiny fraction, but otherwise his expression didn't change. I wondered if mortification could be lethal, and if so, how long it would take for me to perish.

The answer was *too damn long.*

Of all the possible outcomes to confessing my feelings that I'd imagined, and I'd imagined *a lot,* dead silence was the one thing I hadn't counted on. Tears pricked my eyes as my embarrassment mounted.

Once the silence stretched to the point where I knew Varro wasn't going to speak, I clapped my hands. "Now that we've cleared that up, let's never talk about it again. I'm going to go hide in my bunk and not come out. I'll see you in thirty years."

My legs were shaking, along with the rest of my body, but somehow, I managed to stand. I glanced longingly at the door. Running away clearly didn't solve anything, but damned if I didn't want to try again to see if the result would be different.

Unfortunately, Varro had already proven that he could find me anywhere on the station.

But maybe this time he wouldn't bother.

I hadn't taken more than a tentative half step toward the door before Varro's fingers wrapped around my upper arm, halting my progress. I refused to turn to him. I felt as fragile as glass, but his grip was exquisitely gentle.

"Please let me go," I whispered.

His grip gentled further, but his fingers remained lightly touching my skin. "I didn't know," he said, his voice rough.

I nodded, glad, at least, that my feelings hadn't been so obvious. "That was the point."

"No," he said, something fierce and dark in his tone, *"I didn't know."*

I turned my head just enough that I could see his face from the corner of my eye. He was scowling, a thunderstorm of emotion on his brow. His eyes were nearly black, the dark streaks swallowing the brown.

"Well, now you do. I'll see you for dinner. It's my turn to buy."

I tugged my arm free and climbed the ladder to my bunk before he could say another word.

WITH THE PRIVACY CURTAIN PULLED, I COULD ALMOST PRETEND THAT I was somewhere—*anywhere*—else, but the earlier awkward silence would be burned into my brain forever. I pulled out my comm and sent Tavi a message. I wrote and deleted five options before settling on the most basic. *I confessed to Varro.*

Just writing it sent my nerves fluttering again and a sick sort of dread pooled in my stomach. I was not looking forward to dinner, but I was an adult, and I would deal. People confessed their feelings all the time and hardly any of them died from it.

While I waited for Tavi's response, I reconnected my slate to the FHP network and checked my security settings. I wasn't sure my mind would settle long enough for me to get anything done, but the familiar lines of code drew me in like old friends.

This, at least, I could control.

I don't know how long I was lost in the world of servers and code and tiny exploits that cracked open narrow pathways that led closer to the information I hunted, but it was Tavi's voice that dragged me back to the world.

My comm implant piped her staticky, exasperated voice directly into my ear—like telepathy, but powered by technology. "Kee, if you don't answer your messages, I'm going to come kick your ass and charge the docking fee to your account."

The slate was busy running a scan that didn't need my input, so I picked up my comm. I didn't bother with a verbal response because trying to voice chat at a distance was infuriating thanks to the signal delay.

My comm screen was filled with nearly two hours of messages from Tavi starting with *WHAT HAPPENED????* They escalated from there.

I started writing before I could overthink it: *He'd noticed I'd been avoiding him and thought it was his fault. I clarified that it was not. Now I'm hiding in my bunk and hoping he gets very specific, temporary amnesia.*

It took over a minute for Tavi's response to come

through. *Are you okay? We're heading back toward the station now, but it'll be late before we arrive. Should we dock?*

I could *feel* Tavi's love and concern through the screen, and I had to blink away tears. No matter what, she was always in my corner.

No, don't dock, I wrote. *I'm making progress on the thing we talked about, but I need more time. I will deal with Varro.*

I'll be in voice range in six hours. I expect you to answer your comm. If you need anything before then, let me know. I will pay for a hotel for you if you need it.

I touched the screen and wished I could hug her. *I'm okay,* I wrote back. *Embarrassed, yes, but at least now the secret is out. I'm safe with Varro. Things will be awkward, but I'll make it work. Talk soon!*

Talk soon, she responded.

I set a reminder for when Tavi would be in voice range and another one to remind me about dinner. I felt better after our brief chat, but I knew the real interrogation was still to come. Tavi was one of my closest friends, but she was also the captain. She needed to be sure that Varro and I would be okay together on a small ship because one bad relationship could break a crew.

Would I be okay on a ship with Varro now that he knew?

The full-body cringe I felt every time I remembered his blank expression after my confession said no, but I was stronger than that. I would get over him *and* the embarrassment. The plan hadn't changed, despite a few minor setbacks.

I returned to my slate. The scan had finished, but it hadn't returned as many results as I'd expected. I frowned at the data. I had hoped that the wireless network would be connected enough for me to slip into their systems from the outside, but that didn't seem to be the case.

Usually, FHP systems were built by the lowest bidder, which led to a few cut corners—corners I could exploit. But in this case, someone had done a decent job of securing and isolating their networks, either because Bastion had been a military base first or because it was so close to the Valovian Empire.

I would keep poking at the data I could see from the wireless network, but my gut told me that I'd be breaking into the back wall of my bathroom after all.

THE INCESSANT CHIME OF MY DINNER ALARM DRAGGED ME AWAY from the slate's screen. I sat up and turned the alarm off, but frustration simmered in my veins.

I'd made infuriatingly little progress in the last four hours. Whoever was running security for the FHP knew what they were doing, and despite some early hopeful signs, I hadn't found any hints of docking data or flight plans or anything else that might be useful in hunting down Morten.

The FHP *did* seem to be increasing the number of soldiers stationed on Bastion, which could be significant. It could also just be a temporary adjustment as they shuffled around patrols.

Partial data was just that—*partial.*

Without more information, I couldn't make any assumptions, no matter how eager my brain was to connect more troops to Morten and his push for war.

I set the slate down before I fell back into it. The temptation was certainly there, especially since the other option was facing Varro. But my stomach wanted food, and I needed to stretch my muscles after staying in place all afternoon.

I steeled my spine and pulled the bunk's privacy curtain open with a decisive yank. The room was quiet, and I didn't see Varro. Was he sleeping? And if so, could I sneak out without him noticing?

The ladder creaked as I climbed down, and I imagined that my muscles were making much the same noise. I should've stretched more. I usually set a timer for every hour or two, just to give myself a few minutes to move around, but with everything that had happened this afternoon, I'd forgotten.

The lower bunk was empty and the bathroom door was open. So where was Varro? Had he decided to find his own room after all? If he left without leaving a note, then we were going to have a very frank conversation about the basic requirements of friendship.

I checked the control panel near the door, but Varro hadn't left a message. I killed the stab of disappointment and squinted at the floor, trying to remember if I'd heard the outside door open. All I really remembered was the server that had taken eight different cracking attempts to breach, only to find out, once I was in, that it was a room reservation system for meeting rooms and the gym.

I'd still pulled the data, because I'd gone to so much trouble to get it, but it wasn't exactly the bounty I'd been looking for.

Varro could take care of himself. I would eventually figure out where he'd gone, but for now, I needed to move and get some food. I wrote a short note on the control panel, just in case he returned, then strapped on my weapons and stepped out of the room. I waited to see if I would feel Varro's gaze, but the hallway felt empty.

After all of his warnings about safety and his promises to stand guard, he'd left me as soon as things got a little uncomfortable. The hurt of it bled like poison into my veins. I'd been uncomfortable for weeks—*weeks*—and had still tried my best to be a good friend. He hadn't even made it half a day.

Maybe Tavi *should* come back and get him. At least then I wouldn't have to worry about running into him as I stalked out of the residential section.

The recycled air, with its faint metallic undertone, did nothing to soothe my fraying temper. The station had a garden, tucked away somewhere on one of the fancy upper levels. As far as I knew, access wasn't restricted, but if it was, I wasn't above tweaking their systems to get in, because right now, I needed a bit of peace. Dinner could wait.

I joined the small crowd waiting for the elevator. When the doors opened, I slipped inside and pressed the button for the highest level. The woman next to me gave me a polite smile. "Are you staying at the Eminence, too?"

I guessed, from her expensive clothes and top-of-the-line comm, that she was here for the fashion exhibition because she'd just named the hosting hotel. "No," I said. "I'm just visiting."

She looked me up and down, expression shrewd, then flicked a holographic card at me. "Too bad. You'd be perfect for my new line, you know."

The card activated as soon as I touched it, projecting a series of suits and dresses a few centimeters above its surface. The clothes ranged from sleek, severe lines to floaty, lacy creations that appeared to defy gravity. Some of them seemed to glow with an inner light. "They're beautiful," I murmured.

The woman swiped her fingers through the hologram until she came to one of the delicate, fluttery dresses. "I'll pay you two thousand credits to wear that dress for an evening while mingling with guests."

My gaze flashed to hers. She looked vaguely familiar, but that was a lot of money just to mingle. Her light brown skin glowed with health—and lots of pampering—but she had creases at the corners of her eyes and around her mouth. Her dark hair was pulled up in a complicated updo, but it was shot through with streaks of silver. I wasn't a good judge of age, but I'd guess she was in her late sixties.

But just because she had money didn't mean she was legit. I didn't need to get myself disappeared just because I'd bought into an image. I glanced at the card, looking past the flashy holograms. Anna Duarte. I sucked in a breath. The House of Duarte was one of the biggest names in haute couture, founded forty years ago by the woman standing in front of me.

And it was the human half of the upcoming fashion and technology exhibition.

"I see you've heard of me," she said with the kind of supreme self-confidence that only the very rich and very secure ever achieve.

"I have," I said slowly. "I've also heard that you rarely leave Constantinia. What are you doing on Bastion?" I knew, but sometimes letting people explain themselves led to better information.

"My Valovian counterparts from Rarku Dropror refuse to journey farther than Bastion, so our collaborative debut must take place here." Her nose wrinkled as if she smelled something unpleasant, but she waved a lazy hand. "Surely you've seen the signs?"

I nodded absently. The Valovan phrase translated to Midnight Luxury, which was a Valovian fashion designer brand. I hadn't heard of it before I'd started researching the exhibition, but that didn't really mean anything because I didn't keep up with fashion. From my brief searches, it seemed like it was well known on Valovia.

The elevator dinged at the upper level, and I realized that most of the crowd around us was actually security for Ms. Duarte. Eli would have my head for being so unobservant—if I told him, which I wouldn't.

"The exhibition is tomorrow evening, but we are eschewing a catwalk—too boring. I will need you for five hours, plus some time in the morning for fitting and alterations. You will have a guard, and if anyone touches you, the guard will break their fingers. All you have to do is smile and flirt. Or look sad and mysterious. Either will work with the dress. In return, I'll pay you two thousand Fed credits."

One of the women in the group held the door while Anna waited for my response.

I absolutely did not have time to wear a pretty dress and make cow eyes at fancy people. But I *wanted* to, and the credits would go a long way to making my stay on Bastion more affordable.

"Okay, I'll do it," I agreed. I could wear a pretty dress *and* gather information at the same time. Win-win. Probably none of the people attending would know anything about Morten or the Sun Guardian, but they might. And if there really was something happening behind the scenes, I might learn more about it.

"Good. Alina, get her information and measurements,"

Anna said without looking away from me. "Tomorrow morning, eight sharp, at the hotel. Direct questions to Alina." Then the self-proclaimed matriarch of the fashion world swept from the elevator without a backward glance.

At the last moment, I remembered that Varro would murder me for agreeing to go without him, assuming he was still around.

"Wait, can I bring a plus one?" I blurted.

Anna turned and her eyes skimmed down my body again. "Do they have something more appropriate to wear than"—she waved at my clothes—"whatever this is?"

"He will," I promised.

"Very well. Alina will handle the invitation. Anything *else*?" When I meekly shook my head, the fashion maven spun and strode away, her heels clicking against the floor and her entourage in tow.

Had that really happened?

A slender young woman with olive skin and a colorful head scarf waved me out of the elevator. "I'm Alina," she said with just a hint of an accent that she was trying hard to suppress. "What's your name?"

"Kee Ildez," I said automatically, forgetting to give her my alias. My career as a fashionable spy was off to a stellar start.

She made a note in her comm, then looked me over. "I can get rough measurements over your clothes, but it would be better if you undressed to your undergarments. That way the fitting in the morning will be shorter. Do you have time now?"

I lifted one shoulder. I wasn't on a schedule, exactly.

"Follow me," she said as she set off at a brisk pace. "We

have a conference room in the hotel set up for fittings. Have you modeled for a designer before?"

I chuckled at the absurdity of that question. "No."

Alina nodded. "Don't worry. Ms. Duarte likes finding fresh new faces, though there will be plenty of professional models as well, if you have questions." She stopped and peered at me. "You're not an introvert, are you?"

"No."

"Perfect. Just mingle like you would at any party. Make sure to move enough to show the dress in motion and stand up straight when you stop. Most people will be more interested in the dress than you. Don't take it personally. No one is allowed to touch you or the dress. If they try, your guard will deal with it."

My eyebrows rose at the second mention of a guard in the past few minutes. "Are the guards necessary?"

"Generally, no. Occasionally a guest will have too much to drink and become unruly, but that's about it. However, no one has held a huge fashion event on Bastion before, let alone in collaboration with a Valovian fashion firm, so we're being extra cautious."

I put two and two together. "You're worried someone is going to disrupt the event." I frowned in thought. There hadn't been any credible threats as far as I'd seen, but maybe Anna's team was keeping the information under wraps.

Alina's eyes dropped away from mine. "We're just being extra cautious," she said again. "Ms. Duarte doesn't want anything to ruin the unveiling. She's spent nearly three years getting this collaboration off the ground, and officials from both the FHP and Valovia will be on hand to oversee its success."

Well, shit. My fun evening of dress-up had just turned into something potentially dangerous. And worse, now I'd have to explain to Tavi how I'd managed to get myself mixed up in the very event I'd promised to avoid.

Lady help me.

CHAPTER EIGHT

After getting poked and prodded by Alina, then scanned in my underwear for my measurements, I continued on to the garden. My stomach growled its protest, but I needed some time to think, and I'd promised myself greenery.

I let myself through the old-fashioned wrought-iron gate and into a tiny green oasis. A path meandered through flowers and shrubs, and there was even a small lawn with a fountain in the middle. A half-dozen seats were scattered through the area, most empty.

The few people in the garden nodded at me as I passed. I picked an empty bench in the back corner and lowered myself to the seat. I cocked my head at the faint but unmistakable sound of birds chirping. It had to be a recording, because the station wouldn't let animals roam free, but it was well done and added to the ambiance.

Some of my tension bled away.

I set a ten-minute timer on my comm. I would like to stay longer, but I still had too many things to do tonight, not the least of which was talk with Tavi in a couple of hours.

My timer hadn't yet gone off when I felt the cool brush of a mind against mine and Varro's furious voice echoed in my head. "Where are you?"

I didn't know how far his telepathy worked, but I couldn't feel his eyes on me, so he wasn't *too* close. I debated the merits of just not telling him, but I decided that would only delay the inevitable. "Upper-level garden," I thought back as loudly as I could.

"Stay there."

I rolled my eyes hard enough that I hoped he caught it, but the touch of his mind vanished without a word. I didn't know why he was in a snit. He was the one who'd disappeared without so much as a note. If anyone should be angry, it should be *me*.

But try as I might, my temper refused to rise. And without anger as armor, I felt terribly exposed, raw and vulnerable. The urge to run was nearly irresistible.

I canceled my timer, then fidgeted with my comm, but my eyes kept sliding toward the garden's entrance. Sitting still became its own form of control. I slowed my breathing and relaxed one muscle at a time.

It didn't help much, but it gave me something to focus on.

A few minutes later, I felt Varro before I saw him, which was impossible—*and yet*. My gaze was already on the correct path when he stormed into view, angrier, even, than when he'd found me about to be mugged.

The dark streaks in his irises had nearly swallowed the normal tawny brown. His jaw was clenched tight, and his hands flexed at his side, as if he'd like to shake some sense into me.

He stopped a few steps away, and I could feel the thrum of his power in the air, like static against my skin. "You left without letting me know," he said, his voice deadly calm. But his eyes continued to darken, and I swore I could *feel* the worry and anger swirling through him.

Staying seated was nearly impossible, but I tamped down my urge to flee. Varro would never hurt me, but I wasn't running from him; I was running from the emotions that rose when he was around. "I left a note," I corrected. "And if we want to get technical, you left first."

"I went to get dinner," he bit out between clenched teeth. "Which I told you I was going to do."

"And did I acknowledge it?"

His gaze dropped to the side as he finally broke eye contact. "No. I thought you were refusing to speak to me."

I sighed and rubbed a hand over my face. "I was busy with my project. I didn't even hear you. I didn't hear you leave, either. When I finally resurfaced, I thought you'd left because of what I said." That was as close as I was getting to referencing the whole incident.

He looked up sharply. "I wouldn't. I *didn't*."

"I see that. We were both wrong."

He dipped his head in acknowledgment, but he didn't say anything else and his eyes remained dark. Still angry, then, but controlling it. And he didn't press me about my confession, thank the Blessed Lady. If I pretended hard enough, maybe I could erase it from existence.

I patted the seat next to me. "I got an interesting offer on my way up here, but I'd like to enjoy the garden for a while longer before we talk about it. Join me?"

I held my breath until he settled onto the bench beside me, leaving a few centimeters between us. At least he hadn't sat at the far end. Maybe we'd make it past this weird awkward phase without too much embarrassment.

It took several minutes for the hum of his power to fade away. I let the peace of the garden wash over me for a bit longer before taking a deep breath and letting it out slowly. "I don't suppose you brought any dress clothes with you?" I asked quietly.

I could feel the weight of Varro's gaze. "No, why?"

"I met Anna Duarte on my way up. She's a famous fashion designer, and tomorrow night she is unveiling her new collection, which is a collaboration with Rarku Dropror."

Varro sucked in a surprised breath, and I turned to him. "You've heard of it?"

He nodded. "It's a major luxury brand on Valovia. Empress Nepru and other members of the imperial family often wear their designs. Rumor has it that the imperium owns a partial stake."

"Do you think any imperial family members will attend the unveiling?" I asked with a frown. If so, we might actually have to worry about Morten showing up.

"I doubt it. They rarely traverse the wormhole into FHP territory, and they would not grace Bastion with their presence. But there will likely be other important Valoffs there. Are you planning to attend?"

"I am. Anna saw me in the elevator and liked my look, so she asked me to wear a dress at the unveiling. I can bring a guest, as long as you wear appropriately fancy clothes. So we need to rent you a suit, assuming you want to go."

"I go where you go." The challenge in his gaze and

voice said that he thought I would argue, but I was perfectly happy to have him at my back in a room full of unknowns.

"Okay," I agreed easily, then tilted my head at him. "I thought you would try to convince me not to go."

"If you think it's worth doing, then it's worth doing."

Such a simple statement should not make such a huge impact, but his faith in my decisions warmed me from head to toe, and it was proof that I hadn't broken our friendship beyond repairing.

I blinked away the sting of tears and said, "When I first heard about the exhibition, I suspected that it was a front for some other meeting, but I haven't been able to find any information backing up that suspicion. And with two high-end designers attending, maybe it's exactly what it says it is."

Shrewd understanding dawned in Varro's eyes. "You were planning to attend all along."

I shook my head. "I was planning to lurk around the fringes, but Anna's offer was too good to pass up. If nothing else, it'll be a fun evening that will help pay for our stay, but the collaboration with Rarku Dropror means that it might not be a bad place to gather intel."

I paused and debated not telling him the rest, but he deserved to know. "Plus, they've hired guards. I don't know if they've had a threat or if they're just being cautious, but there's a chance of trouble. I haven't seen any rumors, but maybe they're keeping it quiet."

His eyes narrowed. "Will I be able to bring a weapon?"

"Doubtful, but I might be able to smuggle one in for you. If things go sideways, can't you just mojo your way out?" I wiggled my fingers.

Varro's mouth quirked into a self-deprecating grin.

"While I appreciate your faith in my ability, it's no guarantee, especially against unknown Valoffs."

My stomach growled, reminding me that I still hadn't eaten dinner. Varro stood and offered me a hand. "I left our food in the room, but it should still be good."

I slipped my hand into his, and he pulled me to my feet. My breath caught. We were so close that I could see the dark streaks in his eyes had receded to their normal size. He opened his mouth, his expression intense, but my stomach growled again, and he stepped back without a word.

I knew wishing did no good, but I would've given up my precious new slate to know what he'd been about to say.

DINNER WAS SURPRISINGLY EASY. THERE WERE A FEW AWKWARD pauses as we tried to dance around the Conversation That Shall Not Be Named, but for the most part, it was fine. If my heart felt like it was being chipped away, piece by piece, well, that remained my problem, not his.

He had handled my blurted confession with considerable grace and wanting more wouldn't change reality.

I cleaned up the trash from dinner, then climbed up to my bunk for my chat with Tavi. The privacy curtain wasn't soundproof, but I could use my subvocal comm so Varro wouldn't overhear.

Which was good, because I desperately wanted Tavi's advice.

A few minutes after my alarm went off, Tavi's call came through. She was close enough that she'd sent a video request. I made sure the audio would be routed through my comm implant, then accepted.

Tavi's familiar face on-screen was nearly enough to send me straight into tears.

"How are you doing?" she asked, her brow wrinkled with concern.

"I am okay," I said. The subvocal mic worked by translating the tiny movements of my throat muscles into words. When used properly, I could communicate completely silently, like a form of technological telepathy.

"Should I be worried about eavesdroppers?" Tavi asked.

I shook my head. "He's here, but I'm using my implant. He can't hear you. Or me."

"Tell me everything."

The story poured out of me, from the moment Varro had helped me with the muggers to the meeting with Anna Duarte. Tavi listened with quiet patience, letting me get everything out without interruption.

When I finally wound down, she took a few seconds to organize her thoughts. When she spoke, her voice was velvet-wrapped steel. "You let yourself be cornered in a hallway, when I know for a fact that you're smarter than that."

I sighed. "I tell you my entire story of woe, and that's what you want to focus on?"

"We'll get to the other stuff once I stop having a heart attack. Kee, you *promised* that you would be careful." Tavi took a deep breath. "Eli is going to shit a brick."

"You could just not tell him," I tried.

Tavi's raised eyebrow told me that wasn't going to work, but her face softened as she let me off the hook—for now. "Are you okay, really?"

"I'm . . ." I searched for the right word. "I'm sad, I think. I came here to get my head on straight and ended up worse off than before."

"What can I do to help?"

I smiled fondly at the instant offer. Tavi would move mountains to help one of her crew. "Nothing. I just have to ride it out."

"It's not so bad to have your feelings out in the open," she said, her voice gentle.

I snorted. "Not for you, maybe, since Torran is head over heels for you. Now imagine if he *wasn't*."

Her face contorted into a grimace before she could help herself. "I see your point. Would you like me to pick up Varro? Torran can order him back and make it stick. I think they're talking right now." She hesitated. "But I would have to send Eli or Chira to replace him. You need someone to watch your back at this event you're going to. In fact, maybe I should dock so we can have the whole team there."

Eli would absolutely have my back, though he might also kick my ass halfway across the station for the little lapse in attention that led to the near mugging. But he would join me, even though Tavi needed him on the ship.

I couldn't pull him away from his own job just because things were a little awkward between me and Varro. Same for Chira. She was Torran's first officer, and her duties were on the ship.

And both of them would try to talk me out of going to the exhibition.

"Don't dock," I said quickly. "My invitation is only good for one. I'll take Varro. He's handled this situation really well. I'm the only one who's a mess."

Tavi's eyes flashed. "You're not a mess. I can't believe he left you hanging in silence. I thought for sure . . ." She trailed off and shook her head. "We're going to stick close for a few days. What have you found about the event? Is there something more going on?"

"Not that I've found, but they are hiring extra security. I'm going to keep searching for the reason when we're done chatting."

Tavi's expression hardened until I was staring at my captain rather than my friend. "Agreeing to attend was impulsive, even for you. Are you *sure* you should go? Out of all of the people on the station, why did Anna pick you? What if it's a trap?"

I swallowed the defensive words that wanted to escape because I heard the worry under her grim tone, but her lack of confidence in my decision stung. Yes, I could be impulsive, but I wasn't stupid—I wouldn't have agreed to go if I thought I'd truly be in danger.

Unless Tavi was seeing something that I'd missed?

I frowned at the screen, looking at the event from all angles, trying to see if I'd overlooked anything, and Tavi quietly gave me time and space to order my thoughts.

"I've done a lot of research," I said slowly, "and there just hasn't been any info. If it's a trap, then we're fucked, because it means Morten and his crew have the ability to coerce the biggest fashion designer in the galaxy. I checked the records, and it's really her. I don't know why she chose me, but apparently picking random models out of crowds is also a standard habit of hers." I'd verified that, too.

"You're beautiful. Of course she would want you!"

Tavi's staunch defense made me smile, but I didn't let her distract me. "There might be an attack or something else could go wrong, but I don't think it's a trap—at least, not for us. And if Morten *is* involved, then I might be able to mitigate the damage if I'm there. And catch the asshole. That would be nice. If it's not Morten, then I still might be able to glean some useful intel. We know Morten is working with at least a few Valoffs."

Tavi nodded, face grim. I knew from her expression that she was mentally working through all of the ways it could go wrong, and she would worry until she knew we were safe.

"Agreeing to go was impulsive," I admitted softly, "but it is the right decision. I may not be the strongest member of the team, but I'm not helpless, and I'll have Varro with me. With his ability, he might be able to pick up something from the crowd. But I will keep digging tonight. If anything looks sketchy, we won't go. You have my word."

"I don't think you're helpless, Kee, I just want you to be safe; you know that." Tavi paused and rubbed her eyes, clearly torn between her desire for more information and her desire to protect me. "Keep me posted. I want an update before you leave for the party. And remember to sleep." Her expression softened. "If you ever need to chat, I'm here. Anytime, day or night."

Tavi was a large part of the reason I'd survived the war. She'd helped me through a few hellacious months, and I knew she still worried about me. I nodded, throat tight. "I'll let you know what I find."

"Be careful."

"I will."

She waved, then disconnected, and my slate's screen went dark. I slumped back on my bunk and stared at the ceiling. I'd sounded confident while talking with Tavi because I didn't want her to worry, but now *I* was worried.

Had I missed important data because I was too wrapped up in my personal issues to notice?

I didn't *think* I had, but the whole team counted on me to deliver information, so I needed to be certain.

I pulled back the privacy curtain and hung my head over the side of the bunk. Varro looked up from where he sat, leaning against the wall at the head of his mattress.

"Are you done talking with Torran?" When he nodded, I asked, "Did you learn anything interesting?"

"They are planning to remain close by until after the party tomorrow night. If we need a quick exit, we can take a transport out."

Tavi hadn't mentioned that part, but it was a good reminder. "I'm going to spend some time making sure we're not walking into a trap, but I need to be upstairs at the hotel by eight in the morning. Wake me up if I sleep through my alarm, okay?"

"I'll ensure you're up in time if you promise to get more than four hours of sleep."

"I'll try," I said. "Depends on what I find."

"Can I help you search?"

"Sure, just a second." I lifted my head and the blood rushed out, leaving me dizzy. Note to self, don't hang upside down for more than a few seconds. I gathered my comm and slate, then climbed down and joined Varro on his bunk.

"I'm going to be doing a little illegal breaking and entering, but if you could search the publicly available station message boards, that would help. Let me send you a few places to start."

He picked up his comm. "What am I looking for?"

"Anything that seems slightly off. Hiding information

in plain sight is tricky and not too many people can do it well. But don't worry if you don't find anything because I doubt they are using the public forum."

One eyebrow rose, but he didn't complain about doing what amounted to busywork. It was still work that needed to be done and by giving it to him, it freed my time to work on something else.

We settled into comfortable silence, each occupied with our tasks. I carefully withdrew from the FHP network and reset my security protections, then dove into my regular dark-net information sources. If something was going down on Bastion tomorrow, I would find it.

But the further I dug, the less I came up with.

If it was a trap, then it was the most tightly held secret in the galaxy. That didn't rule out interference from Morten, since I couldn't find him, either, infuriatingly enough. But it wasn't a trap in the sense that the fashion exhibition had been set up to cover for something else.

Anna Duarte really had been working with Rarku Dropror for three years.

I kept digging, certain that I was missing something, but hours later, I hadn't found any new evidence. I rubbed my eyes and admitted that it was time to give up for the night. When I checked with Varro, he hadn't had any success with his searches, either. I wished him good night, then reluctantly climbed up to my bunk and dropped into sleep.

My dreams were plagued by soft brown eyes and quiet, stricken whispers.

CHAPTER NINE

The next morning found me once again at the Eminence, surrounded by what could only be called controlled chaos. Three dozen tailors worked with more than a dozen models in various states of dress. As far as I could tell, most of the tailors were only perfecting the fit on their models with tiny adjustments, but my dress was a little more serious.

Anna Duarte frowned at me as I stood on a pedestal, a quartet of people around me, all frantically making adjustments. Alina stood next to her, dutifully taking notes. "Lose the bra," Anna said at last. "The dress will give you enough support and the lines are distracting."

I refrained from pointing out that the bra had been her idea in the first place. She'd taken one look at the bra I'd worn up here and demanded someone find me something "less hideous."

She was a charmer, no doubt, but I liked her.

And the dress was even better in person than the hologram had made it look. It floated around me in gauzy layers as delicate as gossamer. Every time I moved, the dress changed color as the nearly invisible embedded light panels reacted with a pale rainbow of hues that matched my hair exceedingly well—Anna Duarte had an excellent eye.

I didn't know how she'd done it, but the panels drew energy from the movement itself, so the dress didn't have a single battery pack. It felt as light as it looked, which truly was a marvel. Perhaps the Valovian designers had contributed the technology, which made me wonder what other surprises I'd see tonight.

I smiled as unseen hands undid the back of the dress's bodice, then unhooked my bra and peeled it from my body. Nudity didn't bother me, but even if it did, none of the people around me were paying me the slightest mind. I could've been a mannequin for all the effect my bare breasts had on the room.

Once the bodice was refastened, Anna nodded in satisfaction. She spoke to Alina without taking her eyes from the dress. "I want her hair down and gently curled, makeup soft. Do something about the dark circles." Anna's eyes flashed up to mine. "How are you in heels?"

I looked down. The dress hit just below my knees in a fluttery handkerchief hem that offered little peekaboo slits up to mid-thigh. I didn't feel like the dress *needed* heels, but I'd wear them if I had to. "How high?"

Her smile was all teeth. *"High."*

"Depends. How does your dress look on the floor? Because that's where it'll be when I break my ankle."

Every person around me stilled, but Anna just laughed. "At least you're honest." She gave me another considering look. "How are you with bare feet?"

I wiggled my toes. "As long as we're going to be in some fancy room in this hotel, fine. I wouldn't want to walk around the station without shoes, though."

She nodded and turned to Alina. "No shoes, but find some adhesive protectors for the bottoms of her feet. Have someone give her a pedicure. She will be our nymph for the evening."

After another half hour of poking and prodding, I was left to change back into my own clothes with a stern admonishment to return at seven for hair and makeup before the exhibition started at eight.

Before I left, Alina handed over a black, gilt-edged envelope. "That's the invitation for your guest," she murmured. "I also put his name on the guest list, but it'll be far easier for him if he has the invitation."

"Did all of the guests receive paper invitations?" I turned the heavy paper over in my hands, luxuriating in the feel. The expense of sending out hundreds of these across the galaxy would've been *astronomical*.

"Of course. Ms. Duarte likes to make a statement." Someone called Alina's name and she hurried off, calling over her shoulder, "Don't be late!"

I slipped out the door to find Varro waiting exactly where I'd left him. I'd tried to get him to stay in our room this morning, but he'd insisted on accompanying me.

He straightened. "All done?"

"For now. I have to be back this evening." I handed him the envelope. "This is your ticket in. Don't lose it because they told me the paper invitations are important."

Varro accepted the envelope and tucked it into one of the larger pockets in his pants. "I found a shop that rents formal wear. It's on this level."

I winced. "Nothing on a cheaper level?"

He shook his head. "Seems there's not a lot of demand."

"Never mind," I said with a wave, heading for the exit. "I'll pay, of course, since this is my idea."

In the corner of my eye, his expression hardened. "It's already taken care of."

"Did you go while I was at my fitting?" I asked. I'd hoped to help him choose, but maybe this way was better. I'd see his choice tonight, and I needed every minute between now and then to lock my feelings into an appropriately armored box.

"I didn't leave," he said. "I just prepaid for the rental. I still need to go for a fitting, and I was hoping you would come with me because I don't have a great deal of experience with human formal wear."

The door slid open and we stepped out of the hotel. "What do you wear on Valovia for formal events?"

Varro lightly touched my back and directed me to the left. I shivered at the innocuous touch and my heartbeat picked up. Clearly I was going to need *two* armored boxes—one for my feelings, and one for my unruly body.

Thankfully, Varro didn't notice my distraction. He said, "We wear *zafore,* a long, formal coat that buttons down the front and is usually embroidered."

The Valovan word was unfamiliar, but words for clothes hadn't been a priority during the war. I was fluent enough to communicate, and I'd learned a lot from watching Valovian vids, but there were gaps in my knowledge. I made a mental note to practice more.

"A suit shouldn't be too different, but it might be a little more restrictive."

Varro grunted an acknowledgment and we lapsed into silence. I used the break to try to get my pulse under control.

I had nearly managed it by the time we made it to the understated boutique with a trio of suits in the window. My pulse climbed again, but this time it was at the thought of exactly how much this was going to cost. I'd have to figure out a way to repay Varro. Or maybe I could persuade an employee to let me pay while Varro was changing.

As soon as we stepped in the door, a slim young man in an exquisitely tailored suit approached with a smile. He had pale skin and reddish hair, cut short.

"May I help you?" he asked. To his credit, he didn't bat an eyelash when he caught sight of Varro's distinctly Valovian eyes.

"I have a rental for tonight. I need a fitting."

"Ah, Mr. Runkow, welcome. My name is Tyler, and I will be assisting you today." Tyler turned to me. His eyes were a bright, vibrant green that could not possibly be natural but looked amazing. "And you are . . . ?" he trailed off delicately.

"I'm Kee. I'm here for moral support and unsolicited opinions."

Tyler's eyes crinkled at the corners, but he just dipped his head in acknowledgment. "Right this way, if you please." He indicated that we should follow him with a wave.

The fitting room he led us to was bigger than the cabin we were staying in. A pair of plush chairs and a tiny drink table sat in the back left corner while the right corner was shielded by a folding fabric screen. In the middle of the room, a trio of mirrors surrounded a short pedestal, like the kind I'd spent the morning perched on.

"Mr. Runkow, what did you have in mind?"

"Ask her," Varro said, and Tyler obediently turned to me with a raised brow.

"We're attending the House of Duarte fashion exhibition tonight. He needs to look good enough to get through the door without breaking the bank. Cheaper is better."

"What will you be wearing?"

"One of Anna Duarte's dresses."

If the news shocked him, Tyler didn't show it. "Do you happen to have a picture?"

I took out the card Anna had given me and scrolled through the holograms until I found the dress I would be wearing. Tyler looked thoughtful for a few moments, then nodded. "I have a few things I think will work. Mr. Runkow, if you would undress," Tyler said with a little gesture at the fabric screen, "I will get your measurements."

Varro moved behind the screen, but his height meant that I could still see his head and shoulders, so when he pulled his shirt off, I was treated to a visual feast of tan skin and flexing arm muscles.

I nearly swallowed my tongue. By the time I remembered how to speak, Varro was clearly working on his pants. "I'll just . . . wait outside," I stammered weakly. If only I could remember how to make my legs move.

Varro looked up and met my eyes and something hot and dark licked through his expression. "Would it make you more comfortable?"

I found my voice and answered his question with a question of my own. "Would it make *you* more comfortable?"

"No. I would prefer it if you stayed," he said, and I could almost *feel* his satisfaction when I nodded in agreement.

This is hell, I thought darkly. That was the only explanation, but I sank into one of the chairs in the corner, my legs shaky. The angle meant I could see only the top of Varro's head. I worked on getting enough oxygen into my lungs.

I was an adult. I had survived years of war. I could survive the sight of Varro's naked shoulders. And the thought of him mostly bare behind that thin fabric panel. *I could just walk over there and* . . . I jerked my thoughts back into safer territory.

Tyler finished his measurements and stepped out from behind the screen. "Please wait here. There are robes on the bench so you don't have to re-dress. If you would like something to drink, press the button on the wall and someone will bring it. I will return shortly."

He left and the door clicked closed behind him, leaving the room shrouded in awkward silence. I closed my eyes and prayed to the Blessed Lady for strength.

I heard a soft button press, then a few seconds later a pleasant voice asked, "How may I help you?"

"Could we get two glasses of water, please?" Varro asked.

"Of course. Just a moment."

I cracked my eyes open and found Varro swathed from shoulders to knees in a fluffy black robe. I'd seen him in workout clothes that were far more revealing but something about this felt incredibly intimate.

He sat in the chair next to me, the robe straining over his thick thighs. I dragged my eyes away. Nope. Not going to look. That way lay danger.

The door slid open and an older man in a perfectly tailored suit entered carrying two cut crystal glasses and a heavy carafe of chilled water on a gilt-edged tray. Time had worn creases into his tanned skin and whitened his blond hair, but the signs of age just gave him an air of quiet authority. He set the tray on the little table, then poured two glasses of water with steady hands. He met my eyes. "Will there be anything else?"

"No, thank you," I murmured. I was starting to suspect that the suit rental was going to cost far more than I would like. I should've known just from the location, but I'd been holding out hope.

The man withdrew and Varro handed me one of the glasses. "Have some water."

I sipped at the drink, thirstier than I'd thought. When I poured myself a second glass, a small smile ghosted over Varro's lips. "Yeah, yeah," I grumbled, unnerved by how he always seemed to know what I needed. After a second, I added, "Thank you."

"You're welcome."

Tyler bustled back into the room followed by another person carrying at least four suits. The assistant hung them on the rack near the changing screen, then slipped out the door.

"Mr. Runkow, I brought a few options, but if none of them are to your liking, we will find something else. First." He pulled a light gray suit from the rack. "What do you think?"

"I would prefer a darker color," Varro said.

Tyler nodded, as if he'd expected that result. He put the gray suit back and pulled out another that was a deep, charcoal blue. "I believe this will be a good foil for Ms.

Kee's dress. Black is classic but severe. This is a little softer. Would you care to try it on?"

Varro rose and disappeared behind the screen. Time passed in tiny, precise increments, accompanied by the sound of rustling clothes.

"When you are ready, please step out and I will check the fit," Tyler said.

"I don't know how to tie this," Varro said from behind the screen.

"If you're decent, we'll fix it out here."

Varro emerged from behind the screen and every cell in my body froze before bursting into vibrating excitement. The suit looked like it had been tailored specifically for him. It hugged his broad shoulders and accentuated his trim waist and thick legs. The stand collar was unusual enough for a second glance, but it looked both modern and fashionable.

Tyler made quick work of the plain navy tie. "Slide it behind the waistcoat and step up on the platform."

Varro did as asked, and the view from the back was just as good as the front. Tyler moved around him, checking the fit in various places. "I knew this was going to be the one," he murmured. "It looks like it was made for you. Nothing too tight or uncomfortable?"

Varro shook his head, then met my eyes in the mirror—once I'd dragged them away from his ass. I barely remembered to snap my jaw shut.

"Do you approve?" he asked.

"It looks amazing," I managed to say without turning into a stammering mess. But it also looked *expensive.* I turned my attention to Tyler. "How much?"

"Mr. Runkow has already taken care of the expense,

but I assure you, you will be pleasantly surprised. The owners were quite eager to have one of their suits at the exhibition tonight. All we ask in return is that you mention us if anyone asks."

I tipped my head at Varro. "Does that work for you?"

"Yes."

"Then it works for me."

"Excellent," Tyler said with what looked like true delight on his face. "Mr. Runkow, if you'll change back into your normal clothes, I'll have this packaged up for you. You'll need to return it by tomorrow afternoon. Don't worry about cleaning it—we will take care of that. Oh, and you can leave the tie tied and slip it off over your head."

"I can tie it," I volunteered. "My dad taught me how, unless you've done something complicated."

Tyler shook his head. "This suit doesn't need a fancy knot. Simple will work just as well."

Varro looked at me and then pulled the tie free and let the ends hang over his waistcoat. It should *not* have been sexy, but it was. He looked just rumpled enough to give him a dangerous edge—not that he needed any help in that department.

To get my mind away from subjects better left alone, I returned my attention to Tyler. "I'm surprised you had a suit that fit so well."

"We get a lot of military folks who want to dress up for special occasions, so our stock sizing is wider than usual. Happy customers are repeat customers, so it works out for us as well as them."

The mention of the military was enough to remind me that Varro and I weren't just here to play dress up. I'd been too busy looking up details about the party to keep digging into the FHP servers, but I still needed information about Morten, which meant splicing into the hardline network behind my bathroom wall.

And if that failed, I would be getting intimately familiar with the FHP half of Bastion.

I just hoped it wouldn't come to that.

CHAPTER TEN

Varro and I returned to the room I'd rented. I had hours until I needed to be back upstairs for the event tonight, so I planned to spend the afternoon on research. I was tired of the slow progress I'd made so far, and while I hated to keep Varro cooped up all day, searching for information was the whole reason I was on the station. He could leave if he got bored.

I stared at the wall hiding the bathroom from view. Time for extreme measures.

After I unlocked the main part of my pack, I pulled out a fiber-optic splicer and a quartet of meal bars. I also pulled out a tiny cutter and other tools I might need to remove the bathroom wall.

Varro watched in silence.

I handed him three meal bars, since I hadn't wanted to stop for lunch, and unwrapped one for myself. Keeping him fed was the least I could do.

He ate one of the meal bars, then waved at the pile of tools I'd laid on the bed. "What is all of this?"

"I'm going to punch a hole in the wall in the bathroom, then splice into the FHP's mainline network. This little device"—I held up the splicer—"will not only get us in, but it'll also give me remote access to the network."

"Is it dangerous?"

"Only if I mess it up. In that case, we'll need to change rooms with some haste."

I finished my meal bar while Varro started on his third, then pulled up the station's networking diagram on my slate. It'd taken quite a bit of work to find these, but now I wouldn't have to guess which cable to splice into.

I left Varro on the bunk and headed into the tiny bathroom. The narrow section of wall between the toilet and shower would be my best bet. Everything on a station was designed for easy replacement. If I was lucky, the panel could be removed without damaging it.

If not, well, that was where the cutter came in.

I found and removed four screws, but the panel still didn't budge. After some gentle encouragement—in the form of a thin pry bar and a lot of elbow grease—I managed to pop it off without needing to cut a hole in it.

I set the panel aside and peered into the narrow gap that had been revealed. Two dozen cables crisscrossed the opening in a dozen colors. Electrical wiring and plumbing pipes also crowded into the space. Getting the splicer into position far enough back to replace the panel would be a tight fit.

And after it was installed, I wouldn't be able to remove it without alerting the FHP. Technically, it was supposed to be able to reconnect the fiber without interruption, but I'd never had that part work successfully.

I turned around to find Varro watching me from the doorway. He pointed at the wall. "How do you know how to do this?"

My nose wrinkled. "A combination of misspent youth, military service, and a natural inclination to learn everything I can get my hands on." I laughed. "At least until it gets boring."

"Do you know which cable you need?"

"I'm pretty sure it's this orange one"—I pointed to one of the cables near the top—"but I will double-check with the schematic."

"And that will be enough to get into the FHP network?"

"I hope so. If we're extremely lucky, it'll give me access to the security systems as well as the internal systems. Then, when we decide to visit the military side later, it will be a lot easier to hide."

Varro frowned, but he didn't contradict me. "Do you really think the FHP is behind Morten's kidnapping of Cien?"

"I don't know." Bitterness rolled through me at the admission. "I'd like to imagine the FHP is above kidnapping a child—especially the grandson of Empress Nepru—but I know that's not true. Someone powerful is hiding Morten and his allies, but I don't know who it is. And the fact that I don't know proves just how powerful they are. Not one person on his team has leaked the tiniest bit of information. That would be impressive if it wasn't so fucking frustrating."

"You'll catch them."

"Damn straight I will," I agreed with a grin. "But I wish it were faster. Speaking of, hand me my slate and let's get this show started."

I pulled up the networking schematic, triple-checked

the cable, then clamped the splicer around the correct one. I pushed it back in the wall so that it would be out of the way, then took a deep breath. "Cross your fingers," I murmured.

The click of the activation button sounded loud in my ears. A red light blinked into existence, flashing slowly. As long as the light was flashing, I could cancel the splice.

Thirty seconds later, the light went solid amber. There was nothing I could do at this point but hope that everything went okay. I whispered a quick plea to the Blessed Lady and watched the light like my life depended on it.

Which it might, truth be told.

Just when I'd started to sweat, the light turned green, which meant a successful splice—failure was solid red. I blew out a long breath. "We're in," I said. "Now I just hope they haven't changed their network configuration or we'll be in trouble."

The splicer didn't broadcast its network, but I'd preconfigured it with my slate, so it was a moment's work to connect to it. "Let's see what we have."

"Would you like me to put the wall back?"

"Not quite yet. I need to make sure the connection is working." I tapped on my slate and brought up some of my security protocols, but I didn't bother to route my traffic through a proxy. An outside connection would be more suspicious than not.

An initial scan proved that I was at least connected to a functioning network. Step one: check. I glanced at Varro, still patiently waiting. "You can put the wall back, if you don't mind. Try not to bump the splicer if you can help it."

He nodded, and I squeezed past him, ignoring the tempting heat of his body. I settled onto the lower bunk and started delving into my new playground. My schematic had been correct—this was definitely the secured FHP network. Despite the turmoil of the last few days, this access alone was worth the trip.

As much as I wanted to rush headlong into every database I could find, I had to be careful. Just because I had spliced into the network didn't mean I was past all of their security. I had to make sure I didn't trip any intrusion detection alarms, which meant a slow, methodical search.

After a moment's thought, I tied the splicer's connection to the public network. I was technically opening a hole in the FHP's security, but if anyone found the splicer and made it past my protections, then they would've found their own way in eventually. And now I could access the FHP network from anywhere on the station.

That done, I set a pair of alarms to remind me when I needed to leave so I wouldn't be late for the exhibition, then lost myself in the search. It might take a while, but I *would* find whatever the Feds were hiding.

IT TOOK ME AN HOUR TO LOCATE THE SECURITY CONTROL SYSTEM, and then another four hours to carefully, gently work my way into it without setting off any alarms. But once I did, I had access to every locked door in the station, as well as all of the camera and sensor feeds, including the ones on the civilian side. I wondered how many people knew that the Feds were capable of spying on them even when they weren't in the military zones.

I delicately inserted a new user into the system with override control for all of Bastion's locks, then tied it to the secondary chip on my comm. A burner comm would've been better, but I activated the secondary chip only when I needed it, so I couldn't be tracked by it. And I couldn't give them any biometric data, or an audit would reveal exactly who had been poking around in their system.

Now that none of the doors in the station could keep me out, I started peeking at a few of the different vid feeds, but Varro tapped me on the shoulder. "It's time for dinner. You need to eat before the event."

I waved a hand, most of my attention focused on the slate in front of me. "You go ahead. I'll eat a meal bar."

"You had a bar for lunch."

I hummed in agreement. "I don't mind. That's why I brought them."

"If you come to dinner with me, I'll take you to the bakery I found that sells cookies as big as your face."

I was already pulling up another vid feed when the sentence finally sank through my focus. I blinked up at him. "Really?"

He held his left arm across his chest and dipped his head. "On my honor."

Trust Varro to find the one thing more tempting than breaking into FHP servers. I carefully eased my way out of the system I was in, then disconnected the slate and set it aside. "Do they have snickerdoodle?"

"They did yesterday. I had planned to take you after dinner but . . ." He trailed off and rubbed a hand over the back of his neck.

But instead he'd had to chase me up to the garden because I'd thought my confession had driven him away, and he'd thought I was refusing to talk to him. Clearly our communication needed some work.

I stood and stretched, releasing the tension from my neck and shoulders. "Okay, a quick dinner, a cookie or two, and then we'll head upstairs for the party. Is there anything else you need to do to get ready?"

He shook his head, then led me from the room to the same mess hall we'd eaten at before. The woman who'd offered to get me to safety wasn't there, but she must've spread the word that we were okay, because while we got a few hostile looks, it wasn't nearly as bad as the last time.

We sat at an empty table and people left us alone. As soon as the first few bites of the vegetable pasta I'd ordered hit my stomach, I realized just how hungry I was. The warm food was far better than the meal bar I'd been planning on, and the extra energy would be useful for the exhibition.

"Thank you," I murmured. When Varro cocked his head in question, I added, "For getting me out of the room. I needed this."

He nodded but didn't gloat. His ability to be right without turning into a smug asshole was one of the many things I liked about him.

"Let's talk about the plan," I said. "I'm going to be wandering around in a fancy dress all evening. What are you going to do?"

"Follow you," Varro said, expression hard and flat.

I shook my head and lowered my voice. "I'll have a guard. You need to mingle with the other guests, see if you can find out anything about Morten or the Sun Guardian."

"Unless your guard is a Valoff, they won't be able to protect you sufficiently in a mixed crowd. I will stay with you."

I grinned at him. "My shields aren't *that* bad. I can defend myself for the few minutes it will take you to cross the room."

If anything, his expression hardened more, but he didn't

contradict me directly. "Your safety is my priority." He held up a finger before I could protest. "Captain Zarola's orders."

Exasperation warred with gentle warmth. Tavi was keeping me safe even when she wasn't here. "Fine," I allowed. "You're going to stick with me, but what *else* are you going to do?"

Varro's eyes glinted. "Eavesdrop."

"But—" I bit off the rest of the sentence as his meaning became clear. "You mean?" I wiggled my fingers like I had when I'd asked him if he was using his ability to make the crowd part.

"Exactly. I won't need to leave your side."

"Won't the other Valoffs know what you're doing?"

His smile was quick and dangerous. "No."

Something between admiration and dread crawled down my spine. "Could you read my mind without me knowing it?"

Varro's expression shuttered, but he nodded cautiously.

"Show me? I'm going to think one word over and over. You tell me what it is."

"Kee—"

"I swear I won't hold it against you if you pick up anything else. I just have to know, okay?"

He sighed and something like defeat crossed his face. "Tell me when you're ready."

After strengthening my mental shields as much as I could, I thought about the word I would pick. It had to be unique or it could be a lucky guess. Once I had it, I said, "Go," then mentally repeated it.

Less than a second later, Varro said, "Credenza."

I sucked in a surprised breath. There was *no way* that could've been a guess. Normally when a Valoff made a mental connection, it felt cold in a way that was easy to recognize but hard to explain.

But I hadn't felt the touch of his mind *at all*. Goose bumps rose on my skin. I knew better than to ask a question I didn't want to know the answer to, but I couldn't help myself. "Every time you seem to magically know exactly what I need before I do, are you reading it from my mind?"

Varro's face smoothed into a blank mask that hid his true feelings. "No."

"Not even by accident?"

"No. My shields block outside thoughts. I know what you need because I pay attention." He considered me for a moment, then his voice was very soft when he said, "You are afraid."

I immediately shook my head, then paused and lifted one shoulder. "A little," I admitted, then rushed to add, "Not of you, exactly, because I trust you, but of the ability. I always thought I'd *know* when someone was in my head, even if I couldn't do anything about it."

"My skill is rare. And you are not wrong to be afraid. Even other Valoffs fear me and my abilities." His voice was flat but held an undercurrent of pain.

Anger flared. "Are Torran and the others—"

"No. We trust each other implicitly. And if not for Torran, the war would've gone much worse for me."

"He saved you like Tavi saved me," I murmured.

His chin dipped in silent agreement. I had a million questions I wanted to ask, but his closed-off expression told me that this was a sensitive topic. And since I refused to talk about my time before I'd joined Tavi's squad, I let it go and turned back to the original topic. "I felt the mental connection before, when you were shielding for me on Valovia. That felt normal."

Some of his tension bled away and he shrugged. "I can do it either way. I figured that would make you more comfortable."

I smiled at him. It felt a little fragile around the edges, but I fought hard to make it genuine. "Thank you for showing me. And for being so considerate, both on Valovia and by taking care of me. I'm glad one of us is paying attention."

The wariness didn't completely leave his expression, but he tipped his head in acknowledgment.

I redirected the conversation back to safer waters. "So you're going to be working, and I'm going to be prancing around in a glowing dress. Seems unfair."

A tiny smile stole across his mouth. "You're going to be distracting everyone, making my job easier."

I leaned in, my voice conspiratorial. "You may not know this, but I am *excellent* at distracting people."

His face softened for a moment before he schooled his features into a grave expression and inclined his head. "They won't know what hit them."

WE FINISHED OUR DINNER, THEN VARRO BOUGHT ME A COOKIE that was, indeed, as big as my face. He also picked up a medium-size box wrapped in a bow, but he wouldn't let me peek inside, no matter how much I wheedled.

Back in the room, I ate my cookie while Varro changed into his suit. I'd tried to convince him that he didn't need to go upstairs when I did, since he'd be waiting around for an hour before the exhibition started, but there was no arguing with the man.

Varro had put the bakery box in the storage bin with firm instructions not to touch it, so of course the only thing I wanted to do was see what was inside.

I needed a distraction, but I resisted the temptation to look at my slate. My first reminder alarm had already gone off, and if I started poking around in the FHP network again, I would miss the event entirely. The bathroom door slid open, saving me from myself.

At least until Varro stepped into view.

I'd forgotten just how lovingly the suit encased his body, the dark charcoal blue a perfect foil for his tan skin and blond hair.

I might've stared at him forever if he hadn't offered me his tie. "Will you tie this for me?"

My scattered wits were beyond recovery, but I nodded and stood, accepting the silky tie. I looped it around his neck, smoothing it under his shirt's collar. I peeked at his face and found him watching me with intent focus.

My hands trembled under the weight of his gaze.

It would be so easy to tilt my face up and taste his lips. I gathered my fraying control and wrapped the tie over itself. I could hear my dad's coaching in my head as I tied the simple, even knot. I snugged it against Varro's collar, then absently straightened the length by running a hand down his chest.

His hand closed over mine, trapping my palm against his waistcoat. He waited with endless patience for me to gather the courage to meet his eyes. When I did, he murmured, "Thank you." His expression remained unreadable, but the dark streaks in his eyes had expanded.

I pretended that he didn't draw me like a magnet. "You're welcome."

He let me go and I swallowed my disappointment, but he only bent to retrieve the box from the bakery. He held it out to me, his expression solemn even as his eyes burned. "I apologize for yesterday. You caught me by surprise, and I am sorry I hurt you."

Embarrassment flared into my cheeks, but I waved my fingers in a dismissive little gesture that cost me far more than I was willing to admit. "No apology needed, and we *really* don't have to talk about it. Ever."

Varro continued to hold the box out to me. It was *vosdodite,* a Valovian apology gift, and unless I accepted the gift, he wouldn't believe that I accepted his apology.

Did I accept his apology?

I stifled a sigh. It wasn't Varro's fault that yesterday had been excruciating. He really didn't have anything to apologize for, but I reached for the box anyway. All I had to do was accept it, and then we could put this whole thing behind us.

As I lifted the box from his hands, relief washed across his face. I gently placed it on the bed, untied the ribbon, and opened the lid. Twelve huge snickerdoodle cookies—my favorite—waited inside.

"I couldn't make them myself, so this was the best I could do," Varro murmured.

"They are perfect. Thank you." I broke off a piece of one and popped it in my mouth. If anything, these were even better than the one I'd just eaten. I broke off another piece and lifted it to Varro's lips. "Try it. They're delicious."

He stole the piece of cookie directly from my fingers. My gaze snagged on his lips, and my breath caught as I realized exactly what I'd done. I tried to jerk my hand back, but Varro caught it before I could.

His thumb traced a blazing path over my fingers, and he stared at me, expression once again unreadable. Finally, he asked, “Why do you think I’m not interested in you?”

I huffed out an unamused breath. “Perhaps because when I told you I was attracted to you, you stared at me in silence for five minutes.”

One corner of his mouth tipped up. “It wasn’t that long.”

“Well, it felt like two hours,” I grumbled.

“What else?”

I could tell him about all of the times I’d very obviously flirted with him only to get nothing but grunts or polite smiles in return, but why drag up all of that pain? I sighed and looked away. “Does it matter?”

He leaned down, looming over me until his words rumbled directly into my ear. “Yes,” he said, his voice deep and sure, “because, to borrow your words, you could not be more wrong.”

CHAPTER ELEVEN

I blinked, sure I'd misheard. I pulled back until I could see his expression. If he was mocking me, I would dump his apology cookies on his head, then kick him in the shin. *Repeatedly.*

But Varro's face was serious, his expression calm and open. Only his eyes gave away his inner turmoil, the dark streaks expanding against the deep, tawny brown of his irises.

I frowned in confusion. He might not be mocking, but his confession didn't match his past behavior. "I flirted with you and you ignored me. You never once flirted back or noticed me as anything more than a friend. I kept asking you to do things with me, and you did, but it seemed more like duty than fun. And you never asked me to do anything with you."

Varro's expression clouded. "When I get close to someone, my shields have a tendency to . . . thin," he said, old pain echoing in his voice. "It's not something I do consciously, but when it happens, I have a higher chance of catching their thoughts—or of them catching mine. I refused to let that happen with you because I refuse to break your trust. So I kept myself locked down, especially because I thought you were just being nice."

He held himself stiffly, as if he was expecting a blow. And the thought of someone in my head without my knowledge did make me uneasy, but it wasn't an insurmountable problem. Hopefully.

Still, I couldn't quite believe that he actually liked me. I brought my gaze back to his. "To be clear, I wasn't being nice. Well, yes, I was. But I wasn't *only* being nice; I was flirting. And you ignored me."

His eyebrows rose. "When I made you food, you complained about the ingredients."

"I was *teasing*! And you cooked for anyone who was around."

He shook his head. "I cooked for *you*. They just benefited from being nearby."

Nervous butterflies took flight in my belly, and I frowned, trying to remember if that was true. I'd *thought* he cooked for everyone, because there were usually others around, but he often finished the meal just as I wandered in.

Hope fizzed through my veins. Was it possible that we'd both thought we were being obvious, and we'd both been oblivious? My fingertips tingled with a combination of nerves and excitement, and I couldn't help the smile blooming on my lips. "We have *got* to work on our communication."

Varro's gaze moved over my face with the kind of intent

focus that made the butterflies take flight again. "Agreed," he murmured, his voice a soothing rumble.

"So how do we give this a shot," I said, waving my free hand between us, "without you ending up in my thoughts?"

Varro's eyes turned bleak before he hid whatever he was feeling behind a blank mask. "We don't."

I sucked in a breath at the unexpected pain. "So you confessed just to tell me we don't have a chance?"

"I've tried everything," Varro said, his head bowing in defeat. "Anything short of constant, conscious control and my shields will eventually slip."

"What does that mean exactly?"

"I will be able to sense your emotions and hear some of your thoughts, especially if you're thinking about me. And the same goes for you—you'll be able to faintly sense my thoughts and feelings. Would you like a demonstration?"

I hesitantly nodded. A moment later, emotions washed through me that I instinctively knew weren't mine. Longing, desire, fear, and hope were a jumbled mess that closely mirrored my own tumultuous emotions. Then Varro's voice whispered in my head, "You're the most beautiful woman I've ever seen," and I could *feel* the sincerity behind the words.

The wild, reckless hope I felt was all mine, but by the way Varro's eyes widened, maybe he'd caught a piece of it. "I want to try," I breathed. I pressed my fingers to his lips when he would've interrupted. "I know it will be an adjustment, and if you don't want to, then we won't. But I'm willing to try if you are."

He must've replaced his shields because I didn't catch any of the feelings I could see flickering across his face as he stared at me. Finally, he asked, "You're sure?"

"I am." Since this seemed to be the day for confessions, I whispered, "I wanted you the moment I saw you, and I've been fighting my feelings for you for weeks."

He groaned and his expression heated. "May I kiss you?"

"Yes, *please,*" I demanded.

Varro let go of my hand and leaned down, his searing gaze fastened to my face, his focus absolute. I had no doubt that if I showed the slightest hesitancy, he would pull back, but that was the last thing I wanted. I bit my bottom lip and his eyes turned black as the dark streaks overtook his irises.

My eyes slid closed as his lips brushed against my mouth. I savored the simple, dizzying pleasure for a moment, then I gripped his shoulders and pulled him closer. He wrapped his arms around me with a low sound, and his mouth settled more firmly over mine. I moaned as sparks exploded along my nerves, and I caught the faintest hint of his desire as his shields faltered.

I pressed closer, needing more, when my second reminder alarm went off, shattering the moment. Varro straightened, and I groaned out a curse. I opened my eyes and reluctantly let him go.

After a deep breath, I ducked my head and focused on silencing the alarm, then checked the time and cursed again. "I've got to go or I'll be late, but this conversation isn't over."

His hot gaze raked over my face, and a tiny smile pulled at the corner of his mouth. "I'm glad," he growled, his voice deep.

I closed my eyes against the surge of desire that made me want to forget about the fashion exhibition altogether and instead spend the evening exploring his body. But once again, I was racing ahead of myself. When I wanted something, my focus became absolute, and many people recoiled from that level of attention, especially when they were still deciding if they were even interested. I'd driven away more than one romantic partner by moving too fast and being too "clingy."

It was something I knew was an issue for me, which was why I'd tried so hard to keep my distance from Varro after he'd ignored my attempts at flirting. But now that I knew he *was* interested, I would have to be even more careful. Just because we had chemistry to spare didn't mean that we needed to immediately tumble into bed—or that he'd even want to.

I was on Bastion to do a job, so I took a deep breath and put my desire aside.

Once I was sure that I wouldn't reach for him, I looked him over, struck again by how good he looked in a suit. "Tuck the tie behind your waistcoat, and I think you're ready. Lucky you. I've still got an hour of prep ahead of me."

I stuffed a few more supplies in my pockets while Varro fixed his tie and pulled out his paper invitation, then I handed him my comm. "Will you carry this for me? I'm not sure I'll be able to carry it with the dress, and if things go wrong, it will be useful."

He accepted it with a nod and slipped it into the inside pocket of his jacket. "If you're ready, I will accompany you upstairs. May I shield for you tonight?"

I wrinkled my nose, worried about what he might pick up from my turbulent thoughts, but if he was right about his shields naturally thinning, then I needed to get used to it. Still . . . "Do you think it's necessary?"

"If you're right about the number of Valoffs who will be attending, then it's a good idea. I will keep it light, and they will think you just have a better-than-average shield for a human. But if they try to breach it, I will know."

"Okay," I agreed, even though the butterflies were back in my stomach.

He crossed his chest with his left arm. "Thank you. If you need me, mentally shout, and I will hear it."

I really, really hoped that wouldn't be necessary.

IN THE ROOM THE HOTEL HAD SET ASIDE FOR FITTINGS AND PREP, this morning's chaos had been amplified by nine million. Half-dressed models—both human and Valoff—shouted at the people helping them, harried tailors looked like they hadn't slept in a week, and assistants crisscrossed the room carefully carrying clothes worth more than I made in a year.

"Kee, over here," Alina shouted from somewhere in the din. I finally spotted her a little off to my left, standing with a trio of tailors and the dress.

"You're late," she said, when I finally worked my way through the crowd to her side.

I rolled my eyes. "By two minutes. That's practically early."

She shook her head at me but didn't argue. "Let's get you changed."

I stripped out of my clothes and the people around me got to work. They poked and prodded and sewed and adjusted until the dress draped my body in perfect, floating waves of color.

Then I was off to have someone fix up my hair, face,

hands, and feet. And through it all, I could feel Varro's presence in the back of my mind, a slim buffer between me and everyone else.

By the time Alina returned to stick the adhesive protectors on the bottoms of my bare feet, I felt a little like I'd survived a sparring round with Eli—and the night hadn't even started yet.

She silently led me to a full-length mirror, and I gasped in surprise. My makeup was subtle, but it made my light brown eyes look huge. Most of my hair was loose around my shoulders in colorful waves, but a circular braided section around the top of my head formed an anchor point for a delicate, intricate crown inset with jewels that matched the ever-changing color of my dress.

I really did look like a nymph queen who'd just emerged from a sheltered wood.

"How does everything feel?" Alina asked from behind me. "Anything loose or uncomfortable? You'll be stuck like this for the next several hours, so the time to speak up is now."

I took a few steps and then bounced on my toes. The crown stayed rock solid, and the dress fluttered around me. The foot protectors felt a little weird, but I figured it was just something I would have to get used to.

"Everything feels good," I said.

"If you need to go to the bathroom, do it now. I'll find your guard. We've paired you with Nick. They're one of our most experienced guards, so you're in good hands. They will ensure no one touches you."

I nodded. "Sounds good, but I will take that bathroom break. I'll be right back."

I made my way across the room to the row of locked

boxes where all of the models had secured our belongings. I keyed in the code to open my box, then surreptitiously slid a tiny plas blade and an adhesive holster from between the layers of clothes.

Barely bigger than a knife, it wasn't the full-sized blade I usually carried, but it was the only thing slim enough to conceal under my gown without altering the flow of the skirt. I locked the box, then went to the bathroom and applied the holster to my outer right thigh.

The underskirt was just full enough to slide past the blade and holster without catching. I checked my appearance in the mirror, but I couldn't tell that I was armed even though I knew where to look. Good enough.

When I returned to the main room, most of the tailors and beauticians had cleared out, and models were starting to find their guards. I found Alina standing next to a pair of people in dark suits. One had pale skin and short, black hair and the other had tan skin and long, blond hair.

The blond inclined their head at something Alina said, then moved off. My breath caught. I wasn't close enough to say for sure, but I'd bet a great deal of credits that they were Valoff. I hadn't known that security would be a mix of humans and Valoffs, but with the mix of models, it made sense.

Alina waved me over. "Kee, meet Nick. They're your guard for the evening."

Nick was a few centimeters taller than me, with a lean build and sharp eyes that never stopped moving. If they were armed, I couldn't tell.

I smiled in greeting. "Nice to meet you. I've never done anything like this before," I said with a wave around the room, "so if I do something stupid, please let me know."

Nick met my eyes and grinned. "Will do."

"Have you ever had problems at one of these things?"

"A few, especially once the alcohol kicks in. But don't worry. I won't let anyone touch you."

Before I could respond, Alina interrupted. "If you two are good, I have a few more things to take care of."

Nick nodded, and I waved her off. "I'm good. Thanks for all your help."

"You're welcome," she said, already on her way to head off some new disaster.

I glanced at Nick, then decided to be upfront. "My plus one is liable to stick close to us tonight. He's Valoff. Is that going to be a problem for you?"

Nick's grin deepened. "As long as he doesn't try to touch your dress, it won't be a problem."

THE HOTEL BALLROOM HAD BEEN TRANSFORMED INTO A DARK, MAGical paradise. The lights were dim and intimate, the better to show off the illumination in the clothes.

Varro was waiting just inside the door. When he caught sight of me, I felt a stab of stark yearning, and it took me a second to realize that it'd come from him. Hot, dark eyes caressed me from the top of my crown to my bare toes, a stroke I could nearly feel.

"You are stunning," he breathed.

A pleased blush warmed my cheeks at the undisguised admiration on his face. "Thank you. You're not too bad yourself."

Nick cleared their throat delicately, and I laughed. "I think that means it's time to earn my pay," I stage-whispered to Varro.

After a quick introduction, I moved deeper into the crowd with my two bodyguards in tow. Nick and Varro nodded warily at each other, then seemed to come to an unspoken understanding. Nick stayed closer to me while Varro orbited at a slightly greater distance.

But no matter where he was physically, I could always feel Varro's mental shield protecting me—along with tiny flashes of his emotions, too brief to identify.

I stopped to watch in awe as one of the other models spun into a graceful pirouette on pointe shoes. Their dress flared around them and digital flames engulfed their body, so realistic that several people gasped in surprise.

My own dress floated around me like a gossamer cloud, glowing with gentle, rippling color. I'd never felt more like a fairy princess, and I found it difficult to keep my mind on work.

A stranger reached for me, but before their hand made contact, Nick was there to block it. "No touching the art," Nick said for the tenth time in as many minutes. I had a feeling we'd both be heartily sick of the phrase before the night was over.

"But this fabric is incredible," a masculine voice said. "Surely one little touch won't hurt anything?"

I glanced at the older human man as he tried to slide past Nick. He wore a black tuxedo that looked expensive, as did the heavy watch on his wrist.

"If you touch any of the exhibits or models, you will be forcefully removed from the room," Nick said flatly.

The man sniffed and reached for me again. "Anna Duarte is one of my—"

Varro loomed at my side, but before he needed to intervene, a security guard appeared at the man's elbow. "Come with me," he said.

"This is an outrage!" the man shrieked. "Do you know who I am? I will not allow—"

From his expression, the guard either loved or hated his job, but either way, he wrapped a hand around the man's elbow and dragged him away in the middle of the tirade.

"Thank you," I murmured to Nick.

They grinned at me. "This job has its perks. Kicking out self-righteous assholes is one of them."

"What if he really *was* important?"

Nick made a dismissive gesture. "Ms. Duarte gave us photos of the dozen or so people she considers friends or essential to the show's success. Everyone else is fair game."

I continued drifting through the crowd, stopping to let people admire my dress, and making small talk while they did. So far, I hadn't heard a single suspicious word. I caught Varro's eye and thought very loudly, "Have you heard anything?"

He shook his head.

It should've made me feel better, but instead, anxiety brewed in my stomach. Despite all of my research, I couldn't help but feel like I'd missed something. The crowd ebbed and flowed around me, humans and Valoffs socializing with bright smiles and wary eyes.

A Valovian model wearing an exquisite tuxedo, complete with top hat and walking stick, approached from my left. His silvery hair fell over one of his pale eyes, giving him a rakish look, and his skin was golden tan. When he got within a few meters, his suit, which had been black, started to glow very faintly.

The model smiled and swept into an elegant bow. When

he rose, he offered me his hand and the color from my dress climbed his jacket sleeve, transforming his tuxedo. Varro muttered something under his breath, but neither he nor Nick intervened, so I figured this must be part of the show.

I slid my fingers into the model's hand and he carefully drew me closer. "Pretend to be enthralled," he murmured as a secret grin flirted with his mouth.

Honestly, he was gorgeous, so I didn't have to pretend too hard. I tried to look properly smitten as the color from my dress spread across his suit. Instead of dimming, my dress glowed more brightly as we began to match, pulsing like a heartbeat.

It was absolutely stunning, and I had to work to keep my mouth from falling open in awe. The growing crowd around us murmured their approval and watched with rapt attention.

The stranger dipped his head. From a distance, it probably looked like he was nuzzling me, but instead, he whispered in my ear, "Are you okay with me twirling you?"

Varro's presence in my mind sharpened, and I tried to send him a wave of reassurance, then nodded at the unknown Valoff holding me so carefully.

"I will twirl you away, then I will leave. Watch me until the dress stops pulsing." He pulled back enough for me to see his lips quirk. "Try to look heartbroken."

"Perhaps *you* should look heartbroken," I murmured.

"Oh, *heme,* I will," he purred. "Ready?"

I tried to keep my face set into its lines of longing, but a smile peeked through. "Yes, *darling,* I am."

Surprise flashed across his face that I'd understood the Valovan word. He dipped his head in acknowledgment, then he raised his hand to twirl me away from him. The layers of my dress flared wide as I spun. I stopped facing him with my arm extended, our palms still clasped.

His hand slid from mine, and I let my arm hang in the air for a long moment as he steadily backed away, gentle longing on his face.

The pulses in my dress slowed and the brightness dimmed. Across from me, the colors faded from the Valoff's tuxedo until he was once again clad in black. With one last, lingering look and a touch to his hat, he disappeared into the crowd.

The group around me burst into applause, and Nick had to keep a million hands from reaching for my dress. For once, I didn't blame them. I had no idea that the costumes interacted with each other, and the amount of technical skill that must've gone into it kind of blew my mind.

"What did he say to you?" Varro murmured, close enough that I could almost feel the heat from his body.

I slanted a glance at him. His jaw was clenched tight, and his eyes were still locked onto where the other Valoff had disappeared. I decided to poke him, just a little. "He called me 'darling' in Valovan."

Varro's eyes narrowed and a muscle in his neck flexed.

"But," I continued softly, my voice pitched for his ears only, "I prefer 'bright star.'"

I saw the moment Varro parsed my words because his eyes darted to mine, his mouth opened in surprise, and a flash of pleasure echoed through my mind. He reached for me, but Nick blocked his hand.

"Don't make me kick you out," Nick grumbled. "You know the rules."

Half an hour of mingling later, a chime rang through the air, and hidden spotlights illuminated a small, raised stage at the far end of the room. Anna Duarte and an unknown man stood together, both dressed in the absolute height of fashion. The man had light brown skin and straight brown hair.

"Thank you all for joining us," Anna said, her voice amplified by the speakers in the ceiling. "Tonight's exhibition is the culmination of years of work, and the first in what I hope will be a long and prosperous partnership between House of Duarte and Rarku Dropror."

Light applause rippled through the room.

Anna waited for the room to quiet before she continued. "Tonight, we have one final surprise for you, but I'll let Siarvez Sofdol, head of Rarku Dropror, tell you about it."

The man next to Anna bowed to her in thanks before returning his attention to the crowd. "As Anna said, we have worked closely together to bring you tonight's show, but none of this would be possible without the support of one of our biggest patrons. Please welcome His Imperial Highness Liang Nepru."

I froze in shock and a murmur went through the crowd—I wasn't the only one surprised. Liang Nepru was the empress's fourth child. What in the hell was a member of the imperial family doing on Bastion, even one so far removed from the crown?

A very familiar figure stepped onto the stage and my jaw dropped. Silvery hair, top hat, tuxedo, and walking stick. The man I'd thought was nothing more than one of the other models smiled at the crowd as he moved to stand next to Anna and Siarvez.

"Thank you," he said, his voice deep, just a little playful, and lightly accented. "It is my pleasure to be here tonight, and I thank both House of Duarte and Rarku Dropror for letting me wear this amazing piece of art and technology." He gestured at his tuxedo.

"I believe art—and fashion *is* art—can build bridges and reveal common ground. I hope that this partnership becomes an example that many more companies will follow in the coming months and years. And I am excited to see what Anna and Siarvez will dream up next."

He smiled again, and the audience clapped politely even as the whispers continued. Anna started speaking again, but Varro turned to Nick. "Did you know?"

Nick nodded. "We were briefed. He also had more security than the one visible guard trailing him. I think it was a bit of a last-minute change. His security team approved it only because the guest list was small and his face is relatively unknown, even on Valovia."

I glanced at Varro. "Did you recognize him?"

He shook his head. "I might've without the hat, but like that, no."

I tried to match the playful man in an expensive tuxedo to the empress who wanted us dead and came up blank. Either Liang Nepru was the galaxy's best actor or he didn't share his mother's goals.

So which was it?

I was trying to decide how to get close enough to talk to him again when a wave of force punched me in the chest, stealing my breath, and the wall next to the stage exploded into shards of shrapnel.

CHAPTER TWELVE

Varro tackled me to the ground as a second explosion rocked the room. People screamed in panic, but it all felt distant because of the ringing in my ears.

"Are you okay?" Varro shouted.

His hand cradled the back of my head, so it hadn't smashed into the floor, but the rest of me wasn't so lucky. My back and shoulders felt bruised, but I nodded anyway. I tried to peek past him to find Nick, but Varro's body blocked my view.

"People are starting to panic," he growled. "We have to get up so we don't get trampled. I'll help you."

Varro lifted himself into a crouch and scanned the room for additional threats, his face set into granite lines of fury. After a moment, he stood and helped me to my feet. In the distance, a siren wailed, but the explosion had been well contained. The wall next to the stage was missing, as was one closer to us, but nothing was on fire.

A team of six soldiers in Valovian armor had surrounded Anna, Siarvez, and Liang. At first, I thought they were Liang's security, but several of the soldiers had their weapons trained on the trio they'd surrounded, and three bodies in dark clothes were on the ground, unmoving.

Two of the soldiers seemed to be arguing. A man in a suit crawled out from under a pile of rubble and climbed unsteadily to his feet. He stared and the soldiers around Liang froze.

A telekinetic.

With a telekinetic on our side, we might stand a chance. Liang grabbed for the nearest weapon, and I tried to shove my way through the crowd.

Neither of us were successful.

One of the soldiers broke free and shot the telekinetic in the head. He crumpled without a sound, but the crowd reacted with even greater panic, lurching away from the stage. Varro caught me before I was swept away, then he cursed darkly, his body a line of tension.

The closest soldier shoved Liang away and brought his rifle up again. The prince backed off, lifting his hands.

Nick appeared at my elbow. "We need to get you out of here," they shouted. "There is an emergency exit in the back."

The crowd surged around us, scrambling away from the drama unfolding in the front of the room, but I shook my head. "Do you have a weapon?" My tiny knife wasn't going to do much against Valovian armor.

"You're no match for a squad of Valoffs," Nick argued.

"They're human," Varro said, then tilted his head and focused on the stage. "Mostly. At least one Valoff."

Varro grunted as someone slammed into his side. He

remained planted as the woman bounced off him and sprawled on the floor. I winced as someone stepped on her. Varro bent and hauled the woman to her feet, then gave her a push toward the exit.

"Give me your weapons, then leave with the others," I told Nick. "I'll return the dress later if I can."

"Fuck the dress," they shouted. "You'll get yourself killed."

"If I survived the war, I can survive this," I said with more confidence than I felt. I'd survived the war because Tavi and Eli had constantly watched my back.

A soldier hit both Siarvez and Liang with a plas blade set to stun. Both men fell screaming, and the soldier pulled out an injector and jabbed it into the prince's thigh through his tuxedo, then repeated the operation with Siarvez.

A moment later, the Valoffs slumped into unconsciousness, and two soldiers crouched over them. Each soldier picked up one of the Valoffs, slinging them over their shoulders, while a third stood with a pistol pressed to Anna Duarte's head.

When another soldier approached with an injector, Anna stumbled back, but she didn't get far. The soldier injected her, seemingly with a bit more care, then picked up her unconscious body.

"Give me your weapons," Varro demanded with a flinty look at Nick. "I don't want to take them from you, but I will."

I'd seen Varro furious before—recently, in fact—but this transcended even that. He'd turned from the quiet man who made me protein-packed smoothies into a hardened soldier who barked commands and expected compliance. I shivered at the change, glad that he was on our side.

Nick's mouth pressed into a flat line, but they handed over a plas pistol and a plas blade. Varro handed me the pistol and kept the blade. He looked at me. "Plan?"

I let out an unconscious breath. He still wanted my help. At least I wouldn't have to fight him about that. I wiggled my fingers. "Can you disable them?"

Varro shook his head. "Too risky with a Valoff shielding for them and the hostages."

"Can you hide us?"

"Yes, once we're out of this." He waved at the chaos of the room. "But possibly only from the humans."

Nick pulled *another* pistol from a hidden holster and looked at Anna, dangling over one of the soldier's shoulders. "I will help. What can I do?"

Varro herded us behind a wall of potted trees as the crowd began to thin. So far, the soldiers weren't indiscriminately killing civilians, but they wouldn't ignore our weapons, no matter how shiny my dress was.

I desperately needed to change, but I didn't have time.

"As long as they're staying put, I'm going to try Tavi," I said. "Let me know if things change." Varro nodded, so I activated my subvocal comm. "Tavi, are you in voice range?"

"What's wrong?" she asked immediately.

Our comms were encrypted, but I had no doubt the Feds could tap in if they wanted to, so I had to be careful how much I revealed. "There's been an attack. Humans in Valovian armor took hostages. V and I are going to follow. Can you get anyone here?" And, as much I would like Torran's help, his presence was far too dangerous—if this wasn't Morten's plan, then the Feds would be looking for a scapegoat. "Keep T on the ship at all costs."

Varro crowded me farther into cover as the soldiers on

the stage started to visually sweep the nearly empty room. As far as I knew, Valovian helmets didn't have thermal cameras, but they *did* have excellent night vision, so we had to stay hidden by more than shadows.

"The station is in lockdown," Tavi said. "No one in or out, including transports."

"Shit," I breathed. Varro and I were on our own.

"Fuck, I knew I should've docked," Tavi growled.

I winced but didn't contradict her.

"Kee, don't engage. Your safety is my main priority, even if that means they escape. We can find them again."

"There are some extenuating circumstances that make that a bad idea. I'll be careful. Let me know if the lockdown lifts. And be on the lookout for any ships leaving in a hurry."

"If there's been an attack, there might be a mass exodus as soon as they lift the restrictions, but I'll keep you posted."

I murmured my agreement, then dropped the connection. "The station is in lockdown," I told Varro. "So no backup." And we couldn't count on station security either, since they hadn't bothered to show up yet.

If this was a plot by Morten or the Feds, then security would take their sweet time.

At some unseen signal, the soldiers started moving toward the hole in the wall. "Can you tell which one is the Valoff?" I asked quietly.

"The one carrying Siarvez," Varro said.

I glanced at the group again. A Valoff of unknown ability plus five other soldiers with pistols and rifles, all in near impenetrable armor, versus the three of us in suits and a glowing dress.

Following them would be the height of stupidity.

"Last chance to back out," I whispered to Nick.

They stubbornly shook their head. "You weren't the only one who survived the war."

The soldiers disappeared into the next room. Varro eased around the trees. "Stay behind me and stay silent," he warned.

I ignored him and whispered, "Can you track them after they get out of sight?"

"Yes, for a while. The Valoff is shielding them, but I'm stronger."

"Then let's check on the people they shot. I didn't see any weapons on the telekinetic, but I think some of the others were also the prince's guards. We might be able to score a few more weapons."

Varro led us to the front of the room. "Be quick." He glanced down. "And watch your feet."

The protectors on the bottoms of my bare feet weren't meant to protect against exploded wall—or blood. I carefully approached the first body and shoved aside my revulsion. He didn't need his gun anymore, and I *did,* so I quickly searched him. The Valoff had lightweight armor on under his suit, but that hadn't saved his life.

Stripping the armor would take too long, so I picked up his plas pistol and returned to Varro, who'd been searching another downed Valoff—this one still moving.

"They have the prince," the man gasped in Valovan.

"Help is on the way," Varro said, his tone reassuring.

I glanced at the empty room. Was that true? If so, we needed to go. Varro caught my look and nodded.

Nick dropped a pair of boots next to me. "They'll be too big, but they're better than nothing."

I murmured my thanks and bent to put them on while trying very, very hard not to think about where they'd come from. They were a few sizes too big, and I didn't have any socks, but they protected my feet, and that's what mattered. I laced them tight around my ankles to keep them in place, then followed Varro to the hole in the wall.

I handed him the extra plas pistol I'd found, and he swapped the blade to his off hand. Then he stepped into the hallway without looking.

"Wait," I whispered, alarmed. "Look before you just—"

He turned back with a tiny, confident smile. "The hall is empty. The nearest people are at least two rooms away."

Right, I'd forgotten that he could feel people nearby. That was certainly a handy skill.

"But we need to move," he said, voice low. "The soldiers are getting farther away."

He headed right at a fast jog, and Nick and I fell in behind him. "Are they heading for a landing bay or transport hub?"

"Not yet."

We ran through the empty halls of the hotel. We saw only a handful of people, and none of them paid us any mind. Either Varro was mojoing them, or they were in too much shock to notice their surroundings.

We exited the back of the hotel into a narrow service corridor. Varro tilted his head as if he was listening to something far away, then he turned left. A few meters down the hall, he tried to open a door set into the firewall, but it was locked tight.

He looked like he was contemplating kicking it down, but I held out a hand before he could try it. "Give me my comm."

Varro handed it over, and I quickly activated the secondary chip, then waved it over the lock control.

The door unlocked, and it was my turn to toss Varro a confident little smile. I'd still be fucked if I couldn't fix the logs, since the door had likely made note of the primary chip even from a distance, but we had bigger problems right now.

I jammed the comm in the bodice of my dress and hoped it would stay put. If ever a dress needed pockets, it was this one, right now. As soon as we rescued Anna, I'd lodge a formal complaint.

The door led into a maintenance tunnel, one of the hundreds that snaked through the station. Small, cramped, and sweltering, the tunnels were the perfect way to escape notice—at least from bystanders.

Because of the security risk, the Feds heavily monitored every tunnel route, which meant if they were going to mount a defense, they'd know exactly where to find the fake Valoffs—and us.

I didn't have time to override the security cameras, and I wasn't sure tipping my hand quite yet was the right call. We hadn't done anything wrong, so I just hoped that whoever was watching the video was susceptible to Varro's ability to keep us hidden.

Varro moved at a quick jog and by the time he slowed, sweat was beading on my skin and running between my breasts while my boots chafed the skin of my ankles.

At the next intersection, he stopped. "The team split," he said quietly. "Four are heading down with Ms. Duarte, two are taking the two Valoffs that way." He waved off to our right.

"Which way is the Valoff who's shielding for them going?" I asked.

"With the Valovian captives."

Shit. I tried to remember my mental map of the station, but it was lost under adrenaline and distraction. "Do you know where they're heading?"

"As far as I remember, that's the FHP controlled part of the station."

Well, fuck. If we didn't rescue the prince, we'd have a war on our hands for sure, but I desperately wanted to go after Anna. She'd been kind to me, in her own way, and I hated that someone was using her as a pawn.

"I'll go after Anna," Nick said. "You two rescue the Val-offs."

I didn't have time to argue, as much as I'd like to. "Do you have a comm?" When they nodded, we quickly exchanged contact info.

"Don't try to take them out yourself," I said sternly. "And don't count on support from station security. If you can track them to a ship, I can track them off the station. I have a team on a nearby ship who can rescue Anna without risking her life—or yours—so keep me posted about what's happening. We'll join you as soon as we can."

Nick nodded, then we separated. I hated sending them off alone, but I didn't know what the FHP had planned for Liang, and I didn't want to wait and find out.

Varro and I followed a convoluted route through the twisting maintenance tunnels that I would never be able to duplicate. I hoped Nick had better luck with the team they were tracking.

When Varro stopped at a door in the wall, I glanced at him. "Is this it?"

"As close as I can figure. There's no one directly on the other side, but there are several people moving nearby."

"How far away is the prince?"

Varro tilted his head and narrowed his eyes in concentration. "Not too far. Probably within a hundred meters."

A hundred meters might not be too far on land, but on a station, that distance could feel vast, especially if we needed to sneak through open hallways with others around. If this really was part of the FHP base, then security would be even tighter than in the rest of the station.

I straightened my spine. "Okay, you tell me where to go, and I'll open the doors."

"Try not to make any noise," Varro warned. "The more senses I have to override, the harder it is. I'm still shielding for you. If you need to talk to me, think loudly in my direction."

I nodded and stepped up to the door, but he caught my hand before I could swipe my comm over the control panel. "Wait, someone is approaching."

"One of the soldiers from the attack?"

He frowned in concentration, then shook his head. "Seems to be a standard patrol. We'll wait until they've passed." He touched my cheek, and his fierce scowl didn't quite hide the worry underneath. "And once we're through the door, be careful."

Reason deserted me, and I lifted on my toes. I brushed my lips across his, a barely there ghost of a kiss. "I will be."

He growled something under his breath, then his arms clamped hard around my waist and his mouth covered mine with heated possessiveness.

My body went liquid with pleasure, and I moaned in delight. This was exactly what I'd been craving. His lips parted, then his tongue slid against mine, and shivers raced down my spine. I clutched his shoulders and plundered his mouth with single-minded determination. I wanted him to feel as good as I did, to feel the heat, the need, the *wanting* that I'd been feeling for weeks.

Varro's hand slid over the curve of my ass, and I pressed harder into him, trying to meld our bodies together. His desire, burning and fierce, washed through me and ratcheted my need higher. Tiny alarms started ringing in the back of my mind, but I ignored them until there was only the slick glide of his lips and the hot clutch of his hands.

When he broke away with a gasp, I chased his mouth. He cursed under his breath, then wrapped his hands around my waist again and gently pushed me away, until our bodies no longer touched.

I frowned as I tried to get my fuzzy brain to work. Had I misinterpreted his interest? Had the desire I'd felt from him actually been just an echo of my own feelings? Or, more likely, had I stormed straight past his comfort level because I'd been too focused on pleasure to see the signs?

I never, ever wanted to make him uncomfortable, and shame bowed my head. "I'm sorry," I whispered. "Sometimes I get carried away, but that's no excuse. I—"

Varro pressed a finger to my lips, silencing me. When I peeked up at him, his eyes were almost completely black, and they pulsed with hints of hidden color.

"No," he growled, his voice low and rough. "If it were up to me, I would already have your legs wrapped around my waist and my c—" He bit off the rest of the sentence with another curse, then visibly sucked in a deep breath and held it for a long moment before continuing. "But we are in danger here, and I can't concentrate well enough to keep you safe while you unravel me, so we must wait."

"So I didn't make you uncomfortable?"

He shifted and a tiny grin pulled at the corners of his mouth. “Not in the way you’re thinking.”

It took me a second to connect the dots, then my eyes dropped to the large bulge pressing against the front of his pants.

I licked my lips and his hand flexed against my waist, but I dragged my mind back to the conversation at hand. “Please let me know if I ever *do* make you uncomfortable. I try to watch for the signs, but sometimes I get overwhelmed and too focused on something else.”

“Kee, I was with you all the way.” He cut me off before I could interrupt. “But I will let you know if I’m not.”

My chin dipped in gratitude, and I tried to ignore the hot throbbing between my legs. I’d had a range of partners, from mediocre to fabulous, but none had sent me up in flames as quickly as Varro.

And I had a feeling that if I wasn’t careful, he would burn me to the ground.

CHAPTER THIRTEEN

I crept through the hall behind Varro, trying to keep my boots from clomping against the hard metal floor. A female soldier passed within half a meter of us, and I glanced longingly at her uniform. As much as I wanted to change, I wouldn't kill someone just for new clothes, and anything less was likely to give away our presence.

So far, we'd gone undetected, but I wasn't sure how long our luck would hold.

I'd scoped our route via the security feeds before we'd left the maintenance tunnel, and as far as I could tell, we were still on the base's periphery. Most of the rooms here were for storage and maintenance. There were a few soldiers in the halls, but not as many as we'd find deeper in the heart of the FHP part of the station.

Someone didn't want their Valovian guests to have an audience.

That worked well for us, but without knowing why they had abducted Siarvez and Liang, it was difficult to make a plan. However, waiting wouldn't make it any easier, so I hoped the element of surprise worked in our favor. No one expected us to pop out of thin air, and that gave us a tiny advantage.

Quiet, furious voices echoed down the hall, and Varro slowed as we reached the next intersection. "The two we've been tracking are just ahead, as are three more humans. The captives are nearby, but not with the others," he said, his voice a murmur in my head.

"You don't understand," a male voice hissed in a Valovian accent, obviously trying to whisper but not quite succeeding. "That's the prince in there. I didn't sign up for this."

"You are being paid well," another male voice answered, likely human. "You knew there might be complications."

"This isn't a complication; it's a disaster. If anything happens to him, the empress will *destroy* everyone involved, and I'm not strong enough to contain him when he wakes up. Every Valoff in the station will know exactly what you've done because *he* knows that it was humans who attacked. War will be the least of your concerns."

"So we'll kill him now," the human said.

The Valoff muttered a string of curses.

"We'll keep him drugged," a female voice interrupted. I couldn't place her accent, but it didn't sound Valovian. "This is a boon and the commander is already working on a way to use it to our advantage, so there will be no rash decisions. My team will handle it from here," the woman continued. "Return to the others and continue with the plan." The command was impossible to miss.

"You don't understand—" the Valoff tried again.

"We have plenty of experience dealing with Valoffs," the woman said harshly, the threat crystal clear.

"C'mon," the human man said. "Let's go."

I didn't hear anything else, but Varro silently pulled me into the nearest doorway. "Don't move," he told me telepathically.

The unseen woman barked, "Check on the Valoffs. Keep them unconscious and let me know if their vitals change. If they wake up, it's your heads." Sharp footsteps echoed down the hall, heading away.

Before I could relax, two people in Valovian armor rounded the corner. The visors on their helmets were open, revealing their faces. The man closest to us had light eyes streaked with a darker color—a Valovian trademark.

The Valoff stared right at us and a tiny flicker passed over his face before he turned his gaze elsewhere. I held my breath, every muscle locked and ready to launch into motion. Had he seen us?

The human continued past without even glancing in our direction. "You shouldn't argue with Collins," he muttered. "She's the commodore's right hand, and she'll fuck you up."

"She's playing with fire."

"Better her than us," the human said, his voice fading out as they disappeared down the hall.

"Did he see us?" I thought loudly in Varro's direction.

"No, but if he gets curious and comes back, that might change. We should move. There are only two humans remaining, and they are both likely in the room with the captives."

If we could quietly take them out before they called

for backup, we might be able to rescue the two Valoffs. My comm piped an alert to my implant. The trigger I'd put on the door to the maintenance tunnels had just gone off. The two soldiers must be taking the same route as the others, and they weren't wasting any time.

"Nick, you're about to have incoming," I said subvocally over the comm. "The two we were tracking are returning to the group."

Nick sent me a short acknowledgment, and I turned to Varro. "Can you hide a door opening?"

He shook his head. "I can hide us as we enter, but they'll see the door open."

I gritted my teeth against the violence to come. I was no stranger to violence, but it never got any easier. Varro needed my help, so I pushed aside my hesitation. "Let's do it before anyone else shows up."

Varro led the way around the corner and stopped in front of a sliding metal door. The control panel glowed red—locked. I'd have to reveal my override ability again, but I'd hidden the secret account fairly well. Maybe they wouldn't be able to revoke my access before we made it off the station.

I caught Varro's eye, and he nodded at me. "Move far enough into the room that the door closes," I thought at him. "I'll take whichever is on the right." His chin dipped, and I activated the chip in my comm, then swiped it over the control panel. The light turned green and the door hissed open.

The room was set up as an impromptu medbay. The two Valoffs were strapped to hospital beds while two humans stood over them—a blond man and a brunette woman, both in FHP uniforms.

The soldiers turned to the door with frowns on their faces, but when no one appeared, the man rolled his eyes. "Goddamn doors are acting up again. You'd think we could afford tech that actually worked once in a while."

The door closed and relocked with a soft metal rasp. I asked the Blessed Lady for forgiveness, then snapped my pistol up. The man was on the right, and my line of fire was clear. I dropped him with a single shot.

By the time I swung my pistol left, the woman was already on the ground, unmoving. "Check the Valoffs," I said. "See if you can get them awake."

I scanned the room. A pair of rucksacks were stacked in the corner. I opened the first one and clothes and rations spilled out. These two were likely supposed to be on assignment somewhere else. Interesting, but not my main concern right now.

The shirt I shook out was too big to be the woman's, so I moved to the next bag. *Jackpot.* I pulled a spare uniform from the bag and started putting it on. The woman, whose body I was trying very hard not to look at, was a little taller and broader than me, but it was better than the dress I was wearing.

I turned my back to Varro and wiggled out of the dress, then pulled on a long-sleeved shirt. Or, rather, I tried to, but it got caught on the crown I'd forgotten about. After a moment of flailing, I freed myself and unpinned the crown from my hair, then pulled on the shirt and pants.

There weren't any spare boots, and I refused to strip hers from her corpse, so I put on a double layer of socks and slid my feet into the boots I'd been wearing before. Hopefully the socks would prevent some of the chafing issues I'd had before.

The dress and crown were far too distinctive to leave behind, so I carefully wrapped them together into a bundle that would hopefully protect the delicate crown. I emptied the woman's backpack, then stuffed the bundle in the bottom and tossed in a pile of rations, just in case. If everything went according to plan, we'd be back on *Starlight* before food became an issue. If not, well, at least we wouldn't starve.

By the time I slung the bag over my shoulder, Varro had both of the Valoffs unstrapped from their beds, but neither of them was moving. Had they been dosed again or was the first dose still keeping them asleep?

With them out, my chances of slipping away to do a little snooping were approximately zero. While the post-attack confusion would be the perfect time to poke around, Varro couldn't carry them both, and as much as I wanted to know what Morten was up to, I wouldn't hand over two hostages to the FHP.

Varro's eyes cut to my new clothes and pack, then back to the Valoffs. He frowned, probably trying to figure out how he would carry them both and shield for all of us.

As if I'd let him do *all* of the work.

"I can carry one of them if you can help me get him over my shoulders." There was no way I could deadlift that much weight, but once it was balanced, I could carry it.

I hoped.

Varro's eyes swept down my body, judging my fitness, but he didn't argue. He helped me drape the Valovian prince over my shoulders in a fireman's carry that left one of my hands free—two if I wasn't moving. I took several tentative steps while Varro picked up Siarvez.

For having such a lean build, Liang was surprisingly

heavy, and having him wrapped over my shoulders wasn't super comfortable—likely for either of us. As long as I didn't fall down, I'd be okay, but I'd have to be careful not to bash his head into walls and doorways. I didn't need to accidentally give him a concussion on top of everything else.

Unfortunately, being so close to my dress meant Liang's tuxedo glowed with a rainbow of colors. Without Varro's ability, we would draw all kinds of attention. I just hoped the prince didn't decide to wake up and stab me in the face before I could prove that I was on his side.

"Will you be okay carrying him?" Varro asked after he'd gotten Siarvez situated over his shoulders.

"For a while. And let's try to avoid climbing stairs. Or descending stairs." I grinned and waved a hand. "You know what, let's just avoid stairs in general."

Varro nodded solemnly, a hidden smile in his eyes. "Let me know if you need help."

The alarm on the door from the maintenance tunnels went off again, and I sighed. "Now what?" I pulled out my comm to check the video. An unknown woman with ivory skin and braided blond hair stepped into the hallway. She wore an FHP admiral's uniform, but why would an admiral arrive via maintenance tunnel?

"We've got incoming," I said. "A woman just entered from the same tunnel we used. She's dressed as an FHP officer, but admirals don't usually skulk about."

Varro's eyes went distant, then his face blanched and he cursed darkly in Valovan. "We need to move right now," he whispered, his face once again all hard edges and fierce concentration. "That's the telekinetic from Cien's rescue. If she catches us, we're dead."

I captured a screenshot of the video. The angle wasn't

great because her face was mostly covered by her hat, but it was better than what we'd had before, which was nothing. The cool feeling of Varro's mental shield increased. He was trying to keep us hidden from the other Valoff's senses.

Torran had barely prevented the telekinetic from killing Tavi, and without him here to help, Varro and I had precious few seconds to make ourselves scarce. Torran thought she was one of the empress's elite Sun Guardians, but even if she wasn't, she was still too strong for the two of us. We couldn't fight her and win, not alone.

Varro pulled me into the hallway and turned away from the intersection leading back to the maintenance tunnel entrance. He broke into a light jog, and I struggled to keep up with Liang's additional weight. We were heading deeper into the FHP base, but it was better than meeting a telekinetic head-on.

I kept an eye on her progress. She moved with confidence, not stopping to check directions at the intersections she passed. "Do you think she's here for the prince? Should we leave him somewhere she'll find him?" I wasn't sure noise of any sort was safe right now, so I thought the questions as loudly as I could.

"I don't know," Varro responded telepathically. "She protected Cien, but she wasn't at the party earlier. I don't know where she came from. It's possible she has her own agenda."

The heavy weight of the Valovian prince pressed into my shoulders. Were we saving him by keeping him with us, or were we preventing him from getting the help he needed?

On my comm, the telekinetic passed the room where we'd found Liang and Siarvez without stopping. She wasn't here for the prince—or she knew he wasn't in the room any longer.

Either way, we needed to stay ahead of her.

At the next intersection, I tapped Varro's shoulder and pointed right. Varro and I circled back toward the maintenance tunnel entrance while the Sun Guardian moved deeper and deeper into the FHP part of the station. Varro kept us hidden by using his ability, but the Sun Guardian's apparent rank and confident stride meant that FHP soldiers saluted and moved out of her way. No one wanted to draw an admiral's attention.

Varro and I slipped through the hallways, avoiding people when we could and freezing in place to make it easier for Varro to shield us when we couldn't. It felt like we'd been on the run for ages, but according to my comm, less than ten minutes had passed when we arrived at the entrance to the maintenance tunnel.

After Varro verified that there was no one on the other side, I unlocked the door and we eased into the tunnel. I'd lost track of the Sun Guardian a few minutes ago, but she'd been aiming for the heart of the base. Was she planning to carry out a solo attack? She was powerful enough to do it, but what would she gain?

War would be a given, but I'd thought the empress was trying to pin the blame on the Feds, not start the war herself. It was much easier to rally public support for war around defense rather than aggression. And after three years of relatively stable peace, most people would not be delighted to return to the horrors of war.

There was no way for me to warn the FHP soldiers about the Sun Guardian without causing even greater chaos, so I hoped that they were paying attention. Nick, too, would be on their own until we got the prince to safety. Hopefully the Valoff would wake soon and contact his guards. Until then, we were all the protection he had.

"Let's head back the way we came. If the soldiers had the surveillance turned off for this section, then we might be able to sneak through."

Varro nodded and took the lead.

I followed him and activated my subvocal mic. "Nick, how's it going?"

"The group is still heading for the lower levels, but it's slow going because they're sticking to the maintenance tunnels. The other two haven't returned yet."

"We have the prince and Siarvez. We need to get them to safety before we can join you. There's also a telekinetic floating around. She has blond hair and is wearing a Fed admiral's uniform. If you see her, do not engage. She'll kill you before you know you're under attack."

I wasn't sure if Nick was *trying* to send me the flurry of curses that followed or if their thoughts were just too vehement for the subvocal mic to ignore.

With another admonishment to be careful, I cut the connection, then looked at Varro in front of me. His suit was looking more than a little rumpled, and I winced. Hopefully the shop would agree that an attack constituted unusual circumstances and wouldn't charge him for damages.

But the two of us were far from inconspicuous. I had a man taller than me whose tuxedo constantly changed colors draped over my shoulders. Varro carried one of the most famous fashion designers in the Valovian Empire. We couldn't move through the station like this or even Varro's ability would be hard-pressed to keep us hidden.

But we'd have to risk it because the Feds would be

scouring the tunnels soon enough. The smart move would be to catch a transport directly to *Starlight,* but with the station in lockdown, none would be running. I could potentially override the transport lock, but then I'd just be dragging trouble directly to Tavi's doorstep.

We needed somewhere to hide until we could escape.

A memory rose of the woman who'd been concerned that Varro was holding me against my will. She'd given me her contact address, but I didn't even know her name. It was a risk—possibly a huge one, considering her reaction to Varro—but I didn't have anything else. Returning to our room would potentially lead the Feds straight to my splice into their network. And once we had the prince secure, I still had to track down Morten.

I fired off a message to the address the woman had given me. We were nearly back to the main part of the station when the reply came. It was just a location and nothing else. A quick search showed that it was in the main module of the station on one of the lower levels just above the docks.

Getting there would be tricky, and there was no guarantee that we wouldn't find a host of guards waiting for us. I'd told her that trouble was following me, but I hadn't exactly given her *all* the details, so even if there weren't guards there when we arrived, it was possible she'd call them after she saw who our passengers were.

There were eyes everywhere on a station. With enough time, I could blind some of them so we could slip through unnoticed, but time was in short supply. Anna was still captive and the telekinetic was roaming around, too. We needed a home base so we could just breathe for a second and make a plan without constantly looking over our shoulders.

With that thought in mind, I moved up until I could tap Varro on the back. When he turned, I held up the comm. "We need to head here," I thought at him. "The woman who offered to free me from you is giving us a temporary place to hide."

His brows drew together. "Is that a good idea?"

"Do you have a better one? We can't get to *Starlight* until the station comes out of lockdown. And we can't get rid of him"—I pointed at the prince on my shoulder—"until he wakes up."

After a moment Varro reluctantly nodded in agreement.

We exited into the service corridor behind the hotel. The hallway was empty and the whole floor felt eerily quiet. We needed to work our way down about fifteen levels. Stairs would be the safer route, but I couldn't navigate that many flights while carrying more than my body weight.

"There is no one in the immediate vicinity, but there are several people in the hotel, all human," Varro whispered into my mind.

"We need to get to the elevator. Or go down a level via the stairs then catch the elevator. Whichever is easier for you to keep us hidden."

"Can you manage a set of stairs?"

I wrinkled my nose but nodded. I'd manage. Somehow.

We crept through the level on soft feet. FHP soldiers had finally arrived and guards were posted every ten meters. The rest of the level was empty. People were either being confined in their rooms or station security had actually evacuated the entire level.

Two soldiers guarded the entrance to the stairs. They were too close for us to slip past them.

Varro approached, but before I could warn him not to

hurt the soldiers, his voice whispered into my mind. "Don't move or make a sound."

I halted in place. It was weird, standing in the open, in plain view, and yet remaining unseen.

One of the soldiers jerked his head to the side. "Did you see that?"

"What?" his female partner asked.

"Something moved over there."

"It's probably just your imagination. Stay put." Her head whipped to the side. "Never mind, I saw it, too. Call it in, and we'll check it out. I'm on point."

The two moved away from the door. As soon as they disappeared around a corner, Varro darted forward, and I followed on his heels. The door didn't automatically open, and the control panel lit red.

I used my comm to override the lock, and we entered the stairwell. The stairs were wide and well lit. The stairwells weren't only for emergencies, so they were maintained along with the rest of the public spaces.

I put my comm away and clutched the handrail. The first step nearly buckled my leg, but I clenched my teeth and kept moving. I hit the landing halfway to the next floor and paused for a breath. There was no way I'd be able to climb back up, so down was the only option.

Varro moved easily, like he wasn't carrying a whole other person, and I hated him just a tiny, tiny bit. He stopped at the door leading to the level. "Two people standing on the other side," he said telepathically.

I sighed as I reached him. "Down another level?"

"Can you make it?"

I nodded, and we started down again. Every step burned as my leg muscles fought not to collapse under the extra weight. Eli would never, ever let me live it down if I dropped the Valovian prince on his priceless head because I hadn't spent enough time in the gym.

Then, two steps from the next level, the entire stairwell went completely, relentlessly dark.

CHAPTER FOURTEEN

The inky darkness disoriented me, and I stilled, clutching the handrail. Logically, I knew that the landing was only two steps down, but it might as well have been a kilometer. The sound of doors unlocking echoed from above and below, and I wondered just how fucked we were.

"Are you okay?" Varro asked, his voice soft.

"I'm still here," I said, deflecting. "The emergency lights should come on in a second."

Sure enough, a faint glow started high on the wall in front of me and grew until I could see—not well, but better than nothing.

Varro frowned up at me. "What's happening?"

"I'm not sure. The doors unlocked, which means that the safety feature tripped. I don't know if the whole station lost power or just part of it."

Varro tilted his head. "There is no one guarding the door."

I forced my trembling legs to carry me down the two steps to the landing. "Let's peek outside, then."

I slid the door open and peered into the dim twilight of emergency lighting. I blinked, hoping that the scene would change, but no, it remained the same. I checked my comm, but I couldn't connect to any of the cameras I'd been monitoring—or any other system, Fed or public. The network itself remained up, but every system appeared to be down.

So we were *super* fucked, then.

I blew out a slow breath. "As far as I can tell, the whole station is down, so no elevators, which means the stairs are about to be entirely too crowded."

I felt a flicker of his concern as he asked, "Can you make it the rest of the way?"

I clenched my jaw. "No. Not fast enough." Shame burned through me, and angry tears filmed my eyes, but Varro merely nodded, expression soft.

"We'll go as far as you can. We need to put distance between us and the upper level. Tell me when you are done and we'll find a place to rest."

I'd made it down two more levels and was nearly ready to call it quits when the prince jerked. I clutched at the handrail and barely kept us both upright.

"Varro," I called urgently. "I think my passenger is waking up." By the time I reached the next landing, Liang was starting to actively fight me. Luckily, he was still pretty out of it, and I had him wrapped around my shoulders, but it wouldn't last for long.

Varro put Siarvez down in the corner of the landing, out of the way of the growing trickle of people. Then he plucked Liang from my shoulders and set him beside Siarvez. I moaned in relief as my spine decompressed.

I could literally skip the rest of the way down the stairs now.

Liang blinked fuzzily at Varro, who'd crouched down in front of him. "Who're you?" he slurred in Valovan.

"Your rescue plan," Varro responded in the same language. "What do you remember?"

Liang frowned, then his gaze sharpened. "There was an attack. Humans dressed in Valovian armor."

"Good." Varro nodded. "We"—he hitched a thumb at me over his shoulder—"rescued you from them."

Liang looked up. His eyes were a pale, striking blue with deeper blue streaks. Along with his fine bone structure, silvery hair, and golden tan skin, he was beyond gorgeous, even if he looked a little rough around the edges right now.

His eyes narrowed on my hair. "You're the woman from the party," he said in Common. "With the glowing dress."

I nodded warily as his gaze raked over the rest of me.

"You're FHP." I could hear the derisive snarl beneath the words.

"Not for several years," I said quietly. "But a glowing dress wasn't the best disguise, so this was the better option." I eased closer and waved at him. "I'm Kee."

His gaze flickered to Varro, and he had the slightly distant look of a Valoff using telepathy.

"Kee carried you out of the FHP base and down four flights of stairs," Varro said, his voice firm. "You owe her."

Liang reluctantly lifted his hand in a reciprocating wave, his chin tilted at an imperious angle even though he remained seated. "I'm Liang."

"Can you manage the stairs?" Varro asked. "We have

a place to hide until you can summon your guards, but it's down a few more levels."

Liang's eyes narrowed on Varro. "Who are *you*?" he asked in Valovan.

"I'm Varro Runkow." When the prince merely waited, Varro sighed and added, "General Fletcher's weapons specialist."

Liang went so still that he had to be controlling some sort of reaction. After a moment, he said, "I can manage the stairs. Help me up."

Varro stood and hauled the prince to his feet, then bent to pick up Siarvez. The crowd in the stairwell was growing by the second.

"Keep an eye on Liang," Varro said telepathically. "He's hiding it, but he's still woozy from the drugs."

The warning didn't come a second too soon. Someone bumped into Liang, and he stumbled. I wedged my shoulder under his right arm before he completely lost his balance, and his weight once again strained my leg muscles.

"It's okay to need help," I told him quietly.

He wrapped an arm around me without a word, and we headed down. I could still feel Varro's presence in my mind, and the crowd seemed to unconsciously flow around us. I wondered if he was still shielding all of us from sight.

The stairs were easier with Liang on his feet, though he leaned heavily on my shoulder. By the time we made it to the correct level, I was sweating and trembling with exhaustion, and Liang wasn't in much better shape.

Only Varro seemed unaffected, even though he'd shouldered the biggest burden—literally.

Darkness shrouded this level, too, punctuated only

by the emergency lighting. Was the whole station down? I checked my comm, glad that I'd saved an offline copy of the station map because the public servers remained inaccessible.

If the station stayed down for much longer, people would start to panic. Life support and the atmo barriers in the landing bays were on triple-redundant backups and isolated from the rest of the systems, but that was thin comfort when you were stuck in the dark.

Not to mention that nearly all the doors would be unlocked by default as a safety precaution. The station balanced on the edge of chaos. One tiny push and everything would go to hell.

I tried my subvocal comm as we moved through the hallways toward the address I'd been given. "Tavi, can you hear me?"

"What the hell is happening over there? Are you okay?" Tavi responded, her voice vibrating with worry.

"We're okay. Someone took out the station's systems. Not sure how yet, but everything except for emergency backup power and life support is out."

"The open comms are going crazy. Ships are demanding authorization to leave, but the docking department doesn't have access to any of their systems. They're ordering everyone to stay put to prevent collisions, but I'm not sure how long that will hold."

Ships colliding in the landing bay was a good way to end up with a hole in the station, and then it truly would be chaos. We needed to get out of here.

"Let me know if ships start leaving," I said. If they did, I'd risk overriding a transport, assuming I could get access to the control system. Perhaps we'd be missed in the confusion. "We have a place to lie low and regroup, so don't worry about us."

I didn't need to see her to know that Tavi was rolling her eyes. The captain would always worry about us. "Be safe. Keep me updated when you can."

I agreed and ended the connection. The hallways around us had gotten narrower, and I checked that we were still heading the right way. We weren't quite in the maintenance tunnels, but we weren't far off, either.

With Liang still using me as a crutch, I stopped at the indicated door and pounded a fist on the metal and polymer panel. Backup power wasn't wasted on door controls, so doors had to be manually opened and closed—and there was no way to see who was on the other side without opening the door.

The door cracked open a bare centimeter. I caught a flash of movement, then the door eased open a little farther.

"Are you responsible for all of this?" the woman questioned with a scowl and a wave at the door. Her ebony skin and dark hair gleamed in the emergency lights.

"No."

She eyed me for a long moment, then looked at my companions. Liang leaned heavily against my shoulder and Siarvez remained unconscious, draped over Varro's broad shoulders. The woman frowned. "What's wrong with them? And why is his suit glowing?"

"Someone wanted to use them as hostages, but we rescued them. They've been drugged. They were both part of the fashion exhibition." When her frown didn't lift, I continued, "I'm Kee. I swear we didn't attack the station. Please help us."

The woman blew out a long breath, then nodded. She

slid the door open enough for us to pass through, then closed it and manually locked it behind us.

The room was filled with various boxes and crates, but she led us around the largest pile and then ducked under a tarp. Inside the impromptu tent, a pair of cots, two chairs, and a low table were clustered together.

"You can call me Devora," the woman said. She gestured to Liang. "Put him down before he falls down."

I helped the prince sit on the edge of the cot, then sank down next to him, grateful for a break. Varro put Siarvez down on the other cot, then sat in the chair closer to me.

Devora paced across the narrow space. "Tell me what happened."

I gave her a quick overview without getting into specific details like Liang's identity. The less she knew, the better for all of us—including her. Her expression remained flat through the entire saga.

Once I was done, she shook her head. "You're in deep shit."

I laughed. "I know. Will you help us or should we go?"

"I will help as long as you swear to leave me out of it if you get caught."

"We will," I agreed.

She waited for Varro and Liang to dip their heads in agreement before she continued. "What do you need?"

"Do you know what's happening with the station?"

"Not exactly, but the rumor mill suggests it's malware in the main system. Luckily the vital backup systems seem to be unaffected. Comms are still up, but most everything else is down."

I nodded in unconscious agreement. Malware would explain it. But who had planted it? To take out the whole station, you'd need access to one of the main systems—ideally more than one—so the defensive measures in place wouldn't have time to activate.

My breath caught. The Sun Guardian. She'd waltzed straight into the heart of the Fed's domain. She could be the hacker, but even if she wasn't, all she had to do was plug in a device as close to the datacenter as possible. The script would take care of the rest.

Depending on the strength and maliciousness of the attack, security could have the station back up and running somewhere between minutes and weeks. Weeks of downtime meant a full-scale evacuation, something that had never happened on Bastion before.

Was this the opening salvo in a new war?

I rubbed my face. There were still far too many unknowns, starting with Anna Duarte. I activated my subvocal comm again. "Nick, how's it going?"

"Not now," they chided and closed the connection.

That didn't exactly fill me with confidence, but at least they were still alive. I turned to Liang. "Can you contact your people?"

"My people are dead."

I blinked at him. "You don't have a ship waiting for you?"

"I came as a surprise guest of Rarku Dropror for the fashion exhibition. I traveled with Siarvez."

"So the e—" I bit off the word before I gave away too much in front of Devora. "Your family doesn't know you're here?"

Liang shook his head, and I pressed my fingers to my temples. "This is a disaster," I muttered. "I just wanted to wear a pretty dress for an evening of fun, but nooooo." I remembered who I was sitting next to and winced. I peeked at him. "Sorry, that was incredibly insensitive. You've lost far more than I have. Are you okay?"

"No, but I will be."

That sounded ominous. I didn't blame him for wanting some vengeance; I just hoped it wouldn't lead to war. I needed to ensure that Varro clarified exactly who was to blame because I doubted Liang would believe me while I was wearing a freaking FHP uniform.

I waited a second, but Liang didn't elaborate, so I turned my attention to Devora. "Do you know of a way to leave the station without drawing any attention? I have a ship nearby, but they can't dock because of the lockdown."

Her nose wrinkled, then she shook her head. "Transports are grounded, too. Until they get the main controls back online, only the emergency escape pods will be active, and taking one of those won't be inconspicuous. Plus, the pods are automatically routed to the lunar base orbiting Expedition, so you'd have to travel all the way there before you could switch ships."

"Which would give the FHP plenty of time to send a message ahead to have us detained."

Varro blew out a heavy breath. For the first time tonight, he looked tired, and my heart clenched in sympathy. He glanced at Liang. "How much security does Siarvez have aboard his ship?"

Liang's jaw clenched. "Not enough to dissuade trained soldiers."

Varro nodded as if that was the answer he'd expected. "Will the captain take them in?" he asked me.

"Of course." Tavi took in strays like nobody's business. She'd saved my life countless times during the war, starting when she'd approved my transfer into her squad. I squared my shoulders and tried to look intimidating. "But *I* won't bring that drama to her door without some assurance that the Valoffs won't hold her responsible in any way."

In other words, I wanted to be sure that the empress wasn't going to put a bounty on Tavi again just because she'd decided to help.

Varro and Liang communicated silently for a moment, then Liang turned to me. He put his left arm over his chest. "I swear that no harm will come to you or your crew, from me or anyone in my family."

Valoffs placed high value on personal honor, so it would have to do. Now we just had to figure out how to get off the station.

A loud alarm pierced the air as my comm received an emergency broadcast. A second later, Devora's comm added to the cacophony. I checked the screen while attempting to silence the alarm, and nearly dropped the whole device.

My own face stared back at me from the alert.

The photo was several years old, probably pulled from my FHP records, but it was definitely me. I skimmed the message, blinked, then read it again, but the words didn't change.

Neither did the second picture, one of Liang and me at the party standing close together, while I smiled up at him. We'd been surrounded by a crowd. Anyone could've snapped the photo, but I had to give them credit—they'd moved fast considering there was no way they would've known beforehand that I would be at the party.

Unless . . . I shook my head. I refused to believe that Anna had somehow orchestrated a random encounter with me just to invite me to a party to become a patsy. Someone had recognized me, and then decided that I could be useful after all.

Not only were they blaming the attack on me—and Liang—they were blaming me for the malware, too. I was now the proud owner of a fifty-thousand-credit bounty. At least Varro had avoided being implicated—so far.

Devora looked from her comm to me and back again.

I jumped to my feet, unable to sit still. She backed up, her expression wary, and I held up my hands. "I swear it's not true," I said, panic bleeding into my words. "None of it. If you turn me in, they'll kill me and make it look like an accident. Then they'll go to war with Valovia."

"What's going on?" Varro demanded.

I held up my comm with the alert still visible. "The FHP is blaming Liang and me for the attack and the malware that took down the station. They're also saying that we abducted Anna; that it was all a plot by the Valovian Empire to destabilize Bastion and the FHP."

Devora sighed. "We need to get you off the station."

I nearly slumped in relief. "Thank you." Now if only leaving were so simple. With the bounty, I couldn't override a transport because the Feds would be on Tavi before I completed docking with *Starlight*. I could try to steal a whole ship, but that wasn't as easy as it sounded—and it sounded damn hard.

We could try to take Siarvez's ship, but just getting it out of the landing bay would be nearly impossible, assuming we could get to it at all.

My mind spun in a thousand different directions, trying to find something, *anything,* that would work. My comm implant crackled to life, and I held up a finger to let everyone know I was talking with someone else.

"You're suddenly very popular," Nick said.

"Tell me about it. Where are you? Did you find their ship?"

"You could say that. It's the *Renegade Tide*." They rattled off the ship's identification number, and I added it to a note in my comm.

"How many are onboard?"

"Twelve, including myself and Anna."

"You're on the ship?" I hissed in disbelief. "Did they catch you?"

"Not yet."

I squeezed my eyes shut and asked the Blessed Lady for patience. Unfortunately, she must've been busy because I still wanted to yell at Nick until I lost my voice.

"I think they're trying to get permission to launch, even with the lockdown. I can't hear very well from where I am, but someone mentioned Expedition."

"Get off the ship. We can track it without you risking your life."

"I'm staying. I'll update you when I can."

I knew obstinance when I heard it, so I just sighed and wished them good luck.

"What now?" Varro asked.

"Nick is on the ship with the attackers and Anna, and the ship is trying to launch."

"The station is in lockdown," Devora protested. "They won't let any ships leave because it'll start a panic."

I shrugged. "The Feds make the rules and they can make the exceptions, too."

Siarvez groaned and clutched at his stomach. His eyes cracked open, and he frowned at the tarp over our heads. "Where am I?" he asked in Valovan.

"The exhibition was a blast," Liang said drily. "Remind me never to join one of your ventures again."

Siarvez rolled his head over until he caught sight of Liang and me. His eyes were dark, perhaps brown, and he squinted at us, then scrambled to sit up. He ran a hand through his short, brown hair, mussing it further. "Your Majesty," he said, dipping his head.

Varro tilted his head at Liang. "Get him caught up while we figure a way out." Liang bristled at the command, but he moved to Siarvez's cot. The two Valoffs spoke in low tones in their native language. I wasn't *trying* to eavesdrop, but I wasn't trying not to, either.

However, Varro rose and pulled my attention away from the quiet conversation. The grim lines were back in his face. He was hurting but hiding it. I touched his arm and leaned in. "If you need to stop shielding for me so that you can rest, you should," I murmured quietly.

He immediately shook his head. "Either of the Valoffs would be able to find you because your mind glows."

"Maybe they're busy elsewhere."

Varro lifted one shoulder, then briefly caressed my fingers. "Shielding for you is no burden."

"Then what's wrong?"

He shook his head again. Whatever it was, he didn't want to discuss it in front of company. He turned his attention to Devora. "I have an idea of how we can safely leave the station, but I'll need your help."

She dipped her head. "I'll help you if I can. In return, I'd like to request a favor."

"I'm listening."

"Fix this," she demanded. "Make sure the Feds and the Valovian Empire don't have anything to fight about. Find out who attacked and ensure they won't do it again."

Varro's expression turned dark and fierce. "I intend to."

CHAPTER FIFTEEN

Devora left to gather supplies, and I paced in the tiny room. Nervous energy pulsed under my skin, preventing me from sitting still. So many things could go wrong, not the least of which was Varro's plan—a plan that involved us jumping into open space from a perfectly good space station.

With my face plastered on every comm in the station, I couldn't be caught in public, but that didn't mean I was happy about my confinement. "I wish I had my slate," I grumbled to no one in particular.

Varro looked up at me. "I can get it for you."

I immediately shook my head. "It's too dangerous. I'm just sad because it was a gift. But I rented the room for three weeks, so I might be able to return to get it later if the FHP doesn't find it first."

"I can move through the station undetected. Let me do this for you."

"I appreciate it, but I would never forgive myself if something happened to you."

Varro stood. "If it feels dangerous, I won't enter the room. Can you give me the key to open the door?"

I frowned at the request. "With the system down, the doors are unlocked."

"I know, but I'd still like the key in case the system comes up before I get there."

I wavered. I really did want my slate, as selfish as that made me. It was the nicest piece of tech I owned—by far. And while I wasn't *too* worried about the Feds being able to break into it, there was always the possibility that they'd get lucky and find more information than I'd like.

Varro stepped closer. "I would like to change, too. And I'll drop the suit with a courier to be returned. Give me the key."

"Do you have a comm?"

He nodded and pulled out his comm. He turned it on, then unlocked the slim device and handed it to me. His comm was dual tech, so even though it was made for Valovian systems, it also worked on the human networks. Which meant that now that it was on, it received the same alert we'd received earlier.

I silenced the alarm and transferred the key, then held the comm up instead of returning it. "If anything at all feels the least bit suspicious, you will not risk entering the room."

Varro bowed slightly with his left arm across his chest. "I promise. Do you want anything else besides your slate?"

I handed him the comm. "If you have the opportunity, I would take my whole pack. Don't bother packing my clothes, but my pack has other tech I wouldn't mind getting back. But don't take a risk for it. My slate is the highest priority."

Varro looked at Liang without saying anything, and I realized that they were communicating telepathically. Liang bowed with his arm across his chest.

Varro brushed his fingers across my cheek, and a hint of protectiveness whispered through his mental shield. "If anything happens while I'm gone, stick with Liang."

"Please be careful," I murmured, my heart in my throat.

"I will be, and I'll be back before you know it," he said. "And if you're very lucky, I'll even bring you a cookie or two."

I smiled. "I do love cookies, but I'd rather have you back safe and sound."

"You will," he agreed quietly, then he slipped from the room. I locked the door behind him.

Without Varro to distract me, the silence became oppressive. Pacing did nothing to steady my nerves, but sitting still was equally unviable, so I paced and worried and tried not to think about everything that could go wrong.

Why had I thought I could handle this on my own? I should've let Tavi dock. She would know what to do right now rather than being an anxious mess.

Liang stepped in front of me, and I pulled up short to avoid running into him. I let my eyes drift down his body, looking for the problem. "Are you okay?"

His eyebrow rose. "Are you?"

"Nope," I admitted cheerfully.

"Can I do anything to help?"

I grinned at him. "Sure. You can procure a ship, get the station back online, rescue Anna, stop a war . . ." I trailed off and made a show of looking at him. "Are you sure you don't want to take notes?"

Liang's expression turned rueful. "Maybe there's something I can do that's actually possible?"

"Why did you freeze when Varro told you who he was?"

A rusty chuckle burst from Liang. "You don't pull your punches, do you?"

"Not usually." I gave him a pointed look and waited.

Liang paused, clearly deliberating how much to say. "Even though we're telepathic, most Valoffs assume that our minds are safe behind our shields. Varro Runkow breaks that assumption."

Realization dawned. "He's your boogeyman." When Liang agreed with a nod, a wave of sadness washed over me. How lonely must it have been knowing that the people around you feared your abilities? Tavi, Eli, and I had always assumed Torran was the most dangerous person on the ship, and in a way, he was. But he was the obvious danger. Varro's ability was far more subtle.

"You don't fear him," Liang said, expression curious.

I shook my head. "Varro would never hurt me." Before Liang could ask the questions I saw on his face, I waved a hand at his gently glowing suit. "How'd you get involved with the exhibition?"

Liang's grin told me he knew what I was doing, but he was going to let me get away with it—this time. "Siarvez and I went to school together. We've kept in touch over the years, and I've worn his designs many times. When he started working with Ms. Duarte, I was intrigued."

"That doesn't explain why you're here without the usual pomp and circumstance."

Siarvez rose and joined us. "It's because he is too arrogant and too stubborn to listen to his advisors," he said, voice fondly exasperated. Siarvez raised his hand in greeting. "I don't believe we've met. Siarvez Sofdol, at your service."

I waved at him. "Kee Ildez. Nice to meet you. I was wearing a color-changing dress earlier. It was incredible." Siarvez inclined his head, and I turned back to Liang. "So your advisors recommended bringing more people?"

"My advisors refused to let me attend," he said flatly.

"Oh," I breathed, putting the pieces together. "So that's why your family doesn't know you're here, and why you don't have your own ship full of guards." My eyes narrowed. "You're not pro-war, too, are you? This wasn't a setup to rekindle the conflict?"

Siarvez laughed as if I'd said something hilarious, but Liang just looked frustrated. "No, but I fear that the result may be used for that purpose. I need to return to Valovia with haste, before the empress makes her next move."

"I've already promised to rescue Anna, so if you go with us, it'll be a few days before we can find you another ship."

He nodded. "It will have to do."

AFTER LIANG AND SIARVEZ RETURNED TO THE CHAIRS IN THE HIDDEN part of the room, I confirmed with Tavi that she was willing to take them on. She was, but then she railed at me for five solid minutes about our plan to get to the ship. I let her get it out of her system because I could hear the frantic worry beneath the words.

"It's the only way," I said for the fifth time, trying to keep my voice soothing. "I'm sure you got the alert."

She sighed. "I didn't expect them to blame you. Brilliant on their part, I must admit, but a pain in my ass."

"I could stay here—" I started, trying to keep the reluctance out of my voice.

"No," she bit out. "Try it and I'll be the one jumping out of the ship to come kick your ass."

She would, too. I blinked away tears of relief. With the bounty, my presence on *Starlight* would cause Tavi problems, but she refused to take the easier path and leave me here.

"Thank you," I whispered.

"Kee, you're family. I'm not leaving you behind because the Feds are assholes. We'll make it work. Let me know where you need me, and I'll be there."

I promised her I would and then cut the connection. With nothing better to do, I returned to pacing, but that just gave me far too much time to think about everything that might go wrong.

Again.

Varro returned just as I was afraid that even pacing wouldn't be enough to keep me in the tiny room. I opened the door and immediately checked him for injuries, but he looked fine. He was back in his own clothes, and he had my pack slung over his shoulder.

He held the box of cookies he'd given me as *vosdodite.* "For you."

I took the box with a relieved sigh, then stepped aside so he could enter the room. He closed and locked the door behind him.

"Did you run into any trouble?"

He shook his head. "No, but the station is getting restless."

I sympathized. It felt like I'd been trapped in this dim room for *hours,* though it'd actually been less than an hour.

The smell of sugary goodness wafted from the box as I opened the lid and picked up a cookie. At the first bite, I closed my eyes in delight. The rest of the night had not been great, but a good cookie could cure all ills—at least temporarily.

A hot flash of desire whispered through my mind, and I opened my eyes to find Varro's gaze locked on my face, his expression intense. Answering heat flickered through me, and I bit my lip. Varro's eyes dropped to my mouth, but before he could do more than look, Liang emerged from under the tarp.

"Is everything okay out here?" he asked, either blissfully unaware that he was interrupting or doing it on purpose. From what I'd seen of him so far, it could go either way. His eyes lit on the box. "Are those cookies?"

I ignored the unsubtle plea in the question and tilted the box toward Varro. When he hesitated, I said, "I'm not going to be able to take them with us. You might as well enjoy a few before I let the others at them."

Varro accepted two cookies with a solemn nod.

The prince practically vibrated with impatience, but he still managed to give me his best puppy eyes—if puppies were somewhat commanding even while pleading. "May I?"

I picked up a second cookie then handed him the box. "Help yourself, but share with Siarvez. And save some for Devora."

Liang raised an eyebrow at the order but didn't argue.

Once he disappeared back under the tarp, hopefully to share his sugary bounty, Varro handed me my pack. "Your slate is inside. I grabbed your clothes as well, if you want to change."

My heart swelled. "You didn't have to do that."

"I know, but I wanted to."

I wrapped one arm around him and squeezed him into a half hug. "Thank you."

He squeezed me back. "You're welcome."

I finished my cookies, then quickly changed into my own clothes. I felt better once I was out of the FHP uniform, and my feet appreciated being back in my own boots.

I unlocked the inner part of my pack and returned the slate to its padded spot, then transferred the bundled-up dress and crown into the bag along with the rations. I would have to figure out how to carry the pack with me when we went on our little adventure in space.

Someone tapped on the door and Varro moved to open it. He could sense whoever was on the other side, so I hoped it was Devora. Sure enough, she slipped into the room on silent feet.

"Are you all ready?" she asked. "I've got what you need, but we have to go soon because they're calling all maintenance personnel in, even the workers who just got off shift. If I don't show up, they'll be suspicious."

"We're ready," Varro said, and the other two Valoffs appeared from under the tarp.

Liang held out the box of cookies to Devora. "For you."

Her eyebrows rose, but she accepted a cookie with a nod. I shouldered my pack and checked that I hadn't left anything behind. "Can you dispose of the uniform?" I asked.

Devora nodded, so I left it in the corner with the pack I'd stolen.

We followed Devora into the hallway. I could still feel the cool presence of Varro's mind surrounding mine. He was shielding for everyone, including the other Valoffs, who weren't strong enough to hide themselves from view.

I wondered how Varro still had the energy to shield all of us. When he'd told me he was more powerful than many Valoffs, I hadn't understood exactly what that meant, but I was beginning to.

Devora moved through the narrow hallways with easy familiarity. We cut through the station and down a level in the maintenance tunnels, until we ended up in what was obviously a small maintenance workroom.

One that had a large, heavy airlock leading out of the station.

So far, the room remained empty, but if all the maintenance personnel were being called in, then that could change at any moment. But at least the lack of surveillance finally worked in our favor—no one would know who had helped us escape.

"Have you spacewalked before?" she asked.

Varro and I nodded, while Liang and Siarvez shook their heads. Heading into open space was dangerous enough without taking two complete newbies with us. There were a million ways this could end poorly.

"Can you hide them until it's safe for them to try for their ship?" I asked.

Devora sighed. "I can't guarantee it. Rumors are already floating about random searches."

"We'll be tethered together," Varro said. "The captain is bringing the ship as close as possible without setting off alarms. We'll make it."

I wished I had half his calm confidence.

Devora moved to the storage lockers at the edge of the room. "These are the suits we can spare. Two of them are powered, two are emergency suits. I suggest the two of you with experience use the powered suits so if anything goes wrong, you can retrieve the other two."

Nervous dread made its home in my stomach until I felt like I was going to see a return of the cookies I'd eaten. I loved space, but only when I was safely in a ship or station. Floating around in a squishy suit where one wrong move meant death was not my idea of a good time.

I'd had minimal extravehicular activity (EVA) training, just enough so that I could fix something on *Starlight*'s hull if I needed to. My training hadn't included untethered transfers between vehicles, but no one else complained, so I swallowed my fear and started getting suited up.

As I worked my way into the heavy EVA suit, I wondered how I'd let Varro convince me that this was a good idea. Somehow, he'd blinked those gorgeous brown eyes at me, and I'd agreed to jump out of the station into open space with nothing but a few thin layers of fabric and polymer to protect me.

But now his eyes were busy with his own suit, so I had plenty of time for a whole host of second thoughts. I'd forgotten that he was shielding for me, and my increasing anxiety must've bled through the connection because Varro telepathically asked, "What's wrong?"

"Just having a minor freak out over here, nothing to worry about."

He met my eyes from his seat down the line. "I'll keep you safe. I wouldn't suggest this if I didn't think it would work."

I swallowed and nodded at the absolute confidence in his tone. "I know. But that doesn't make it any less scary."

Nick's urgent voice came through my comm implant

and I touched my ear. "The engines are spinning up. We're launching soon. Are you ready?"

"Almost," I replied. "We'll be right behind you. Can I give Varro permission to contact you telepathically, if possible?"

After a long silence, they said, "I suppose it's for the best, so yes. I'll try to let you know before they capture me."

"Be careful. If you get caught, play dumb. We don't know who the attackers are yet, but they went to quite a bit of trouble to look like Valoffs, so pretend that they are. If they think you don't know anything, especially that they're humans playing dress-up, maybe they'll leave you alone until we can rescue you."

"Will do. You be careful, too."

The connection died and my anxiety climbed higher. "Nick thinks their ship is launching. If one ship leaves, there'll be a rush for open space. We need to be on *Starlight* now."

Varro's expression went distant. "The ship is almost in position."

Once we finished suiting up, Devora checked all of us to ensure the seals were properly fitted and tight. She met my eyes through my helmet's clear shield. "I can't leave the airlock open, so once you're out, you will have to make it to your ship or down and around to one of the landing bays."

"Thank you for your help."

"I'm counting on you to catch the assholes who did this," she said, her expression fierce, "because I refuse to go to war again. Good luck."

I inclined my head in acknowledgment, then Varro, Siarvez, Liang, and I tethered ourselves together with two lines between each of us—a primary and a backup. Varro was at the front with Siarvez just behind him, then Liang, then me.

I lashed my pack to my waist and one leg. It wasn't super comfortable in gravity, but it would be out of my way once we stepped into space, and it wouldn't interfere with the suit's propulsion.

We moved into the airlock. It was big enough for all of us, with plenty of room to spare. Devora closed the door behind us, then asked over the comm, "Ready?"

I relayed the question to Varro, and he telepathically asked the other two Valoffs. A moment later he said, "We're ready when you are."

I asked the Blessed Lady for success, then gave Devora a thumbs-up. She activated the airlock and machinery rumbled to life as the air was removed from the chamber. My suit's statistics were displayed on a small, transparent screen embedded at the bottom of the face shield. I had thirty minutes of oxygen and fifteen minutes of propulsion.

I tugged on the tethers tying me to Liang. Both held firm.

If everything went according to plan, I wouldn't have to do anything at all. Varro would direct us toward the ship, and we'd float along behind him like ducklings in a row.

The status lights turned green, and the airlock door swung inward, leaving nothing but the black of space visible. Terror wrapped clawed fingers around my throat. I froze as I tried to get my panic under control, but a tug on the tether pulled me forward one halting step at a time.

"Everyone okay?" Varro asked, looping me into the telepathic conversation.

A chorus of affirmatives came back. All of our suits

had handled the switch to vacuum without a hitch. We'd cleared the first hurdle.

At the edge of the airlock, I squinted into the distance, trying to find *Starlight*. It took me longer than it should've because there were quite a few options, and I wasn't used to looking at the ship from the outside. *Starlight* had all of its external lights on, and it was tilted on end relative to our position.

The distance between us seemed impossibly vast.

Varro's voice whispered into my head. "Ready?"

No. The thought was so loud, it wouldn't surprise me if he'd picked it up. I took a deep breath, viscerally aware that I was using precious oxygen I might need later. "Yes."

"I will keep you safe, Kee, I swear it."

I smiled, even though he couldn't see it. "I believe you. I don't jump out of space stations for just anyone, you know."

A warm wave of affection washed over me, and my breath caught. I wanted to hug that feeling close and keep it in my pocket forever. I held on to the memory with both hands as Varro stepped off the station.

CHAPTER SIXTEEN

Floating in open space would be incredibly peaceful if it wasn't so fucking terrifying. Weightlessness was spectacular, but the sound of my panicked breathing sort of ruined the ambiance.

Four meters ahead of me, Varro finessed his EVA suit to keep us on a trajectory to *Starlight*. Siarvez and Liang were spaced out between us, because I'd been the last to leave the artificial gravity of the station.

I didn't dare try to look over my shoulder at how far away the station was, but *Starlight* grew larger in front of us. We had to be nearly halfway by now.

Movement in the corner of my eye drew my attention. I carefully peered down—or at least toward my feet, since up and down weren't too relevant in space—and found a stream of ships pouring from one of the lower landing bays.

I didn't know what had set them off, but the exodus had started.

The ships had to be flying under manual control because an autopilot would wait for more clearance. So far, they were staying below us, but all it would take was a single ship to break upward and we'd be directly in their path.

"Varro," I mentally shouted.

"I see it." I couldn't read anything from his tone, but the tether around my waist pulled tight as he eased us slightly faster. Too fast and we'd slam into *Starlight,* assuming we didn't miss it altogether. Too slow, though, and we'd slam into some *other* ship that had decided to head our way.

Below, two of the ships edged too close together. The hit didn't look too bad, but the captain on the right overcorrected and unleashed a chain of chaos. They slid along the ship on their starboard side, sending a hail of debris spinning off into space.

I could immediately tell which ships had experienced crews because they did nothing. They knew their hull shielding would protect them and altering course was far more likely to cause problems with so many ships in close quarters.

But the inexperienced pilots panicked. And panic was incredibly difficult to predict.

Three ships pulled up, toward us, while three more broke off in other directions. More ships collided, sending even more debris into play. The tiny pieces of metal didn't matter to the ships, but they mattered a very great deal indeed to four people protected only by thin spacesuits.

Varro hit the thrusters on his suit again, deciding that

speed was less dangerous at this point than everything else.

"Kee, things are devolving. Get here," Tavi urged over the comm.

"We're working on it," I gritted. I checked the ships below us. Two would obviously miss us, but the third was going to be close.

And then the first piece of metal glanced off my arm.

My suit was protected by a tightly woven outer layer that resisted tears and abrasions, but the emergency suits that Liang and Siarvez wore were not nearly as robust. If I didn't do something in the next ten seconds, their suits would be so shredded that the inbound ship wouldn't be our biggest problem.

I pulled myself along the tether until I reached Liang. His eyes were wide with fear, but he didn't fight me when I hooked a leg around him and kept pulling on his tether until I'd reached Siarvez.

"Hold on to him!" I shouted at Liang, hoping that Varro would relay the message. I pointed for good measure, and Liang wrapped his arms around the other Valoff.

"What are you doing?" Varro asked.

"Debris. I'm going to shield them as much as I can because my suit is stronger. You get us to the ship." I wrapped an arm around Liang and then very delicately used my suit's thrusters to turn so that I was underneath the two Valoffs in the emergency suits, my back to the drama happening below. I wouldn't be able to see, but the back of my suit was more protected than the front.

"Hold on," Varro said, voice grim.

I clutched at Liang and hoped his grip on Siarvez would hold. With a jerk, Varro changed our direction. Thirty seconds later, a ship passed us with less than five meters to spare.

I breathed a sigh of relief, but it was too soon, because the ship also brought a sparkling cloud of debris with it. I could feel the tiny impacts against the back of my suit, and the warning beeps as the self-healing fabric sealed each tiny breach.

Then agony stabbed through my right calf, and the warning beep turned into a solid tone. My suit was punctured, and no amount of self-healing would fix it.

I watched the minutes of my oxygen decrease with alarming speed. "Varro, my suit's cut," I thought at him, strangely calm.

"How bad?"

"Bad." I couldn't tell if the light-headedness was due to panic, lack of oxygen, or something else, but I somehow managed to keep ahold of Liang.

"Hold on," Varro said.

I laughed at that. As if I could do anything else. My calf throbbed and burned, and I wondered if I was bleeding. Would I drown in my own blood before my oxygen ran out? That didn't sound like a very nice way to go.

The oxygen numbers fell far too fast, and my breathing turned shallow. I should've told Tavi I loved her before I left the ship. And Eli, too. They knew I considered them family, but the words were nice to hear.

And why had I waited so long to confess to Varro? Stupid pride.

"Don't die," Varro urged. "We're almost there." His mental voice was calm, but I could feel a tangled jumble of emotions that weren't mine. He wasn't as calm as he sounded.

I didn't tell him that my oxygen level was nearly zero and my lungs weren't working quite right. It would only worry him more, and he still had to rescue the prince and prevent the war.

Something clamped tight around my body and white-hot agony blotted out everything else.

CHAPTER SEVENTEEN

My eyelids felt like they were welded shut, but the novelty of being alive gave me the strength to pry them open. Slightly. A bright overhead light blinded me, and I had no idea where I was. Had we made it to *Starlight,* or was I back on the station? I reached for Varro, but he was no longer shielding my mind.

I opened my eyes again, squinting against the light.

Someone leaned over me, a dark silhouette. "You scared the shit out of me," Eli grumbled.

"How long was I out?"

"Twenty minutes. Your calf was a mess, but Havil got you fixed up pretty quickly. We didn't even have to use the autostab this time."

The autostabilization unit was in the medbay on *Starlight.* It could perform minor medical procedures and keep a patient alive until they could reach help, but it was nowhere near as good as Havil's innate healing ability. Without him, I'd no doubt be sporting a rather vicious scar.

"Everyone else?" I whispered.

"Havil healed them, too. They made it, thanks to you. Your suit was a pincushion. Without your protection, the two in emergency suits would be dead."

I chuckled quietly. "Think they'll throw me a parade on Valovia?"

"Probably not. Ungrateful fucks."

I pushed myself up. The aftereffects of the healing had left me woozy, but overall I felt pretty good for someone who'd thought she was going to die less than half an hour ago.

Once I was sitting up, Eli scowled at me. "If you ever do something so stupid again . . ."

"Anyone ever tell you that your bedside manner needs work?"

"Next time, you can watch while I lie there like a corpse, and we'll see how much *you* like it."

I already knew that I wouldn't like it at all. I glanced around, but Eli was the only one in the room. "Where's Varro?"

"Torran had to drag him away and order him to eat something. Apparently whatever he was doing burns through calories like wildfire, and between that and worrying about you, he was dead on his feet. And Tavi is getting us away from the mess around the station. She's also tracking the *Renegade Tide*."

I looked at my bare legs. Someone had cut off my pants. My right calf was smeared with partially wiped away blood, but the skin was smooth and clear. I swung my legs off the side of the bed and opened my arms.

Eli wrapped me in a hug.

With my face pressed into his shoulder, I told him, "I love you, Eli. You're my brother in every way that matters. I should tell you that more."

A shudder wracked his frame, and he pressed his face to my hair. "You thought you were going to die," he whispered, distraught.

I tried to make my tone light. "The thought may have crossed my mind."

He pulled back, his eyes wet. "I love you, too, Kee, even if you do keep scaring years off my life. And of course I knew you loved me." He grinned. "Who else would put up with me for so long?"

"No one," I agreed solemnly. I peeked up at him with a grin. "Although . . . I do seem to remember a few people who might volunteer." I wiggled my eyebrows. "Any updates you'd like to share?"

"You're as bad as Tavi," he grumbled, but a flush of color spread through his cheeks.

I bit my lip against the tide of questions. Eli would share when he was ready. "I don't suppose anyone brought me any pants?"

Eli rolled his eyes. "It wasn't our highest priority."

I hopped to the ground and winced as my calf twinged. Ooh, that was still tender. I turned to Eli. "Did my pack make it?"

"Yeah, it's in the cargo bay. Want me to grab it for you?"

"Please. I'm going to find some pants then head to the galley."

"Can you make it?"

I took a few steps. My calf ached a bit, but it wasn't terrible, so I nodded.

Eli leveled a glare at me. "Be careful."

"I will be."

I MADE IT HALFWAY UP THE STAIRS BEFORE VARRO FOUND ME, HIS face set in a thunderous scowl. "What are you doing?"

"Hobbling to my room for some pants."

His eyes dropped to my bare legs as if I'd drawn him a map. The scowl darkened when he caught sight of the dried blood that I hadn't bothered to clean off. "You shouldn't be up. Where is Eli? He promised to look after you."

I moved up another step, lifting myself with my left leg and carefully suppressing the wince. After the day I'd had, a flight of stairs *might* have been a little ambitious, even with Havil's healing, not that I'd ever admit it. "I feel fine, and Eli is grabbing my pack from the cargo bay."

"Cho udwist zas hisi las," Varro murmured. "What am I going to do with you?"

My stubborn, precious bright star. Warmth suffused me at the endearment.

He bent and swept me into his arms, then paused, clearly torn between returning me to the medbay and helping me get to my room.

"If you take me back, I'll just escape again, so you might as well help me to my room." Varro heaved a long-suffering sigh, then started up the stairs. I leaned my head against his shoulder. "Are you okay?"

"You nearly died. If Torran hadn't pulled you in, you would've. I couldn't protect you, couldn't keep you safe."

I could feel the tension in his body despite the mild tone. I'd scared him, badly. "You got us out of the station.

The prince is still alive. We're all okay, and that's thanks to you."

Varro didn't argue, but his tension didn't decrease, either.

The door to my room slid open at my touch. The familiar pale purple walls were a soothing balm on my ragged emotions. Because Tavi had given me one of the officers' quarters, I had a decent-sized bed, a tiny desk and chair, and my own private bathroom tucked behind the bedroom.

Varro carefully set me on my feet. His expression remained closed, so I smoothed a hand over his chest and peeked at him through my lashes. "I'm going to take a shower. Want to join me?"

His jaw clenched as something hot and fierce flashed across his face, but he locked the emotion away and shook his head. I *knew* it was too soon, that we weren't there yet, but I still felt the sharp stab of disappointment, because I'd wanted that connection between us.

Perhaps Varro wasn't the only one struggling with my near death.

Before I could apologize, Eli hit the door's buzzer. "I have your pack. Should I bring it in?"

I crossed the room and opened the door. Eli blinked at me for a second, then his gaze moved over my shoulder and a grin pulled at the corner of his mouth. "I see how it is," he murmured.

"Careful, Bruck," I whispered sweetly. "I believe at this point you have more to hide than I do."

Eli dipped his chin, though his grin only grew as he handed me my pack. "Have fun," he said with a wink. He closed the door in my face before I could growl at him.

I set the pack on the bed and pulled out all of the tech I'd taken with me. Most of it was illegal, so leaving it lying around wasn't a good idea. I could feel Varro's eyes on me as I popped open the secret compartment in the bottom of my wardrobe and carefully put everything away.

I hoped he understood that I'd just shown him a great deal of silent trust.

Varro scrutinized me as I moved toward him. "Is your leg bothering you? The wound was deep, and Havil said it might remain tender for a day or two."

"I can feel it," I admitted, "but it's not too bad now that I'm not trying to climb stairs." I stopped just in front of him, close enough that I could feel the heat of his body. I reached up and wrapped my hand around his neck, then rose on my toes.

Varro stiffened and stepped back, avoiding my kiss.

I might not be great at reading signs, but this one was impossible to misinterpret. The rejection slammed into me, and I jerked my hands away like I'd been burned. I should not have assumed, no matter how hot our previous kiss had been. Maybe after everything that had happened on Bastion, Varro had realized that I was more trouble than I was worth.

Or maybe he'd caught a hint of my feelings while he'd been shielding for me and the intensity was too much for him. Once more, I was all in while my potential partner was still on the fence. This wouldn't be the first time my fervor had scared off a romantic interest, because when I fell for someone, I fell with my entire being, and there was nothing I could do to stop it.

Old pain mingled with new to cut like a scythe, but none of it was Varro's fault. We'd shared only a couple of heat-of-the-moment kisses, and they weren't any kind of commitment.

No matter how much I wished they were.

He'd even warned me that we wouldn't work, but I'd recklessly forged ahead anyway. Story of my life.

I locked away the hurt and cleared my throat. "I apologize. I'm going to shower; please show yourself out."

"Kee—" he started.

I waited, tentative hope blooming, but he turned and left without another word.

The hope died, and along with it, my heart.

CHAPTER EIGHTEEN

I didn't feel any better after the shower, but at least I was cleaner. I found Luna waiting outside my door. The fluffy little burbu always seemed to know when someone needed a cuddly friend. I scooped her up and buried my hands in her soft fur.

"Let's go see if we can find Tavi, hmm?"

Luna chirruped at me and affectionately butted her head against my chin. It was enough to bring tears to my eyes. I'd left for Bastion to get my emotions under control, and now I was worse off than before. The irony did not escape me.

I found Tavi on the bridge, scowling at her terminal. "Problems?" I asked.

"A Fed ship is harassing us and being a general pain in the ass, so situation normal." She peered at me. "How are you?"

I lifted a shoulder. "I'm alive."

Tavi's terminal turned red and an audible alarm sounded. "Are they *targeting* us?" I asked in disbelief.

"They've been demanding boarding access to search the ship for you. I've been stalling, but apparently they're done playing. Take Varro and the two Valoffs you rescued and hide in the smuggler's hold."

I grimaced at the thought of being stuck with Varro in a tiny space for who knew how long, but the Feds would destroy *Starlight* if Tavi continued to refuse the search. Tavi misinterpreted my expression. "I won't let them find you, Kee."

"I know," I said. I handed Luna to her. "I'll message you when we're hidden."

She nodded, already turning back to her terminal to deal with the FHP ship. I headed for the galley and found everyone else inside. Varro, Liang, and Siarvez sat at the table with Havil and Anja. Liang and Siarvez had changed into the stretchy, casual clothes we kept on board for rescues and bounties.

Chira, Eli, and Torran leaned against the bar. None of them looked particularly inviting, but Torran watched Liang like one might watch a dangerous snake. Unfortunately, I didn't have time to find out what had caused that look because we had bigger problems.

"The Feds are getting ready to search the ship," I said without preamble, carefully avoiding Varro's eyes. "Liang, Siarvez, and Varro, follow me. The rest of you never saw us." I turned for the door, then paused and looked back at Eli. "Did you dispose of the EVA suits?"

He nodded and straightened. "I'll come make sure you're secure."

I turned to the Valoffs. "If any of you need to use the bathroom, your time is now. We'll likely be stuck for an hour or more."

They shook their heads, so I started for the door before remembering the dress. "Shit, I have to grab the dress I wore. It'll be a dead giveaway." I looked at Liang. "Get your glowing suit and meet us in the cargo bay. Run."

I took my own advice and ran for my bunk. I pulled out the glowing dress bundle. I carefully put the crown in the secret compartment below my wardrobe, then dumped the FHP rations on top. I tucked the pack away, then ran for the cargo bay.

By the time I arrived, Eli already had the smuggler's hold open. It took two solid minutes to open it if one knew the exact number and order of steps. FHP soldiers would likely suspect that we had hidden stowage, but they wouldn't be able to find it without exceptional luck.

A section of wall stood open, revealing the deep, narrow room behind. Shielded from all scanners, it wouldn't show as a hollow space and thermal cameras couldn't pierce it, either.

But it wasn't very big.

Varro, with his broad shoulders, would be hard-pressed to stand sideways. I sighed. We were all going to be squeezed closer together than any of us would like.

Liang arrived clutching his suit. The strange fabric started to glow as soon as he approached. He peered at the tiny room, then turned to me. "Do you seriously expect us all to fit in there?"

"I seriously do. Unless you'd rather be caught by the FHP?"

His grimace turned into a teasing smile. "Want to be my snuggle buddy, *heme*?"

I tilted my head as I considered the offer. It wasn't a bad idea, actually. Liang was charming, but I didn't feel anything for him, and I was fairly sure he wouldn't take advantage of our physical closeness.

A heavy hand landed on my shoulder before I could reply. Liang's eyes crinkled, and he turned to Siarvez with a sigh. "I suppose it's you and me, my friend."

The two Valoffs wedged themselves as far back as they could. They faced each other with a scant few centimeters between them. Varro and I crammed ourselves in behind them.

"Ready?" Eli asked.

I nodded. "Close us in, and let Tavi know we're hidden. I'm turning my comm off, so Torran will have to contact Varro if you need to get us a message."

"I'll let them know. Remember: no movement, no sound," Eli warned before shutting the door. With the glowing fabric, it wasn't completely dark, but it felt like it. I could just barely make out Varro's silhouette in front of me. The room was ventilated, so we didn't have to worry about air, but we didn't have any extra space. Luckily, small spaces didn't bother me, but inactivity *did*. I hoped the FHP gave up quickly.

"This is cozy," Liang muttered from my right. His shoulder brushed against mine.

"Quiet," Varro whispered. "Sixteen humans are approaching the ship. I will shield."

Two squads. The Feds weren't playing around. At least Tavi had Torran to watch her back. I doubted the FHP knew that there was a telekinetic on board or they would've sent more people.

I felt the cool touch of Varro's mind as he once again shielded me. I built my own shield and tried to keep my thoughts very, very quiet. He didn't need to discover my lingering hurt.

Time lost all meaning. The glowing dress rotated through its colors in an endless loop. My right calf ached, then burned, then blazed with searing pain. I shifted minutely, trying to find a position—*any* position—that helped. There was no relief.

Varro wrapped his arms around me and pulled me into his chest. I resisted, but he leaned back, and suddenly there wasn't as much weight on my calf. I sagged against him and cried in silent relief.

Time passed in cycles of glowing fabric. Without my comm, I didn't know what was happening in the rest of the ship, but Torran would let Varro know if we were about to be discovered.

Now that I didn't have the pain in my leg to focus on, my pulse beat a furious rhythm under my skin, and it was all I could do to stay still. Not that there was anywhere for me to go. I was pressed against Varro from head to thigh. My temple rested on his shoulder, and his arms were wrapped around my back, holding me close.

Staying still and quiet were two things I'd never excelled at. And as the seconds slowly ticked past, it became harder and harder. I twitched, and Varro's fingers stroked a delicate, soothing pattern on my lower back. "Just a little while longer," he whispered into my mind.

He was far too optimistic. I was in a sort of loopy half-sleep when Varro finally whispered, "They are leaving."

I turned on my comm and blinked at the time. It had

taken three agonizing hours for the Feds to tear the ship apart to their satisfaction.

"Don't move," I whispered. "I have to find all the surprises they left behind before someone can let us out."

It took twenty minutes to clear the cargo bay. Once Tavi and Anja had disabled all the bugs and trackers I could detect, Varro and I eased out into the open. Siarvez and Liang stumbled out behind us.

Liang muttered something in Valovan too quiet for me to catch.

Varro let me go, and I took a tentative step. I groaned, half in pain, half in relief. My whole body ached, and I wasn't sure I could do more than hobble, but I still needed to find the rest of the sensors before we could enter the main part of the ship.

Tavi handed me a bottle of water, and I very nearly kissed her in gratitude.

"I have a meal bar if you want it," she said. "Or there's some leftover dinner once you can make it to the galley."

We were in the early hours after midnight. It was too late for dinner and too early for breakfast, but hunger hollowed my stomach. I stretched my arms overhead and then bent, working all the muscles that'd spent the last three hours locked in place. My calf burned, and I hated to imagine how bad it would've been if Varro hadn't helped.

"I want real food," I finally decided as I straightened. "Let's find the rest of the sensors those assholes left behind so I can enjoy it."

Varro ate a trio of meal bars and drank an entire bottle of water, but he insisted on continuing to shield for me while I found the rest of the trackers.

It took over an hour for me to sweep the entire ship—

twice. But when I was finished, I was fairly confident that I'd caught all of the trackers the Feds had left behind, even the ones that they'd set to activate later.

Exhaustion pulled at me, but I needed to eat because I planned to sleep straight through breakfast and maybe lunch. I wavered on my feet. Then again, food was overrated. Sleep. I needed sleep.

I blinked up at my muscly shadow. I'd expected Varro to disappear once I was done sweeping the ship, but he continued to trail me, a frown on his face. "I'm going to sleep," I told him. "You should do the same. We're at least a day from Expedition, assuming that's where Anna's ship is heading."

His frown deepened. "You didn't eat."

Pain pricked me at the reminder that he cared enough to notice. My filter, tenuous at the best of times, decided to go on vacation. "Why did you pull away when I tried to kiss you earlier?"

Varro's face shuttered. A muscle in his jaw flexed. "You should not kiss me."

The words had absolutely no give, and they landed like knives. Tears rose, and I sucked in a shaky breath as I ducked my head to hide the reaction. I nearly turned and fled, but some tiny part of me refused to give up.

"Why not?" I asked, peeking at him.

His eyes flashed. "Because I broke a vow to you. I failed to protect you, and you were hurt because of it."

Now it was my turn to frown. "But I'm fine."

"If not for Torran and Havil, you wouldn't have been."

"But I'm *fine*," I reiterated. "I don't blame you. You shouldn't blame yourself."

He shook his head, his expression calm and cold.

I lifted a helpless hand in question. "So that's it? We're

through before we even started?" The tears returned, but I blinked them away, desperate to see his face.

His chin dipped in agreement, and my heart sank. "Couldn't you just give me an apology gift?" I whispered tentatively.

"Not for this."

The hard finality of the answer told me that I wouldn't change his mind, and his shield was once again rock-solid, because I couldn't sense any of his feelings.

I drew a shivering breath past the lump in my throat and held it for a long moment. When I felt like I could move without shattering, I murmured a farewell and escaped to the safety of my room, where I could let myself grieve in privacy.

CHAPTER NINETEEN

I awoke after lunch to an empty stomach and aching heart. I ignored both and got ready for the day. I didn't have time to mope, because I needed to figure out what the attackers' plan was—and if Morten was involved—before they arrived at their destination.

I'd wasted far too much time on personal problems over the past few days, so I walled off my pain, painted on a sunny smile, and ventured out of my room to find some food.

In the galley, I found Tavi and Torran sitting at the bar, speaking in low voices, while Luna finished her lunch. The fluffy little burbu chirruped in greeting, and I cooed back at her, some of my tension unknotting.

"Any updates?" I asked Tavi. We were still on course for Expedition, but she could tell me if anything had come in that wasn't in the ship's log.

The captain turned to face me. She frowned as she looked me over, but she didn't comment. "The FHP ship is still shadowing us. Are you hungry? There's leftover pasta from last night or I can make you something."

I waved her off and went hunting for the pasta. Once I'd warmed up a large bowl, I joined her and Torran at the bar and picked up the conversation. "Do you think the FHP knows we're onboard, or are they just being their normal asshole selves?"

"Varro hid your jump from the station," Torran said. "But they still suspect you're here. They just don't know how."

Tavi nodded. "We'll have to be very careful when we land or dock, depending on where the *Renegade Tide* ends up."

I'd tried to contact Nick earlier with no luck, so I hoped they were okay.

Tavi leaned close. "What's wrong?" she whispered. "You look worse than when you arrived. And if you'll recall, you arrived bloody and unconscious."

My smile turned genuine. "Thanks for that, Captain. You have a real way with words. Torran is a lucky man."

She pinned me in place with a look, not letting me off the hook that easily. "You're deflecting. Did Liang or Siarvez threaten you?"

I frowned at her. "What? No." My anger ignited. "Did they threaten *you*? Because Liang swore he and his family wouldn't harm you or the crew." I hadn't thought to make Siarvez vow, too. If my mistake had put Tavi and *Starlight* at risk, I'd never forgive myself.

Torran interrupted whatever Tavi was going to say. "What was the exact wording of the vow?"

“You’ll have to ask Varro. Exact wording isn’t my forte. But it was close to what I just told you.” I hesitated. “Is that bad?”

Torran shook his head. “It’s far better than I hoped.” He gave me a small smile. “You must have impressed him.”

“Well, I *was* trying to look all intimidating when I demanded he promise not to hurt anyone on *Starlight,* so he was probably too scared to do anything else.” I leaned around Tavi and dropped my voice to a stage whisper. “And don’t tell the captain, but I was channeling her scowl.”

Torran nodded knowingly, a sparkle in his eyes. “That would do it.”

Tavi barked out a laugh and swatted at my shoulder. “Remind me to put you on cleaning duty for insubordination.”

I shook my head. “I’m pretty sure you meant garden duty for being so awesome.”

Tavi’s face softened. “I missed you, Kee.”

Torran slipped from the room, and I knew that Tavi wouldn’t let me evade this talk, as much as I’d like to.

“I missed you, too. When I thought I might die, I realized I should tell you and Eli that I love you more often. You’re my family, and I want you to know how important you are to me.”

Tavi wrapped her arms around me and pulled me into a gentle hug. “I love you, too.” She leaned back but kept a hand on my arm. “Now tell me what’s wrong. Truly.”

The whole story spilled out of me like water from a bucket. I told Tavi everything that had happened since I’d last talked to her, from confession to kiss to rejection. She listened quietly, without judgment, and I felt better once I was done.

"What will you do?" Tavi asked gently.

My shoulders slumped. "I don't know. I tried to tell him that I don't consider the vow broken, but he wouldn't listen."

"Would you like me to ask Torran for advice? I'll keep it as generic as possible, but he'll guess that I'm talking about you."

I winced but nodded. "If you don't mind." Maybe another Valoff would see a way for us to make it work. "So Liang and Siarvez haven't caused trouble?"

"No, they've been perfect guests so far." Tavi clasped my shoulder. "You did well on Bastion, Kee. I don't love that you were injured, but you rescued an imperial family member and fucked up the FHP's plan."

"If only I knew what that plan was," I muttered.

"You'll get there."

Tavi's confidence bolstered my own. "Of course I will," I agreed with a smile that almost felt genuine.

"Do you think the attackers knew the prince was going to be at the show?"

I tilted my head in thought. "I don't know," I said slowly. "The Valoff they were working with definitely didn't know, but the other soldiers might have. They certainly took out Liang's guards quickly enough."

"Do you think Anna is complicit?"

"No. I considered it because there are definitely some convenient coincidences, but no. She was legitimately scared and angry when the soldiers attacked."

"Anna did not know I planned to bring Liang," Siarvez said from the doorway. "Security was briefed just before the party."

I jerked around in surprise. Siarvez entered the galley

with Liang and Varro behind him. Varro's gaze raked over my face and his eyes narrowed slightly before his expression turned bland once again. I hid my pain behind my sunniest smile.

"Eavesdropping is rude," Tavi said.

Siarvez lifted one shoulder in a careless shrug. "Eavesdropping implies ill intent. I merely overheard your conversation as we arrived. I believe you wanted to speak to us."

"I did. I want to know if you plan to repay Kee's kindness with treachery."

I suppressed my groan. Tavi was as subtle as a hit with a plas blade.

Liang swept forward, his eyes locked on me. "Do you think I'll betray my vow?" He stopped a meter from me, a scowl hovering on his brow.

Even sitting on the barstool, I was still shorter than him, and while he was leaner than Torran and Varro, I wouldn't underestimate him. I'd carried him down several flights of stairs. I knew just how solidly he was built.

I waved my hands in what I hoped was a universally placating manner and switched to Valovan. "No, of course not. But the captain wasn't there, and she's overprotective."

"Kee," Tavi growled. She didn't speak Valovan and had yet to find a reasonably priced translator module, so she didn't understand what I'd said.

I flashed her a smile and switched to sign language. "Try not to piss off a member of the imperial family by implying that he won't honor his promises," I signed. "We need him on our side."

Liang watched the interaction with a thoughtful expression. "She doesn't speak Valovan," he said at last. "And then you communicated with her in a language *I* don't understand to balance the scales. Clever. Annoying, but clever."

Torran returned to the room, his posture casual but his expression sharp. He moved around the table and leaned against the wall closest to Tavi. The very last thing I needed was a brawl in the galley because of a misunderstanding.

"Everyone take a deep breath," I ordered in Common. "We're on the same side." I hoped.

Liang's eyes cut to Tavi, and he looked every bit the haughty prince. "Kee saved my life twice and asked for nothing in return. I will not repay that debt with betrayal."

I smiled softly at him. "I didn't save your life because I expected something in return. You don't owe me anything."

Liang shook his head. "A life is no small thing. The debt stands."

"She saved my life, too," Siarvez added, "and I also remain in her debt."

"So you'll both swear that you had nothing to do with the attack?" Tavi asked, voice deceptively mild. When both Valoffs easily vowed their innocence, some of Tavi's tension drained away.

I looked at Liang and debated the wisdom of showing a bit of our hand. When he caught my look and raised an eyebrow, I asked, "Can I trust you?"

His smile had an edge, and he wielded it like a blade. "Not many do."

I shook my head. "That's not an answer. Can *I* trust you?"

He stared at me for a long, long moment. I held his gaze and let him consider the question. "No," he said slowly. "I will not hurt you if I can avoid it, and I won't lie to you, but you should not trust me."

I grinned at him. "Okay, good, because I do."

Tavi huffed out a laugh, and Liang blinked at me in surprise. "But I just told you *not* to trust me."

"Exactly. Do you really go around trusting people because they tell you to?"

"No?" It came out sounding like a question, as if Liang wasn't sure of the answer. Sometimes I had that effect on people, so I didn't hold it against him.

"You could've lied and chose not to."

His expression sharpened. "But what if I *did* lie and this is all an elaborate plan to win your trust?"

"Then I guess you win. Congratulations." I flourished my hand in his direction. "You may now unleash your evil plan."

Liang looked at Tavi, who only shook her head. "Kee's logic isn't always logical, but it's always right," she said. She squinted at him. "Are you sure you're related to the empress?"

Liang sighed. "Unfortunately."

Varro watched the whole interaction without a hint of emotion. I tried to pretend indifference, but I was hyperaware of him even when I wasn't looking at him.

I pulled up the picture of the Sun Guardian and held my comm toward Liang. "Do you recognize this woman?"

Tavi sucked in a surprised breath, but she didn't try to stop me.

Liang squinted at the picture, then shook his head. "I don't think so, but if I had more information, I might be able to place her." His tone was entirely casual, but his eyes were not.

I grinned at him. "Now who's being clever?"

His expression turned unrepentant. "I did warn you not to trust me."

I studied him to give myself a moment to consider my next step. I hadn't lied—I *did* trust him, but only to a certain point. "I'll tell you, if you promise you won't repeat the information to anyone who's not currently on this ship." I glanced at Siarvez. "Both of you."

"I hope you know what you're doing," Tavi said over the comm. The subvocal mic had picked up her silent words, so Liang wouldn't know she had concerns.

"Me, too," I replied.

Siarvez lifted a shoulder and made the promise, but it took a bit longer for Liang's curiosity to overwhelm his caution. "Very well," he agreed at last. "I will not repeat what you're about to tell me to anyone not on the ship."

I glanced at Torran and he dipped his head. Good enough. "We believe that she is one of Empress Nepru's Sun Guardians."

Liang's mask was instantaneous and perfect. "Do you think me a fool?" he asked, his voice soft.

I shivered at the threat, and both Torran and Varro moved closer. Varro's expression had flattened into watchful nothingness, and his hands flexed at his side.

"No," I said, returning my attention to Liang. "I *thought* you might want to help us stop another war, but it seems that I was wrong." I waved airily. "No matter. I'll find her eventually; I just need a bit more time."

"She'll kill you," Liang bit out.

My eyebrows rose. "I know. She nearly killed Tavi. Why do you think Varro and I ran with you? We couldn't be sure she wouldn't kill you, too."

"She was on the station?" At my nod, Liang looked

troubled. He closed his eyes and blew out a slow breath. "If I tell you who I *suspect* she might be, our debt will be settled."

I agreed easily. I'd already told him he didn't owe me anything, but if agreeing resulted in answers, then I wasn't above using his honor against him.

"*If* she is Fiazeffere—and I'm not saying that she is—then she is likely Sura Fev. Sura is the only one I know of with that hair and skin tone. But I do not know all of the empress's guardians."

Sura Fev. I repeated the name to myself, then entered it into my comm. I *probably* wouldn't forget it in the next ten minutes, but I'd found it was far easier to save important information somewhere that wasn't my brain.

"Thank you," I murmured, already thinking about the searches I needed to start.

Liang sighed. "I truly don't know if it's her, so don't thank me for making a guess."

I dragged my attention away from my comm. "Is Sura telekinetic?"

One of Liang's eyebrows rose. "Many Fiazefferia are."

It wasn't exactly a confirmation, but it wasn't a denial, either. I didn't blame Liang for being cautious, so I smiled at him. "How does it feel to be debt-free? Is it everything you hoped?"

He stepped closer, until he was decidedly in my personal space. I tipped my head back to hold his gaze. The darker blue streaks in his eyes expanded ever so slightly. "If I had to owe anyone a debt," he murmured, "you are quickly becoming my first choice."

Liang was objectively gorgeous, especially when he was intentionally flirting, but I only felt a fond affection for him—much like what I felt for Eli—and none of the sparks and heat I felt around Varro.

Liang's lips quirked into a tiny, rueful grin, and I felt the lightest brush of a mind against mine. When I nodded permission, Liang's voice murmured into my mind. "Sura Fev *is* a telekinetic, but you didn't hear it from me." He paused and something fleeting and a tiny bit sad passed across his face. "Varro is lucky."

I couldn't quite suppress my wince, and Liang's head tilted in question. "No?"

"He's upset that I was hurt during the jump and being stubborn," I thought back.

"Perhaps I can help with that," Liang said. Before I could question him, his presence left my mind and his expression turned mischievous. He leaned in and brushed a lingering kiss over my cheek, his lips barely touching my skin.

"You good?" Tavi asked over the comm.

"Yes," I assured her.

Liang jerked back, Varro's hand on his shoulder. The prince flashed a wicked grin at me, then turned to Varro with an icy glare. "Do you mind?"

"Not at all," Varro rumbled. Liang must've switched to telepathy, because Varro's face darkened, and his gaze briefly landed on my face before flitting away again. His jaw clenched. "Do what you will."

I wasn't sure if Varro was speaking to me or Liang, but he spun and left the room. I frowned at Liang. "What did you say?"

"Nothing that he didn't need to hear," Liang said.

Siarvez snorted. "One of these days, your version of diplomacy is going to earn you a black eye." The words had bite, but Siarvez's face was soft with exasperated fondness. Tavi had turned that exact expression on me more than once.

"It's not my fault that he doesn't appreciate what he has," Liang said gently, eyes on my face.

And that was my cue to exit. I turned to Tavi. "If you need me, I'll be in my control room."

The captain smiled and let me escape.

CHAPTER TWENTY

I sank into my chair with a sigh that felt like it came from the bottom of my soul. I rubbed my chest. As much as I tried to pretend otherwise, Varro's indifference hurt. I'd hoped that we would at least remain friends, but it seemed as if even that was impossible now.

I chuckled bitterly. My time on Bastion was supposed to make me feel better, not leave me in exactly the same sorry state I'd been in before. But the Blessed Lady rarely sewed one's thread into a neat, straight line, so I just had to keep moving forward and hoping for the best.

Despite everything, my time on the station had been worth it—I'd rescued Liang and got to spend time with Varro before I'd scared him off. I hadn't completely stopped the attack, but I'd foiled some part of the attackers' plan.

And now I had a huge bounty on my head, so that was

fun. That meant I was doing *something* right, even if it was just pissing off people in the FHP.

I had a million things that I needed to do, and I wasn't sure which was the most important. I closed my eyes for a second and took a deep breath. I needed to start with something routine so that I actually *would* start and not just sit in decision paralysis until dinner.

I opened my eyes and checked the familiar screens in front of me. They confirmed that *Starlight's Shadow* was running well within spec and that the FHP ship trailing us still hadn't given up.

Ahead of us, the *Renegade Tide* continued toward Expedition. I hoped that they were aiming for the planet rather than the moon, but I doubted it. Unlike Bastion, the lunar base orbiting Expedition was almost entirely a military installation, the Forward Observation Station Odyssey I. There was a small civilian port for ships that didn't want to risk Expedition's atmosphere, but access was restricted.

If Anna and Nick disappeared into the lunar base, it wouldn't be easy to extract them. We'd still try, of course, but it would better for all of us if it didn't come to that.

I needed something to hold over the FHP. I needed *leverage.* My first thought was Liang, but I hadn't gone to all the trouble of rescuing him just to hand him over. Plus, I tried not to use people as bargaining chips. It was one of the many things that differentiated me from Commodore Frank Morten.

With the prince off the table, the only thing left was the malware infecting Bastion. If I could fix it faster than the Feds, then that fix would be the perfect leverage. I added it to the top of my list.

I stared at the blip on the screen that was the *Renegade*

Tide. Remotely hacking a ship wasn't easy. That wasn't to say I couldn't do it, but I might not get it done before we arrived at our destination. It would be far easier if Varro could reach Nick telepathically—assuming Nick had figured out where they were heading and hadn't been captured. I made a note to ask Varro to try, then added hacking the ship, too.

Leaving things off the list was how they ended up lost to the ether.

Finally, I needed to search for information on Sura Fev, the alleged Sun Guardian. And while that would take the longest overall, it was the easiest to get started.

My searches for Commodore Morten had returned results that I needed to go through—another thing for the list—but I started building new queries for the Sun Guardian. I didn't have real-time access to Valovian systems—they were too far away—but I had some data cached from our time on Valovia. All ships had a local data store, but I'd upgraded *Starlight*'s far past the norm. The ship constantly pulled down new data whenever it was within range of a network, including Valovian networks.

And if that wasn't enough, the FHP also had a treasure trove of data stored up—I just had to get to it. Bastion would've been my first choice, but with it down, I moved on to Expedition.

The signal delay was annoying, but I worked around it.

I started with public data because it was easiest. The screenshot I'd captured wasn't good enough for facial recognition, so I had to go through photos of Empress Nepru's entourage manually after filtering for those that contained blond women. The empress always had a phalanx of guards with her, but most of them were her normal security and not the nearly mythical Sun Guardians.

I looked at photos long enough that everyone started looking the same, so I took a break and worked on finding other information instead. In the public articles, the empress's guards were never named and only a couple of her advisors were named. None of them was Sura Fev.

But the name *did* return quite a few hits. I set the searches to pull relevant data and let them run. The number of photos kept increasing. I'd need a better way to filter them or I'd have to get the whole ship involved in manually sorting through them.

Behind me, the door slid open, letting in the distant sound of voices. They didn't sound upset, so I didn't let it distract me. I squinted at the screen. The facial recognition algorithms might not be able to recognize Sura from the photo, but I could run them on the rest of the photos. Surely the empress's guards didn't change that often. Once it was done, I'd have to look at only a few people rather than a thousand photos.

Pleased, I set it running, then turned back to my list.

"It's time for dinner," Varro said from out of nowhere.

I yelped and clutched a hand over my chest to keep my heart from lurching away in fright. I spun and scowled at him. "When did you get here?"

"A few minutes ago. You were looking at pictures and muttering, so I didn't interrupt. You didn't hear me arrive?"

I wrinkled my nose. I *had* heard the door open, so I couldn't entirely blame him. I stood and stretched, sighing in relief as my spine decompressed.

Varro watched me with an unreadable expression. Finally, he said, "You could've asked for far more from Liang for the debt he owed you."

"Seeing as how I didn't think he owed me anything at all, I'm fine with just the name."

Varro's mouth flattened into a hard line before he said, "Be careful. He's charming, but he's also a member of the imperial family. Charm is his weapon."

I blinked away the hurt. "Do you really think I don't know that?"

Varro rubbed a hand down his face, then gripped the back of his neck with a flex of muscles that threatened to derail the conversation—at least from my side. "No," he growled, frustration clear. "You're one of the smartest people I know."

"Then why won't you believe that I don't hold you responsible for my injury?"

Anguish flashed across his face before he hid it away. "Just because you are kind doesn't absolve me of responsibility."

I blew out a slow breath. "So what would? What do we have to do to move past this?" I dredged up a teasing smile. "Perhaps you could kiss my toes for a week. Or follow me around espousing my greatness. Or carry me from place to place like my own personal palanquin."

Varro froze, and my eyes narrowed. "What?"

He shook his head, but something in his expression remained carefully intent.

I tilted my head. I should probably talk to one of the other Valoffs before I tried something that could just make the situation worse, but Varro was here now, and they weren't.

From my perspective, the broken vow was nothing—there's no way he could've predicted I'd put myself between the debris and Liang and Siarvez. But from his perspective, he'd not only broken a vow, but he'd also allowed me to be injured. It didn't matter if I thought it was ridiculous, because he *didn't*.

"Varro," I said slowly, "you broke a promise to me. I require restitution."

His expression remained grave, but his eyes lit. Perhaps I was on the right track. I couldn't ask for something too easy, or I'd insult him. But I also couldn't ask for something too hard, because I just couldn't.

"Here are my requirements. You will take over my cleaning duties for a week so that I can spend more time searching for Fev and Morten. And you will bake me a dozen cookies a day for that same week."

Varro placed his left arm over his chest and bowed low. "Consider it done."

I bit my lip, but I couldn't stop the question. "Was that what I was supposed to do?" When he nodded, I shifted nervously. "It wasn't too much was it? I could help you with the cleaning. I don't mind—"

Varro cupped my cheek with his palm and swept his thumb over my lips, silencing me. "It was perfect."

CHAPTER TWENTY-ONE

Each of the tables in the galley easily sat ten people, so Liang and Siarvez joined the main table, sitting at one end next to Eli and Chira. If Eli was impressed to have a Valovian prince sitting next to him, you wouldn't know it from his expression, which budged from cool politeness only when he glanced across the table at Chira.

Havil sat on my right, with Torran, Eli, and Liang on my left. On the other side of the table, Anja sat across from Havil, followed by Varro, an empty chair for Tavi, Chira, and Siarvez.

Tavi settled into her seat, and we all dug in. Torran had cooked tonight: thinly sliced vegetarian protein and roasted vegetables in a sweet and savory sauce served over brown rice.

It was delicious.

Tavi caught my eye. "Everything okay?" she murmured over the comm.

"I think so. Varro is going to be doing my cleaning chores this week, in addition to his own."

Tavi frowned. "You know I prefer everyone to pull their fair share."

"I think he needs this to repay the broken vow. I'm not sure, but he seemed happier when I asked him to do it. I tried to take it back, to offer to help, but he wouldn't let me. And it'll give me more time to search."

"One week only," Tavi allowed. "Then you'll have to find something else."

"I hope a week will be the end of it."

Tavi looked skeptical. "I talked to Torran. It seems minor to us, but a broken promise of protection is a big deal to a Valoff. Torran was surprised Varro didn't offer a life debt, but he figures Varro knows you would hate it, so he's trying something else. But much like a life debt, it won't be over until Varro thinks his honor is repaired."

My nose wrinkled. As much as I'd teased Tavi about her debt, I really *would've* hated Varro declaring a life debt to me. And I hoped he didn't expect me to order him around for more than a week, because that was already pushing it.

Aloud Tavi asked, "Did you find anything on Fev?"

"Not yet, but I set up my initial searches. Hopefully I'll have something soon. Until then, who wants to lay odds on where *Renegade Tide* is heading?"

Eli groaned. "It's going to be the fucking lunar base, isn't it?"

"I don't know," I admitted. "I tried to contact Nick, but their comm wasn't accepting connections."

Varro frowned from his place across from me. "Have they been caught?"

"I don't know. I was planning to ask you to try to contact them telepathically—they gave me permission—if we're close enough."

Varro's expression went distant. "I will try," he said quietly.

Anja leaned forward. "I've spent time on Expedition, both the planet and the lunar base. I know my way around." The mechanic shook her head. "FOSO I isn't going to be the easiest place to infiltrate, especially not with a bounty on your head."

Forward Observation Station Odyssey I was named for Expedition's main moon, Odyssey. It had been built before Bastion and had been the FHP's stronghold in this sector before the station took over that responsibility.

"I don't suppose Lexi is still kicking around in this part of the galaxy?" I asked hopefully, looking at Tavi. Our favorite thief would be useful if we were going to be breaking into an FHP base.

Tavi shook her head. "Last I heard, she had a job on Ailved. I'll send her a message to see if she has any ideas, but we might not hear back before we arrive."

"If I understand correctly, you think Anna's ship is heading for an FHP base," Siarvez said. "Why would they take her there?"

Tavi looked at me, and I subvocally asked, "How much can I tell them?"

"Whatever you think is best. You've spent more time with them than I have."

I sighed. I wasn't sure *what* was best. Liang could help us, or he could run straight back to his mother and tell her exactly what we knew. "From what I've gathered," I said slowly, choosing my words with care, "the FHP and the Valovian Empire are attempting to goad each other back into war. That's why the soldiers who attacked Bastion *looked* like Valoffs, even if they weren't."

Liang leaned forward so that he could see me around Eli and Torran. He looked curious. "How do you know they *weren't* Valoffs?"

I shrugged. "Oh, one of them was, for sure."

That surprised him. He had already known the attackers weren't all Valoffs, but he hadn't expected me to know that one of them *was*.

"With the confusion from the explosion, I couldn't tell they weren't until they spoke," Siarvez said. "So the Valoff must've been shielding for the humans."

Varro had been able to tell from a distance, but he was a stronger telepath than most of his peers. That meant the Valovian guests probably couldn't be counted on to say the attackers were humans in Valovian armor because they might think the soldiers actually were Valoffs.

This situation was a mess all the way down.

I shook my head and got back on track. "We think the FHP is behind the attack. Or if not the FHP directly, then a former soldier who's working behind the scenes for FHP Command."

"Why would FHP take out their own station?" Chira asked.

Tavi tipped her head toward the Valovian first officer. "That part doesn't make any sense," she agreed. "They could've made it *look* like the station was down without actually taking it out. Losing Bastion, even temporarily, is a serious blow."

"If the attack was Morten's doing, then perhaps the telekinetic moved without his knowledge," Torran said.

"That's not good," Tavi murmured.

It wouldn't be the first time Fev had deviated from Morten's plan. While Morten thought that she was working for him, she seemed to have her own agenda as an agent for the empress.

But if Fev was working on her own, then the empress had ordered an attack on an FHP installation, and that was a dangerous escalation—one that played directly into the narrative the FHP was building about the Valoffs being a threat. We needed to get Anna rescued, Morten and the Feds stopped, and Liang home before the treaty compliance dissolved further.

"But still, why Anna?" Siarvez asked. "She's not a strategic target."

"But she is," I argued. "She's not a strategic *military* target, but that doesn't mean she's not the perfect target. If you were trying to persuade people to return to war, what lever would you use?"

"Fear," Tavi said. "Or pride."

"Exactly. Anna Duarte is well known in certain powerful circles. She's seen as untouchable. Her collaboration with a Valovian designer initially set off a slew of controversy, but more recently it's been changing to cautiously optimistic hope. Valovian soldiers attacking and abducting her, even though she's been working with one of their own, is the ultimate betrayal."

Eli nodded and picked up the thread. "And once the Feds get the rich and powerful on board with war, they know that the rest—the people who will actually be fighting and dying—don't matter." Bitterness laced his tone. It was a lesson we'd all learned early and often.

"But won't she know it was humans who abducted her?" Liang asked.

Eli shook his head. "We don't have telepathy. If they don't take off their helmets, she won't know. Then when soldiers in FHP uniforms show up to 'rescue' her, she'll believe the lie."

"Anna is smarter than you're giving her credit for," Siarvez said, voice sharp. "And before they hit me, I warned her that the attackers were human." Eli, Tavi, Anja, and I all winced. "What?" he demanded.

"If the Feds can't use her, they'll kill her," I said quietly. "Her ignorance was the thing keeping her safe. If she lets on that she knows they're not Valoffs, then she becomes a liability."

Siarvez paled and his face crumpled. "I've killed her," he whispered, distraught.

"Maybe we're wrong," I rushed to assure him. "And even if we're not, they won't kill her on the ship." I hoped. "We still have time."

Liang leaned forward and glanced around the table before letting his gaze settle on me. "Will this be enough for the FHP to break the treaty?"

I looked at Tavi, waiting for her to answer, but she tipped her head toward me. I swallowed as my pulse sped up. Usually, I fed information to the captain and let her draw conclusions and make plans. Being put on the spot was a bit harrowing, but I had all the information; I just needed to use it.

I mentally played out various scenarios while everyone at the table waited for me to gather my thoughts. "No," I said slowly, "they won't break the treaty immediately. They still need to sway public opinion before we go to war again. But once the news spreads . . . probably. Especially with the actual attack on Bastion."

Liang nodded, as if the answer was what he'd expected.

"But if we rescue Anna, we can change the narrative," I added. "Using her is a double-edged sword for the Feds, because her opinion carries weight. And if she goes public with a true accounting of events, then the FHP looks like the villain rather than the hero."

"What can I do to help?"

I grinned at him. "I don't suppose you're secretly a telekinetic? Or a thief? Or just a really good lock pick?"

"Sadly, no," Liang said with a shake of his head.

"Can you talk the empress out of war?"

Liang snorted. "I'd have a better chance of turning telekinetic."

"Well, we'll figure something out," I said with a wave. "Don't worry about it. For now, the most important thing is staying out of the FHP's clutches—for both of us."

AFTER DINNER, HAVIL AND ANJA WERE ON CLEAN-UP DUTY. AND AS much as I wanted to head down to the rec room and lose myself in a vid, I didn't have time. We'd arrive at Expedition around lunch tomorrow. I had to have a solid plan by then, which left precious little time for relaxation.

I settled back in my control room and stared at the monitors. The *Renegade Tide* had to know that we were following them, but it remained to be seen what they planned to do about it. Tavi had an incredibly rocky relationship with the Feds. They'd paraded her around as the Hero of Rodeni despite the fact that they knew full well that the battle had been won only because they'd blown up a building full of civilians—over Tavi's protests.

Tavi had let them prop her up as a hero because it was

the only way the Feds would process our expedited discharge paperwork. Her silence had bought our freedom. But if she had nothing left to lose, she'd reveal the truth of what had really happened on Rodeni, and she had precautions in place for just such an event.

I knew, because I'd helped her set them up.

But that would be the last resort, because there was no returning from it. The Feds would hunt us down, claiming that she'd turned traitor, especially considering her and Torran's relationship.

We needed a plan that kept everyone safe—or at least safe-*ish*.

The facial recognition algorithm was still chewing through the various photos I'd collected, but I peeked at the results anyway. A handful of people came up multiple times, but Sura Fev was not among them. I started going through the individual results, which were still numerous.

I'd made it more than halfway through the list when a blurry, ivory-skinned blond woman stared back at me. I pulled up the surveillance screenshot, then squinted at the two faces on screen. *Maybe?*

I opened the full photo and found that the blonde was in the background of a shot of the empress when she had visited Bastion for part of the treaty ceremony. The blonde faced the camera, but because of the depth of field, she wasn't entirely in focus. I copied the photo to my comm and went looking for Liang.

After several minutes of searching, I finally found him and Siarvez in the garden arbor with Torran. The three of them looked comfortable, like they were in conversation, but I waded in with a perfunctory greeting and held the comm up with the picture zoomed in on the blonde. "Is this her?" I asked Liang.

His head tilted as he studied the photo. "Yes," he said after a moment, "I believe so."

"Thank you." I turned to leave, then spun back around. "You wouldn't happen to have a better picture, would you?"

A sly smile crossed his mouth. "And if I did? What would it be worth to you?"

"Nope, I'm not playing that game. I'll find her on my own. Have a good night."

I turned to leave again when Liang's voice made me pause. "I don't have a photo," he said quietly. "The identities of Fiazefferu are closely guarded. Be careful with that information."

I smiled at him over my shoulder. "Thank you. I will be." I bid everyone good night and left them to continue their conversation.

A blurry photo that showed the telekinetic's entire face was better than nothing. Once I reclaimed my seat in the control room, I tweaked my facial recognition algorithm to search for her specifically. It would bubble the closest results to the top, so I'd have even fewer photos to look through next time.

Hopefully.

That done, I turned back to my list. The malware infecting Bastion was the highest priority, but I wasn't sure if I should spend my time planning how to access the lunar base instead. I wrinkled my nose. I needed Tavi's and Torran's help to plan our entry, and Torran, at least, was busy right now.

I added an item for access planning to my list, then set a timer for an hour. I'd get started on the malware, then switch when the timer went off. That would give Torran plenty of time to talk to Liang and Siarvez.

I connected to Bastion's network, but they hadn't brought up any of their servers, which meant they hadn't figured out the malware on their own—yet. There was still time for me to use the solution as the leverage I needed to get my bounty removed.

Most malware had a backdoor written into it, so it was just a matter of finding it. I pulled up the list of servers I'd connected to before and started scanning the most likely ports for an open connection.

Nothing.

I grumbled at the screen, but if it was easy, the Feds would've already figured it out. I cracked my knuckles and got to work. No Valovian hacker was going to get the better of me.

I SQUINTED AT THE SCREEN AS I WAITED OUT THE BRIEF SIGNAL DElay. The ship was quiet and still around me. My alarm had gone off at some point, but I'd silenced it without taking my attention away from the tricky piece of software that had made its home on Bastion's network.

I had to give the Valoffs credit—they didn't do anything halfway. As far as I could tell, the malware was designed to encrypt every drive it came across using a very specific, very niche exploit, one that I was kind of mad I hadn't found first.

Hopefully the Feds were smart enough to keep their backups separated from their main network or they were in for a world of hurt. There *should* be a way to decrypt everything with the right key, but finding it could take longer than restoring the servers from backup.

Luckily, I had found something interesting, a way to potentially bypass the need to brute-force the key at all. The malware communicated using a very old protocol, one that I almost hadn't caught because no one used it anymore, and most modern monitoring software didn't even register it.

I followed the tiny, hidden stream of packets to a server that had a similar signal delay as Bastion itself. Somewhere near the station—probably in a ship, if I had to guess—was a server that held the very key I needed. All I had to do was find my way in.

And do it in such a way that I didn't accidentally infect *Starlight*'s systems. I made sure all of my security precautions were in place, then I got to work.

Finessing one's way into an unknown server required a combination of luck, skill, persistence, and nonlinear thinking. It was something I'd been doing for most of my life at this point, but the thrill never went away. It was a careful dance, and I lost myself to it completely.

I didn't know how much time had passed when someone touched my shoulder, but I was so immersed in the data on the screen that I didn't even bother to startle. My head felt light and disconnected, my eyes were heavy and gritty, and my stomach appeared to be trying to gnaw its way out of my body. I blinked at nothing, momentarily distracted by my physical aches.

"Have you been here all night?" Varro asked, and worry whispered across my mind.

I twisted to look at him and my spine cracked with a series of audible pops. Varro's hair was damp and he was wearing different clothes. I squinted at him as if I could tell the time just by looking hard enough. "Is it morning?"

His mouth flattened into a hard line. I guess that wasn't the answer he had hoped to hear. Too bad, because I was *this close* to cracking the server, and I couldn't afford to be interrupted now.

I turned back to the screen and considered my next steps. One by one, I cleared the final hurdles until, at last, the security gave way.

I. Was. In.

I jabbed a fist in the air and shouted in triumph. I spun around to share my excitement with Varro, but the room was empty. Disappointment rose, but it was drowned out by the elation of victory.

There was no time to gloat. Their security was top-notch. My intrusion would be found sooner rather than later, so I had to act fast. But after a night of fighting for access, I knew exactly what I was dealing with.

I flipped the heavy manual switch that physically disconnected my terminal from the rest of the ship's network and systems. I trusted my security setup, but I wouldn't take any risks. By physically isolating the connection, I ensured that a mistake or unexpected threat would just take out one terminal and not the whole ship.

After spending countless hours getting into the system, finding the private key I needed to break the encryption was almost ridiculously easy. I copied it into a secure enclave, then poked around to see if I could find anything else interesting.

Sadly, it seemed like whoever had set up this server had done the same thing I had—isolated it from the surrounding network. Not only that, but the server itself had been freshly set up to deliver and control the malware.

And to store what appeared to be a whole host of highly

classified FHP data. Someone had been busy before Bastion's servers had gone down.

I started copying the data, more interested in speed than stealth. The transfer was less than half done when my security alert went off. My prying had not gone unnoticed, but they'd traced me only as far as the first proxy.

I didn't have time to go through the files to find the most important ones, so I let the transfer run. I didn't want the Valovian Empire to know exactly who had hacked them, so I'd have to kill the connection once they reached the second proxy, assuming my security scripts didn't do it first.

A few minutes later, a second security alert went off and then the transfer stopped. *Oh, shit.* That was way faster than I'd expected. My hands flew into motion.

My second proxy would be in the process of wiping itself, not that I kept anything incriminating on it, but better safe than sorry. I pulled up my list of proxies and marked it as dead. Even with the wipe, there wasn't a guarantee that the other hacker wouldn't get in and leave a surprise for me. Better to count it as a total loss.

I disconnected from the third proxy, wiped it as well, and then breathed through the spike of adrenaline. Whoever had been monitoring their system knew exactly what they were doing, and they had spent plenty of time cracking into human systems. Maybe the Valovian Empire had such a person, but I added a list item to make some subtle inquiries to see if anyone in the dark net had heard of a less-than-legal job offer lately.

Adrenaline and fatigue fought for supremacy, leaving me feeling both jittery and exhausted. I double-checked that the private encryption key was safe, then copied it to a removable data drive and unplugged that from the system.

This was the leverage I needed, and losing it would make the last ten hours a waste of time.

At some point, I would need to go through the classified data I'd been able to transfer, but it could wait until I'd gotten a couple of hours of sleep. The door opened as I was contemplating whether or not I could sleep in this chair. It wasn't a very comfortable bed, but I was so tired that I wasn't sure I cared.

"I brought food," Varro said. "You can eat while you work."

I turned and grinned at him. He held a tray with a smoothie and a plate of food I could eat with my fingers. He'd gone to a lot of trouble for me, so I was rather abashed when I said, "I'm done. I need to talk to Tavi."

Varro balanced the tray on one hand and offered the other to me. "Let's move to the galley. I'll get the captain for you, and you can eat and talk at the same time."

I wasn't sure I could, actually, but I let him pull me up. Every muscle protested as I straightened. Even with a nice chair and an attempt at ergonomics, I tended to slouch after sitting for too long, and my body didn't appreciate it.

I stretched my arms overhead, then followed Varro from the room.

CHAPTER TWENTY-TWO

Varro settled me into my usual spot at the table, placed the tray in front of me, and told me to eat while he went to find Tavi. It was a sign of my exhaustion that I didn't remember he could just contact her telepathically until after he'd already left.

By physically going to find her, he was giving me time to eat, so I pulled the tray closer.

I ate with mechanical motions, barely tasting the food, but the smoothie soothed my scratchy throat. As the adrenaline faded, weariness took over. A check of the time proved that it was still early morning. Most of the ship was probably either in the gym or asleep.

Sleep sounded good. Maybe I'd rest my head on the table for a second, just until Tavi arrived.

I'd finally found a semi-comfortable position when I heard footsteps in the hallway. Tavi entered wearing workout clothes and looking far too energetic for this hour. I felt more tired just looking at her.

Varro followed her in, but he frowned at me. I snagged a piece of toast off the plate and nibbled on the crust. His frown didn't disappear, but his expression turned slightly less grumpy.

Tavi's gaze took in my slumped position, the toast, and the half-eaten plate of food next to me. "Rough night?"

"Long but productive night," I corrected without lifting my head. "I found the encryption key the Feds need to fix Bastion's servers."

Tavi sucked in a breath and a smile broke across her face. "Incredible job, as usual. What are you going to do with it?"

"Once I can blink without falling asleep, I'm going to barter it to the Feds in return for dropping my bounty. Maybe. I might poke around in their network for a while first." I waved the piece of toast. "I haven't decided."

"Eat your breakfast," she admonished, and Varro nodded in agreement.

"I am." I took a bite just to make the statement true. "Oh, and I also found a cache of what I believe to be classified FHP files, but I haven't looked at them yet. I didn't get everything because whoever was monitoring the server figured out they had a breach faster than I would've liked, but it should still be interesting reading."

Tavi's eyebrows rose. "Do you think the attack was a cover to grab the files?"

"Could be." I sat up with a groan and shoved the rest of the toast in my mouth. When I was finished chewing, I said, "Or the files could be a nice bonus to an attack they were planning anyway. I might know more after I look at what we've got."

"First, sleep," Tavi said, using the tone of voice that meant she expected to be obeyed.

I tossed her a jaunty salute. "No argument there. We're about six hours from Expedition. I need at least two hours of sleep, then we need to make a plan. The Feds aren't just going to let us waltz in after Anna."

"Four hours, no less," Tavi said firmly. She raised a hand and cut off my protest. "Torran and I will get started on a plan, but we're going to need you to get us past their security. If you're dead on your feet, you're no good to us." She turned to Varro. "Make sure she finishes her breakfast before she falls asleep."

"I don't need a babysitter," I growled, but she was already on her way out the door.

Varro sat down across from me. I tried to scowl at him, but I was too tired to make it stick. "Thank you for making breakfast," I said.

"You're welcome."

I stared at him while I continued to eat. Finally, I asked, "Are you going to stop being mad at me after you do my chores for a week?"

Varro shifted and his eyes narrowed. "I'm not mad at you. You are not at fault."

I might be dead on my feet, but I knew a dodge when I heard one. "That didn't answer the question. What do I need to do to prove that I don't think you're at fault, either?"

"Let me do things for you."

I shook my head. "I'm not going to order you around. And Tavi said a week of chores is all she's going to allow. So I'll ask you again—is that going to be enough?"

Varro's expression flattened. "You nearly died."

"Are you trying to fulfill a life debt without actually pledging a life debt?"

For an instant, shock crossed Varro's face before he smoothed it away and narrowed his eyes. "Has Torran been meddling where he shouldn't?"

"One, he's your friend and he cares about you, so of course he's going to wonder what's going on. Two, it was Tavi who was meddling, not Torran. And three, that's *still* not an answer."

Varro sighed and dropped his gaze to the table. "I am trying not to make you uncomfortable, but it seems I am not being very successful."

He paused to gather his thoughts, and I kept my eyes open by sheer force of will. This conversation was too important to have half asleep, but I was afraid if I postponed it that it wouldn't happen at all.

"To humans, a promise of protection holds no more importance than any other promise," he said slowly. "If you promise someone protection, it means you'll *try* to keep them safe, but you may not be successful. Both parties innately understand this."

That was a little simplistic, but mostly accurate, so I nodded.

"With Valoffs, it's different. If a Valoff promises someone protection, then that person will be protected *at all costs*. Even a minor injury is considered a broken vow, which is why Valoffs rarely promise protection."

Understanding dawned. "Is that why Torran is still so torn up about Tavi's injuries during the rescue?"

Varro nodded. "He failed to keep her safe, despite the fact that he promised to protect her *and* owed her a life debt."

"But he did everything he could. Surely that's enough?" I wasn't talking about Tavi and Torran anymore.

"No," Varro said, his voice firm but gentle. "It wasn't enough." He wasn't talking about Tavi and Torran, either.

I sighed. "So what happens now?"

"Now you sleep."

The idea sounded so good that I didn't realize he'd dodged the question *again* until I was already in my bed—alone.

DREAMS AND SHADOWS CHASED EACH OTHER OVER ALIEN LANDscapes and war-torn vistas. But I didn't want nightmares tonight. With a thought, the view shifted and phantom arms slipped around my waist. I sighed and leaned back against Varro's broad chest.

This dream was my favorite.

Varro nuzzled my temple, breathing my name against my skin like a prayer. I turned and tipped my chin up. He met my mouth with a groan, and now that I knew what his lips tasted like, I could feel the warmth of his skin and the firm pressure of his mouth.

The kiss burned hotter than in any dream before, and when his tongue stroked into my mouth, my toes curled in delight. His hands kneaded my ass, pressing me against his growing hardness. "This is torture," he growled.

I frowned at him. That wasn't usually how this dream went.

He palmed my breast, scattering my thoughts. He gently pinched my aching nipple and the shock of pleasure sent desire blazing brighter, turning my blood slow and molten. With a thought, my shirt disappeared, lost into the swirling fog surrounding us.

Varro stared at my bare breasts as if they held the secrets of the universe. A woman could get used to devotion like that, especially when he bent his head and drew a pebbled nipple into the heat of his mouth. Pleasure drowned me, setting every nerve alight.

When he pulled back to move to my other breast, a bed appeared, and I fell back on it, crooking a finger at him. My pants vanished while he remained frustratingly clothed.

He crawled onto the bed, looming over me but not touching. "You're everything I've ever wanted," he confessed. "And I can't have you except like this."

I tilted my head and my brows drew together in confusion. Something about that sounded wrong.

Then Varro's lips were on mine and his hands were roaming across my skin and nothing mattered except getting closer. I spread my legs and moaned in pleasure when his fingers stroked through my slick heat. I lifted my hips in a silent plea and he pressed two fingers into me slow enough to make me whine with impatience.

Just when I thought it couldn't get any better, his head dipped and he brushed his lips over my neglected nipple once, twice, before drawing it into his mouth with gentle suction. My back bowed as pleasure exploded.

But why was he still wearing pants?

"Get naked," I demanded, pulling at clothes that I couldn't seem to grasp. I frowned at his shirt. That had never happened before.

Varro reared back, his expression shocked. "You're not a dream."

"I am dreaming," I insisted. "But you're supposed to be naked. Why aren't you naked?"

Horrified realization bloomed on his face. "I fell asleep in the garden. I invaded your dreams."

It took a second for the words to break through the desire. "Wait, *you're* not a dream?" The shock was enough to send me toward wakefulness. The bed disappeared, and Varro wavered.

I reached for him. "Wait, come back!"

"Sleep, Kee," he murmured.

He vanished and everything faded to black.

FOUR HOURS OF SLEEP WAS JUST ENOUGH TO MAKE ME FUNCtional, if not exactly perky. I dragged myself through my morning routine and tried not to dwell on the memory of Varro's horrified expression. I'd been able to lucid dream for as long as I could remember, but this was the first time someone else had joined me.

And despite his worry, I wasn't so sure that *I* hadn't pulled *him* into my dreams.

I opened my cabin door with the intention of finding him and stopped short. Mission accomplished.

Varro was leaning against the opposite wall, his face a distant, hard mask. He straightened, then bowed low. "I am deeply sorry," he rumbled. "I cannot turn back time, but I have taken precautions so that my shields will not fail again."

He held himself in the bow, awaiting my judgment. He'd told me before that he would need to use constant control to prevent his shields from slipping.

He was going to torture himself to protect me.

I crossed the hall and urged him to stand with careful hands on his shoulders, not sure that he would appreciate my touch. "Varro, I've dreamed of you before," I confessed. "It's one of my favorite dreams. Why do you think I was so comfortable with you?"

"I was influencing—"

I pressed my fingers against his lips. "You weren't, I promise. But what if I accidentally pulled you into my dreams? We both know my shields are terrible." I swallowed and looked away. "And while I *knew* that you didn't want me in real life, I did nothing to alter the dream, though I could've." Tears filmed my eyes and I blinked them away. "I should be the one apologizing."

Before I could, Varro's hands cupped my face, his touch gentle. "No."

"But—"

"No." Varro's voice was as hard as the deck under my feet. "You are many things, Kee Ildez, but a strong telepath is not one of them. There is no way you made it past my shields, even thin ones. The fault is mine."

I dropped my eyes to his shirt and whispered, "I didn't mind. And I wouldn't mind if it happened again."

His groan was filled with longing, and when I lifted my gaze, his eyes were nearly black. "Kee—"

I cut him off before he could list all the reasons it was a bad idea. "If I can only have you in dreams, then I accept."

Varro shook his head. "You deserve so much more."

"I do," I agreed quietly. He remained silent and the rejection stung.

Still, I couldn't let him torture himself on my behalf. "If you want to make it up to me, then swear that you won't hurt yourself ensuring the shield between us is strong—unless that's what *you* want. Don't do it to protect me, because I don't need or want the protection." *I want you.* I managed to bite off the confession before I made this conversation even more uncomfortable.

Varro stared at me for a long moment, his gaze slowly tracing my face, then he dipped his chin. “As you wish.”

It was not nearly what I wished for, but I’d learned long ago that wishing rarely made a difference. The lesson never stuck, however, because what was life without hope?

I summoned a smile and tucked my hopes away, close to my heart. “Thank you.”

CHAPTER TWENTY-THREE

After a brief stop by my control room, I joined the rest of the crew on the bridge as we approached Odyssey, Expedition's moon. The main screen showed the cratered gray and tan lunar surface. Expedition hung in the background, a green-and-white marble floating in the black of space. The planet not only had breathable atmosphere, but it also had a temperate climate.

There was a reason the Feds fought so hard to keep it.

The moon, however, barely had any atmosphere. The lunar base was essentially a space station that happened to be built on the lunar surface.

Luna chirped a greeting from her place atop Tavi's terminal, and I cooed a greeting back at her, then moved close enough to scratch her under her chin. The little burbu flopped over, exposing her fluffy belly, but I knew a trap when I saw one.

Tavi looked up at me. "Did you sleep well?"

"I slept like the dead," I fibbed. "In fact, I may still be part zombie."

"There's hot chocolate waiting for you at your terminal."

"You're my favorite captain, have I ever told you that?"

Tavi laughed. "Thanks, but it was Varro's doing."

I was determined to keep things normal between us, no matter how much my heart ached over his continued rejection. He was sitting next to my navigation terminal, so I turned to him and said, "You're my favorite weapons expert, have I ever told you that?" If it came out a little huskier than I'd planned, I hoped everyone just blamed it on my short night.

Tavi elbowed me in the side, distracting me. "I see how it is," she groused.

I laughed and dodged out of elbow strike range before she could get me again. "If you'd like to try to win back my love, I accept payment in chocolate and sugary desserts."

"What about me?" Eli asked from his place at the tactical terminal. "Am I your favorite?"

"Of course you are! You're my favorite pain in the ass."

Next to him, Chira snorted out a laugh before hiding her smile with a hand. Eli turned to her with a betrayed look and a dramatic hand on his chest. "You, too?" he demanded.

Her eyes danced, but she smoothed her expression into innocence. "Sorry," she said with a ridiculously fake cough. "My drink went down wrong."

"You don't even have a drink!"

Chira cracked into laughter and the rest of the room joined her. I was happy to see that the reserved Valoff felt comfortable enough to join our playful banter. While I'd enjoyed getting to spend time alone with Varro, I'd missed this. I was happiest when I could see for myself that all the people I loved were happy and safe.

I glanced around at the rest of the room. Anja sat in her usual spot at engineering, with Havil at the nearby science and medical terminal. Torran was at the communications terminal. The operations terminal—Lexi's usual spot—remained empty.

Liang and Siarvez sat in the back of the room, not part of the crew, but not completely excluded, either. I'd walked right past them without noticing.

I waved at them, then dropped into my chair and picked up the hot chocolate. The first sip tasted like heaven, and I dipped my head at Varro. "Thank you, this is exactly what I needed."

He nodded, and a small, pleased smile touched his lips. "You're welcome."

I enjoyed the view for a moment longer, then turned to my terminal. A quick check confirmed that the *Renegade Tide* was on final approach to the lunar base. *Starlight's Shadow* wasn't the fastest ship, but it was faster than the *Tide.* Tavi had made up a little time overnight, but we were still two hours from landing.

The FHP ship that had been following us had broken away at some point, but that didn't mean much because there were plenty of others to take its place. Traffic was always heavier around planets and stations, but this level seemed unusual.

"Do you have a plan?" I asked Tavi.

"We've been discussing the best way into the base, but all of the options are kind of terrible, especially when the

Feds have a two-hour head start and you have a bounty on your head."

I hoped I would be able to remove the bounty, but I wasn't sure it was a good idea to do it right before breaking into an FHP base—if we got caught, I might need that leverage.

Speaking of leverage . . . "Do you think they'll hand over Anna in return for the key that unlocks Bastion's systems?"

Tavi idly petted Luna while she thought. "No. Since the Feds know you were at the fashion exhibition, they have to assume that you know who really attacked. They would likely rather see Bastion take weeks to recover than let you talk to Anna—assuming she hasn't already let on that she knows they're human. And if they know you have the solution, they'll be even more motivated to capture you."

I shuddered to think how far the FHP goons would go to pry the information out of me. On second thought, I wanted to be somewhere far, far away when I demanded they remove my bounty in return for the key.

"Varro and I could get in," I said at last. "We did it on Bastion. I just need to find a way into their system." Doing it in two hours would be a stretch, but maybe I'd get lucky.

"I'm not sending you in alone," Tavi said. Eli nodded in agreement.

"A smaller team might be better," Torran argued. Tavi scowled at him, but he just held his hands up with a smile. "I know you don't want to send anyone into danger without you, but Varro can shield for Kee, and they'll be virtually invisible. And to help their chances, we can create a distraction."

"What kind of distraction?"

"Whatever you think is best."

Tavi rolled her eyes, but she couldn't quite suppress the tiny smile that peeked through. Eli, however, wasn't sold. "It's too dangerous."

"Taking a larger team isn't going to make it safer," I said. "It just means the Feds are more likely to notice us."

"Then you stay on the ship, and I'll go with Varro."

My gut instinct screamed denial, but I held back the words. It wasn't a bad plan. I could support from the ship, possibly even better than I could on the ground.

I still hated it.

"Varro is the only one who can hide Kee if the FHP starts searching for her," Torran said.

Eli frowned. "Why only him?"

Torran didn't say anything, but Varro disappeared from view. Even knowing it was possible and seeing the results firsthand, it still amazed me.

"What the fuck?" Eli demanded.

"He's tricking your mind into believing he's not there," I said. "It's how we made it through Bastion."

Torran's team didn't look surprised, which made sense, because Varro had been with them for years, but the humans all looked as stunned as I'd felt the first time. I glanced back at our guests. Liang was frowning at Varro's location with a look of concentration, and Siarvez's expression was impossible to read. At least neither of them looked ready to bolt at proof of Varro's mental strength.

Eli stood and crossed the room. When he got close to Varro's chair, he slowed. As he reached out, he said, "Varro, if you're there, don't let me poke you in the eye." When his hand connected with an invisible obstruction, Eli cursed again.

"Are you touching him?" Anja asked.

"I think so," Eli said. Varro blinked back into view with Eli's hand on his shoulder. Eli shook his head again. "That's freaky," he murmured. "Does it work on other Valoffs?"

"Depends on their strength," Varro said, "but generally not as well, unless I use a lot of energy. However, I just hid from everyone in the room. You can verify with them."

Eli looked at the Valoffs in the room, who all nodded. "Damn, that's handy."

Varro's mask was in place, but I could see tiny signs of wariness. I remembered how reluctant he'd been to tell me just how strong he was, so I decided to change the subject.

"When Varro's shielding for me, we can both hide in plain sight," I said. "Electronic surveillance gets tricky, but I should be able to handle that part."

Eli considered Varro. "How long can you maintain the illusion?"

"It depends on the number of people around and how strong they are. Hiding in a crowd is far more difficult than hiding from one or two people. As long as we're careful, I should be able to hide us long enough to find Anna and Nick and return."

"I'm still not sure that sending Kee into a base full of people who want to make her a patsy is the best plan," Tavi said after Eli returned to his terminal. "What are our other options?"

Her lack of confidence after my success on Bastion stung. I would never be the strongest member of the team—far from it—but I thought I'd proven that I could get the job done. *Hadn't I?* With no clear answer forthcoming, I shoved the question away and turned to Varro. "Have you been able to contact Nick?"

He shook his head, his mouth a flat line. I hoped distance was the issue and not that Nick had been hurt or killed, but there were too many unknowns. I was all for sticking it to the Feds, but storming an FHP base without enough information was a good way to end up dead.

"Tavi, did you contact Lexi?" I asked. "Have you heard back?"

"I contacted her," the captain said with a sigh, "but I haven't heard back. We probably won't for at least a day or two. The fastest route to Ailved is three wormhole traversals."

Standard communication was slow, but speedier priority messages got expensive fast. I plotted the course on my terminal. It would take *Starlight* six days to reach Ailved. If Lexi booked passage on one of the express ships, she might make the journey in three days, but that was assuming she dropped everything and headed our way. Even then, she'd be too late.

But if everything went wrong, she'd at least know where to look for us.

"What if they're not planning to keep Anna on the lunar base at all?" Chira asked. "They know they're being followed. They could switch ships and leave before we even arrive."

"They know they're being followed . . ." Tavi repeated softly, her gaze distant. "If I knew I was being followed, what would I do?"

"You'd lead them into a trap," Eli said.

Tavi nodded and her expression hardened as she looked at me. "How sure are you that Nick isn't working for the Feds?"

"Fairly?" I winced as it came out like a question. "We

didn't exactly have time to have deep, meaningful conversations, but I got the feeling that they weren't a fan of the FHP. And that they'd do about anything for Anna, including sneaking aboard an enemy ship."

"But what if they didn't?" Tavi questioned. "What if they just fed you enough information to get you to chase the *Tide* to the lunar base?"

"Nick and Anna were on a ship that left Bastion," Varro said. "I don't know if it's the ship we are chasing, but I kept tabs on them when we were close enough."

Tavi tapped her fingers on the arm of her chair. "Can you tell if they're on Odyssey?"

"Not yet, but I should be able to once we approach."

"Okay," Tavi said, holding up a finger, "option one: the Feds are behind the attack, and Anna and Nick are not in on it. The *Renegade Tide* isn't an FHP ship, which gives them a veneer of separation, but then they make a run straight for an FHP base. Why?"

"I don't think they expected the secondary attack that took down Bastion," I said. "Maybe they weren't planning to move Anna off the station at all, but without knowing who attacked or why, they decided to regroup somewhere safer."

That jogged my memory, and I sat up straight. "I have Bastion's docking records. On my slate. I pulled them down before I got into the FHP servers, then forgot about them because of everything else."

"Docking records for how long?" Tavi asked.

"Since we were on Valovia."

Tavi shook her head. "Only you would have something so incredible and then completely forget about it," she said with an affectionate smile.

I stood and grinned at her. "This time it wasn't even my fault. If you'll recall, the whole station went sideways. I was a little busy."

I hurried to my bunk, grabbed the slate, and then returned to the bridge, holding it aloft like a trophy. "You all can thank Varro for going back for it. I'd forgotten just how much info I'd pulled before everything went to hell."

The docking ticket datastore contained nearly a hundred thousand entries, but both the ship's name and identifier were included with each record, so a simple search turned up all of the relevant records.

Renegade Tide had been to Bastion a half dozen times in the past few months. I kicked off a search for the corresponding flight records based on both the ship's name and ID.

"Well, don't keep us in suspense," Eli prompted.

I blinked at him, then shook my head. "Right, sorry. *Renegade Tide* has been making irregular stops at Bastion over the last three months." I pulled up the most recent docking ticket and checked the dates. "They arrived four days ago and paid for a week's stay."

"So they didn't plan to leave today?" Tavi asked.

"Not according to their docking ticket, but that doesn't necessarily mean anything. It could be a way to deflect suspicion, though the docking ticket would've updated with their actual departure date—if the station was up."

"Still, that makes option one viable," Tavi said. "Maybe they didn't plan to move Anna at all. Or option two: the Feds are behind the attack, and Nick and/or Anna are in on it."

"I don't know about Nick, but Anna is definitely not involved," Siarvez said, speaking up for the first time. "She genuinely believes that collaboration is better for both humans and Valoffs. She approached me. I wasn't the first designer she approached, but I was the first one who agreed with her vision."

"Did she know about your connection to the imperial family?" Torran asked.

"I suppose it's possible, but she didn't learn about it from me, and she never asked me about it. I know what you're thinking, but this isn't a long con. I've worked closely with Anna for three years, and I wasn't entirely trusting at the beginning." He grimaced with a combination of embarrassment and shame. "I violated her privacy by peeking into her head. She's genuine."

Torran's expression hardened. "I hope you admitted your failing and apologized."

Siarvez ducked his head. "It took a year, but I did, and I made it right."

"So Anna is likely in the clear, but Nick could still be betraying her," Tavi said.

"I suppose it's possible," I allowed, "but I didn't get that feeling at all. Nick was surprised by the attack, and they tried to get me to leave via the emergency exit with the rest of the crowd."

"I don't think Nick is involved," Varro said.

They continued debating it, but my attention drifted back to my slate. My flight record search had returned. I squinted and double-checked that I'd input the parameters correctly. Everything looked right, so I checked the results again.

Renegade Tide was one of the few ships that had standing authorization to fly into Valovian space—authorization that they'd taken full advantage of.

CHAPTER TWENTY-FOUR

Tavi was the first to notice my slack-jawed stupor. "What's wrong?"

"The *Renegade Tide* is Morten's ship," I said, my voice barely more than a whisper.

"What? Is he on it?" Tavi demanded.

"I don't know. And I'm not *positive* that it's his ship, but it has standing authorization to traverse into Valovian space. And it arrived from Valovia a little over a month ago, about the same time we returned."

Tavi sucked in a breath. "That's a hell of a coincidence."

"But it could still *be* a coincidence," Eli warned, ever the pessimist.

"If we assume that it *is* his ship," Tavi said over Eli's protests, "then that leads me to believe that he didn't plan to move Anna, at least not on the *Tide*. He wouldn't want to burn his ship by getting it directly involved."

"Maybe he expected another ship to pick her up, but they didn't make it because of the lockdown," Chira suggested.

Tavi shook her head. "Morten would've expected the lockdown. It's standard procedure after an attack or accident that might threaten a station. But he wouldn't have expected the entire station to lose power."

I turned to Liang and Siarvez. "Did the soldiers give you any idea what they wanted with you or Anna? They were prepared to take you all, but what was their reasoning?"

Liang shrugged. "They didn't say much. They spoke a few words to order us around, but mostly they seemed to be communicating silently. I couldn't speak to their reasoning."

Tavi sighed. "There are too many unknowns."

"There usually are," Torran said softly.

"What would you do?" she asked.

Torran had been one of the most successful generals in the Valovian military. His grasp of strategy was second to none, but since he'd joined *Starlight,* he'd been very careful not to usurp Tavi's authority as the captain.

"If Varro can sense them on Odyssey, then I would attempt a rescue with a very small team—possibly just Varro and Kee, because the Feds don't know that they're on the ship. As soon as we land, FHP soldiers are going to demand another search. The two of them can slip out while you argue with the authorities. If Varro can't sense Anna and Nick, then I wouldn't risk a landing."

Tavi nodded, her face thoughtful. "We'll need to be careful. If Sura Fev continued working with Morten after Cien's rescue, then she likely told him that I was the one who interrupted his plan—assuming he didn't already know. The Feds can't come after me without cause, but that doesn't mean they won't try *something.*"

"What do you mean by 'Cien's rescue'?" Liang asked, his voice deceptively mild.

Oh, shit. It was easy to forget that he wasn't part of the crew.

Torran turned toward Liang almost lazily, but his face was set into granite lines, and his expression chilled the blood in my veins. "I rescued Cien from Valovian rebels and safely transported him to his mother."

If Liang was concerned, he didn't show it. He switched to Valovan. "Is that the official story or what really happened?"

"Both." Torran's voice had zero give.

Liang dipped his head. "As you say. I'm glad he's okay." Liang was also Cien's uncle. The fact that he didn't know Cien had been taken meant the empress had kept the kidnapping extremely quiet.

Tavi watched the interplay with a worried frown, but Torran must've reassured her telepathically, because she nodded. "I agree," she said, returning to the previous conversation. "If they move Anna to the lunar base, it's worth it to try to rescue her, even if it's likely to be a trap. We'll just have to be more prepared than they are."

"I'm still going to try," I said, "but odds are I won't be able to crack their systems in two hours. Not if they're as diligent about security as Bastion. Unless . . ." I stared into the middle distance as I thought. "Assuming the comm link between the station and the lunar base is up, I might be able to route a request through the FHP network to give myself access, since I'm already in on Bastion. I'll have to see if other traffic is transmitting, though, or they'll notice it immediately."

"Try it," Tavi said. "If it doesn't work, do you have a backup plan?"

"Knock out a soldier and steal their ID?" I asked with a raised eyebrow.

Tavi laughed. "Not the most elegant plan, but not a bad one if it comes to that. We'll need to move fast, especially if you don't have control of the surveillance. Once we get Anna on board, we'll need something to keep the Feds from attacking and destroying us in a 'tragic accident.'"

"With Anna *and* Liang on board—or at least presumed to be on board—we'll be a priority target, especially if we've just broken into their base," Eli said.

"Anna could broadcast a message saying she's safe onboard *Starlight*," I suggested. "It might give the Feds pause to blow us up right after she said she was safe."

"They could blame another attack on the Valoffs," Eli argued.

"If they do that, then at some point they just start looking incompetent," I said. "We need to make sure we're on the right side of that line."

Eli didn't look convinced, but he stopped arguing. And while a broadcast from Anna *might* work, it would certainly be better for us if I could alter the surveillance video to mislead the Feds long enough for us to make our escape.

"I'm going to start working on the system access," I said, standing. "I'll let you know if I get in, but you shouldn't count on it for your plans."

Tavi nodded. "Keep me posted. I'll let you know if we find Anna's location. Keep trying to contact Nick over the comm."

I bobbed my head in agreement. "I will."

MY PLAN TO ROUTE AUTHORIZATION THROUGH BASTION DIDN'T work as well as I'd hoped, but it wasn't a complete failure, either. The signal traffic between Bastion and FOSO I was far heavier than I expected for a station whose entire system was down.

The Feds must have a backup communication system that hadn't been infected. They'd gotten it up faster than the rest of the station, which made my job a little easier. Still, I hadn't quite gotten the access I needed when the control room door opened, and Varro stepped inside.

I used his entrance as an excuse to stand and stretch. When I was done, he handed me a plate holding a dozen peanut butter cookies. I set the plate on my desk and picked up a cookie. It was still warm, and the first bite was gooey and delicious. I looked at him in amazement. "When did you have time to make these?"

"I made the dough earlier, so I just had to bake them, which only took a few minutes. After I confirmed that Anna and Nick are on Odyssey, Tavi and Torran took over planning, so I slipped out."

"So they definitely are on the moon? Did you have any luck contacting Nick? They never answered any of my attempts."

Varro shook his head. "I could sense them, but they didn't respond. It could be that we are still too far away."

He didn't sound convinced, so I prompted, "Or?"

"Or they're unconscious. Same with Anna."

That wasn't the news I was hoping for, but at least Anna and Nick were both still alive—for now. I forced myself to smile. "Well, Anna should weigh less than Liang, right? I'm becoming quite proficient at carrying people. As long as we don't have to navigate another tower of stairs, I'm golden."

My smile faded as I peered at Varro. He didn't look as rested as I would like. "How are *you*? You have to do all the hard work. You should be saving your strength rather than making me cookies. Maybe we should move our agreement to next week."

"No." The word was quiet, but it had iron behind it.

"Varro—"

"Kee, I know this is difficult for you, and I'm trying to be flexible, but it's a matter of *honor*. It can't be postponed or fixed later."

I swallowed my protests and nodded. He was accommodating my sensibilities, so the least I could do was return the favor. I hated seeing people I cared for hurting or in distress, but *I* would be hurting him if I didn't let him repay the debt.

I bowed my head. "I'm sorry," I whispered. "I know this is important to you, but I forget that when I'm worried about you. Feel free to ignore me and do what you need to do."

Varro cupped my jaw and tipped my head up until he could meet my eyes. *"Cho wubr chil tavoz,"* he murmured.

My life is yours. That sounded a lot like a life debt to me, but I bit my tongue against the immediate protest. Torran had slashed his wrist open when he'd vowed his debt to Tavi, so it wasn't the same, but perhaps the words made Varro feel better.

"Lota ze utaro tu," I replied. *I will treasure it.*

Varro's expression softened. "I know you will," he said. "You are too kind for your own good."

"I'm definitely not," I argued with a smile. "Because I'm totally keeping this entire dozen cookies to myself, and if anyone asks about the delicious cookie smell wafting in the hallway, I'm going to pretend that it's all in their head."

Varro's chuckle warmed my heart and soothed away some of my worries. His happiness made him even more gorgeous, and I stroked my fingers over the back of his hand.

His thumb swept across my cheek and heat kindled in his eyes. I vibrated with the desire to kiss him, to continue where we'd left off in the dream, but the fresh memory of rejection held me back. I'd already chosen him, but he needed to choose me, too, and that wasn't a decision I could make for him.

But I couldn't force myself to pull away when his fingers lingered on my skin, his touch a pleasure all its own. If this was all I could have, then I would enjoy it while I had it.

"Hisi las," he murmured, brutal yearning on his face, "tell me to leave."

I swallowed. "Is that what you want?"

"Lota dikov valu," he confessed in a bare whisper. *I long for you.*

My breath caught. "Then have me."

A groan tore free from his chest. "You deserve better than me. Someone safer."

"I want *you,* Varro," I murmured. "It's always been you."

He closed his eyes, but his fingers remained on my jaw, his touch featherlight. His body was a line of tension, but I didn't press. He had to make this decision without my influence. After a long moment, his lashes lifted and he stared at me with eyes gone nearly black.

Hope stole my breath, but I remained rooted in place by sheer force of will.

Varro's touch softened further, until he was barely grazing my skin. I could've pulled away with nothing more than a deep breath, but I remained riveted as he slowly bent toward me. I forgot about debts and rejections and enemies and rescue plans. There was just me and Varro and this fragile, searing connection between us. I lifted my face and met him halfway.

The moment Varro's lips met mine, I ignited.

At my pleased moan, Varro's hands moved to cup the back of my head. With each glide of his tongue, desire sank burning claws into my nerves, until I trembled in his grasp, overwhelmed in the best possible way. His shields wavered, and I could *feel* his need and longing and iron-clad control echoing across our link.

I did my best to send my own pleasure back to him, to let him feel how much I wanted him. He groaned again and his arm flexed around me, caging me exactly where I wanted to be while he devoured my mouth.

Desire—his and mine—flooded into my mind, mixing until I couldn't tell where I ended and he began. But desire wasn't the only emotion whispering across our link. His sharp longing was tempered by tender care, and the depth of those feelings brought tears to my eyes.

Varro pulled back, his eyes black and his breathing ragged. "Too much?"

I shook my head with a smile, and the small, hurt part of me unclenched. He hadn't been rejecting me because he didn't care. And my feelings weren't one-sided. Varro was just much better at hiding his true feelings behind a shield of honor. And if I could sense his feelings this clearly, then he could sense mine as well—and he wasn't pulling away in disgust at the intensity of what I felt for him. Instead, he was confirming that I was still with him.

"It's perfect," I murmured, pulling his head down to mine. "You're perfect."

His hands stroked down my body and settled on my ass, pulling me closer until I could feel him pressed against me, hot and hard. I moaned into his mouth and slid my hands over his chest, feeling the muscles tense and bunch under my fingers as the edge of his control frayed under the onslaught of our shared pleasure.

Yes.

More.

I could've spent hours exploring his body, but distantly, I heard my terminal start beeping as one of my scripts found a potential exploit. It was designed to catch my attention, but I would've happily ignored it.

Varro, however, did not. He broke the kiss and nuzzled my jaw. "I think your terminal is trying to tell you something," he growled, his voice deep and rough.

I took a moment to rein in my wild pulse and burning desire. "I guess I should check on it," I agreed with a sigh when the beeping refused to stop. Before I pulled away, I guided Varro's lips to mine for a fleeting kiss that was both an enticement and a promise. Now was not the time to explore everything between us, but *soon*.

I'd never looked forward to anything more.

Varro reluctantly drew away, and I let him go. I turned and silenced the alarm but left the window active, so I wouldn't forget to check on it. Then I turned back to Varro and tried to remember what we'd been talking about.

My gaze landed on the cookies, and I frowned. "I suppose I should see if the rest of the crew wants a cookie while they're still warm. You should grab a couple before I put out the call."

Varro shook his head. "I made another two dozen cookies for the rest of the crew, so you don't have to share yours."

I blinked at him. "You know I can't eat a dozen cookies a day, right? I was planning to share from the beginning. You don't have to make extras."

Varro's expression didn't change. "Your cookies are yours. You're welcome to share, of course, but I'll continue to make extra, so you don't *have* to."

I started to protest but took a breath instead. "Is this one of those things you need to do?"

He nodded, his expression wary.

"Okay. Thank you." I held up the plate with a smile. "Would you like a cookie? They're delicious."

CHAPTER TWENTY-FIVE

Powered by freshly baked cookies, I managed to work my way into FOSO I's systems by the time we started the landing process on Odyssey. I didn't have quite the same level of access that I'd had on Bastion, but it was as good as I could do in the limited timeframe.

I didn't have time to give myself access to the door locks, but I did manage to get access to the surveillance system. Varro and I were huddled in the corner of the cargo bay while Liang and Siarvez were once again secured in the hidden stowage compartment. Varro would provide an additional layer of shielding for them until we were out of range.

Varro stood beside me, physically shielding me with his body in addition to the mental shielding, but I still felt exposed. I knew the Feds would be swarming the ship as soon as we touched down, and it felt weird to be standing in the open with a fifty-thousand-credit bounty on my head.

It helped that I had about a thousand camera feeds to flip through while we waited. Anna and Nick were somewhere in the base and while Varro could lead us to them, I'd like to see what to expect before we got there.

Starlight jolted lightly as it settled onto the landing bay deck, and Tavi's voice came through my comm implant. "As expected, they're already demanding access for a search. Are you ready?"

"Are we ready?" I asked Varro. The cool feeling of his mind covering mine increased slightly and he nodded. I relayed the message to Tavi.

"I know this was partially my idea and that it's the best plan, but I still hate it," Tavi grouched. "I don't like sending you off on your own."

"Varro will be with me." I crossed my fingers and asked the Blessed Lady for luck. "We'll be in and out before you know it."

"I hope so," she murmured, "because I'd hate to have to tear this base apart looking for you."

"No you wouldn't," I said with a laugh.

"No, I wouldn't," she agreed. "But I figure we probably wouldn't come out ahead in the end, so come back safe and sound. And if you have to leave Anna and Nick behind to escape, I expect you to do it."

"You know I won't," I disagreed cheerfully.

I could hear her sigh over the comm. "I know, but I had to try."

"We'll be careful," I said. "Varro won't let me take any silly risks."

"I'm counting on it."

I laughed at her honesty. It was killing her to stay behind when she knew I'd be in danger, but she and Torran had talked through a dozen different plans and this one made the most sense.

But that didn't mean she had to like it.

Varro and I were both dressed in sturdy pants, boots, and long-sleeved shirts that hid the lightweight, flexible armor vests we wore. We'd discussed wearing a full set of armor, but if Varro's shielding failed, then we'd immediately stand out, so we'd traded some protection for the ability to blend in. For the same reason, I'd concealed my colorful hair under a knit hat. Anja told us the lunar base always ran a little cold, so the hat wouldn't look too out of place. From a distance, we would pass as soldiers on downtime.

I also carried a specialized comm, a plas pistol, and a plas blade. We were hoping for complete stealth, but heading into an enemy base unarmed was just asking for trouble.

Tavi and Torran came through the hatch into the cargo bay, and the rest of the team followed them. Tavi's expression had flattened into the hard mask that meant she was furious. I shivered, glad she wasn't pointing it at me. I'd caused that expression only a handful of times, but each and every one was permanently etched into my memory. Tavi might have a soft, fluffy heart of gold, but she could also be damn scary.

Tavi headed our way while Torran took up a position near the cargo bay door. He leaned against the wall, but his casual pose wouldn't fool anyone who caught sight of his face. Whereas Tavi's anger burned bright, Torran's turned ice cold.

Tavi touched my shoulder, then did the same to Varro. "Stick to the plan," she said, looking at both of us. "If anything goes wrong, we'll get you out."

"I'll keep her safe," Varro promised.

"You have *got* to stop doing that," I muttered. "Or at least put some qualifications on it. 'I'll keep her safe unless she does something reckless, which she will.' Something like that."

Tavi covered her laugh with a cough, but Varro's expression turned quietly intense, and he crossed his left arm over his chest. "I will protect you," he said. "No matter what."

Goose bumps raised the hair on my arms at the unmistakable vow in his words. I *had* to keep my impulsiveness under control or Varro would get himself killed while trying to protect me, and I couldn't live with that on my conscience.

"We'll stick to the plan," I said. "In and out with no one the wiser."

"Have you found Anna and Nick?" Tavi asked.

"Not yet, but I'll keep looking."

Varro tilted his head and his expression turned distant. "I can sense them, but they're far away."

I pointed at my comm. "From the video I've seen, the base doesn't look like it's on alert. We should be able to slip through without any trouble, once we have a cloned ID that will open the doors."

A long series of bangs against the cargo bay door interrupted our conversation. Tavi sighed. "The Feds are being patient, as usual. You ready?"

I nodded and everyone moved into position. It was harder for Varro to hide us from particular minds than from everyone, so the humans on our team wouldn't be able to see us, but the Valoffs *would*. It would take far more energy for Varro to hide us from Torran and the others, and there was no point when all of the Fed soldiers were human.

Varro and I stood next to Tavi at the control terminal beside the cargo bay door. Torran stood on the other side of the door. If everything went to hell, he was our ticket out.

Tavi glanced around the space. When she got to us, she frowned, and a look of pained concentration crossed her face. "That's weird as hell," she murmured. "I can't even see your aura."

Thanks to an FHP experiment, Tavi could see colorful auras surrounding Valoffs if she focused hard enough. The experiment had nearly killed her, and in the end, the ability had proven entirely useless to the war effort because aura color didn't correspond to a particular skill or power level.

Plus, using the ability always gave her a splitting headache, which wasn't ideal in the middle of battle.

Tavi looked around once more, ensuring everyone was in position, then opened the cargo bay door. A young man with fair skin, freckles, and sandy brown hair marched up the ramp. His uniform marked him as a lieutenant. "Captain Zarola, you have kept us waiting far longer than the—"

Torran straightened away from the wall. He was nearly ten centimeters taller than the lieutenant and probably fifteen kilograms heavier—all of it lean muscle. The lieutenant came to a nervous stop.

A Valoff alone shouldn't garner that reaction from a trained FHP soldier, so the lieutenant knew that Torran was telekinetic. At least the Feds weren't *completely* awful at information gathering.

Unwilling to turn his back on the obvious threat, the lieutenant spoke to Tavi without looking directly at her.

"We believe you are harboring dangerous fugitives and per Section 211, Article VII of the—"

"Just get on with the search, Lieutenant Walters," Tavi said with an impatient wave. "I don't have all day, and I've already lodged my complaint with the oversight committee."

Walters glanced around the cargo bay. I held my breath as his gaze passed over Varro and me without stopping. He cleared his throat and gestured at Torran. "If you would just have your, uh, crew step away from the door."

"General Fletcher is fine where he is," Tavi countered. "He is not obstructing your search area, and he enjoys fresh air."

Walters paled at the name, which meant that while FHP Command had told him a telekinetic was on board, they hadn't told him *exactly* who he'd be facing. They really were throwing him to the sharks with this assignment, but Walters steeled his spine and waved the eight soldiers behind him up the ramp and into the ship.

Torran planted himself against the wall, crossed his arms, and watched the advancing soldiers like a cat watching especially delicious mice.

Varro and I crept forward. Now came the tricky bit. While the Feds had sent a relatively green lieutenant to lead the group, the search team they'd sent looked far more capable. Half of the soldiers wore thermal imaging glasses, and two carried sensitive audio monitoring equipment.

And we needed to slip past them without getting caught.

As soon as all the soldiers were inside, I used my system access to loop the surveillance camera feeds that included *Starlight*. Varro's ability might keep us hidden in real-time, but if something went wrong and the Feds went back and looked at the footage, I didn't want Tavi implicated.

Six of the FHP soldiers swept through the cargo bay in two teams of three. Each team cleared half of the room, with the soldiers wearing thermal cameras paying special attention to the walls and floor—they were looking for our hidden stowage.

They wouldn't find it that easily, but it was a good effort.

The remaining two soldiers stayed near the door with the lieutenant. That wasn't ideal, but we'd planned for several different scenarios. I'd love to steal the lieutenant's ID, since he likely had better access than the rest of the soldiers, but that was just asking for trouble, especially if someone in security noticed doors opening when he was supposed to be on *Starlight*.

Varro touched my shoulder, then moved in front of me. We skirted around Tavi. Varro nodded at Torran, and the former general stepped away from the wall with a frown. "You're blocking my air."

Lieutenant Walters backed up a hasty step before remembering that he was supposed to be in charge. He threw his shoulders back and puffed up his chest. "I have orders to prevent anyone from leaving the ship until the search is complete."

"So we're prisoners?" Torran asked softly. I shivered at the menace in his tone—and I knew he was on our side.

Walters didn't stand a chance. True to form, he signaled the soldiers at the door to back him up. The two soldiers fell in behind him with their weapons held in white-knuckled hands. At least they knew enough to be wary of an angry telekinetic.

"The FHP," Walters started, his voice shaking. He

cleared his throat and tried again. "The FHP has the legal authority to temporarily detain any ship and crew suspected of aiding and abetting criminal activity."

Torran took another step forward, leaving just enough space for Varro and me behind him. As we slipped past him, Torran asked, "And what criminal activity are we accused of, exactly?"

Varro and I carefully crept down the ramp as the lieutenant spluttered. "As I explained to your captain, we have reason to believe that you are harboring dangerous fugitives—"

His voice faded as Varro and I moved deeper into the landing bay. We'd successfully accomplished the first step of our plan. Now we just had to steal an ID, find Anna and Nick, bust them out, and get back to the ship without getting caught.

Sure, no problem.

CHAPTER TWENTY-SIX

The lunar base's landing bay was far larger than any of the individual landing bays on Bastion, a huge half circle that connected to the main part of the base at several points along the curve. Overall, the landing bay was smaller than Bastion's total capacity, but it was still so vast that the other wall was lost in the distance.

Varro and I wound our way through a scattering of ships that looked like they were in long-term storage. Empty berths were piled with ancient cargo containers, some of which spilled into the walkways. Had the Feds put us in an unused part of the station because they'd expected trouble?

Or, more worryingly, because they didn't want witnesses?

Tavi and I had agreed to limit comms to emergencies only, but any of the Valoffs could communicate with Varro without tipping off the Feds, so we'd have some idea of how the search was going.

Once we were far enough away, I removed the surveillance loop. If we were lucky, no one would be the wiser. If not, at least they couldn't pin our appearance on Tavi. It was far too much work to loop all of the station's videos in a way that wouldn't be immediately obvious, so I had to hope that we'd remain undetected for the rest of the trip.

I trusted Varro to lead me in the right direction as I went back to flipping through the security camera feeds on my comm, looking for any sign of Anna or Nick. The cameras showed frustratingly little. If only I'd had another few hours, I'd feel far more prepared to break into a Fed base, but time was a luxury we didn't have.

I really wished Lexi were here. I might be tech savvy, but Lexi had far more skill at the actual *breaking* and *entering* part of breaking and entering. And if that didn't work, she could straight up charm someone into opening a locked door for her. But we still hadn't heard from her, and low-level worry gnawed at me. I knew she was too far away for a quick response and that she could take care of herself, but I still missed her.

Varro stopped, and I looked up from the comm. We were entering a busier part of the landing bay, and several soldiers in FHP uniforms appeared to be loitering around an open cargo bay ramp.

"Will one of them work for an ID?" Varro asked telepathically.

I watched the soldiers for a second. They were all deeply engaged in conversation and not very concerned with their surroundings. "Let's aim for the soldier on the right," I said. That would put us closest to the edge of the ship, giving us a little physical cover in addition to Varro's ability. "I need to be within a meter."

Varro nodded and threaded his way through the cargo and ships around us until we approached the soldiers from the hidden right side. He stopped and waved me around him. I tiptoed closer to the soldier, holding my comm in front of me.

I'd left my main comm on the ship, partially because it had far too much data on it to carry into an enemy base, and partially because I needed some highly specialized modifications that I hadn't had time to add to it yet. One of them let me clone another comm's ID chip signature. It wasn't my preferred method of entry because it would open only certain doors—the ones the soldier was authorized to use—but without system-level access to the lunar base's security system, it was the best I could do.

I extended the comm until it was less than a meter from the soldier, but frustratingly, it didn't detect anything. I eased closer until Varro put a warning hand on my shoulder, but even though I was well within the necessary meter radius, the comm still didn't find a single ID.

If they were relying entirely on biometrics for security access, then we were going to be fucked before we'd even started.

Okay, new plan.

"We need to find a door and see how they get through," I thought loudly in Varro's direction.

He carefully drew me backward until we had put a little distance between us and the cluster of soldiers, then his voice whispered into my head. "What happened?"

"My comm didn't recognize any ID signatures. So they're either using straight biometrics for security or the ID standard is one my comm doesn't know to search for."

"What do we do?"

"See which it is. Worst case, we wait until someone goes through the door we want, then we follow them."

Varro shook his head, but he didn't complain. I once again cursed my lack of access. If only I'd been better, *faster,* then we wouldn't be in this situation. If I'd gotten into the security system, we could already be halfway to Anna. I glared at my comm as if I could fix it via sheer willpower.

It did not work.

In my peripheral vision, Varro frowned at me. "Stop beating yourself up," he whispered telepathically. "You're doing great."

I transferred my glare to him.

He put a reassuring hand on my shoulder. "Don't worry. We'll find a way in even if I have to abduct an entire soldier to get it done."

I smiled, just as he'd meant for me to do. "Hopefully it won't come to that."

He nodded, a glimmer of satisfaction in his eyes. "I can still feel Anna and Nick in the distance. They haven't moved. We'll head that way until we find a door."

"Sounds good. I'll keep searching through the camera feeds."

IN THE END, WE DIDN'T HAVE TO ABDUCT A SOLDIER AND CARRY them around like our own personal ID card to get out of the landing bay because the first door required no ID at all—it was the public entrance.

FOSO I was broken into several independent modules connected by airlocks and hallways rather than one huge structure. The public module was a small complex with only three floors and an assortment of shops and lodging.

Varro and I carefully wove our way past the crowd of civilians, contractors, and bounty hunters until we found the entrance that led into the base's huge, central military module that housed most of the barracks, galleys, rec rooms, and offices needed to keep a station of FOSO I's size running smoothly. It was the busiest module on the base, so it would give us the best chance to catch someone going through the door.

But that also meant we were under constant risk of discovery.

I wedged myself against the wall, waved Varro behind me, and waited for someone to open the door. I needed to see what they were using for identification. A moment later, a young woman in an FHP uniform approached the entrance and waved her comm over the control panel. The heavy door slid open, then closed behind her. If we were fast and quiet, we could've followed her through, but a key would be better.

At least they weren't using biometrics.

I glanced over my shoulder. "The next time someone approaches, I need to be within a meter of the control panel," I thought to Varro. "Can you shield me that well?"

His chin dipped, and we eased closer to the doorway.

I let several young soldiers pass without doing anything, and I could feel Varro's mounting frustration, but they wouldn't have the access I needed. Patience would pay off, assuming my nerves could take the strain.

Varro jerked me back as the soldier next to us stumbled, clearly drunk. My pulse lurched, and I held my breath as he passed within a half meter of me.

"What are you waiting for?" Varro demanded in my head.

I glanced back toward the public area of the base, and the crowd parted, revealing the perfect mark. "Her. She's a commodore. Her access will open nearly every door on the base."

Unfortunately, it also meant that many people wanted to talk to her. When she finally got free and approached the door, my hands trembled as I held my comm as close to the control panel as I dared. I silently sucked in a deep breath. I would have one shot at this, so I had the comm scanning for every known frequency.

"We'll follow her through," I thought to Varro and got back a silent acknowledgment. If I didn't get the key, I'd come up with a new plan once we were on the other side of the door.

The commodore swiped her comm over the panel, her hand centimeters from mine, and my comm vibrated as it picked up the key. *Jackpot.*

Relief nearly buckled my legs, but we weren't done yet. The door slid open, and Varro and I eased through behind the oblivious officer. I didn't dare relax until we'd put three hallways between us.

I let Varro take the lead, since he could sense Anna and Nick while I continued swiping through the security feeds. We had crossed into one of the smaller modules that was used for training and storage by the time I found Anna's vid feed. A few swipes later, I found Nick.

I tapped Varro's shoulder. "I found them," I thought.

He squinted, looking down the hallway in front of us. "They're not too far. Either in this section or the next."

A check of the map proved that he was correct. Anna and Nick were being held in two separate rooms in the next module, right on the outer edge of the base. Their rooms were as far as possible from the landing bay, and I was amazed that Varro had been able to sense them at all.

The outer modules were used almost exclusively for storage of dangerous supplies because if something was going to explode, it was far better for that explosion to be on the periphery than smack in the middle of the base.

And because those supplies weren't needed very often, it would be relatively easy to sneak in a hostage or two without anyone finding out.

I went back to the vid feeds. Anna appeared to be awake, sitting on the edge of her bed, but Nick was laid out on a pallet on the floor, unmoving. Nick might've been merely sleeping, but the bruising on their face indicated otherwise.

I shoved the worry aside and focused on finding us the safest path to their area of the base.

I handed Varro a meal bar to eat while I checked the cameras around the impromptu holding rooms. A soldier in an FHP uniform without any rank insignia patrolled the hallways in the area, which was a little unusual, but the fact that Anna and Nick weren't in the brig told me that Morten was keeping their presence quiet.

So perhaps he didn't have FHP's complete support for this little scheme, which meant we still had a chance to stop the war before it started.

I checked the station map for the fourth time, plotting the main route, backup routes, and escape routes. The repeated checks let my brain know that this was *important,* and maybe we should hold on to the information for longer than five seconds. It didn't always work, but it was better than nothing.

I led us on a slightly longer path that bypassed some of the busier corridors between the two modules. By staying in the relatively empty areas, we could move much faster without having to worry about running into someone. We were closing in on Anna's room—it was closer than Nick's—when Varro's mental voice whispered urgently, "Stop."

I jerked to a halt and carefully put my foot down without making a sound. "What is it?" I looked around for what had spooked him, but we were in a narrow, empty hallway. The low ceiling, plain gray walls, and scuffed floor proved that we weren't in an area that the public was expected to see.

Varro pulled me into a shallow alcove that contained safety equipment and a floor cleaning robot. We were out of the hallway, but we were wedged in beside the robot. Mere centimeters separated us, and I could feel the heat of his body.

"There's another Valoff nearby—the one from the station," Varro said telepathically. "He must be shielding because I just noticed him."

"Moving?"

Varro nodded, then footsteps echoed down the hall. I froze in place, barely daring to breathe. Varro pulled me closer. "I've got you," he murmured into my mind. "You're safe."

True to his word, the footsteps passed us without stopping. While we waited for the coast to clear, I shifted back and handed Varro another meal bar. He quirked an amused eyebrow at me. "Where do you keep coming up with these?"

Heat climbed my cheeks, and I ducked my head. "Torran said using your ability burns through calories, and I had some spare pockets. I wanted to take care of you, like you always do for me."

Varro's fingers ghosted along my jaw, tilting my head up. The intense look in his eyes stole my breath, and I curled my fingers into tight fists to keep from reaching for him.

"Thank you," he replied.

Longing and desire and worry jumbled together until I couldn't stay still. I clutched his hand before he could pull it away. "Don't get hurt because of me," I pleaded.

"I won't risk myself unnecessarily, but I will keep you safe," Varro said, his mental voice inflexible. He took a deep breath and his expression softened. "Please don't ask me to do otherwise."

I closed my eyes as I fought the words that wanted to escape. I *knew* this was important to him, but I still hated it. If he was hurt because of me, I would never forgive myself.

The thought made me pause. I guess I understood how he felt after all. I squeezed his hand, then silently let him go. Varro brushed gentle fingers over my cheek. "Kee, I need you to promise me something."

The grave tone of his mental voice sent shivers of dread down my spine. "What?" I thought warily.

"I need you to promise that if I tell you to run, to escape, that you'll do it, no matter what."

I started shaking my head before he finished. "I won't." I cut him off when he would've insisted. "I can't blindly promise that. I *won't*. Please don't ask me to." When he reluctantly nodded, I continued, "But I won't take unnecessary risks, either."

His chin dipped and a wry smile tilted the corner of his mouth as his realized that I was echoing his own words back to him.

"Is the Valoff gone?"

Varro's head tipped, and he frowned in concentration.

"I think he's making a loop," he said at last. After a moment, he shook his head. "No, now he's stopped with another group."

I pulled out my comm and checked the nearby cameras. One of the feeds showed a few soldiers, but I couldn't see anyone in Valovian armor. I handed the comm to Varro because his memory was better than mine. "Do you recognize him?"

Varro pointed at one of the people on-screen. "That's him."

The Valoff was sitting in what appeared to be a hastily built bunk room with three other soldiers. All of them wore basic FHP uniforms without rank or insignia. I checked the camera name, then the map. Their room was across the hall from Anna's room.

Well, that was not ideal, especially because I doubted that my cloned ID had access to Anna's door, which meant it would take me a little bit to finesse it open.

Varro blew out a frustrated breath. "If that was a patrol, then we will hopefully have a few minutes before they go out again."

"Can you shield us from the other Valoff long enough for us to get into Anna's room?"

Varro nodded. "But if they open the door, it'll be more difficult. Has Nick moved at all?"

I pressed my lips together and shook my head. Varro cursed darkly.

We'd planned to rescue Anna first for two reasons: Morten's plan wouldn't work without her, and we weren't sure what state Nick would be in.

If we could get Nick up and moving, then they could help watch our back while we rescued Anna. But if we couldn't, then they would be a liability and we'd lose the element of surprise. If things got dicey, we were supposed to leave Nick behind, but Tavi knew me well enough to plan a half dozen contingencies for getting them both out, dicey or not.

"We stick to the plan. Anna first, then Nick," Varro said. His expression went distant. "The soldiers are still searching *Starlight*. They haven't found the prince, but not for lack of trying. If we move fast enough, we might get back to the landing bay before they're done."

"Okay, let's go get Anna. It will take me a few minutes to get the door open, and it might be a bit loud. Are you okay shielding?"

Varro crammed the meal bar I'd given him earlier into his mouth, nodded, and then helped me out of the alcove. He led me down the hallway toward the next intersection, then stepped around the corner without looking first, something I would never get used to.

The corridor curved in front of us—we were on the outer ring of the module. Varro slowed as we approached Anna's door. She was on the interior side of the hall, which put the soldiers on the exterior wall. If I had a grenade and a death wish, I could take them out fairly easily.

The cool feel of Varro's mind increased and he nodded at the door. "She's the only one inside. I'm not blocking her, so she'll be able to see us."

The door's control panel glowed red—locked, not that that was a surprise. I was tempted to try the commodore's ID, but if I was holding someone I didn't want found, I'd put an alarm on their door that triggered when anyone unexpected tried to open it.

No, I was going to have to do this the old-fashioned way.

Lexi had taught me how, but I desperately wished she was here now to do it for me.

I removed the pouch of tools from my belt and got to work. Lexi's directions whispered through my memory. First, I needed to carefully pry the control panel's cover off so I could get at the internals. I winced when it popped off with a loud scraping noise, but Varro just waved at me to keep going.

Next, I needed to short two wires while disconnecting a third. It was the trickiest part, and mistiming it meant the door would stay locked *and* set off the alarm. The tiny, delicate wire cutters wobbled in my grip. I took a deep breath and shook out my hands.

Slowly, carefully, I clamped onto the first half of the shorting circuit, then positioned the clamps and cutters at the appropriate wires, one in each hand. I asked the Blessed Lady for help, then squeezed both sets of handles.

The control panel went black, and an agonizing second later, the door slid open. I nearly whooped in joy before I remembered that we were supposed to stay quiet. I did a tiny victory dance, then peeked into the room.

Anna Duarte no longer looked like a pristine fashion maven. Unlike Nick, she had a bed rather than a pallet, and she was sitting on the edge of it. Her stretchy jumpsuit was a shapeless blob and her dark, silvering hair was a tangled mess. But her chin remained at a haughty angle and there was fire in her gaze.

"Who are you?" she demanded when Varro and I entered the room.

I frantically waved my hands. "Stay quiet," I whispered. "We're your rescue squad. I was the nymph at your party."

She stared at me without blinking, then she tilted her head in consideration. "What are you doing on Valovia?"

"Is that what they told you? You're not on Valovia; you're in the lunar base on Odyssey, Expedition's moon."

"I was taken by Valoffs," she insisted, a canny gleam in her eye.

Ah, perhaps Nick had been able to warn her to play along after all. "I'll explain later, but for now we need to find Nick and then leave. This is Varro. He's a Valoff, but he's an ally. He needs to shield your mind, so we won't be caught."

Her chin rose impossibly higher. "No."

"Your options are let Varro shield for you or stay in this cell and rot." I wouldn't actually leave her, but sometimes tough love was necessary.

Anna grimaced. "Fine." She rose on unsteady legs, but she crossed the room on her own. "Where is Nick?"

"They are a few doors down, but there is a roomful of soldiers across the hall, so we need to be very quiet. Varro can communicate with you telepathically. Is that okay?"

Anna's lip curled, but she nodded shortly.

We followed Varro into the hall. We needed to move quickly because I couldn't close Anna's door, so as soon as a soldier stepped out of the room across the hall, they'd know something was up—if whoever was monitoring surveillance didn't alert them first.

As if he shared my thoughts—which he kind of did, right now—Varro drew his plas pistol while I worked on Nick's door. Finally, after what felt like an age, the door slid aside. Anna made a tiny, distressed sound, and a glance inside revealed that Nick remained flat on the pallet, their face and arms mottled with bruises.

"Are they . . . ?" Anna asked aloud. She hadn't quite mastered telepathic communication, and I didn't have the heart to call her on it right now, not with the devastation plain on her face.

I crossed the room and carefully shook Nick's shoulder. They didn't stir, but when I put my hand in front of their nose and mouth, I could feel the barest whisper of breath. "They're alive," I whispered, "but I don't know how bad of shape they're in. I'll have to carry them out."

"I will do it," Varro said.

"You're already doing all the work. I can carry Nick." I smiled up at him. "There aren't even any stairs this time."

He grumbled at me, but he helped me get Nick draped over my shoulders. Nick didn't make a sound, which worried me. We needed to get them back to Havil as soon as possible. Hopefully they were just drugged, but if they had head trauma or an internal injury, then carrying them around would do them no favors.

After Varro made sure that I was stable, he telepathically said, "The soldiers haven't moved from their room, but we should take another route back to the ship. Do you have a preference?"

I pulled up the map on my comm and showed him the backup route that I'd plotted. He studied it for a second, then nodded. He ushered Anna into the hallway, and I followed on his heels.

Varro froze so suddenly that I ran into him. Before I could figure out what had happened, he crumpled to the ground with a deep groan, revealing the grinning soldier holding the glowing blue plas blade. “Run!” Varro gasped into my mind.

I jerked back, but the soldier was already mid-swing. I had just enough time to press the emergency button on my comm, then I went down with a scream.

Nick’s weight drove me into the floor, and everything went dark.

CHAPTER TWENTY-SEVEN

I came to with someone slapping my face—and not gently. I growled and lunged forward before I'd even opened my eyes, but I came up short as a plas blade's nonlethal fury cut my legs from under me.

When I could think again, I blinked at the floor. It was the same gray as the walls. I turned my head to the left. A pair of boots blocked part of my view, but the rest of the room appeared empty. We could be anywhere on FOSO I, but it wasn't the brig or the medbay.

"Get her up," an unfortunately familiar male voice commanded.

Two soldiers lifted me to my feet, and I raised my eyes, already knowing who I'd see.

If the universe were fair, Commodore Frank Morten would be a wizened husk of a person, as shriveled outside as he was inside. Instead, he was a tall, broad man, handsome in the way a snake was mesmerizing, with fair skin that glowed with the remnants of a recent tan. His short, brown hair was graying at the temples, and his brown eyes were as cold as an arctic tundra.

I had the intense, nearly irresistible urge to punch him directly in his smug little smile.

But for all that I hated him, Morten wasn't careless. The very second I tried anything, the two men beside me would spring into action, and I didn't feel like getting hit with a plas blade again—or worse.

Morten was wearing a strange helmet that almost looked like a crown, with wire-wrapped sides and an open top. I squinted at it. It kind of looked like an electromagnet. I glanced at the two soldiers beside me. Both of them wore similar helmets.

My memory of the attack in the hallway was fuzzy at best, but Varro, who could detect two people from all the way across a huge lunar base, hadn't sensed the trap. I'd bet a great deal of money that the helmets had something to do with it, which meant I needed to disable them as soon as possible.

And then steal one to study.

I couldn't feel Varro's presence in my head, but I refused to believe that he was dead. He was a valuable hostage, and Morten was nothing if not pragmatic. I was more concerned about Anna and Nick. If Morten found out that Anna knew the truth about the abduction, then her life was in terrible danger.

"I should've known I'd find you here, Specialist Ildez," Morten said with a mocking shake of his head. "You never did know when to give up."

I waved a dismissive hand at him. "Unlike you, who so

often gave up at the first sign of trouble." My smile sharpened into a blade. "I believe there is a word for it: *coward*."

Morten's mouth tightened in fury. "You would know. Attacking a peaceful civilian gathering is not exactly a heroic action."

I rolled my eyes. "Is that how we're playing it? You and I both know that I didn't attack the fashion exhibition. I was wearing a fucking glowing dress when the wall exploded. But it's interesting that you think the attack was cowardly, considering you planned it. I mean, I agree, which is not a sentence I ever expected to say to you, yet here we are. It's a day full of surprises."

The soldier on my left shifted on his feet. I glanced at him. "If you're uncomfortable now, just wait until Morten blames you for some screwup of his. You should get out while you can."

"Enough," Morten barked. "Where is the prince?"

My smile was sweet enough to cause cavities. "Who?"

"Liang Nepru, your coconspirator."

"Oooh, I didn't know I had a coconspirator. And a prince! Aren't I a lucky woman." I looked around with wide-eyed awe. "Where is he? When can I meet him? Is he handsome? I bet he's handsome."

The soldier on my right choked back a laugh, and Morten's jaw clenched. He drew his plas blade and activated it on the nonlethal setting. "Perhaps this will jog your memory."

I bared my teeth at him. "Do your worst, asshole."

The two soldiers next to me stepped back, and Morten jabbed the blade into my stomach. And it was only as it hit that I realized someone had removed my armored vest—not that it would've protected me from a plas blade.

Agony raced along my veins. My legs folded without my permission, and I didn't bother fighting the scream as I fell. I had just enough control to prevent my head from bashing into the floor, but even that tiny exertion was enough to exhaust me.

I focused on breathing as my muscles stopped twitching. My throat felt as raw as my nerves. *Blessed Lady,* that hurt. Tears pricked my eyes from the combination of pain and fury.

An intense feeling of worry trickled through me, then Varro's voice whispered into my head, "Are you okay?"

Relief nearly sent me under. "Are you? Where are you? What about Anna and Nick?"

"Cell. Four guards. Drugged. Don't know."

I could feel his agony echoing across our link. His shields must be very low, and Morten's soldiers had done something terrible to him. My fury burned hotter.

"Are you ready to be cooperative yet?" Morten asked, interrupting my silent conversation.

"I've *been* cooperative," I said, my voice scratchy. "When I get uncooperative is when you need to worry. And while I know the Feds aren't big on due process, torture is still illegal."

"Don't worry, we won't leave a mark on you," Morten said with a nasty little smile. "Just tell me what I want to know and it'll all end."

"Go to hell."

The next hit wasn't any more pleasant. If anything, it hurt *worse.* I screamed as my nerves, already raw, overloaded. At least I didn't have to worry about giving myself a concussion, because I'd never moved from the ground.

"Where is the prince?" Morten asked again.

It took a second before I could form words. "What prince?"

I lost track of how many times we went through the same routine, but my voice gave out from the screaming, and my muscles twitched constantly even when not being hit by the plas blade. The only thing that kept me going was the fragile thread linking me to Varro. It kept getting fainter, which was a concern, and I could feel his murderous rage every time I was hit. I hated that he had to feel my pain, but I was too exhausted to even attempt a shield.

"Maybe we should take a break," a male voice suggested hesitantly. I didn't bother to open my eyes to see which of the soldiers had dared to contradict the increasingly enraged Morten. The fact that it had taken him this long to voice a complaint told me everything I needed to know.

"Bring me Zarola," Morten snarled. "This little bitch might not care about herself, but she'll care when her captain starts taking the hits for her."

I loathed that he was right. I didn't know if I could watch Tavi scream over and over, even though I knew a plas blade wouldn't kill her. My nightmares were haunted enough without adding any more fuel.

"On what charges, sir?" the same male voice asked.

"Do I look like I fucking care?" Morten snarled. "Get it done."

"Yes, sir!"

The door slid open and footsteps left the room. I remembered pressing the emergency button on my comm. It would've sent a message to Tavi, letting her know that things had gone to hell, then locked itself behind a triple layer of encryption, making it as good as useless to Morten.

I just hoped the message had made it through, because someone had taken the device from me, along with my weapons, and my comm implant alone wasn't strong enough to transmit through the shielding on the room.

But even if the warning hadn't arrived, Torran wouldn't let Tavi go without a fight, and the two of them were a formidable team. Not to mention the whole rest of the ship would fight, too. Tavi would be okay. I had to believe that, or Morten had already won.

I stayed on the ground and pretended to be more hurt than I actually was. Not that I was in *great* shape, but I could stand up if I tried hard enough.

Maybe.

Morten stomped around the room and spat curses beneath his breath. The other soldier shifted but stayed out of his way. Two trained soldiers, both armed with plas blades at the very least, versus me, armed with nothing but aching, overworked muscles.

It wasn't the best odds I'd ever seen.

I waved a lazy hand in the air. "I knew you had delusions of grandeur, Morten, but I didn't expect you to start wearing a crown. Surprised Command lets you get away with it."

Morten laughed. "Who do you think funded the research? They're better than mental shields at blocking Valoffs, as your unfortunate partner found out. His clever trick doesn't work against these."

"I have no idea what you mean."

Morten scoffed. "Enjoy your petty rebellion while you can. Once it's your captain screaming, you'll tell me everything I want to know."

I *had* to escape before that happened. With luck, I might be able to surprise and overpower either Morten or the soldier, but both was beyond my ability. I needed a better strategy than "throw myself at them and hope," but my mind remained frustratingly blank.

With nothing else to do, I kept talking. "Did Command agree to let you take out Bastion? Because that seems incredibly stupid."

Morten's smile was drenched in smug superiority. "Didn't you hear? That was all you. You've been working with the prince to destabilize the FHP."

I laughed. "Do you even know who it really was? Because I do. And you are *fucccckkked*." I drew out the word with relish.

Morten stalked toward me, a furious scowl on his face. "I'm going to enjoy breaking you."

"Not as much as I'm going to enjoy watching your plan blow up in your face."

He hit me with the plas blade, and I screamed. The pain seemed to go on forever, and it whited out everything else. Eons later, I felt someone pressing their fingers against my neck and my body felt bruised.

"Her pulse is weak," a male voice said. "You nearly killed her." There was only the mildest rebuke hidden in the words, and I would've laughed at his cowardice if I could've spared the breath.

I blinked up at the soldier, who was kneeling on my right side. He had wavy blond hair, and his pale skin had a milk-white pallor—too much time in space. I didn't have to feign confusion very hard because my brain felt as scrambled as my body. I reached my left hand up and caressed his cheek. He was several years younger than me, maybe midtwenties, and handsome in a boyish way that he still hadn't grown out of. Maybe he never would.

His eyes softened, and I steeled myself for the violence to come. “Aaron?” I whispered, frowning fuzzily and making up the first male name that came to mind. “Where are we?”

The soldier shook his head and bent fractionally closer. “I am not—”

I hooked my fingers around his weird, prototype helmet and jerked it from his head, swinging my arm in a wide arc until the delicate metal slammed into the ground hard enough to bend and break. I used the rebound to change direction, swinging it back toward the soldier.

He blinked at me, surprise slowing his reaction. Morten shouted something, distracting him further, but the warning came too late. The helmet smashed into the soldier’s head with a sickening *crunch*. He slumped to the ground, unconscious or dead, I didn’t know which.

One down, one to go.

I rolled away from Morten’s plas blade. It bit into the gray floor mere centimeters from my head. My muscles screamed, but I lurched to my feet, running on adrenaline and hope.

Morten spread his arms and waved at the closed door. “What’s your plan now?” He waved the plas blade. “I’ve got this, and you’ve got nothing. If you give up now, I won’t break your captain’s fingers one by one while you watch.”

My legs trembled, barely supporting me, but I managed a smile. “You don’t have Tavi *or* the prince. You have nothing except a crippled station and a traitor in your ranks. And I’m sure Command would be interested to know exactly what you’ve been up to lately.”

Morten sneered, his eyes glinting like diamonds. “I have *you*. And the Valoff you were with. I’m sure the researchers will be delighted with a new specimen, especially one who is so strong."

Bone-deep terror for Varro sliced through me, and I clenched my fists against the urge to do something stupid. Morten was baiting me into making an impulsive mistake. I had to resist, as much as it went against my nature.

I tilted my head. "Odd, that you didn't mention Command. And that I'm being held in this room rather than the brig. Plotting a little treason of your own, are you?"

Morten laughed. "I have the full support of the people who matter."

I really, really hoped that *Starlight* was still pulling down all of the base's security footage. I'd put it on a three-hour loop to keep the storage space down, so now I had to get back to the ship in the next three hours because *someone* would find this footage interesting. If the orders weren't coming from FHP Command, then there was a possibility that the FHP Senate wasn't behind it either—at least, not entirely.

Morten lunged for me, and I stumbled back and fell on my ass without the plas blade ever touching me. Morten shook his head in disgust. "I don't know what Zarola ever saw in you."

Eight years ago, that simple sentence would've shaken me to my foundations and left me in tears. But Tavi had been the one to show me that being a shit soldier didn't mean I was worthless. She'd put her neck on the line for me countless times because she believed in me, unequivocally.

The very least I could do was return the favor. Morten's pitiful attempts to wound me would never be enough to make me doubt Tavi. My mouth curled into a mocking smile. "Yes, I suppose loyalty isn't something you'd recognize. Perhaps that's why you're so confused. I could explain it to you, if you'd like."

Morten raised the blade and took a menacing step toward me. I scrambled back, but there wasn't anywhere to go in the small room. Morten jerked to a stop, a scowl darkening his brow. A few seconds later, an alarm pierced the air. I recognized the pattern—the base was under attack.

The room's door slid open, and a female soldier darted in wearing one of the prototype helmets. "Commodore, there's a telekinetic in the landing bay!"

"Neutralize him! I warned you that Captain Zarola would not come quietly, and that General Fletcher would need to be put down."

The soldier shook her head. "It's not General Fletcher. It's a woman, and she's demanding to speak to *you*."

CHAPTER TWENTY-EIGHT

I laughed so hard that tears gathered in the corners of my eyes. I held up a shaking hand and pointed at Morten's expression. "You should see your face right now. Did you think you could abduct the prince *and* a top Valovian fashion designer and just get away with it?"

Comprehension stole across his face, chased away by dawning fury. "*You.* You did this."

I shook my head. "No, this was all you." And maybe a teeny, tiny, impulsive little message left behind on a foreign server. I just hadn't expected Sura Fev to react quite so quickly—or to be so close. I also hadn't counted on her going for a direct confrontation. Stealth seemed more her style, but my limited dataset was apparently bad at predicting her future behavior.

Tavi might actually kill me if my meddling caused the

FHP and the Valovian Empire to return to war. And, honestly, I wouldn't blame her.

Morten looked at the soldier. "Has Station Command been alerted?"

She struggled to keep her expression respectful as she pointed to the ceiling where the alarm still blared. "Everyone's been alerted. The station is prepping for a full-scale attack."

Morten pointed at the soldier still unconscious on the floor. "Drag him out."

The woman followed the order without complaint, and Morten kicked the broken helmet out the door after them. Then he turned to me with a look that could be described only as *murderous*.

"Once I'm done dealing with this latest disaster, I'm going to come back for you." He'd passed fury into something darker and deadlier. "And then I'm going to destroy your crew, one by one, while you watch."

He didn't give me a chance to respond. He hit me with the plas blade and held it against my skin with a cruel smile, until the pain overloaded my brain and consciousness fled for protection.

BY THE TIME I CAME TO, SOMEONE HAD TURNED OFF THE ALARM. I WAS alone in the room, and the door, when I tried it, was firmly locked. I couldn't raise anyone with my comm implant and without my actual comm, I had no idea what was happening in the rest of the base. Varro also didn't respond to my mental questions, and worry burrowed under my skin.

First things first—I needed to escape. I wasn't going to wait for Morten and his sadistic little plan to return.

Whoever had set up this room as a temporary holding cell had locked the inside control panel. It wouldn't open the door without the appropriate code, and even the standard emergency override failed.

I scoured the floor for bits of metal. None were big enough to pry with, but I found a piece of wire that I could use to short the circuit and open the door. Unfortunately, I didn't have any of my other tools.

I wedged my fingernails under the control panel's cover and managed to pry it off while only breaking two nails. My fingers throbbed, and it was almost enough to prevent me from thinking about shorting a live circuit.

Almost.

I held the wire up to the control panel and bent it until it would contact both leads at once. I would have to touch it to the two hot leads while also ripping out the third wire with my bare fingers. Sure, no problem.

I bounced on my toes and took a few deep breaths. This was going to hurt like getting hit by a plas blade again, if not worse, but there was nothing to be done for it. I gripped the wire I needed to remove with my right hand. Before I could lose my nerve, I touched the bare wire I'd bent into shape to the two hot leads with my left hand and yanked on the wire in my right.

Sharp, hot pain flared in my left hand and lanced up my arm. My muscles locked, and I hoped that I'd done it right or I was about to electrocute myself to death.

Just as I was beginning to worry, the control panel went dark, and the door opened. The pain changed from a lightning strike to a deep, lingering ache. Delicate red burn marks climbed my left hand and wrist, and flexing my fingers caused the ache to flare into an inferno.

Okay, I wouldn't be using that hand for precision work for a while.

I eased toward the doorway and peeked around the edge. The hallway beyond was empty with the exception of the soldier I'd attacked. Rather than taking him to the medbay, they'd dumped him at the edge of the hall, still unconscious—or dead.

I tried not to think about it too much as I quickly searched him.

Someone had removed his weapons, but they'd left the broken prototype helmet and his comm. *Ha!* I held the comm aloft like the prize that it was. It was standard-issue, and it looked new. I flipped the device over and removed the back panel by pressing on the hidden tabs with aching fingertips. Inside, a tiny piece of tape had a set of marked-through alphanumeric codes.

I grinned to myself. When I'd been a soldier, my squad had done something similar with our FHP comms because Command insisted on frequent password changes with ridiculous rules. No one could remember them, and I'd gotten tired of cracking into everyone's locked devices, so we'd come up with a new, far less secure system.

Clearly, we weren't the only ones with the idea.

I memorized the code and replaced the back cover, then unlocked the device. Once I was in, I quickly disabled the tracking apps the FHP installed on all of their standard issue comms.

The map proved that we hadn't moved far from where Varro and I were attacked, which meant the roomful of soldiers was just around the corner—assuming Morten hadn't taken them as backup against Fev.

I froze in indecision. I had no idea where Morten had

stashed Anna, Nick, and Varro, but I refused to return to *Starlight* without them. I'd made a back door into the surveillance system, but it would still take several minutes to access it, and I'd have to search through the surveillance feeds again.

Finding Anna and Nick would be so much easier if Varro were here.

I concentrated on how the telepathic communication felt, focused on the faint hint of the link between us, and mentally shouted, "Varro!"

He didn't answer, so I tried my comm implant. "Tavi, can you hear me?"

She didn't answer, either. I could contact her with my stolen comm, but I'd save that for a last resort because the Feds were likely monitoring it. I picked up the broken helmet, bent it back into shape, and put it on my head. It wasn't much, but it might make a soldier hesitate for a second, which was better than nothing. And if that didn't work, the helmet had proven it was a decent weapon, too.

I moved to the next door in the corridor and swiped my stolen comm over the locked control panel. The door slid open, revealing a storage room full of crates. At least I wouldn't have to electrocute myself to open doors now.

I carefully crept down the hallway, continuing my mental shout of Varro's name. At the corner, I hesitated. The soldiers' impromptu bunk room was just a few meters down the curved hall to the left. With no weapons, terrible mental shields, and four-on-one odds, I couldn't let them catch me.

A feather-light touch of coolness whispered across my mind. "Kee," Varro said, his mental voice quiet and strained.

"I'm coming for you. Where are you?"

"Leave me," he said with a sigh.

"Not happening. I will open every door in this Lady-damned base if I have to, don't you think I won't. Save us both time and tell me how to find you."

A glimmer of humor and frustration sparkled through the link. His shields were still paper-thin. Worry pressed on my temples.

"Cho udwist hisi las," he murmured, slipping into Valovan. Our connection wavered.

"Varro, focus. Where are you?"

"You are nearby." A flash of pain crossed the connection, then he said, "So are Anna and Nick. The other soldiers are farther."

I looked at the corner. *Which way?* I turned right and moved at a fast walk.

"Turn around," Varro whispered. "Twenty meters."

I turned around and mentally measured the distance, trying to look everywhere at once as I crept past the open door that marked the room where Anna had been held.

At approximately the twenty-meter mark, two doors stood across from each other. I hesitated. *Which one?*

"On your right," Varro murmured. I would be worried that he was picking up thoughts that he shouldn't if his mental voice didn't sound so drained.

"How many soldiers are with you now?"

"One."

I took a deep breath. I could take out a single soldier, especially with surprise on my side. Eli and I hadn't spent all of that horrible time in the gym for nothing. I would be okay.

Pep talk complete, I swiped the comm over the door's

control panel before doubt could steal my confidence. The door opened, and I dashed into the room on shaky legs. I took in the scene with a single glance. Varro was lashed to a bunk at his shoulders, waist, thighs, and shins. His wrists and ankles were also shackled to the bed's frame, and based on the way his shirt clung to his chest, they'd removed his armored vest, too.

The beginnings of bruises littered his skin, and he wasn't moving.

Fury stole my breath. A single soldier sat in a chair on the far side of the bunk. He frowned at me, straightening.

"What—" he started.

I waved my arms and sprinted farther into the room—and closer to the soldier. "Hide," I whisper-shouted. "The telekinetic is on a rampage, and she's headed this way."

His frown deepened. "What? The commodore said everything was under control." I was almost to him when dawning recognition crossed his face. "Hey, you're—"

My fist slammed into his cheek with all the force I could put behind it. Pain spiked up my arm, but his head snapped back, and his prototype helmet hit the ground with a metallic *clang*. I lunged for the plas blade clipped to his thigh, but he was no green recruit. He dove from the chair, putting distance between us.

The punch had stunned him, but not enough. He came up with a plas pistol, and while his aim wavered slightly, it wasn't enough to be sure that he'd miss me with less than two meters between us.

"Stop right there," he demanded.

I raised my hands. Tavi and Eli had tried to teach me how to disarm an opponent at close quarters, but I was really, really bad at it. We'd practiced with paint guns, and I'd usually ended up looking like a murder victim.

I had nearly decided to risk it anyway when the soldier's eyes rolled back in his head, and he slumped to the ground. At the same time, a deep, painful groan tore itself from Varro's throat.

"Hurry," Varro gasped. "I can't keep him out long."

I quickly searched the soldier, confiscating his weapons and comm. Then I activated the plas blade set to stun and walloped him with it three times in a row. By the third time, he'd stopped screaming.

The bed wasn't designed to restrain prisoners, so the shackles didn't have a control panel. They locked with an electronic key. I swiped the comm I'd stolen from the first soldier over the nearest cuff, but the shackle didn't unlock. Same thing with the comm from the soldier on the ground.

With the clock ticking, I didn't have time to find a way around the lock. The plas blade shimmered red as I activated its lethal cutting edge. "Hold still," I told Varro. He nodded his agreement, his eyes closed and his head barely moving.

I sliced through the restraints holding him to the bed. The plas blade was too wide and unwieldy to cut the cuffs from his ankles and wrists without risking his skin, so I cut through the thick cable tying them to the bed frame.

"Can you walk?" I asked.

Varro's eyes opened. Wide, dark streaks of power or pain pulsed against his brown irises. "You go ahead. I will catch up."

A grin trembled on my lips as I tried to hide my worry. "No can do, I'm afraid. We're in this together."

Agony and concern and fear shivered along the mental

connection we shared. I wasn't even sure if Varro remembered that it was there. He levered himself up with a deep grunt and pain echoed across the link.

"What's wrong?" I demanded.

"Broken ribs," he said with a shallow gasp. "And whatever they dosed me with is still making my head spin."

"Can you tell where Nick and Anna are?"

Varro squinted into the distance, then nodded. "They're close. There aren't any soldiers nearby." His mouth twisted bitterly. "At least not any that I can sense."

At the reminder, I swapped my broken helmet for the one on the ground that I'd knocked off the soldier at my feet. A tiny red light pulsed on the inside of the headband. I needed to be able to communicate silently with Varro, so I found the power switch and flipped it off. The light blinked out. Once we were back to the ship, I'd study the design and figure out how it worked. For now, escaping was our main concern.

Varro stood, and I handed him the plas pistol. I was far worse with a blade than a gun, but he was barely standing. He wasn't in any shape for hand-to-hand fighting right now, and if he fell, I wasn't sure that I could carry him.

"Ready?" I asked, already heading for the door. I had to keep him moving.

Varro stopped me with a hand on my left arm. His eyes traced over the burn marks on my hand, and his expression hardened into grim lines of remorse and determination. "If you have the opportunity to escape alone, you must leave me."

I shook my head in mute denial, but he just squeezed my arm. "I could feel your pain," he whispered hoarsely. "I could feel it and I couldn't do anything about it." Fury, anguish, and grief chased each other across his face. "I know I have failed you an unforgivable number of times, but please don't ask me to suffer through that again."

I bowed my head against the raw pain in his voice. "You didn't fail me," I replied quietly. This was something he needed to hear and understand, so I straightened my shoulders and met his eyes, willing him to listen. "I know you don't believe me, but this *is not* your fault. Neither was my injury on the jump from Bastion. I *chose* to shield Liang and Siarvez from the debris. I *chose* to enter the lunar base. And I *chose* to provoke Morten in the hopes that he would fuck up. I'm sorry that I wasn't strong enough to shield you from my pain, but I would do exactly the same thing again."

Varro's expression remained frustratingly blank, but his thumb swept over my arm. "Kee—"

I lifted my chin and stared at him with steely determination. If I had to, I would use sheer will to bend the future into the shape I wanted. "A telekinetic woman—presumably Sura Fev—is in the landing bay keeping Morten distracted. You and I are escaping, and we're taking Anna and Nick with us." I sharpened my tone into a command. "I will *not* leave you behind, so if you want to keep to me safe, keep up."

Varro's jaw clenched, but he inclined his head.

I hit the soldier on the floor with another trio of stuns from the plas blade. He barely twitched. It would be safer to kill him, but I couldn't murder him in cold blood. I prayed that the Blessed Lady would keep him locked in dreams until we'd escaped.

Varro and I eased into the hallway. I led despite his protests. He didn't want to admit it, but I kept getting flashes of pain across our connection, and based on the way he was moving, broken ribs were the least of his concerns.

We arrived at Nick's door without incident. I activated the nonlethal setting of the plas blade, then waved my stolen comm over the door lock. I swept into the room, blade first. I'd barely crossed the threshold before Varro hauled me back with a pained grunt.

A fist breezed past my nose, barely missing me. I instinctively swung the blade, but Varro hauled me farther back before I could make contact. "That's Nick," he hissed.

Nick spun toward us, but their reaction time was slow. I raised my hands and deactivated the blade. "Nick, it's Kee. From the party. We're here to rescue you."

Nick blinked at me, then sagged against the doorjamb. Bruises darkened their pale skin in a nebula of painful purples and grays. "Where is Anna?"

"We're getting her next. She's just down the hall. We have to move quickly because a telekinetic arrived. She's keeping Morten busy, but we don't know for how long. Can you walk?"

Nick's lips pressed into a flat, white line, but they nodded. "Do you have any spare weapons?"

Nick didn't look to be in any better shape than Varro, so I kept the plas blade and shook my head. "No. We barely have these. We're going to have to rely on speed and stealth and hopefully some distractions from the landing bay to get us out."

Nick nodded and fell in behind me, in the protected middle of our little squad. Well, *kind of* protected. None of us was in the best shape right now, and if we met more than a soldier or two at once, we'd be hard-pressed to defend.

But Morten had seemingly taken his soldiers with him, and the halls remained clear. I worried about what that would mean when we finally made it to the landing bay, but that was a problem for future me.

I tried not to think about Tavi and the rest of the crew. *Starlight's Shadow* could cause a lot of trouble for the lunar base if they pushed Tavi too hard, but I hoped it hadn't come to that yet.

I opened Anna's door, and the woman in question lunged out, brandishing a chair. I stumbled back into Nick and the two of us nearly went down. Anna finally recognized us and lowered the chair. Her arms remained steady the entire time. Of the four of us, she was certainly in the best condition right now.

When she caught my wide-eyed stare, she tossed her head and sniffed. "Don't look so surprised. It takes effort to look this good. I work out five times a week, and I'm not waiting around for someone to kill me because I ruined their stupid little plan."

She looked at Nick and her expression softened. "I'm glad to see you up. I was worried about you."

A flush of color touched the unbruised part of Nick's cheeks. "Same to you." Nick had to be half Anna's age, but I was fairly certain that more than professional pride had driven their quest to save her.

I mentally wished them luck, then herded our little group into motion. I chose a roundabout path, just in case Morten finished up with Fev and came looking for us. I didn't think the entire base was in on his plot, but orders from a commodore were hard to ignore, so it would be better to make it to the public part of the base without getting caught again.

I thought loudly in Varro's direction, "Have you heard anything from Torran?"

"No. Whatever the soldiers gave me severely weakened me. I can't reach him, and he hasn't contacted me, either."

My worry deepened, both for Varro and for Tavi. If Torran was too busy to check on one of his crew, then things were not going well in the landing bay. I pushed my trembling legs a little faster.

I rounded the next corner and pulled up short just before I smashed into someone. I'd gotten careless, used to Varro's early-warning system, but based on the pain that kept trickling across our connection, he was doing well just to be moving.

A glance revealed a young woman, barely into her twenties, with lightly tanned skin and short black hair. She wore an FHP uniform, but she didn't have a prototype helmet on, so I surreptitiously shoved the plas blade in my pocket, widened my eyes, and clutched my hands together.

"Thank the Lady," I cried. "I've been trying to get Ms. Duarte to safety for *ages,* but after the alarm and the attack, we got all turned around and the soldiers escorting us fled. Please help us. Our ship is in the landing bay, but I don't know where we are."

The young woman looked us over, a frown on her face. "This is a restricted area."

"It's a maze!" I wailed. "My brains are still scrambled from the pirate attack, and then we get here, where Ms. Duarte was assured safety, only for *another* attack to occur." I lowered my voice to a conspiratorial whisper. "This job is cursed, but at least she's rich. She founded the House of Duarte fashion line, you know. I'm going to retire in three years, assuming I live that long. I'm sure she'll make it worth your while if you help us."

The soldier's eyes lit up. I would've been shocked at how easily money swayed her, but credits made the galaxy go 'round, especially when FHP pay wasn't great. And based on her age, she was fairly new, so she might still be in her mandatory service period, which meant her pay was even worse.

"Take me to my ship," Anna demanded, her tone imperious. "I tire of Odyssey's so-called hospitality."

The young soldier wavered, then gestured for us to follow after a quick glance around. "I know a shortcut. The public module is in an uproar, but we can bypass it."

Trusting her was a risk, but she hadn't seemed to recognize any of us, and her presence lent us a veneer of legitimacy. I nodded, and we followed her down the hall.

CHAPTER TWENTY-NINE

By the time we eased into the eerily quiet landing bay, my muscles were knots of tension. But true to her word, the young soldier had led us exactly where she'd promised. She turned to Anna with a look that was half hopeful, half expectant.

Anna unclasped one of her earrings. "Unfortunately, my comm was lost in the confusion, so I can't repay your kindness right now. But this earring is iridium and opal, mined from asteroids, and hand-crafted by Lucius Southgate himself. The set is very dear to me. I will give one to you as collateral, until I can return with an appropriate gift."

Anna carefully put the earring in the soldier's hand, then curled the young woman's fingers around it. "Do *not* lose this or try to sell it," Anna commanded. "If you do, I will unleash my extensive, *expensive* legal team on you until even your ancestors will feel the weight of my fury. Do you understand?"

The soldier swallowed nervously, then nodded.

"I will return within the month. Give your contact information to my assistant." Anna looked around as if Alina would somehow materialize from thin air, then seemingly remembered where we were and waved a negligent hand at me. I hid my grin. She played snooty well—and it wasn't entirely an act—but she'd also brandished a chair at me. She was going to have to work harder to make me dislike her.

I took down the soldier's contact information in my stolen comm, then she vanished back the way we'd come, Anna's earring clutched in her fist. "Think she'll give it back?"

"She will," Anna said, her confidence clear. "And in return, I will buy out the rest of her mandatory service."

I frowned at the fashion maven, nonplussed. "You would offer her an indentureship?" I'd heard enough horror stories about the practice that I'd taken my chances with the FHP military *during a war.* Perhaps Ms. Duarte had found a way to make me dislike her after all.

Anna's eyes narrowed. "No. Buying out her contract is my repayment. I'll offer her a job, if she wants one, but she'll be free to do whatever she likes."

I blew out the breath I'd been holding and inclined my head. Anna's expression softened, veiled pain in her eyes. "I've never offered indentureships, and I never will. The entire practice should be outlawed." Her tone suggested more than moral grandstanding, and I wondered if she'd been lured in by the promise of avoiding military service by a conglomerate who cared about nothing but the bottom line.

With one problem solved, for now, I turned to Varro,

who was leaning against the wall while trying to look like he wasn't. White lines of pain bracketed his mouth and perspiration beaded his forehead. His tan skin had taken on an unhealthy pallor. My worry sharpened, and I hesitated to ask him to do more.

"There are at least a dozen soldiers close to *Starlight*," he said. "I tried to contact Torran, but his shields are too strong right now, which likely means they are under attack."

"Fev or Morten?"

Varro shook his head. "I don't know. I'm sorry."

"It's okay. Let me see if my implant can connect to Tavi now that we're close." The implant connected, but when I said, "Tavi, can you hear me?" I got nothing back.

A few seconds later, Tavi's voice crackled in my ear. "Kee? Is that you?"

"Yes! Where are you? What's going on?"

There was another long pause. "If you're talking, nothing is transmitting." More quietly, she said, "Please let that be it."

I touched the tiny, flexible patch on my throat that was supposed to pick up the minuscule vibrations from my vocal cords. Either the repeated hits from the plas blade or nearly electrocuting myself had burned out the sensors. I could hear, but I couldn't speak.

"If you can hear me," Tavi said, "tell Varro to stop shielding you."

I relayed the message and as soon as Varro's presence dimmed in my mind, a cold, unfamiliar mind touched mine. "Kee, it's Torran. Are you okay?"

"My subvocal mic is fried," I thought back. "I have Varro, Anna, and Nick with me, but we're in bad shape.

Mobile, but only just. Is Fev still here? Was she the reason the alarms went off? Can we return to the ship?"

I could feel Torran's relief and amusement across the mental connection. "Fev was never here. When you didn't come back, and we couldn't contact you, Chira donned her armor and pretended to be a telekinetic with a little help from me. We figured we'd draw out Morten, at least, and we did."

Dread pooled in my stomach. Morten didn't like to be wrong, and he liked looking foolish even less. Having just been on the receiving end of his ire, I worried for Chira. "Is she okay?"

"So far, but we need to leave before Morten realizes she's not an envoy sent by the empress. Tavi, Havil, Eli, and I are hidden near the public entrance to the base. Where are you?"

I glanced around, but the landing bay was too vast to make out any details, so I checked the map on my stolen comm. "We're on the opposite side from *Starlight*. You're in the middle, so stay there, we'll meet you. We could use the support to get to the ship."

I turned to the group. "We're going to meet up with Tavi and Torran near the public entrance, then we've got to hustle for the ship. They've tricked Morten into thinking Chira is a telekinetic, but the ruse will only last for so long."

Everyone nodded, and I led the group through the landing bay at a fast walk. We already stood out, so running would only draw more attention. And I wasn't entirely sure that Varro, Nick, or I *could* run for any length of time.

The landing bay was surprisingly free of other people, but I kept my head down because my bounty was still active, and I didn't have the time or energy to evade someone looking to make a quick fortune.

Tavi, who'd always been bad at following instructions she didn't like, met us halfway. She slipped from the shadows between ships with Torran, Havil, and Eli on her heels. All of them were in the lightweight armor we preferred while bounty hunting. It wasn't as protective as Valovian armor, but it also stood out far less.

Eli, Tavi, and Havil carried plas blades on their hips. Havil and Tavi also had plas pistols, while Eli carried a plas rifle slung across his body. Torran did not carry any visible weapons, but his telekinetic ability made him the most dangerous person in the group—by far.

Torran and Eli stopped in defensible positions where they could watch our surroundings while Tavi and Havil came closer. Tavi's expert gaze took in our group with one sweep, then she pulled me into a gentle hug. "I'm so glad you're okay," she murmured into my ear.

I squeezed her back, then grinned at her when she let me go. "It takes more than a sadistic asshole with a horde of minions to keep me down."

"And I see you were crowned queen while you were gone."

I touched my helmet. "When it's on, it blocks telepathy. It's one of Morten's experiments." I cast a nervous look around the landing bay. "But, speaking of, we need to leave ASAP. He's going to be *pissed* when he finds out what you did. Where is Chira?"

"She's near *Starlight*. Anja is keeping an eye on her from the ship, as well as guarding Liang and Siarvez. A small space liner landed just as we needed a distraction, so we pretended Chira arrived with the other passengers because her ship was damaged on Bastion."

I raised an eyebrow. "And that worked?"

"Would *you* argue with a telekinetic here on orders from the empress?"

"Good point," I said with a laugh.

Behind me, Varro groaned low in his throat and pain flashed through the tiny connection we still shared. I spun to find him trying to push Havil's hands away. "Heal her first," he said in Valovan.

The mild-mannered medic blew out a frustrated breath and responded in the same language. "Kee will survive her injuries without my help. If I don't heal you, your ribs are going to pierce your lungs, and you'll drown in your own blood. How will you protect her then?"

Varro relented with a poorly disguised scowl. He pulled up his shirt with clumsy fingers, and my breath hissed through my teeth in sympathy. I'd always admired the hard expanse of Varro's chest, but today it was turning a mottled, bruised purple beneath his tan skin, hinting at deep internal bleeding. Several distinct impact points looked like they had come from kicks with booted feet.

My fury at Morten notched higher. He might not have been the one to deliver the blows, but Varro had been hurt on his orders.

Havil laid his hands on Varro's chest, and intense, fiery pain blossomed in my mind, like I'd been stabbed with a hundred blades. I bit my lip, determined to withstand it, but a whimper broke free anyway. Varro's gaze darted to me, shock momentarily overpowering the agony on his face.

Abruptly, my pain disappeared, and I could no longer feel the connection between us. The lack left a ragged hole, and I felt like I'd lost something vital.

I swayed in place, and Tavi caught my shoulder. "Are you okay?" she demanded.

I couldn't quite summon a smile. "Today's been a lot."

Havil grunted and his jaw clenched. "I can get you stable," he gritted out, "but there's too much damage to heal you all the way."

"Don't overextend yourself," Varro said. "We may need you yet."

A few moments later, Havil eased away from Varro, sweat on his brow. "Your ribs are barely knit. Don't get hit in the chest."

I caught a glimpse of lingering bruises in an angry greenish-yellow before Varro pulled his shirt down. "I'll do what I have to do," Varro said, voice flinty. Then, more quietly, he added, "Thank you."

Havil shook his head but didn't argue.

Eli's voice crackled over my comm implant. "We've got incoming."

Tavi's attention snapped to him. "Have they spotted us?"

"Not yet. But we're going to have to circle around to avoid them."

Eli and Torran joined us. Torran and Tavi took the lead, with Anna and Nick just behind them. Varro stopped to wait for me, but I waved him and Havil on. Eli brought up the rear of the group. When he caught up to me, he bumped his shoulder against mine. "Glad to see you're still kicking," he murmured. "I hope you gave them hell."

It was easy to see the worry in his eyes, so I winked at him. "Thanks to your lessons, two soldiers didn't know what hit them. Then I channeled your flirtatious smirk to charm a third into helping us. So I'm three for three today."

I'd conveniently left out a few minor details, and from Eli's expression, he knew it, but he didn't call me on it. "I told you practice would save your hide."

"Yeah, yeah. I bow to your superior knowledge—and pretty face."

He rolled his eyes, but the smile that hovered on his mouth was soft and relieved. He nudged me forward. "Go tell Varro you're okay so he stops glancing over his shoulder every two seconds. I'll watch our backs."

"My mic is out. I can hear comms but not respond."

Eli nodded. "Torran told us."

I left Eli and moved up next to Varro. "You should've told me that you were in so much pain."

He slanted an unreadable look at me. "You should've told me that my feelings were constantly bleeding through our connection."

I peeked at him as Tavi and Torran led us through a maze of ships and cargo containers. His jaw was set, and he avoided my eyes, so I told him the truth. "I didn't mind."

The muscles in his neck flexed. "I failed to protect you. *Again.*"

"I'm not that fragile," I bit out. "Yeah, I hated feeling your pain, but *not* because you failed to protect me from it, but because you were hurt, Varro. And, ultimately, you were hurt because of *me.* If I'd done my job and gotten better access into the base's system, then I could've set alerts on the vid feeds so we wouldn't have been ambushed. Hell, I could've unlocked Anna's door from the ship."

The admission stung, and I swallowed as tears welled in my eyes. "Everything that happened today is my fault," I whispered, "including your broken ribs." It was a confession that cut on the way out, slicing into me with blades of truth. One more kick in the wrong place and Varro would've *died*.

Varro stopped and spun toward me, righteous fury on his face. "No. None of this is your fault," he growled. When I opened my mouth to disagree, his hands clamped around my shoulders, and he gave me a gentle shake. "Not. Your. Fault."

Despite his gruff certainty, it was hard to let go of the negative feelings, and I realized that we were probably more alike than not in this case. "If it's not my fault, then it's not *your* fault, either," I said as gently as I could. "If you continue to shoulder the blame, then you can't criticize me for doing the same."

"It's not the sa—"

I pressed my finger to his lips. "It is. To me, *it is*."

He stilled, his expression deep and fathomless, and I pulled him into motion as Eli caught up with us. If Varro and I were going to make something of the simmering attraction between us, then we'd need to discuss the whole fault thing more deeply, but now was not the time.

As we threaded our way through the landing bay, I pulled out the comm I'd stolen and started working my way into the back door I'd left for myself in the surveillance system. Without Varro shielding for us, anyone who looked at the cameras would be able to tell exactly where we were.

I planned to make that a little more difficult.

It took several minutes, but eventually I gained access to the surveillance system again. Before I could get distracted looking for Morten on the eleventy-billion feeds, I looped all the landing bay cameras and changed their access settings.

If we were lucky, it would take the Feds a few hours to

find and fix my changes, but even if we weren't, it should keep them occupied long enough for us to make a hasty departure.

I jogged to catch up with Tavi, wincing as all of my muscles protested the extra work. "I've turned off surveillance in here," I warned. "So we don't have to worry about Morten spotting us, but I didn't have time to save an unedited stream anywhere, so we won't have proof if he attacks unprovoked. And I can't keep an eye on him, either."

Tavi split her attention between me and our surroundings. "So you're saying we should hurry?" When I nodded, she asked, "Can you run?" She looked over my shoulder. "Can they?"

My nose wrinkled. "Me, yes, for a little while. Anna, yes. Varro will do it even if it kills him, which it might. Nick, maybe, and not for very long. They're in pretty bad shape."

"Havil is also still recovering," Tavi murmured. "How long will the cameras be out?"

"Twenty minutes to two hours." When her eyebrows rose at the wide window, I shrugged. "Depends on if the Feds have anyone decent on staff. Better to plan like they do."

"We'll take a faster route, but we'll save running for a last resort. Will you be able to tell if they undo your changes?"

"Not immediately, unless I happen to be looking at the feed."

"Keep an eye on it," Tavi ordered.

I nodded and dropped back to my place next to Varro. "Everything okay?" he asked.

"Yeah, but I need to search the vid feeds for signs of

Morten. Will you keep me from wandering off or breaking my nose on an inconveniently placed ship?"

Varro cupped my elbow. "Of course."

I nodded my thanks and dove back into the surveillance videos, flipping through them at high speed. I started with the rooms near where we'd been held. The soldier I'd hit with the helmet was still in the hallway, but the one I'd stunned in Varro's room was gone.

Shit. By now, Morten knew we'd escaped, which meant he knew we'd head straight for the ship. I glanced at Varro. "Did you warn the others that some of the soldiers have helmets that make them undetectable?"

His jaw clenched at the reminder, but he dipped his chin.

I continued flipping through the feeds. The base didn't look like it was preparing for an attack. There were more people than usual milling around in the public module, but on the military side it was like the alarm earlier hadn't even happened.

Morten had been concerned that Station Command had been alerted, but now, nothing. Had the commodore somehow spun the whole event as an unscheduled training exercise?

I kept searching, but there was no sign of Morten or any soldiers wearing the prototype helmets. Dread gathered in my stomach. The landing bay was the only place I couldn't see in real-time, but I started looking through the looped video feeds. It wouldn't give me Morten's exact location, but it would at least confirm that he was here.

I had made it through only a few of the feeds when Varro pulled me to a stop. He gestured, and I crouched down beside him. Our group was hidden between two cargo containers and a hulking ship on our right. We were covered by a deep shadow, even in the bright lights of the landing bay.

Varro held a finger to his lips, and I sighed in relief as I felt the cool touch of his mind. It was strange, but I'd gotten so used to having him in my head that after he'd severed the connection, I'd felt like part of me was missing. That part was back, and I wasn't going to let him block me out so easily a second time.

"A group of soldiers are waiting for the ship up ahead to spin down," he whispered telepathically, pointing at the ship in question. "There's not much cover, so it's safer to wait than to try going around."

I glanced at the small FHP ship that had just landed, then frowned as I examined it more closely. A couple of years ago, I'd done a deep dive on ships, both Fed and Valovian, and this ship matched neither. It was close to FHP spec, but some of the lines were wrong. My brain was phenomenal at certain types of pattern recognition, and this ship didn't match any known patterns.

I squinted at it, trying to figure out what was tripping me up. It could be a prototype, but then it shouldn't look like a ship designed and built on blueprints that were two decades old.

Tavi caught my frown. "What?" she whispered.

"You notice anything odd about that ship?" When she shook her head, I asked, "Is your comm still connected to *Starlight*?"

She handed it over and raised an eyebrow when I typed in her passcode from memory. "Remind me to change that," she muttered.

I grinned at her. "Wouldn't do you any good."

"You'd remember the new one faster than me," she agreed with a quiet laugh.

It was a moment's work to pull up the list of recently arrived ships. *Triumphant Victory* certainly *sounded* like a Fed ship—and it was, just not *this* one. I started digging into the registration data.

"What's wrong?" Tavi asked.

"That ship is pretending to be *Triumphant Victory,* and the registration data is *good*. Whoever set up its identity knew what they were doing. There are barely any signs that it's forged."

"How do you know it's not the *Victory*?"

"The *Triumphant Victory* was an FHP diplomatic vessel that had a very brief career before ignominiously crashing into a rogue asteroid, killing everyone aboard. The Feds realized a ship named *Victory* killing everyone made them look bad, so they hushed it up."

"When?"

"A couple of years ago. I found it while digging for information on that raider we tracked, the one who kept hiding by forging registrations of legitimate ships."

"So the FHP could've reused the name by now," Tavi said, but even she didn't sound convinced. Names carried weight, and no crew wanted to be on a ship named after a disaster.

We both stared at the ship in question as the engines spun down. On a hunch, I pulled up the docking information I'd gotten from Bastion and searched through it. Sure enough, the *Victory* had landed on Bastion several times before—most recently, the day before the fashion exhibition.

I bit my lip as I stared at the list of dates. I didn't recognize a pattern in them, but *something* seemed familiar. I cross-referenced the docking dates with the dates the *Renegade Tide* had been on Bastion.

They matched.

Not exactly, and not every time, but close enough for astronomically low odds of it being coincidental. Before I could warn Tavi about my suspicions, the cargo ramp lowered, and a blond woman in an FHP admiral's uniform descended, wearing one of Morten's prototype helmets.

My brain took two seconds to get over the terrified disbelief, two seconds I didn't have because the woman turned and looked directly at our hidden group. Our eyes met and surprise crossed her face for a brief moment before a vicious smile curved her lips. "You have something of mine," she mouthed.

Then raw telekinetic power clamped around my body, freezing me in place.

CHAPTER THIRTY

When Torran had trained with us, telelocking us in place so we could try to break the hold, it had always been a gentle touch, a cupped hand rather than a clenched fist.

Sura Fev's telelock held no gentleness.

I gasped as she crushed the air from my lungs. My bones *ached* as her power bore down on me. She jerked me toward her, and sheer, animal terror whited out my thoughts.

Death had found me at last.

Varro roared, a sound I heard in my head as much as my ears, and it slammed me back into the present. I couldn't give up, couldn't let him fight on his own. My team needed me.

A strong Valoff could break a telelock with mental power alone, but I wasn't a Valoff, and I wasn't that strong. The best a human could do was fight the physical restriction. The harder I fought to move, the harder it would be to keep me locked.

I strained my already exhausted muscles, fighting against the hold. The cool chill of Varro's mind spiked into an icy ache. "Be ready," he gritted.

I was halfway across the distance separating us when a wave of plas pulses swept past me. Fev's eyes narrowed in annoyance. She pulled a nearby cargo container in front of her without ever letting me go.

Blessed Lady and all of her handmaids, just how strong *was* she?

The soldiers who had been waiting for her turned and ran. None of them had Morten's prototype helmets on, which meant they'd probably thought she really *was* an admiral and now her cover was blown.

As if she'd heard my thoughts, a second cargo container smashed into the group of fleeing soldiers, pinning them to the hull of a low-slung cargo hauler—all without her being able to see them.

A chorus of pained screams abruptly cut off, leaving nothing but terrible, damning silence.

I swallowed the bile that coated the back of my tongue and fought harder to free myself from her hold. The fact that I wasn't already dead meant she wanted something from me, but I wasn't about to wait around to find out what it was.

Varro rushed forward with Torran on his heels. I could almost feel the electric buzz in the air as Torran *pushed* the cargo container blocking Fev from view toward her. It moved a few centimeters before she snarled and the telelock faltered.

Varro caught me before I could hit the deck, and his power swept over me in an icy wave. He let my feet drop, then hustled me to the left while Torran and Fev wrestled for control of the container.

A telekinetic had just taken out a group of FHP soldiers, and yet the alarms stayed stubbornly silent. My surveillance loop had damned us to fighting this battle alone.

And damned those soldiers to die.

I swallowed against the urge to be sick and averted my eyes as Varro ushered me past the smashed cargo container and the ship it was pinned to. We lost sight of Torran as we rounded the corner. I knew the former general could take care of himself, but worry pressed on me.

"What about Tavi and the rest?" I asked Varro, breathless from both fear and exertion. Fev wanted Tavi for the empress, which meant we had to do everything in our power to get her to safety.

"The captain is taking the rest of the group a different way."

"Morten is somewhere in the landing bay," I warned.

His mouth flattened. "He's attacking Chira with a team of at least sixteen."

"What?" I demanded. "Is she okay?"

"So far, but they're wearing those fucking helmets, so she's having trouble avoiding them. A couple of soldiers tried for *Starlight*, but Anja unlocked the weapons systems, so they only tried once. They'll attempt to catch us before we make it to the ship."

So we had a telekinetic behind us and two squads of undetectable soldiers in front of us. Great, no problem.

If Morten knew we were here and still hadn't set off the alarms, then he didn't want the rest of the base to interfere. There might be an opportunity there, but a situation was rarely made better by adding *more* Feds.

Varro's head tilted. "Fev retreated to regroup. Torran is

going to meet up with Tavi because with me shielding for you, she is the next likely target."

"We have to help her!"

"It's better if we split Fev's attention. I'll let my shielding slip just enough for her to get a hint of our location. Do you know why she's after you in particular?"

"I'm assuming because Morten plastered that picture of me and Liang all over Bastion. I'm not sure if she's here on a rescue mission or what, but I'm betting the prince is involved. The question is: Is she here on the empress's orders or Morten's?"

Varro scowled as he peeked around the edge of the shipping container. "I've never heard of Fiazefferia turning traitor. It's possible that it has happened in the past and the imperial family covered it up, but fanatical loyalty is one of their most well-known traits. If Fev is here, it's very likely on Empress Nepru's orders."

We sprinted for the next piece of cover—a medium passenger ship—and the cool feel of Varro's mind slipped. He grimaced and leaned against the ship's stabilizer leg to catch his breath. I looked at him in alarm. "What's wrong?"

His expression smoothed into blandness, but he couldn't hide the hitch in his gait as he pushed himself back into motion. He moved like everything hurt, but all he said was "Nothing."

I put a hand on his arm and pulled him to a stop. "Don't give me that shit. What is wrong?"

"Fev briefly locked me. She may have broken one of my ribs again."

I knew the weasel words were there for my benefit, to prevent me from worrying, but based on the lines of pain on his face, she'd *definitely* broken at least one rib.

"Would she help us if she knew we'd rescued Liang?"

Varro started moving again and cautiously led me through the maze of ships and containers while he thought. Without being able to sense Morten's soldiers, he was being extra careful. Finally, he stopped in the shadow of a small ship and said, "I don't know. Maybe, but it's possible the empress wants Fev to retain her place on Morten's team unless there is no other option."

"So Fev might not help, but she might let us escape if she knew we meant Liang no harm?"

Varro frowned at me. "It's a risky gamble."

I grinned. "Don't worry, I'm not going to waltz up to her and suggest it, I'm just contingency planning."

Planning gave me something to do other than worry, especially since I still had Tavi's comm, so she'd have to rely on her implant for communication with the rest of the team. We *should* all be close enough for the implant to work fine, but my brain liked to run worst-case scenarios: What if she was taken captive and needed her comm to call for help?

Most of the thoughts didn't make logical sense—her captors would certainly take her comm anyway—but contingency planning kept my brain occupied so it didn't have as much time to run disaster scenarios.

The cool feel of Varro's mental touch slipped again, and he gritted his teeth. I peered at him, noting the line of tension running through his body. "You're not doing that on purpose, are you?"

His hands clenched, but he gave a sharp shake of his head. "Whatever drugs they gave me still aren't completely out of my system. It's fucking with my concentration."

I pointed to my prototype helmet. "What if I use this instead of forcing you to shield for me?"

"You're not *forcing* me to do anything," he ground out, eyes flashing.

I shook my head and pulled off the helmet I'd been wearing since I'd stolen it from the soldier in Varro's room. "Let's argue semantics later, okay?" I turned the helmet over and found the power switch. With a flick, the tiny red light came on.

When I put the helmet back on, Varro's presence disappeared from my mind, leaving a void. I stumbled and Varro looked ready to snatch the helmet off again. "What's wrong?" he demanded.

I tapped my temple. "I miss you. Can you sense me?"

He frowned in concentration, then his expression hardened. "Barely, and only because I know you're beside me. I could probably get better at sensing you with practice, but, for now, I can't communicate with you as long as you're wearing the helmet."

"I'll take it off if we get separated," I promised. Losing telepathic communication was a steep price to pay, but there was an easy fix: once I removed the helmet, I could mentally shout for backup. Of course, that backup might arrive in the form of a furious Sun Guardian, but I was trying to focus on the positives.

Varro edged around the ship, then cursed under his breath. "There's no cover ahead. I can't sense anyone, but that doesn't mean anything." He leaned a little farther out. "Circling around will add at least five minutes."

I eased up next to him and assessed the situation. We were getting closer to *Starlight* and the part of the landing bay that was used for storage—and unwanted guests. But between the two sections was a fifteen-meter span of open space that the ground-based cargo haulers used to move containers to FOSO I's receiving dock.

On our way into the base, we'd cut through this area closer to the inside wall, which had plenty of containers sitting around waiting to be unloaded. Going back that way would probably be the safest, but it would also be the way Morten's soldiers would be watching because it was the quickest route from the public entrance.

I bit my lip in indecision. "Thoughts?"

Varro's eyes skimmed over the ships and containers on the far side of the gap. Nothing moved. "With the helmet, Fev won't be able to track you, so it's only Morten's soldiers we have to worry about."

"Are they still after Chira?"

Varro nodded slowly. "Some of them."

The open area was *long*. The odds that Morten had soldiers covering the entire thing was minuscule. "Is Tavi ahead of us?"

Varro nodded and pointed to our right. "They crossed somewhere down there a few minutes ago."

"If they weren't attacked, then I say we risk it. Time is of the essence now."

I could tell that Varro agreed, but he wasn't very happy about it. Finally, he sighed. "As fast as we can," he said. "If anything happens, I'll draw their attention. You get to *Starlight*."

"Or we could work together," I suggested.

Varro turned to me, his expression intense. "Get to the ship. I can take care of myself if I know you're safe."

I sighed. I knew it was the best option, but I didn't like

it. "I'll do it, but I'm absolutely going to come looking for you if you disappear, so be careful, okay?"

Varro's expression softened. "I'll be right behind you." He turned his attention to the other side of the open space. A look of pained concentration crossed his face, then he shook his head. "I can't sense anyone, but that doesn't mean it's clear. You ready?"

I took a deep breath and shook out my arms and legs. Everything hurt, but I nodded anyway.

"Stay behind me." Varro turned and rushed into the clear space at an uneven sprint. He was obviously hurting, and he was still *way* faster than me, but I pushed my tired body into motion. Once we were clear, I was going to get a massage and find somewhere with a soaking tub.

Or a beach. Oooh, a beach would be nice. Maybe I could persuade Varro to join me for a few days of sea and sand and a room with only one bed.

We were more than halfway across the gap, and I was just starting to hope we'd make it undetected, when a soldier peeked out of cover, prototype helmet firmly planted on his head. Varro shot at him, but the pulse narrowly went wide, and the soldier ducked back behind the cargo container.

And then a trio of soldiers sprang up and returned fire. Varro darted left, drawing their attention. I fought the urge to follow him, but with nothing but a plas blade and some stolen comms, I wouldn't be much help, and it wouldn't do him any good if I got myself shot. Instead, I sprinted straight for cover, legs and lungs burning.

Varro hit one of the soldiers while darting back and forth with more agility than one would expect from someone with his build, but I'd spent enough time watching him spar with the rest of the crew to see that he was hurting.

I crossed the line of ships and cargo containers, and Varro slipped from view. It felt like I was leaving bleeding pieces of my heart behind, but I didn't slow. The soldiers would've reported to Morten upon first spotting us. This area would be crawling with his lackeys in no time flat. Varro could take care of himself. I had to do the same.

Unfortunately, I hadn't lied when I'd told Tavi that I would be able to run for only a short time, because all too soon, my legs were wobbling like jelly and my lungs were burning like fire. I darted across one last walkway, then eased between a pair of cargo containers to catch my breath and check the map.

I leaned against the container, breathing as quietly as I could, considering it felt like I was two lungs short. I pulled out Tavi's comm with shaky hands. My whole body was a little shaky, a combination of worry, adrenaline, and exhaustion.

The map proved that I was closer to *Starlight* than I'd thought. It would still take five or ten minutes to work my way through the maze of ships and containers, but I might've slipped past at least a few of Morten's soldiers.

I checked the surveillance footage. It was still looped, so either no one had noticed or they hadn't been able to undo my changes. I debated the merits of ending the loop myself, but if we had to fight our way out, then it would be better if there wasn't video evidence of us attacking a bunch of FHP soldiers. Still . . .

I quickly wrote a little script to undo the vid loop and fix the access changes, then tied it to a shortcut key on Tavi's comm. Better to be prepared than not.

After peeking around the corner of the container, I eased out of cover and pushed myself into a slow jog. I had half hoped that Varro would somehow magically catch up to me, but he remained stubbornly missing. I'd promised him that I would go to the ship, and I intended to keep the promise, but worry plagued my steps. In fact, being on my own meant I could worry for everyone at once.

I rounded a corner and came face-to-face with a soldier in an FHP uniform and prototype helmet—one of Morten's. The soldier started in surprise and instinctively backpedaled to avoid the collision. Rather than doing the same, I drove forward, pulling the plas blade from my pocket. I flicked it on and changed it to nonlethal.

The soldier raised his pistol, but I got there first. He went down with a shout. Well, that certainly wasn't stealthy. I removed his helmet and sliced it in half. If nothing else, I could give the Valoffs on our team a fighting chance.

And maybe Varro would figure out where I was.

I hit the soldier a couple more times with the nonlethal setting, then stuck the deactivated plas blade in my pocket and picked up his gun. I pushed my tired body into a run. I needed to put some distance between us.

Unfortunately, the universe had other plans.

Morten appeared at the next intersection, flanked by four soldiers. I spun, but two more soldiers blocked my retreat. The left and right sides of this narrow corridor were blocked by two-meter-tall cargo containers. While I'd like to bound over them like a superhero, that was not within my ability. I'd neatly trapped myself.

Kee Ildez, master strategist.

Morten's smile was as smug as it was punchable—and it was *highly* punchable. "Drop the pistol," he called.

I hit the shortcut button on Tavi's comm. If I was going to be horribly murdered, I at least wanted Morten to have to justify my death to a military tribunal. They wouldn't do shit, but it would be a minor inconvenience for him, and that was better than nothing.

I raised the pistol in defiance, but kept it carefully pointed at the ceiling—no reason to give him the perfect excuse to shoot me. "No."

Morten's eyebrows rose. "What is your plan here, Specialist Ildez? You're surrounded."

I slowly removed my helmet and set it on the ground. Almost immediately, I felt the cool touch of Varro's mind and the weight of his worry. "Are you okay?" he asked.

Relief swamped me. I might be in deep trouble, but at least Varro was okay.

"Maybe *you're* surrounded, Commodore," I said rather than answering Varro.

"Hold on," Varro whispered into my mind. Apparently he didn't need an answer to know that I was in trouble.

But, in truth, Varro wasn't the Valoff I was hoping to attract. It might be stupid, but if Sura Fev thought I knew where Liang was, she might keep me alive long enough to tell her, even if that meant stealing me from Morten. If nothing else, I might be able to determine just how deep her loyalty to Morten went. I was probably leaping headfirst into fire, but I didn't have many options left.

Morten waved to one of the soldiers beside him. "If she doesn't drop the pistol in the next three seconds, shoot her in the leg."

"Too cowardly to do it yourself?" I taunted. "Or maybe you're worried you couldn't hit me."

Morten just smiled with anticipation.

I eyed the distance between us; I could probably hit him, but then I'd be the one committing murder in full view of the cameras, so I spun and flung the gun at the two soldiers behind me, then rushed after it.

The soldiers didn't flinch, and by the time I was within reach, both had their plas blades drawn, glowing deadly red. I stumbled to a stop and held up my hands. "Now now, let's talk about this. You wouldn't want to commit a war crime, would you? Morten isn't worth it."

"Back off," the one on the right said.

Another soldier rounded the corner behind them. It took me a second to recognize her because Sura Fev had removed the rank insignia from her uniform. Now she looked like the two soldiers in front of me.

"Step aside," she said, command in her tone.

The soldier on the left spun to face her while the one on the right stayed focused on me. The two of them stood back-to-back, which made sneaking past them all but impossible. Morten continued to find experienced soldiers who wouldn't go down easily. I started adjusting my plans.

"Let her through," Morten called.

The soldier facing Fev waved her through. I expected her power to clamp around me at any moment, but she merely flicked her gaze from my bare head to my boots. "Still alive, I see," she murmured, her voice pitched for my ears only.

This close, I could see that her eyes were pale blue, but they lacked the distinctive streaks most Valoffs had. She also moved more like a human than any Valoff I'd ever met. Someone had gone to lot of trouble training her for deep cover. Hopefully that meant she was still loyal to the empress, or this was going to end poorly.

"Morten and Fev are both here, along with six other soldiers," I thought to Varro. "And the landing bay cameras are recording again, so the security office can see what's happening. Tell Tavi."

"I will. Hold on. We're coming for you," he whispered. A jumble of concern and frustration and care drifted across the link and I wondered if he knew just how much he was sharing.

I'd missed the first part of Fev and Morten's conversation, but I started paying attention again just as Morten said, "I didn't expect to see you here." There was an odd note in his voice, but he continued, "I thought you were stationed on Bastion."

Fev shrugged. "It's a temporary reassignment." She tipped her head at me. "I might be helpful in questioning the traitor. Unless, of course, you've already uncovered the location of the other suspect."

Morten frowned at Fev. Whatever their association, he didn't fully trust her. "My interrogation was interrupted."

Fev's smile sent shivers down my spine. "Then I'm just in time."

Morten shook his head. "You help is not necessary," he said dismissively. "I will let you know what I find."

Fev's mouth tightened until her smile looked more like a snarl. I could see Morten's death in her expression, but the commodore just waved at the soldiers next to him. "Secure Specialist Ildez for transport."

"On my mark, run past the two soldiers behind you," Varro whispered into my head. "Three, two, one, go!"

I felt the telltale coolness that meant Varro was shielding for me. I turned and sprinted for the soldiers behind me, who looked around in confusion and didn't move.

Sura Fev, however, *did*.

"Where do you think you're going?" she asked softly

as her power clamped around me. I felt a mental spike of icy cold pain as she tried to overwhelm Varro's shield. I winced, but the shield held. My thoughts were safe—for now.

Unfortunately, Varro's shield didn't prevent Fev from immobilizing me with her ability. As she reeled me closer, I realized that enough of Varro's shield had survived that the human soldiers couldn't see me.

Fev glanced around and her puzzlement turned into realization. "Clever trick," she murmured. "Runkow always was an overachiever."

It didn't surprise me that she knew Varro was part of our crew. She clearly knew Torran, or at least knew *of* him, and it wasn't exactly a huge leap to guess who he'd brought with him.

Morten started directing his soldiers into defensive positions. He didn't know Fev had me, but he expected an attack. Fev moved toward the rest of the group, dragging me along beside her.

"Morten plans to execute the prince," I whispered quickly. "Is that a plan you agree with?"

Fev's expression remained perfectly flat. "What makes you think I wouldn't?"

"I know who you are."

Fev's power tightened around me until I groaned in pain. "One word, and I'll kill you."

Varro's presence in my mind spiked, all steely determination and unbending will, and Fev's hold loosened enough for me to suck in a desperate breath. "Liang vowed that my crew and I wouldn't be harmed by anyone in his family if I helped him," I whispered. "And I did. I rescued him and saved his life."

The painful clench of her power didn't ease, but at least it stopped tightening. "Where is he?"

I shook my head. "There's exactly one reason for you to keep me alive. I'm not just going to give it to you. Plus, I don't know if you're actually planning to rescue him or not. I won't give him up."

She pulled me close. "I can break your bones one by one," she whispered.

I raised an eyebrow even as terror clawed at me. "Threats really don't make me want to trust you *more,* you know."

Honestly, I was pretty sure even a vow wouldn't make me trust her at this point, but if I kept stalling, I hoped Tavi would come up with a plan that didn't involve me getting pulverized by a telekinetic one bone at a time.

"Fera, stop standing around and get over here," Morten shouted.

It didn't surprise me that she hadn't given him her real name. "Varro," I thought as loudly as I could, "let go of the shielding that keeps me hidden."

"That's not a good idea," he said, his voice distant. "We're almost in position."

"Trust me. But maybe be prepared for a little chaos."

A second later the feeling of Varro in my head changed, and the soldiers looking our way paled in terror. The two in front raised their weapons in reflex. They were old enough to have fought in the war. They knew exactly what fighting a telekinetic meant—instant, painful death.

Their rifles crumpled in their hands. They looked between Morten and Fev, then turned and ran. Two more soldiers joined them, and Fev let them go. Only the two youngest soldiers had stayed with Morten.

I shook my head. Maybe they'd survive long enough for their brains to grow.

Morten blinked before a calculating look crossed his face. "I see you've been keeping secrets," he said, his voice mild.

"So have you, *Commodore*." The emphasis on the title and Morten's wince made me think that Fev wasn't supposed to know that he was still part of the FHP military—despite what the records might show.

"Get ready to hit the ground," Varro warned. "Chira will take over shielding for you. You'll be visible."

Before I could agree—or ask *why* Chira needed to take over—the feeling in my mind changed. Rather than the familiar cool feel of Varro's mind, I felt something lighter and crisper.

Next to me, Fev snarled. Her telekinetic grip loosened, and I hit the ground in a crouch. I spun and, in a move I'd practiced with Eli a thousand times, swept her legs out from under her. She hit the ground hard, and her prototype helmet fell off.

A plas pulse burned a hole through her shirt, but it was deflected away from her skin by armor hidden beneath her clothes. I pulled the plas blade from my pocket and activated it, but she recovered too quickly. Her power slammed me into the deck, pressing until my joints ground together and pain blossomed like lightning.

She bent and pulled the plas blade from fingers that wouldn't cooperate with the signals from my brain.

My chest refused to expand, and my lungs burned. I gasped for air, drawing in tiny breaths. Okay, that plan hadn't gone as well as I'd hoped.

"Move and she dies," Fev said.

I couldn't see who she was talking to, but Tavi's voice responded. "Let her go. Your quarrel is with Morten."

"You're wrong," Fev responded. Morten laughed, but it turned into a surprised snarl when Fev continued, "My quarrel is with both of you."

CHAPTER THIRTY-ONE

I strained against Fev's hold. She put her foot on my back and leaned weight on it. "Keep doing that, and I'll freeze your lungs," she murmured.

"For the record, this counts as *harm,*" I hissed between clenched teeth.

She leaned more weight on the foot on my back. "Tell me where the prince is, and I'll verify that he actually made the vow."

"No," I gritted out.

She removed her foot and jerked me up, her telelock still vice-tight. "You are a stubborn little thing, aren't you?"

I didn't bother to respond. Now that I could see again, I found Morten kneeling nearby, obviously fighting a telekinetic hold of his own. His two remaining flunkies had disappeared. Tavi was crouched on top of the cargo container on my right, Torran next to her. The rest of the team was out of sight.

Tavi's voice crackled in my ear. "Liang is on his way."

My gaze shot to hers. That was a bad idea for a host of reasons, not the least of which was that the landing bay surveillance footage was no longer looped.

Tavi caught my alarm. "Varro is shielding for him, but we need to move fast because Varro's on his last legs."

So that was why Chira was shielding for *me.* I could still feel the light, crisp presence of her mind, so I thought as loudly as I could, "Tell Tavi to leave me and go."

"Do you really think the captain will leave you behind?" Chira responded telepathically. "I don't know her as well as you do, but I find it highly unlikely."

"My life isn't worth another war," I tried. "Make her understand."

"Even if I thought you were right, and I could somehow persuade her *and* Varro *and* the rest of the crew, Liang wouldn't leave you. He owes you, no matter what he said about repaying the debt with information."

Unfortunately, the point became moot because two people in Valovian armor stepped into view, and Fev made a pleased sound in the back of her throat.

I squinted at the two. One of them was likely Liang, unless Tavi had planned some elaborate hoax, but who was the other one? Based on the height, it could be Varro or Eli, but armor tended to mask differences in build, so it could also be Siarvez or Havil.

At least both of them fairly bristled with weapons. Not that they'd be very useful against a telekinetic, but it was better than nothing.

The armored soldier on the left stepped forward and

opened their visor. Liang's handsome face was set into hard lines of command. "Release her," he demanded, his tone full of imperial hauteur.

Next to me, Fev smirked. "Your mother sends her regards. She appreciates your sacrifice."

I sucked in a shocked breath, and Liang's face smoothed into an expression so bland that he had to be either terrified or furious—maybe both. But his voice was calm and cold when he said, "You swore a blood oath to protect the imperial family. And despite my mother's wishes, I remain part of the family."

Fev's smile grew. "Not for long. I had hoped that this incompetent fool"—she waved at Morten—"would get the job done after I basically hand-fed him the steps, but he couldn't even get that right."

Morten spluttered. "Now see here—"

Fev sniffed dismissively and Morten's jaw snapped shut. "I've heard enough from you to last a lifetime," she said.

"*Thank* you," I muttered under my breath. I knew she was the enemy, but Lady give me strength, the man liked to hear himself talk. "Tell me that felt as satisfying as it looked."

Fev slanted an amused glance at me. "It was highly satisfying."

Liang snapped down his visor. Fev sighed and pulled me half in front of her. At least my feet were on the ground this time, and I was supporting a lot of my own weight. I turned my head, keeping her in view, and she allowed me that much freedom. Was she tiring or was she preparing for something big?

"This one says you owe her your life," Fev said with a wave at me. "Is that true?"

"I didn't say that!" I disagreed. "I said I *saved* his life. Those are two different things."

"Not to a Valoff," she murmured.

Liang inclined his head, confirming her words. Well, shit. I'd thought I could count on Fev's loyalty to the empire if nothing else, but it turns out the empress was willing to sacrifice her youngest son to further her agenda.

"Take off your armor, and I'll let her go, unharmed," Fev said.

"And why should I trust you, *niapsifuv*?"

Fev flinched, and it took me a second to translate: "oath breaker." It was an old word, far less common than *vuw,* the word for "liar," and far more insulting. Though the literal translation was "oath breaker," it was one of those words where the literal translation didn't carry the full weight of meaning. In Valovan, the true meaning was a person without honor. It was one of the gravest insults in the language, which was the only reason I knew it in the first place.

Overhead, an alarm blared to life, surprisingly loud in the cavernous landing bay. Whoever was on duty in the surveillance office had *finally* bothered to look at the video streams. It had certainly taken them long enough. I'd thought I was going to have to send them a freaking hand-painted invitation.

"Be ready," Chira whispered, then her presence disappeared from my mind.

In the next heartbeat, Fev's telelock slipped for a fraction of a second, and I pivoted, putting all of the power from my legs, hips, and shoulders into the punch. Her torso was armored, so I aimed for her face, even though I knew it was going to hurt like punching a wall.

Fev had her eyes closed and her jaw clenched, with one

hand on her head like she had a splitting headache. Someone was attacking her mind, giving me a brief window of opportunity.

I'd take it.

Her eyes opened just before I made contact. She jerked back, but not fast enough. My fist drove into her cheek with a highly satisfying impact that I felt all the way to my shoulder. She stumbled back and hit the ground on her ass, stunned but not out.

And when she looked up, I saw death in her eyes.

Then the unknown person in Valovian armor tackled her while Liang wrapped me in his arms and spun, putting his back to the cargo container barreling toward us. I sucked in a breath, but I couldn't do anything except try to relax and hope death found me quickly.

The cargo container slammed into us. Liang took the brunt of the impact on his back, then cool power wrapped around us and jerked us upward. The container smashed against its neighbor with a metallic groan, centimeters below my toes. Another second and we would've been paste.

"Torran cut that one a little too close," Liang growled, his voice amplified by the armor.

"Are you hurt?"

"I can manage," he said. "We need to get you to the ship."

"Who else is in Valovian armor?" When Liang hesitated, I demanded, "Who?"

"Varro," he said. "He's the only one strong enough to stand a chance against Fev."

"But he's hurt and he's been burning energy all day!" I spun to look back the way we'd come, but Liang caught my arm.

"I promised to get you to the ship," he said. "Torran will help Varro."

I growled and jerked my arm away. "You can help me get to the ship by helping me rescue Varro. I'm not letting him die for me."

Liang sighed. "Fine. But after this we are truly even."

"We were even before. If you don't want to help me, you don't have to. She wants you dead, too."

"I noticed." Liang's voice was as dry as desert air. "Let's do this before I lose my nerve."

The fact that he hadn't *already* lost his nerve said a lot more about him than the mask of the carefree prince that he liked to wear.

"Tell Torran what we're doing."

"I already did," Liang said. "He yelled at me, but he and Tavi will help."

Tavi, at least, knew that I wouldn't leave Varro behind. We moved to the edge of the container, and I finally figured out where we were—on the opposite side from Tavi and Torran. On the floor between us, Varro and Fev continued to fight. Varro was unarmed while Fev had a glowing red plas blade.

From the way he moved, Varro was hurting, and his armor was smoking where Fev's plas blade had had time to cut deep, which meant he wasn't countering her locks as quickly, either.

But Fev also moved like she was hurting, and while I watched, Morten crawled away from her. She dragged him back with her power while fending off Varro. She, too, was tiring if she wasn't keeping Morten constantly telelocked. A crushed pistol was on the ground beside the commodore.

Liang turned to me. "Plan?"

"She's getting tired. How do we use that?"

"Or she's acting that way to draw us back in," Liang countered. "Fiazefferia are trained to fight through all kinds of brutal conditions. She doesn't need to lock us to kill us with that blade."

I tilted my head in thought. We couldn't take her with us because we had no way to subdue her, but leaving her here to wreak havoc on an FHP installation *also* seemed like a bad idea. That left killing her, but we hadn't had very good luck with that so far. Plus, the murder of a Sun Guardian came with its own host of diplomatic issues.

Same with abducting Commodore Morten. It was better to leave him here, escape, and then publicly hit him with the mountain of evidence I'd been gathering. So really, we just needed to buy Varro enough time to slip away. Then, hopefully, Fev would retreat rather than fight an entire base of soldiers when she was already tiring.

I focused my mind on Varro, on how our connection had felt, and waited for a lull in the fight. The last thing I wanted to do was distract him at a critical moment. When the two fighters broke apart to warily circle each other, I concentrated and asked, "How can I help?"

The cool feeling of Varro's mind swept into mine along with a flood of worry and more than a little exhaustion. "Get to the ship," he growled.

"I'm not leaving you behind, so either plan with me or be surprised by what I come up with on my own."

The string of Valovan curses came across perfectly, but the connection wavered when he had to dodge another strike from Fev.

Before I could press him, a bright flash of light, far too close, triggered a deeply ingrained response, and I tackled Liang, flattening us to the top of the cargo container. Across the way, both Tavi and Torran were horizontal, too. Fev and Varro fought on, but Morten had paled in fear.

"What's going on?" Liang demanded at the same time Varro asked, "What happened?"

"Plas cannon," I shouted, knowing Varro would pick up the words, too. "Keep your head down. We need to get off this container."

Without getting up, I twisted to glance behind me, in the general direction where I thought the pulse had originated. I didn't see any obvious soldiers, but that didn't mean they weren't there.

Based on the way the pulse had ricocheted, the soldiers had tuned it for station warfare, which meant it would reflect off metallic surfaces with only minor damage, but it would burn straight through any flesh it contacted. Liang's armor *might* protect him, since the plas cannon wasn't set to its most lethal setting, but I'd rather not stick around and find out.

I had nearly decided to take my chance with Fev on the deck when the obnoxious alarm shut off, leaving us in eerie silence.

I checked my pockets and sighed in relief when I found that I still had Tavi's comm—and it still worked. I pulled up the vid feed. A platoon of soldiers in full FHP battle armor were approaching our location from the center of the landing bay.

Four of them carried shoulder-mounted plas cannons and two more were perched atop stacks of cargo containers to snipe at us from a distance. They weren't taking any chances with a telekinetic and were prepared to light up this part of the landing bay to defeat her.

We needed to get out *right now.*

I could feel Varro's concern, but I didn't have time to reassure him. I pushed myself up into a crouch, then waved until I caught Tavi's attention. I quickly signed, "There's a platoon on its way with six plas cannons."

She signed back, "How far?"

"Not far. A couple of minutes."

Tavi's eyes widened, and a second later, her voice echoed across the comm. "Time to go! Anja, get the ship ready to launch. You have my permission to override every order from flight control. Kee, give me a thumbs-up if you can still hear me."

I raised my thumb.

"Our priority is getting Varro clear," she said. "Don't engage Fev unless there's no other option."

A blinding flash of light passed close enough that I could feel the heat. Tavi's plan was well and good, but if we stayed here, the FHP soldiers would dial in their aim.

I turned to Liang. "I'm going over the edge because I need to help Varro, and I want to snag one of those helmets. You should sprint for the far side, then jump down and head for the ship. The soldiers won't be able to adjust their aim in time."

Varro, who was still in my head, growled, "Go with Liang." His mental voice sounded distressingly fatigued.

"I told you I'm not leaving without you. I will distract her, you disable her," I replied. "Then we'll run for the ship—*together*."

I got back a begrudging acknowledgment and a whispered, "Please be careful."

Rather than getting up and running, Liang sighed and pulled himself to the edge of the container. "Let's do this. Try not to die."

I smiled at him. "Same to you."

We both slipped over the edge of the container. Liang lowered himself with pure strength while I relied on a method I called "controlled falling." Both of us hit the deck on our feet, Liang just did it a whole lot more gracefully.

I unclipped the plas blade from its place on the outside of Liang's thigh. "Why do I get the idea that you're about to do something stupid?" he asked softly.

I gave him my best innocent look, but even our short acquaintance seemed to be enough for him to realize he shouldn't trust it. I tucked the plas blade in my pocket, out of sight.

Fev spun toward us, a vicious smile on her face. Behind her, Varro stood frozen.

"Told you she was faking," Liang growled, stepping between me and the telekinetic.

"She didn't lock us," I whispered back. "She's tired and struggling to hold Varro. We just need enough time to make a run for it. Punch her in the face."

"I doubt she's going to fall for that again," Liang said drily.

"You never were the best strategist," Fev said to Liang, disappointment in her voice, "but I expected better than this. At least I won't have to waste time tracking you down. Die now and I won't kill the rest of the crew."

"Leave now, and we won't kill you," Liang responded.

Fev laughed. "You and what army?"

I looked behind me, hoping to see the FHP platoon, but the universe refused to oblige. If only the flunky in security had checked the vid faster, I could've had a truly epic moment where I spun and grandly declared, "This one!" before running for my life.

"You don't think you're a match for me, do you?" Fev taunted.

"Don't let her rile you," I whispered. "She's trying to goad you into a mistake."

"I'm not *that* bad at strategy," Liang murmured back.

Torran softly dropped to the deck behind Varro, three chunks of metal in his hands. They were roughly cut, about palm-size, and looked like they'd started their life as part of a cargo container.

"Keep her attention," Varro murmured into my mind. "And don't let on that you can see Torran."

I peeked out from behind Liang. "Are you sure you need to kill the prince? What if you just roughed him up a little? Maybe broke his nose?"

"What are you talking about?" Liang demanded, half turning to me. "You're just going to let her beat me up?"

I waved a hand at him. "It's better than being dead, isn't it? Besides, there are quite a few people who think men with formerly broken noses look rather dashing. It might help you!"

"I don't need *help*. I'm *a prince*."

I wrinkled my nose at him and did not dare let my gaze wander over Fev's shoulder, even when I caught movement in my peripheral vision. I tipped my chin up. "With an attitude like that, you certainly *do* need help. Don't worry, I'll get you fixed up."

Fev had apparently had enough of us, because she started forward, deadly plas blade leading the way.

"Do you think she practices that menacing expression in the mirror?" I asked Liang, my voice pitched to carry. In truth, a telekinetic heading my way with a plas blade was the stuff of nightmares, and it was all I could do not to run screaming.

And, sure enough, her power wrapped around me with a crushing grip.

"Hold on just a little longer," Varro said, his voice a soothing balm despite the fact that I could feel his growing pain. He jerked a step forward and the telelock around me faltered. I didn't care what Liang said, Fev *was* tiring.

Then the three pieces of metal lifted from Torran's hand and streaked toward her. She spun and countered the first two, but the third struck her in the chest hard enough to send her flying. Only her armor saved her from death.

"Run!" Tavi screamed. She had dropped from the cargo container and now stood next to Torran.

I jolted into motion, pushing Liang ahead of me.

Morten stumbled to his feet, taking advantage of the opening we'd created. I jerked the plas blade from my pocket and, after an agonizing moment of doubt, activated it to its nonlethal setting.

As much as Morten deserved to die, and as much as his death would be justified by my earlier torture, killing him in full view of the cameras would ensure the Feds hunted me to the ends of the galaxy—and, by extension, Tavi and the rest of the crew. I couldn't be responsible for that. I *wouldn't*.

The plas blade glowed blue, and I slammed it into Morten's face without a drop of remorse. He screamed as he went down, and I took an extra second to hit him again—*twice*—on my way by.

I bent and scooped up Fev's hopefully undamaged helmet and then pushed my tired body back into a run. I didn't bother looking behind me. If Fev was up, I didn't want to know.

Liang had put some distance between us, but Torran

and Varro waited for me before falling in behind me. I could feel Varro's exhaustion as though it were my own, and I tried to send him mental encouragement. We were almost there. Just a few more minutes.

Tavi sprinted ahead to secure our exit route, and a few seconds later, Chira and Havil appeared at the far end of the corridor created by the piles of containers. The captain stopped to wait for the rest of us, and as she looked back, her eyes widened in horror. *Varro!* I spun, but Varro and Torran were only a few steps back. Fev was still on the ground, as was Morten.

It was only when I looked farther, at the other end of the corridor, that I saw what had alarmed Tavi: a squad of FHP soldiers, with the one in front aiming a plas cannon straight at us. Even if the shot didn't hit directly, the two sets of metallic cargo containers on either side of us would ensure the ricochets finished the job—like shooting fish in a barrel.

Distantly, I heard Tavi shout Torran's name, her voice laced in anguish. But even the telekinetic would be too late this time. There would be no escape. I stared death in the face as despair rose. Varro would never know just how much I cared for him, and that thought made me unbearably sad.

At the last second, Varro shoved Torran ahead, then he jerked me against his chest and curled protectively around me, his feelings an impossible jumble.

The world went white.

CHAPTER THIRTY-TWO

Varro's presence disappeared from my mind so abruptly that it left me reeling. He slumped against me, and his weight nearly drove me to my knees. Behind me, Torran cursed darkly, then he grunted with effort. Metal squealed and the cargo container on our left slid sideways, blocking the plas cannon from view.

Temporarily.

I dropped the helmet I'd been carrying and shifted, trying to help Varro stand, but he slid farther down, too heavy for me to hold. I wrapped my arms around him and froze.

There was a hole in the back of his armor. Panicked static filled my brain. *No.* "Tavi!" I screamed, my voice raw. The captain could fix this. She could fix anything.

Someone tried to take Varro from me, and I snarled at them. Torran got in my face. "I can carry him and you can't. If you want him to live, *let him go.*" I reacted to the command more than the words and opened my arms.

Torran lifted Varro while Havil removed the weapon specialist's helmet. Varro's eyes were closed, his skin pale and waxy.

The static got worse.

Havil put his hands on Varro's face and frowned in concentration. "This is beyond me," the medic said, his words clipped. "We need to get him to the ship. *Immediately.* I'll do what I can as we go."

Someone put the prototype helmet in my hand and closed my nerveless fingers around it. "Systems Engineer Ildez, get that helmet to the ship," Tavi commanded.

The command cut through the static, and I snapped my spine straight and saluted. "Right away, Captain!" I blinked and looked around. Now if only I could remember where the ship was.

Tavi seemed to understand my problem. "Follow me," she said. "Eli, watch her back."

MY FINGERS ACHED BY THE TIME WE BOARDED *STARLIGHT'S Shadow*. But I'd held on to the helmet, just like Tavi had asked me to. Every time I looked at it, the static receded and pain sliced deep.

So I stopped looking at it.

"Get us launched," Tavi shouted. "And get me a line to FOSO I's Command."

"I can do it," I volunteered. Anything to get me away from this Lady-damned helmet.

Tavi's face softened. "You need to be in the medbay."

I looked down at myself, searching for an injury, but I was fine. "Captain—"

"Trust me, Kee." The soft pain in her voice cracked me

open, and snippets of memory slipped though. I shook my head and backed away from her. *No.* I didn't want to remember.

"Eli, go with her."

Eli took the helmet from me and put it in one of the lockers in the cargo bay, then led me toward the medbay. The closer we got, the more I dragged my feet.

"He's alive," Eli said softly. "They got him to the autostab in time."

I sucked in a breath as a wall of pain engulfed me. *Varro.* He'd been shot, and rather than helping, I'd completely fallen to pieces. A sob caught in my throat, and I sank to the floor, trying to make myself as small as possible.

As small as I felt.

Tears burned behind my eyes. I tried to hold them back, but the pain needed an outlet. The world went watery, and I buried my face against my knees.

Seconds later, strong arms wrapped around me and pulled me into a broad chest. "Shhh," Eli whispered. He ran a gentle hand down my back, soothing me with touch and love. "Let it out; that's it."

I cried until I felt like I'd made my own ocean, but Eli never complained. At some point Luna had made herself at home in the narrow gap between my lap and Eli's chest. When my tears slowed, she purred and rubbed her face against me. I scratched her head and she purred harder.

Tucked under Eli's chin, where he couldn't see my face, the question I'd always been too afraid to ask slipped out. "How can you trust me to watch your back when you know that I might fall apart at any moment?"

Eli took a deep breath. I tensed, but his voice, when it

came, was gentle. "We all have a breaking point, and today you pushed well past yours. And even when you broke, you still followed orders and helped the team. I would never hesitate to have you watch my back."

"What if Tavi thinks I'm a liability?" I whispered. It was one of my deepest fears.

Eli gently jostled me in reproof, and Luna chittered at him. "You know she doesn't. She loves you, and she sees your strengths *and* weaknesses. She knows how to compensate, because that's what a good commander does, and Tavi is the best. Unless you think she doesn't know how to do her job . . ."

"Of course I don't think that!"

I could hear Eli's smile in his voice. "I know you don't."

I allowed myself to soak up some of Eli's calm confidence and Luna's unconditional love while I mentally faced everything that had happened today. Yes, I had broken down, but only after sneaking into an FHP base, getting tortured, rescuing Anna and Nick, and then watching Varro nearly die.

That was a lot for *anyone* to handle.

But I had.

I quietly turned the idea around in my mind. I *had* handled it, far past what I would've expected. I was stronger than I gave myself credit for—and stronger than my crew gave me credit for, too. I'd let others cocoon me in safety for too long. I was awesome, and it was about time Varro—and everyone else—realized it.

I set Luna on the ground with a final chin scratch and climbed to my feet. I pulled Eli up and stared in trepidation at the closed medbay door. Just because I was awesome didn't mean that I couldn't use a little backup occasionally. "Will you stay with me?"

"You don't even need to ask."

I stepped forward before I could talk myself out of it. The door slid open and I blinked at the scene within.

I'd been braced for chaos, for blood and death. Instead, I found Varro stripped of his armor in the autostab, his chest rising and falling with his breath. He wasn't conscious, but he was alive, and his color looked better than the pale corpse from my memory.

I sagged against the door frame, and though I'd just cried a sea of tears, more wet my lashes. Eli had told me they'd gotten him into the autostabilization unit in time, but I'd half believed he'd been lying to spare my feelings.

Eli nudged me into the room and the door closed behind us. Liang, still in most of his armor, was on the bed beside the autostab, and Torran was laid out on a third bed. Both men appeared unconscious.

"What happened to them?" I asked, with a wave at Liang and Torran. "Are they okay?"

"Used too much energy," Havil said, his voice tired. The medic was slumped in a chair next to Varro. He looked like he needed to be in a bed, too. "And Torran took quite a bit of damage from Fev." Havil waved a hand before I could launch into a thousand questions. "He'll be fine, but he'll be sore for a couple of days, until I rest enough to heal him."

I swallowed and forced the words past stiff lips. "And Varro?"

"Hurt bad, but we got him stabilized. Prince Nepru helped me patch up the worst of it."

"Liang's a healer?" Eli asked in surprise.

Havil shook his head. "Not exactly." He did not elaborate, and his expression did not invite further questions on the topic.

"So Varro will be okay?" I asked, just to be sure.

Havil nodded. "He still needs additional healing, but the autostab will keep him stable until I recover. Captain Zarola was smart to purchase such a machine." The medic slowly tilted sideways and barely caught himself before he fell off the chair entirely. "Now that you're here, will you keep an eye on him so I can rest?"

"Of course." I rushed to his side. "Here, let me help you into a bed."

Between Eli and me, we got Havil situated on the bed next to Torran. The medic drank two electrolyte drinks back-to-back, then lay down and slipped into sleep with a sigh. I pulled a light sheet over him so he wouldn't get chilled, then turned to the autostab.

After the first glance, I'd carefully avoided looking at Varro, in case it was worse than I'd originally thought. I stepped closer, said a prayer to the Blessed Lady, then lifted my eyes.

Varro had not moved, but his chest expanded with every breath. Breathing on his own was a good sign, right? He had an IV in his left arm and the bruises on his chest had once again darkened to deep purple red. Havil must've been more worried about the hole in his back than any broken ribs he might have.

A sheet covered his legs, so I hoped the visible damage was the worst of it.

Eli stepped up next to me. "You okay?"

I nodded, then slanted a glance at him. "Thank you . . . for earlier."

He wrapped his arm around my shoulders and pulled me into a side hug. "Anytime, friend."

With the panic receding, I realized that I'd left Tavi to get us off Odyssey on her own, without any of the information I had. "Shit, what's our status? What did I miss while I was out of it? Have the Feds attacked yet?"

Eli shook his head. "Ms. Duarte blasted out a broadcast thanking *Starlight's Shadow* for the daring rescue. She carefully didn't name exactly who she'd been rescued *from,* but she let everyone know that we were now safe on Odyssey and heading back to Bastion soon."

I whistled. "Smart."

"Yeah. She also sent a private video message to several of her closest friends explaining the truth of what happened. If anything happens to her, they will take it public. Tavi had fun explaining that one to the station commander."

"I bet she did," I agreed with a smile. "Is Nick okay? And everyone else?"

"Yes. After we were separated from you, Tavi and I got Nick and Ms. Duarte aboard without any trouble. She recorded her message while we went back for you. Everyone is a little beat up and exhausted, but okay."

We'd rescued Anna and Nick, we'd kept the prince alive, and we'd all managed to escape. Relief rushed through me, but there were still a few problems remaining. "Any word on Morten or Fev?"

"Not officially, but the *Triumphant Victory* launched just after us. Tavi tried to get the Feds to stop it, but they refused based on the ship's registration."

I rubbed my face. "They should have surveillance footage of Fev getting into the ship."

"If they do, they're not sharing it."

Trust the Feds to fuck up something so simple. "Speaking of, I need to save some of the footage we pulled down. There are quite a few gems in there that the Feds would hate to have go public. We should be able to use them to discredit Morten and head off whatever stupid plan he had to provoke Empress Nepru into war."

I looked at Varro's still form. The thought of leaving him was like a knife to my chest. I turned to Eli. "Would you mind going to get my slate for me? I'd like to stay—" I bit off the sentence before I could devolve into tears again.

Eli nodded, his expression soft. "Of course. Where is it?"

I gave him directions and sent him off. As soon as the door slid closed behind him, I blew out a slow breath. I knew it was too much to hope that Fev had been removed from the board, but I'd *hoped*. At least her ship didn't have any weapons capable of truly threatening *Starlight*.

I sighed and leaned a hip against the autostab. The display showed that Varro's pulse and respiration were well within expected parameters. Havil had left the hood open, so I grasped Varro's hand.

His skin was warm. *Alive.* Tears dripped down my face. "You need to wake up," I whispered, "so I can yell at you for being so stupid. Who just stands there and lets himself be shot with a plas cannon?"

I wiped my face with shaking fingers. In truth, I knew exactly why he'd done it: the rest of us had been in front of him, either armorless or in armor that was far worse than the Valovian armor he'd been wearing. He'd sacrificed himself for the good of the team. And in his place, I would've done exactly the same thing.

But I was still going to yell at him, just as soon as he woke up.

I felt the lightest brush of a mind against mine. I squeezed his hand and held my breath, but the feeling faded away. My shoulders slumped. *Blessed Lady, please let him wake up soon.*

ELI RETURNED WITH MY SLATE AND A PLATE OF PEANUT BUTTER cookies. He handed me the cookies first. "It's all I could find on short notice that wasn't a meal bar, but I figured you wouldn't mind. Torran and the rest will probably need the extra calories when they wake up, too."

When I moved to set the plate aside, Eli glared pointedly. I picked up a cookie and took a bite. "Happy?" I asked around a mouthful of cookie crumbs.

"Yes, aren't you?"

"Yes," I admitted grouchily. The cookie was delicious, dammit.

Once I'd finished the cookie—and a second, for good measure—Eli handed me the slate. "Are you okay here on your own or would you like me to stay?"

His expression held no judgment, and I knew he'd happily do whichever I preferred. I gave him a soft smile. "I'm good. Thank you."

His chin dipped. "You know how to contact me if you change your mind or if you need any help."

I stood and wrapped him in a hug. "Thank you. Really."

"Don't mention it."

Eli left me alone with the four unconscious Valoffs. I made myself comfortable on the last available bed and opened my slate. First, and most important, I checked on *Starlight*'s datastore. Because I'd long ago decided that more data was better than less data, after I'd gained access to FOSO I's system, I'd set *Starlight* to save a local copy of the surveillance feeds on a three-hour rolling loop.

But when I checked, all of the live feeds were blank. Had the FHP revoked my access or had the ship failed to record everything?

I bit my lip as I checked the last few minutes of the landing bay vid feed that included where *Starlight* had been docked. In the last frame before the video went dark, *Starlight* was missing and several soldiers in full battle armor were standing around.

The backup had worked, at least up until someone had blocked my access. I blew out a relieved breath, then stopped the recording and ensured all of the data was safely stored. I'd have to delete the feeds that weren't important to free up storage, but that could wait.

I flipped through the saved vids, looking for footage of the fight. It took me several minutes to find the right camera. I skipped forward until movement on the screen caught my attention. I watched Morten set up his ambush, then the resulting fight.

The view from above gave me some much-needed distance from the fear and adrenaline, but I skipped over the part where Varro had been shot. I didn't need to see it again, not with him still unconscious in the autostab and our connection painfully absent.

On-screen, Fev, tired though she had to be, had swept aside the FHP soldiers with a wave of power. Then she'd kicked Morten in the head, telekinetically picked up his unconscious body, and draped him over her shoulders. The fact that she didn't just carry him with pure power was a testament to her exhaustion.

She stalked out of the frame, moving more easily than I would've expected.

It took me several minutes to find the feed that included her ship. The recording revealed that she had taken Morten aboard with her before launching.

Blessed Lady and all of her handmaids, she'd abducted an FHP commodore, straight from an FHP base, in full view of the cameras. And while she'd been wearing an FHP uniform, it didn't counteract the fact that she was clearly a telekinetic and therefore a Valoff. If she was trying to start a war, she was doing a bang-up job.

Except I'd thought she wanted to be able to pin the blame on the Feds.

I tipped my head in thought. According to Torran, FHP officials had already told Empress Nepru that Morten was no longer part of the military. So perhaps Fev knew what she was doing after all.

But what did she want with the commodore?

I pondered the question as I started collecting clips of my interactions with Morten. The Feds might have let us go based on Anna's threat, but I still had a bounty on my head. They wouldn't leave us alone for long, not unless I forced their hand.

The audio on the vids from the landing bay wasn't great, especially after the alarm had started, but most of it was at least understandable. It took me nearly thirty minutes to find the footage from the storage room where Morten had tortured me.

And it *was* torture. Watching the replay, I could see the vicious satisfaction in Morten's expression every time he hit me with the plas blade. That I'd withstood it for as long as I had just drove home the fact that I was stronger than I thought. I saved the entire clip, then started searching for the room where they'd kept Varro.

When I found it, I wished I hadn't. The soldiers had drugged Varro in the hallway where we'd initially been caught, then again when they got him into the room. Then they'd stripped off his armor and kicked the shit out of his barely conscious body.

Furious, helpless tears filled my eyes, and I paid special attention to all of the soldiers' faces. When I had more time, I would dig up everything I could find on them, and then I would ruin their lives.

And I would do it as gleefully as they'd kicked Varro.

A faint, comforting touch slid through my mind like a gossamer thread. My eyes darted to Varro, but he remained unconscious. But where there'd been emptiness, I could feel the tiniest hint of a connection.

Varro was healing.

I WAS STILL GOING THROUGH FOOTAGE WHEN LIANG SAT UP WITH a deep groan. "Remind me not to get in a fight with a telekinetic again anytime soon," he grumbled, rubbing his face.

I set my slate aside and rushed over to him. "Are you okay? Do you need help?"

He blinked at me in surprise, then bowed from the waist, his left arm over his chest. "I am, thanks once again to you and your crew. Why didn't you give me to Fev?"

"She wanted you dead."

Liang's smile had a bitter edge. "A lot of people want me dead, it appears."

I wanted to give him a hug, but I wasn't sure if he was hurt, or if he'd appreciate it, so I settled for squeezing his hand. "Well, I don't and neither does the crew. But I'm here if you would like to talk about it."

"My mother and I have rarely seen eye-to-eye, but I never expected . . ." He trailed off and shook his head.

When it became clear that he wasn't going to continue, I asked, "What will you do now?"

"I don't know," Liang said with a sigh. "I only hope that I haven't dragged Siarvez into my troubles."

"Well, I can't speak for the captain officially, but if you need help, Tavi will help you."

Liang nodded, and I squeezed his hand again before changing the subject. "Thank you for helping to heal Varro." Liang tried to wave me off, but I wouldn't let him. "I mean it. If he'd died . . ." I had to swallow before I could continue. "I owe you."

"Let's call it even," Liang murmured. "Would you mind helping me out of this armor? Siarvez helped me put it on, but I'd rather not have to climb up to the main level looking for him."

"Are you wearing anything under there?" I asked with a wobbly grin.

Liang's smile matched my own, except his had a light, wicked edge. "Only one way to find out."

CHAPTER THIRTY-THREE

Much to my relief and Liang's amusement, he *was* wearing the typical thin, stretchy base layer under the armor. He grunted when he had to bend to remove his boots.

"You're hurt," I accused. "Where are you hurt?"

"Just bruised," he said, his voice tight with pain. I helped him remove the boots and he sighed in relief. "Thank you."

"You're welcome. But maybe you should stay here until Havil can take a look at you."

Liang waved me off. "Havil will have his hands full with Varro and Torran. I will mend on my own." He turned to me, expression serious. "But let me know when Havil is ready to heal Varro again. I will assist."

"He said you weren't a healer."

"I'm not." He lapsed into silence, and I didn't press. He stared at me, and after a long moment, he said, "I'm an amplifier."

I frowned in thought. "So you amplify another Valoff's ability?"

Liang laughed. "I thought you'd be more impressed. We're quite rare and valuable, you know."

"You must be, because I've never heard of an amplifier. But I'd never heard of a teleporter, either, not until—" I clamped my mouth shut. Nilo's secret wasn't mine to reveal. "Let me try again." I clasped my hands together in front of my chest and widened my eyes to comic proportions. "*Wow!* An amplifier, I can't believe it!"

One corner of Liang's mouth rose in a self-deprecating smile. "You joke, but I've gotten that exact reaction before, more often than not, actually."

I let the act go and gave him a genuine smile. "I think it's amazing, don't get me wrong. I was just too busy trying to figure out how it worked to express my admiration."

"In simple terms, another Valoff gives me a little of their power, and I give it back in multiples. Havil needed to heal Varro, but the medic was already exhausted. So we worked together. Havil essentially used my power to heal Varro, even though I can't heal on my own."

"That really *is* incredible." I looked at Varro. Thanks to Liang and Havil, he was still breathing. "Thank you."

Liang looked away. "It was the least I could do, considering what I owe you."

I gently nudged his shoulder. "I thought we decided we were even."

Liang shook off his melancholy. "True enough. Now I'm going to go upstairs and see if I can guilt Siarvez into cooking something for me. Do I look pitiful enough?" He tipped his chin up and gave me a haughty look.

I laughed, just as he'd intended. "Oh, yes, no doubt. Very

pitiful." I remembered the cookies. "Here, have a cookie to help power you up the stairs."

Liang nodded his thanks, took a cookie, then left the medbay with a wave.

I looked around the room at the remaining unconscious Valoffs. Three more to go.

DESPITE MY INTENTION TO KEEP VIGIL OVER VARRO ALL NIGHT, MY body had other ideas. I didn't so much slip into sleep as plunge into it like a falling meteor.

I awoke with a crick in my neck and the memory of a soothing presence.

As the cobwebs cleared, I realized it wasn't *just* a memory—I could still feel the connection to Varro, faint but stronger than yesterday.

I slid from my bed and rushed to his side, but if he'd moved at all, I couldn't tell.

Tavi brought me breakfast and tried to coax me from the medbay, but I parked myself on Liang's empty bed and refused to leave. The captain—who always knew which battles were futile—handed me a subvocal mic replacement so I could talk to the crew and let me stay with an admonishment to rest.

To keep myself occupied, I spent the morning digging up as much information on Morten and his team as I could, and I talked to Varro while I worked. Occasionally, our connection would flare and I would feel the smallest brush of a cool mind against mine, but Varro remained deeply unconscious.

Torran woke after lunch. He checked on Havil, Varro, and me, then went up to help Tavi. He was bruised to hell and moved like he was hurting, but I *also* knew which battles were doomed to fail, so I didn't try to persuade him to stay in the medbay.

Havil woke an hour later, looking gaunt and worn. He stumbled when he slid from the bed. I dropped my slate and rushed to his side. "Easy there, cowboy," I murmured. "You're not looking so hot. Pretty sure a medic would tell you to stay in bed."

He flashed me a tired smile. His deep brown skin had an unhealthy pallor and there were bruises under his eyes. "Medics make the worst patients," he confided.

I slanted a dry look at him. "You don't say."

That earned me a rusty chuckle, but Havil still moved toward Varro to check the weapon specialist's vitals and stats. I hovered at Havil's side, ready to catch him—or at least slow his fall.

After he confirmed Varro was stable, I sent him upstairs with a cookie and Eli acting as a crutch. Havil grumbled, but he leaned on the first officer's arm. On their way out the door, Eli glanced over his shoulder and mouthed, "Thank you."

I nodded at him, then resumed my place on the bed closest to Varro and continued my research.

The files I'd pulled from Fev's server were especially enlightening. A lot of them were orders to Morten from FHP Command. For someone who wasn't supposed to be part of the military anymore, he sure got a lot of direct orders from someone in Command.

The orders themselves were carefully vague, and sent via unofficial communication channels, but the gist seemed to be that Morten was authorized to do whatever it took to get FHP ships into Valovian space. The Feds wanted access to the Valovian wormholes.

As did the conglomerates.

Powerful forces wanted the resources that expansion into the Valovian Empire would give us, and they didn't care how that expansion was achieved. Morten had taken that authorization and run. When his initial plan of kidnapping Empress Nepru's heir had failed, he'd changed tactics, potentially without Command's support. Either that, or those orders were in the files I hadn't been able to retrieve.

As far as I could tell, Command had *not* authorized Morten to attack Bastion and abduct an FHP citizen. Perhaps because they knew exactly how bad it would look if the truth leaked.

But there was definitely a contingent in Command who supported his efforts, no matter how extreme. There had to be, because Morten could not have pulled off an attack of this size and complexity without someone helping him from a high level.

I needed to find *that* person, hopefully before Sura Fev used Morten for whatever she had planned.

Because I'd tracked *Triumphant Victory.* The ship was faster than *Starlight,* and it was headed straight for the wormhole to Valovian space. I didn't know how Fev had gotten the initial authorization to cross into Fed space, but Morten was probably responsible for her current authorization. Either that, or the Valoffs were deeper in our systems than we'd like to believe.

I rubbed my eyes and checked the time. It was after midnight, and my dinner sat untouched on the end of the bed. I vaguely remembered Anja delivering it, but then the research had pulled me back in.

I set aside my slate and stretched my arms overhead. I should sleep. I still had to persuade Bastion's commander to drop the bounty on Liang and me in return for the key to their systems, and I needed to be sharp for that conversation.

But I'd been holding on to hope all day that Varro would wake, and I hated to surrender before that happened. "I wish you'd wake up and tell me to go to sleep," I whispered to Varro. "If you did, I might even listen to you."

Nothing happened. I tried not to worry. I could still feel the connection in the back of my mind, and both Torran and Havil had been out for over fourteen hours—and they hadn't been badly beaten and then critically wounded while using so much energy.

I understood why Varro remained unconscious, but I still hated it.

The medbay door slid open and Havil and Liang strode inside, both looking far better than the last time I'd seen them. I tried not to get my hopes up, but I was really bad at it.

Havil smiled gently at me. "I'm going to heal him again, but he still might not wake. He expended vast amounts of energy and suffered enormous trauma. Don't be discouraged if he doesn't jump out of bed."

I nodded, throat tight. I swallowed until I could speak. "Should I wait outside?"

"Only if you want to," Havil replied.

I sighed in relief and shook my head.

Havil put his hands on Varro's chest while Liang gripped Havil's upper arm. Havil frowned in concentration, and something in the air changed. It felt like the prelude to a thunderstorm, a heaviness full of potential energy.

Dear Lady, please let this work.

Havil's jaw clenched, then a few minutes later, he lifted his hands and nodded to the man next to him. I slipped from my bed and circled to the far side of the autostab. "Varro?"

For a long, heartbreaking moment, nothing happened. His chest was still bruised, though it was the sickly yellow-green of healing rather than the furious purple-red it had been before. I clutched Varro's hand, unable to give up so easily. "I need you to wake up," I whispered. "Please wake up."

The coolness in my mind grew, swirling with pain and regret and fondness. A moment later, Varro telepathically whispered, "Kee."

I burst into tears.

Varro's eyes blinked open, and he lifted a hand to my face. "Shh," he said. "I'm okay. Don't cry."

"You're not going to be okay when I kill you for risking yourself like that," I threatened. "I was so worried!" I took a deep breath and tried to get my tear ducts to cooperate for once.

It didn't work.

Varro tried to sit up, but Havil's hand on his shoulder stopped him. "Let me remove the IV first. How are you feeling?"

"Like shit," Varro admitted, his voice rough. "But thank you for pulling me through. How long was I out? Is anyone else hurt?"

"Everyone else is fine. You were out for thirty hours, give or take, and it was close," Havil said. He shut down the autostab, removed the IV, and then shook his head. "If you could avoid major injuries for a week or two, I'd appreciate it."

"I'll do my best," Varro said.

"You'd better," I growled.

Havil smiled at me, then turned his attention to Varro. "Sit up, slowly. Let me know if anything hurts more than it should."

Varro pushed himself up with a groan. I wiped my eyes and looked at his back. Smooth, unblemished skin met my disbelieving gaze. I'd *felt* the hole in his armor. I lifted my eyes to Havil. "That's unbelievable. Thank you," I murmured, overcome.

Havil looked up from his examination of Varro's back and met my eyes across the autostab's bed. "You're welcome." He gestured to Varro. "Swing your legs off the bed and face me."

Varro did, and Havil checked his eyes. "Light exercise is fine," the medic said, "but your ribs will remain tender for a while. If you have any sharp pains, come to see me immediately. Do you understand?"

Varro bowed forward, his left arm across his chest. "Thank you."

Havil nodded, then he ushered Liang from the room. I rounded the autostab, until I was standing in front of Varro. My eyes flitted over the fading bruises on his chest. "If you *ever* do something like that again—" I started before my anger wobbled into terror, and my throat closed up.

Varro wrapped an arm around my waist and drew me close, until I was standing between his legs, leaning against his chest. His heart beat a reassuring rhythm under my cheek. He clasped the back of my neck and buried his face in my hair. "I'm sorry I scared you," he murmured.

I huffed out a breath at that vast understatement. I

drew back, and he let my neck go, but his hands settled on my waist, keeping me close.

"We are even," I said, my voice harsh in my own ears. "No more pseudo life debt, no more doing my chores, no more cookies. We are even, and if you can't accept that, then I can't—"

My voice broke and I swallowed the sea of tears that lurked behind my eyes. "You almost died, Varro."

Varro's expression hardened. "You had no armor. You *would have* died. And I would die a thousand deaths to spare you one."

"I don't want you to die *any* deaths! Every time you're hurt, it breaks a piece of me."

Varro's jaw clenched and his hands flexed on my waist. "I apologize. Hurting you was never my intention."

"I know; that's why I'm telling you. I lo—*like* you, Varro. *A lot.*" I barely kept the true confession locked behind my teeth, unsure of the reception. I'd felt the depth of Varro's care, but care wasn't necessarily love. I knew I was racing ahead again, but I'd had plenty of time to think over the last thirty hours. Varro, however, had barely woken. I would not rush him into an admission he wasn't ready—or willing—to make.

"Hisi las," he murmured. *"Cho arbu chil tavoz." My heart is yours.*

The phrase had the solemn weight of a vow. Bright, aching joy filled my chest, drowning out the worry. Varro pulled me closer, heat in his gaze. I raised my head and his lips brushed mine, gentle and heartbreaking.

I'd almost lost him.

I hugged him close, and as if he felt my need for reassurance, his mouth slanted across mine, hot and demanding.

I gasped, and he plundered deep. Desire slammed into me, and I moaned against his lips.

But I couldn't get distracted. Varro was a master of avoiding questions. I pulled back, even as my hormones screamed in protest. "Wait," I murmured.

Varro grumbled a denial, but he let me go.

"Do you agree that we're even? No more debt?"

Varro nodded. *"Cho wubr chil choz." My life is mine.*

I let out a shaky sigh. "Thank you."

"I will still protect you," Varro vowed. "I can do no less."

"That's okay, as long as I can protect you, too. We can protect each other."

"We'll protect each other," he agreed softly. "I wouldn't want anyone else watching my back." He reached for me, then paused as his stomach gave a ferocious growl. He looked down, as if his body had betrayed him.

"Speaking of protecting each other," I said, "it looks like I need to protect you from hunger. I have my leftover dinner, but it's hours old. Let's go see what we can round up in the galley, since I ate all the cookies you made. If nothing else, I make a mean mac and cheese."

"You would cook for me?" Varro asked, an odd, hopeful note in his voice.

"Of course. Just don't expect world-class cuisine or anything. I can handle the basics, but I leave the fancy stuff to Tavi."

MIDNIGHT MAC AND CHEESE WAS ONE OF MY FAVORITE COMFORT foods, so I made it for Varro. Despite the hour, I made a huge pot, because we were getting close to Bastion and the rest of the crew was still up.

Varro tried to help, but I waved him to his seat at the table. He cooked for me all the time, the least I could do was return the favor. I'd barely finished stirring everything together when Eli entered the galley, following his nose. "Tell me you made enough to share," he pleaded.

I scooped out a giant bowl for Varro, a smaller bowl for me, and then tilted my head at the pot and nodded. "Save some for everyone else."

Eli grinned in anticipation, then gently clapped Varro's shoulder. "Good to see you up. You had us worried there for a bit."

"I'm glad to be up. I owe Havil a great deal."

I mixed Varro an electrolyte replacement drink, then gave it to him along with the enormous bowl of mac and cheese. My stomach had tied itself into knots, but I took my own bowl and glass of water and sat across from him in my usual seat.

Varro leaned forward with his left arm over his chest. "Thank you."

I flushed. "You're welcome. Now eat it before it gets cold. Let me know if you want more, and I'll wrestle the leftovers away from Eli. Or if you don't like it, I'll make you something else." I snapped my jaw shut to cut off the rambling stream of words.

Varro nodded and took a bite. His eyes lit. "It's delicious," he murmured. "Thank you."

I smiled at him and dug into my own bowl. It *was* a pretty good batch. Soon, more people trickled in, until we had to pull extra chairs from the second table to accommodate everyone.

Nick looked better than they had in the landing bay. Anna somehow made the plain, stretchy clothes she'd borrowed from our rescue stockpile look chic, and Nick's eyes rarely left her.

Liang was also moving better, and he and Siarvez laughed and joked with the rest of the crew. But I noticed that Liang's smiles weren't quite as bright as they'd been before. His mother's betrayal had to be weighing on him.

Tavi wrapped her arms around me from behind. "I'm happy to see you out of the medbay," she whispered. She continued subvocally over the comm, "Is Varro okay?"

"Yes," I responded in kind. "He's still bruised, but Havil healed the wound in his back. There's not even a scar. It's incredible."

Tavi squeezed me again. "I'm glad."

"How is Torran?"

"Bruised and grumpy," Tavi said with a laugh. "But now that Varro is up, he'll have one less worry."

By unspoken agreement, we kept conversation light while everyone ate, but once the dishes were cleared away, Tavi sighed. "We'll arrive at Bastion in an hour or two. The base is still down, so the traffic is worse than ever." She looked down the table to Anna and Siarvez. "Are your ships still docked or did they make it out?"

"My ship is still docked," Anna said, "but the crew is aboard and waiting on launch clearance."

"My ship launched a few hours ago," Siarvez said. "They should be nearby because I told them to wait on this side of the station."

"Did Bastion take damage from the initial rush?" I asked.

Tavi shook her head. "Nothing serious. They got lucky. So did the ships, honestly. Some minor hull damage and sheared off antennas. You took the worst of it. Those dumbasses nearly killed you."

I wrinkled my nose at the reminder. Varro's expression darkened, so I changed the subject. "Have you heard anything from the Feds?"

"They've been surprisingly quiet," Tavi said. "Makes me nervous."

"I have the key to fix Bastion," I said, "but I'm going to need to talk to the station commander, Rear Admiral Emma Ohashi. She wasn't included in any of Morten's communications, but that doesn't necessarily mean anything. However, some of her underlings definitely *were* communicating with Morten, so going to the top will at least tell us how deep his connections go."

"Do you want to wake her up now or wait until the morning?" Tavi asked.

Could I sleep tonight, knowing that I had to confront a station commander tomorrow? Probably not. "Let's wake her. I'm sure she'll want her station up and running as quickly as possible."

"Will they really be willing to drop my bounty?" Liang asked, leaning forward so he could see me.

"Yes. I have a mountain of evidence against them and no qualms about leaking it publicly. Still, I think you should stay on *Starlight* until we confirm that everything is settled."

"I will stay, as long as the captain will have me." At Tavi's nod, Liang met my gaze and said, "I am once again in your debt."

I shook my finger at him. "Nope. I'm done with debts. I refuse."

Liang's face lit with amusement, but he bowed his head in apparent agreement.

My eyes narrowed. That was too easy, but I didn't have

time to worry about it right now. I turned to Tavi. "Should we go through the official channels, or should we call Admiral Ohashi's personal comm?"

Tavi thought about it for a second, then looked at Torran. "You were a fancy general. What do you think? Which would've made you listen?"

Next to me, Torran tipped his head in thought. "Calling her personal comm will cut through a lot of the bullshit, but it's also a risk." He glanced at me. "Can you record the conversation?"

I smiled. "Of course."

"Then I'd say call her personal comm but be careful. If it becomes clear that she's with Morten, you can go through the official channels to go over her head. So far, the FHP has left us alone because of Ms. Duarte's presence. That should still serve as a deterrent, at least long enough to find someone who isn't a traitor."

Tavi nodded. "I agree. Let me know when you find her address and are ready to make the call."

"I've already found it." I blew out a heavy breath, then added, "I'm ready now."

Somehow, no one called me on the lie.

CHAPTER THIRTY-FOUR

Varro pulled me into a hug, putting a stop to my nervous pacing across the bridge. Tavi was getting everything ready, so our talk with the station commander wouldn't give away more than we wanted. I should've been helping her, but instead I was having an intense case of anxiety.

"Shhh," Varro soothed. He radiated calm. Wrapped in his strong arms, my pulse began to slow. I laid my head on his chest and matched my breathing to his. One by one, tense muscles relaxed and the bottomless pit of anxiety in my stomach shrank to just normal butterflies.

"That's it," he murmured a few minutes later, his voice a rumble against my cheek.

I lifted my head and peeked at the rest of the room. Tavi and Torran were facing away from us, and Tavi had banished everyone else from the bridge, so Varro and I were in our own little bubble.

"Do you think this will work?" I asked, my voice barely a whisper.

"You'll make it work," Varro said with absolute conviction. "If the station commander won't listen to reason, you'll find someone who will."

I grinned at him. "I do tend to be persistent."

He stroked his fingers along my jaw. "And smart. And loyal. And brave."

My breath caught at the raw honesty in his voice. "You think so?"

His thumb brushed over my lips, and his voice deepened. "I know so."

"Kiss me for luck?"

A smile tipped up one corner of his mouth. "I'll kiss you for any reason you like."

"Then kiss me because you want to."

He brushed his lips across my cheek, a tease and a promise. I clutched him closer, and his mouth settled over mine, firm and possessive. Desire burned through my blood. I yielded to his tongue and was rewarded with a groan from deep in his chest.

I could feel Varro's desire echoing across the connection we still shared, and it pushed my own passion higher. I moaned into his mouth, chasing his tongue.

His arms tightened, until I was plastered to his front. He groaned again, then pulled back, kissing me gently before sweeping his lips across my cheek to whisper in my ear, "I believe we've embarrassed your captain."

It took a second for the words to penetrate the fog of lust, but when they did, I chuckled against Varro's shoulder. "I doubt it," I murmured. "She's known Eli too long for that."

Sure enough, when I peeked at her, Tavi was grinning broadly. She winked at me. "We're ready when you are," she said, laughter in her voice.

I kissed Varro again, just a light brush of my lips. "Thank you for calming me down." I glanced up at him from under my eyelashes. "And for heating me up."

A slow, wicked smile bloomed across his mouth, like dawn breaking across the sky. "My pleasure. And I'll be here if you need me."

I squeezed his shoulders in a quick hug, then turned to Tavi. "I'm ready." And thanks to Varro, this time the words didn't feel so much like a lie.

TAVI AND I SAT SIDE-BY-SIDE WHILE VARRO AND TORRAN WAITED AT the edge of the bridge, out of view of the camera. Tavi sent the connection request to Admiral Ohashi's personal comm.

The connection was approved almost immediately. Tavi raised her eyebrows at me just before the video connected. Despite the hour, Admiral Ohashi was perfectly put together. She had dark eyes, pale skin, and dark hair streaked with gray that was pulled back into a low ponytail. She was wearing a white blouse, and she had taken the call from what appeared to be her office.

Her office that had fully functioning lights and equipment. It made sense that the station commander's office would run perfectly on backup power, but that didn't help any of the thousands of people on the station who were making do with dim emergency lights and nonfunctioning doors.

Ohashi didn't smile, but she nodded, as if she'd expected us. "Captain Zarola, Ms. Ildez, what can I do for you?"

I grimaced. "To start, you can call me Kee." Ohashi nodded, and I continued, "You don't seem surprised to hear from us."

"We've been tracking *Starlight* since you left Odyssey. Not only do you have one of the biggest names in fashion aboard, but you are also carrying a Valovian prince who's wanted for the attack on Bastion." She tipped her head at me. "As are you."

I stared at the screen without a flicker of emotion, but I wanted to smile at her. At least someone was paying attention. Beside me, Tavi's face was set into a polite, blank mask. She was letting me take the lead, but she was here to throw her weight behind me when I needed it.

"So you have talked to FOSO I?" I asked, my voice mild.

The corners of Ohashi's mouth turned down. "I have."

"And what did they tell you?"

"That you attacked unprovoked. But they refuse to share their surveillance footage. Apparently they had 'technical difficulties.'" Her eyebrows rose. "Do you know anything about that?"

"Their surveillance system worked fine; they just don't like that it disputes their claims." My smile was full of teeth. "Luckily, I have a backup of the relevant vid feeds if they've misplaced theirs."

Ohashi's smile was as sharp as my own. "While I appreciate the offer, we've been monitoring FOSO I for months. I have my own people in place."

"Which side are those people on, Admiral?"

She didn't pretend to misunderstand. "Frank Morten is a traitor. His behavior does not reflect our goal of maintaining peace between the Federated Human Planets and the Valovian Empire."

"Several of your peers would disagree with you."

Her chin dipped. "As would a third of the senate." I was still recovering from the shock of that revelation when she continued, "But Fleet Command doesn't take their orders from a fascist minority. We've been trying to quietly root out the traitors in our ranks, but they have powerful people protecting them."

"Then it sounds like you *do* take your orders from a fascist minority," Tavi said. Her voice sounded deceptively calm, but I could hear the fury underneath the even tone.

And so could Admiral Ohashi. Her jaw clenched. "Fleet Command has been reluctant to rock the boat," she agreed. "But this latest attack was enough to finally prod them into doing more. However, we need Morten to stand trial for his crimes."

I snorted. "Good luck. That weasel's been avoiding consequences for *years*. But you're welcome to try. He's aboard the *Triumphant Victory* with a telekinetic Valoff, and they're on their way to the wormhole to Valovian space."

"We can't stop the ship," Ohashi said.

"Of course you can't," Tavi muttered.

The admiral ignored her. "Once we approached, they started broadcasting diplomatic registrations, from both the FHP and the Valovian Empire. Both are genuine."

I rolled my eyes. "Well, once they're through the wormhole, he's as good as gone, so you'd better come up with a plan fast."

Ohashi's eyes gleamed in a way that I didn't like at all, and I held up my hands to ward off whatever she wanted. "Nope, leave us out of it. This is your problem. You fix it."

"*Starlight's Shadow* already has authorization to traverse the wormhole. The FHP can't send ships across, but we can send *you*."

Tavi's fists clenched. "No. We've bled enough for the FHP. Do you own dirty work."

Ohashi's expression hardened. "I will draft you if I have to."

"You can *try*," Tavi taunted, her smile glinting like an unsheathed blade. "I wouldn't recommend it, though, unless you want the public to know what really happened on Rodeni—and on Bastion and Odyssey. We will bury you in public outrage, and then we'll disappear."

Ohashi stared her down, but when Tavi refused to concede, the admiral nodded once. "We are prepared to offer you a bounty contract for Morten." She held up a hand to cut off Tavi's protest. "Voluntary, naturally."

"I decline," Tavi said.

The admiral raised her eyebrows. "Don't you want to hear the terms?"

"No."

I suppressed my grin. Tavi could be stubborn and tenacious when she was angry, and right now, she was furious. She still hadn't forgiven Ohashi for the draft threat, and I didn't blame her. Usually, I'd persuade her to listen to the offer, as I had with Torran, but crossing the wormhole to retrieve Morten was just asking for trouble.

Ohashi, however, was undeterred. "Successful retrieval pays a million Federated credits. Proof of death—before he gets to the empress—pays half."

I choked on air and spluttered out a cough. Blessed Lady, that was a fortune by any standard. Federated credits were the most valuable currency in the galaxy, and a million of them would set us up for a decade, at least.

Tavi, however, remained as cool as ice. "And what does it pay when we all die as soon as we traverse the wormhole?"

"In the unlikely event that you perish while hunting Morten, your families will be compensated with a hundred thousand Fed credits each."

Ohashi sighed and rubbed her eyes, looking for the first time like a tired woman rather than an impassive statue. "Empress Nepru can't get her hands on Morten. He knows too much. War would be the least of our problems, especially with the division we're already facing."

"Problems FHP Command and the FHP Senate allowed to fester," Tavi pointed out. "And even now, when you're asking for our help, you're allowing the bounty on Kee and Prince Liang to stand when you have to know they had nothing to do with the attack."

"It's being taken care of," Ohashi said. "It should be removed within the hour."

"And are you going to send out another emergency blast, saying that you accused the wrong people? Because right now, the entire station thinks my systems engineer was responsible for a brutal attack on one of FHP's prized jewels and a fashion industry icon."

A muscle in Ohashi's jaw flexed, but she said, "It will be done."

"Then we can talk about the bounty after it *is* done."

"In a few hours the *Victory* be at the wormhole anchor, which can only hold them for a short amount of time, and it will take you at least ten hours catch up. I need your answer now."

"Then my answer is no. Surely you have another crew stupid enough to try. Hire them."

"Your crew is uniquely suited to this task, and you know it. Sending anyone else would be sending them to their death."

"And yet you are okay sending us to our deaths. Why is that, Admiral?"

"I've seen the footage from FOSO I's landing bay. You held your own."

"Then you've seen FHP soldiers shoot one of my crew members without provocation," Tavi said quietly. The quieter Tavi got, the more furious she was.

Ohashi flinched. "You must admit, wearing Valovian armor in an FHP base—"

"Is not against the law," Tavi interrupted. "Why should I help you, any of you?"

"I know the FHP failed you, and I know that you owe me nothing, but I am trying to prevent a war, Captain. Right now, I have Fleet Command's attention and backing, but I don't know how long I can hold it before the warmongers make a stronger case. Exposing Morten would spur change."

"Or it would get covered up, hidden away, just like everything else."

"It might," Ohashi agreed. "But it might not. Will you stand idly by while the assholes win? When you have possibly the only team in the entire FHP that is qualified to track down Morten in the Valovian Empire?"

Ah, she meant because we had Valoffs on our crew now, specifically Torran. Fighting a telekinetic was an iffy battle *with* Torran on our side, but at least we'd made it through alive. Another team would not.

My heart twisted. Fuck it all, she was persuasive, even if the very last thing I wanted to do was tangle with Fev again. But we'd been trying to prevent a war since we rescued the empress's grandson. Here was an opportunity to expose the rot in the FHP. Maybe. If Admiral Ohashi was playing fair—which I would dig into just as soon as this call ended.

"If we're ideally suited, then you can find some more money in the budget," Tavi said. "But I still won't take the job without talking to my crew."

Ohashi's eyes narrowed, but she dipped her chin in reluctant acceptance. "Was there anything else?"

Below the view of the camera, Tavi wrote on her terminal screen: *Sell her the key she needs. Not less than 100k.*

I grinned. "Yes, there is one more thing, Admiral."

AFTER SECURING A PROMISE FROM THE ADMIRAL THAT SHE WOULD immediately transfer a hundred twenty thousand Fed credits in return for the encryption key, Tavi disconnected the call.

I blew out a breath and slumped in the seat I'd pulled over next to Tavi's terminal. "Well, that was a lot," I murmured, then slanted a glance at Tavi. "What will you do?"

She rubbed her face. "I'm surprised you're not already advocating for going after Fev."

"We started hunting Morten in order to prevent a war. This would just be a continuation of that, only now we'd get a huge payment for doing what we were doing for free before."

"In Valovian space," Varro growled, unable to hold his silence. "Where the empress already wants you dead."

"True enough. But what happens when Fev delivers Morten directly to her, along with the records she pulled from Bastion that prove part of the FHP is willing to do whatever it takes to get into Valovian space, including kidnapping the empress's grandson? Is the empress just going to decide oh, never mind, we don't need a war after all?"

Varro's jaw clenched along with his fists, but he couldn't deny my words. The empress *would* use Morten and his actions to start a war.

Torran looked at Tavi. She dipped her head with a sigh, and Torran said, "I have a way to get to Valovia without being killed. The empress has ordered my return and promised safe passage for *Starlight* and the crew. I have a guaranteed writ, and it has been posted publicly. She will honor it, at least until we land."

Tavi didn't show a flicker of surprise—she'd already known.

"You were planning to go to Valovia anyway?" I asked her.

"No, I was *planning* to avoid it like the black hole that it is, promise of safe passage or otherwise. It's a trap, of course. Just like Ohashi's request."

"You think the admiral is working with Morten?"

Slowly, Tavi shook her head. "But I think she's perfectly happy sending us into danger while she waits here in safety and does nothing about the traitors in her ranks." She blew out a slow breath. "There's no good answer."

A piercing alarm sounded from Tavi's comm, followed a moment later by mine. The emergency alert was a notice that Liang and I were exonerated from all involvement in the attack on Bastion, and our bounties were rescinded. Additionally, it listed the new person of interest as Frank Morten—with a picture of him in uniform.

So Ohashi had decided to throw down a gauntlet after all.

Tavi swore under her breath, because if Ohashi truly meant to root out the rot in the FHP, we would have to help her. And helping her meant putting ourselves in danger, again.

Tavi hit the ship's intercom. "*Starlight* crew, report to the bridge. Everyone else, sit tight for a bit."

A moment later, the door opened. Eli was the first in, followed by Chira, Havil, and Anja. "How'd it go?" Eli asked. He held up his comm with the emergency alert still showing. "You must've done something right."

Tavi briefly explained the meeting, what Ohashi had asked us to do, and the empress's demand that Torran return to Valovia. Eli's disgust was easy to see, but the Valoffs were harder to read.

"So Ohashi wants us to clean up her mess? Typical," Eli scoffed. "Fucking Feds."

"We have the chance to make a difference," I said.

"We have the chance to *die*," he corrected. "You know I love you, but even considering it is madness."

"War affects us all," I said. "Our families, our friends, and millions of other people we don't know but who don't deserve the trauma we went through."

"Who are we to stop two fucking superpowers hell-bent on destruction? Look around. What chance do we have? For once in your life, be realistic," he snapped.

I flinched at the unexpected attack and tears filled my eyes. Varro wrapped an arm around my waist and pulled me against his side, a wall of solid support I leaned on as one of my best friends cut the legs from beneath me.

But after a breath, I straightened. "No," I said, swiping furious a hand across my traitorous eyes. "If being 'realistic' means forgetting about everyone we can help, then I refuse. Maybe we'll get ourselves killed before we make a difference, but if we do nothing, then we're no better than the fucking FHP. Maybe you're okay with that, but *I'm not*."

I jabbed a finger at my chest. "*I* choose to fight for what I believe in, even when the odds are against me, and if that's not realistic, then I don't fucking care. You can't change the world by being realistic."

I could *feel* Varro's pride echoing across our link, but the rest of the crew stood in stunned silence.

Eli blew out a heavy breath and bowed his head. "You're absolutely right, and I'm sorry. I should not have snapped at you. Your compassion is one of your greatest strengths, as you've proven time and again." His mouth twisted into a sheepish smile. "Sometimes I get so caught up in worrying about you that my brain short-circuits, and I forget that you're perfectly able to take care of yourself. I apologize. Please forgive me."

I summoned a wobbly smile. "I *am* able to take care of myself, but that doesn't mean I don't appreciate your care. Just don't try to smother me. And don't yell at me because I'm on team fix-this-shit rather than team status quo."

Eli winced. "You know I don't love the status quo."

"But are you willing to do anything about it?" I demanded softly.

Tavi cleared her throat before the argument devolved further. "Neither option is perfect. We are uniquely suited to retrieving Morten, or at least ensuring Empress Nepru can't use him as a pawn, but we've also already served our time fighting for a government that doesn't care about us. And we've fought Fev twice now and barely escaped both times."

Torran stepped up next to her, and the captain met our

eyes, one by one, her expression grim. "Each of you needs to decide your path forward, no pressure, no expectations. Torran and I are going. If you all decide to stay, then we'll take a passenger ship from Bastion, and I'll leave *Starlight* with you."

A shocked silence followed her pronouncement, then everyone started talking at once, an indecipherable cacophony of sound. Tavi waved her hands until the room quieted. "You don't have to decide right now, but I will need to know in the next hour or so. Think about it. This will be the most dangerous thing we've attempted since the war."

"Third time's the charm," I said. "I'm not letting you go alone."

"You should think ab—" Tavi started.

"None of us are letting you go alone," Chira said. She nudged Eli, who was next to her. "Not even this pessimist."

"No pressuring each other," Tavi admonished. "Everyone needs to decide for themselves."

Eli rolled his eyes. "Like I'd let you all sail off into certain death without me."

The rest of the crew nodded, except for Varro, whose expression remained as impenetrable as stone, and even our connection offered no insight into what he was thinking. It would break my heart to leave him behind, but he had to make his own decision, and I wouldn't pressure him to decide the way I wanted.

No matter how much it hurt.

Tavi's relief was plain, so I put aside my worry, painted on a mischievous grin, and asked, "How many more credits do you think we can wring out of Ohashi?"

CHAPTER THIRTY-FIVE

We returned to the galley, where our four guests were waiting with tense anticipation. "Is everything okay?" Nick asked, gaze darting across the group to gauge our expressions. "I saw the alert. Congrats on no longer being wanted criminals."

Eli grumbled something unintelligible beneath his breath, so I said, "The admiral cleared our names because she wants us to retrieve Commodore Morten from Fev."

Nick's eyes widened. "And you *agreed*?"

"*Thank* you," Eli grumbled. "Finally someone who gets it."

"I thought Fev was headed to Valovian space," Liang said. His expression went distant as he telepathically conversed with one of the other Valoffs. After a moment, he turned to Tavi. "I would like to join you on your trip to Valovia, if you'll have me. For obvious reasons, returning with Siarvez is not the best plan, but I need to get back."

“You are always welcome with me,” Siarvez protested.

Liang smiled softly. “And I appreciate it, but I don’t want to put you in danger.”

“Yet you don’t mind putting *us* in danger?” Eli asked, eyebrows high.

“You’re already going to be in danger, but you also have a guarantee of safe passage. Even if Empress Nepru suspects that I’m on board, she can’t do anything about it until I leave the ship.”

Tavi glanced at Torran. They communicated silently for a moment, then Tavi said, “You’re welcome to come with us, but our main objective is retrieving Morten. If Fev doesn’t head directly for Valovia, neither will we.”

Liang bowed, his left arm across his chest. “I understand. Thank you.”

Tavi nodded, then turned to Anna. “Has your ship launched yet?”

Anna shook her head. “They are still awaiting clearance. Everything is being handled manually, so it takes ten times as long.”

“Would you mind waiting on Siarvez’s ship, assuming he agrees? Once we have a contract with the admiral, we’ll need to leave immediately to catch up with Fev.”

“Anna and Nick are welcome to join me on *Loddat* until their ship is ready,” Siarvez said. “I have a very nice bottle of wine that will help pass the time.”

When Anna inclined her head in thanks, Tavi turned to Eli. “Work with Siarvez to dock with *Loddat* as soon as possible.”

Eli nodded and the two men left for the bridge.

Tavi sighed and rubbed her face. “I can’t believe we’re doing this,” she murmured.

I nudged her shoulder. "You know it's the right call."

"That doesn't mean it isn't fucking terrifying. I'm about to lead everyone I love straight into enemy territory."

"And we all knew the risks when we agreed to join you."

Tavi pulled me into a one-armed hug. "Thank you."

"Has Ohashi sent the money for the key yet?"

Tavi checked her comm and nodded. "One hundred twenty thousand credits, just like we agreed. If we bring her Morten, do you think she really can make a difference?"

"I don't know," I admitted, "but I hope so. And by the time we arrive at the wormhole, I'll know everything about her. If she's not being honest, we'll know before we commit. For now, though, I'll send her the key and see what happens."

Tavi smiled. "Good luck."

I waved to everyone in the galley, then headed for my control room. Varro followed me, and once the door closed behind us, I turned toward him and shoved my hands in my pockets to keep from reaching for him. "Are you planning to stay on Bastion?"

Shock briefly crossed his face before he covered it with a blank mask. "You think I would let you head into danger alone?"

"You shouldn't base your decision on mine." The words cut like glass, but I forced them out.

He tilted his head and stared at me like I was a puzzle he could solve if only he looked long enough. "Why not?"

"Because it *is* going to be dangerous. We might not survive. The empress wants us dead, and we're walking directly into her trap. That's not a decision you should make lightly."

Varro wrapped his arms around me and drew me forward, his touch light enough that I could break free with the merest resistance.

I didn't resist.

His shirt-covered chest was broad and warm against my cheek. I snuggled in closer and squeezed his waist with my arms. I took a deep breath and some of my tension bled away.

"I will always follow you, until you tell me not to," Varro said, his voice a deep rumble. "I hate that you're heading into danger and I might not be able to protect you. But I would never begrudge you following your heart."

"I don't want you to follow me into danger out of a sense of duty," I whispered. "Our debts are settled."

Varro pulled back until he could search my expression. He stroked my jaw with gentle fingers. "You do not understand," he murmured at last, something like relief on his face. "You speak Valovan so well, sometimes I forget that you don't always know our customs."

If he was about to tell me that our debt *wasn't* settled, then we were about to have big problems.

"'*Cho arbu chil tavoz*' is not a phrase a Valoff tosses around lightly," he murmured. "While it literally means 'my heart is yours,' it has a deeper meaning as well."

My breath caught and hope wove delicate tendrils around my heart. "What does it mean?"

"It means that I will commit my life to yours. That I will always be there for you, no matter what. That you are the one for me, my perfect match and partner in all things. It is not a debt; it is a vow: wherever you go, you carry my heart with you."

Tears welled in my eyes, and I blinked them away, unwilling to miss a second of this moment. For the first time, I wasn't the only one rushing headlong into emotion. Varro was right there with me. "I didn't know," I whispered. I choked on a teary laugh. "I thought it just was a nice phrase that meant you liked me."

Varro smiled. "I do like you."

"So what happens if I say it back?" I asked, my voice quiet.

"You will be accepting my vow and making your own. In the future, if we suit, we would pledge a life bond—a marriage."

Varro had essentially just asked me to marry him. Nervous energy fought effervescent joy. I cradled his jaw in my hands. "Varro, I love you. My heart recognized you from the moment I saw you, and your honor, care, and loyalty only proved that my heart is very wise indeed, so I will happily give it to you. *Cho arbu chil tavoz.*"

For a frozen moment, nothing happened. Then Varro smiled, and his whole face lit with the joy I could feel echoing across our link. He reached for me, then paused. "Did you come in here to do something for the captain?"

I blinked at the change in topic, and it took me a second to mentally switch gears. "I need to send the encryption key to Ohashi."

Varro nodded, eyes hot and body taut with longing. "You should send it. We are at least forty minutes from docking with *Loddat,* and I have plans for those minutes."

Heat curled through my system, but I merely raised an eyebrow. "Do you?"

A wicked grin tugged at his lips. "Shall I show you?" I nodded, and rather than reaching for me, he changed something with his mental shield, opening his mind completely to mine. Desire flooded my system, a wave of heat that made me clench my thighs together in need.

"Oh," I breathed. "I see."

He restored the shield, and I reeled at the loss. When I didn't move, Varro nudged me. "The encryption key."

"Right." It took me a long moment to focus, but I found the key and sent it to the admiral along with instructions on how to use it.

"Anything else?"

I looked around, but I couldn't focus on anything. It was like I'd never seen my control room before. "No?" I looked at my comm, but I hadn't set any reminders. "No," I said with more confidence. "I want to say good-bye to Anna, Nick, and Siarvez before they leave, but nothing until then."

Varro's eyes were nearly black as the dark streaks expanded with his emotions. He pulled me back into his arms and whispered, "Good." He lowered his head, and I rose on my tiptoes to meet his lips halfway.

The first touch sent a jolt through my system, and I moaned as my desire climbed higher. I sucked his bottom lip into my mouth and wrapped my hand around the back of his head. His curly hair was soft against my palm, and I smiled against his lips.

"Can you feel how much I want you?" I whispered.

Varro froze and pulled back, wariness on his face. "My shield has been slipping."

I nodded. "More since you were hurt, but it's been happening for a while."

The wariness didn't fade. "You don't mind?"

"I like the connection," I admitted. "I like knowing what you're feeling, knowing that you're there. Even when you were unconscious, I could still feel your presence and I knew you were alive. It gave me hope."

I could feel his relief. Varro pressed a reverent kiss to the corner of my mouth. "I'm glad. Would you like to feel more?"

I tugged him back until I could see his face. "You mean like before? When you let me feel your desire?"

He nodded. "You'll be able to more easily experience what I'm feeling, but I'll also be able to pick up more of your feelings. Is that okay?"

I cupped his jaw. "I *want* you to feel what I'm feeling."

Varro's presence in my mind changed, and his emotions flooded through me. Before, I'd been catching flickers and flashes of emotion, like a distant candle in a large room. Now emotion roared like bonfire. Desire was predominant, but underneath was deep affection tempered by a core of respect. I gazed at him in wonder. I hoped he could feel that my emotions mirrored his own.

He kissed me slowly, thoroughly, as if we had all the time in the world. Our mutual desire flowed between us, growing hotter, burning brighter. He drove me past worry, past thought, past everything except pleasure and joy. One sparked the other in an endless cycle until I ached with the need for him.

If only we had a handy bed. But really, my desk was right here, as was the wall. Hell, even the floor would work in a pinch—I wasn't picky. Varro must've picked up on my thoughts because he pulled back with a delicious smile. His eyes were completely black, and power buzzed in the air around us.

He backed me into the wall, boosting me up so that my legs wrapped around his waist. With his hips pinning me in the most delicious way, his hands were free to roam—and roam they did.

He nuzzled my jaw while his palms glided up my sides, pushing my shirt up as he went. The feel of his skin against mine shorted out my brain, until he was the only thing I knew. This was so much better than any dream.

When he got to my bra, he looked at me, a question in his eyes. I smiled at him, then pulled my shirt over my head, unclasped my bra, and dropped it on the ground.

I hissed as my back touched the cool wall, but the heat in Varro's expression burned away the chill. "I can't believe how lucky I am," he murmured, and I could *feel* his reverence. He cupped my breasts and his thumbs swept across my nipples, sending jolts of sensation sparking across my nerves. "Tell me this isn't a dream."

"Not a dream," I gasped, arching my back, inviting him closer. I sent him a sultry look through my lashes. "But if you'd like to reenact any part of it, I wouldn't stop you."

He breathed out a soft curse and a spike of lust curled my toes. He boosted me higher, then kissed his way down my throat and across my collarbone. I moaned, and he smiled against my skin, then his mouth closed around my nipple and my moan turned into a satisfied groan.

"Yes," I hissed, burying my hands in his hair. Being able to feel his emotions settled some deep part of me that constantly worried if I was moving too fast or feeling too much. If I was, Varro was right there with me.

Distantly, I heard the door slide open, and Varro turned so he was shielding me from view. "Hey, Kee—ah, um, never mind," Anja squeaked, embarrassment in her voice.

The door closed, but the moment was broken. I laughed

and glanced at Varro. "Maybe we should move to my room before we scandalize the ship?"

"I would not object to getting you into a bed," he growled.

"And what would you do when you had me there?" I asked, tightening my legs around his waist. I could feel him, hot and hard against me, and it took all of my focus not to rock mindlessly against him.

Rather than answering, he sent a mental image of me kneeling over him while he did terrible, wicked things with his tongue.

"Yes," I gasped. "Let's do that."

He kissed me, then eased me to my feet and found my shirt. I pulled it over my head, mostly to keep from shocking the crew. Tavi and Eli had seen enough of my skin over the years that they wouldn't even blink, but I wasn't sure how the Valoffs or our guests would react.

I led Varro from the room, impatience in my pace, especially when I could feel his desire as well as my own. I sent Tavi a message letting her know that I was going to be busy until we docked, then turned off my comm.

Once the door closed behind us, butterflies took flight in my stomach. Varro, who was in my head as much as I was in his, ran a hand down my back. "We don't have to do anything you don't want," he reassured.

I smiled at him as my nerves steadied. "I want you, and I want this"—I gestured between us—"but sometimes I get lost in my head and don't notice signs. Let me know if I do something you don't like or are not comfortable with, and I'll do the same."

Varro nodded, and his eyes darkened further. "Get naked," he said, echoing my command from the dream.

The words arrowed straight to my center, but I held on to control with the thinnest thread. "You first."

"As soon as my clothes come off, I'm going to fuck you into oblivion."

Every muscle tightened as I balanced on the edge from his words alone. "Promise?"

His nod was enough to get me moving. I bent and removed my boots and socks, then shimmied out of my pants and underwear, leaving me in only my shirt, which was just long enough to cover everything interesting.

I could feel Varro's control fraying as I played with the hem of his shirt. "Take this off," I whispered. His jaw clenched, but he pulled his shirt over his head, exposing the hard muscles of his chest, still bruised. I touched the darkest one with tentative fingers, my desire dimming. He was still hurt. He shouldn't have been lifting me earlier.

He caught my hand and placed it over his heart. "Havil healed me. These are superficial. You can feel what I'm feeling. Am I hurting?"

I sorted through everything that was coming across our mental connection. He wasn't in *pain,* but he felt the same deep ache that I did. I let my other hand drift to his waistband, then lower. He growled and thrust against my palm before reining himself in.

"It feels awfully cramped in here, maybe you should take off your pants," I suggested in my most innocent voice.

"Kee—" he growled, reaching for my hand.

I pulled away. "And your boots. While you do that, I'll see if I can get my shirt off."

I lifted the hem a centimeter and his gaze glued itself to my bare thighs. When he didn't move, I let the hem fall again. He ground out a curse in Valovan, then bent to remove his boots, socks, and pants.

He left his underwear, a tight pair of black briefs that left nothing to the imagination. I licked my lips and his desire flared brighter. Done with teasing, I pulled my shirt over my head, leaving my body bare.

Varro took a step toward me, then froze, his muscles clenched tight. A deep breath, then he herded me backward, his eyes pitch black. He yanked the blanket and top sheet from the bed, then in a move that proved exactly how strong he was, he picked me up, fell back onto the mattress, and lifted me so that I straddled his chest.

"You with me?" he asked, his voice rough. When I nodded, a sinful smile pulled at his lips. "You may want to brace yourself."

That was all the warning I got before he lifted me up and settled me directly over his mouth. At the first touch of his tongue, I braced a hand against the wall and buried the other in his hair as stars exploded behind my eyes. "Fuck, yes," I moaned.

He pulled me closer, until my entire world narrowed to the movement of his tongue and the gentle rasp of his stubbled cheeks against my inner thighs. My body coiled like a spring, and I tried to pull back, to draw it out, but Varro refused to let me go.

Not that I tried *that* hard.

A moment longer and pleasure crashed over me in a wave that bowed my back and curled my toes. It rippled across our connection before rebounding, even stronger than before. Below me, Varro groaned, and the vibration sent lightning bolting through my belly.

I recovered just long enough to be sure that I could

actually move my limbs, then I carefully crawled back. I leaned down and kissed him on my way by, but I had other destinations in mind.

When I reached his underwear, I looked up in question. He nodded and I peeled it from his body. I stroked him once, twice, then he pulled me up, wrapped an arm around me, and flipped us over, caging me in with his body.

"I warned you what would happen when my clothes came off," he said, his voice dark with promise.

"Yes," I hissed out.

He nudged my legs apart and settled between them. I arched against him, but he pinned me down. Instant heat licked through me, and Varro must've felt it because his smile turned downright sinister. "You like being at my mercy, mine to control."

I whined out a weak denial, but Varro saw through it.

"I'm going to give you what you want, and you're going to take it," he murmured into my ear, his voice pure sin.

A shudder wracked my body, then he was there, pressing exactly where I wanted him. He gave me no quarter, sliding deep in one long thrust, and my muscles fluttered around him.

With Varro caging me in, I felt safe and protected and *adored*. I could let go and let someone else take control, just for a moment.

Tears leaked from my eyes, but Varro, attuned to my every thought and feeling, didn't pull away. "I have you," he murmured.

"I know," I agreed softly, then clenched down on him. "So take me."

The last of his control melted away with a growl. He slipped a hand under my ass, tilting my hips up and hit-ting a place that made me see stars. "That's it," he praised, sending my own pleasure crashing back over me, "take it just like that."

I made a sound that might have been agreement, but I was drunk on pleasure.

Varro found his rhythm, and my world narrowed to the feel of his body and the depth of his care as they worked in tandem to drive me closer and closer to the edge of oblivion, just as he'd promised.

"Mine!" the primitive part of my brain snarled.

"Yours," Varro agreed. He grunted, his control fraying. "Let go. I've got you."

I trusted him to gather up my pieces, so I shattered, screaming his name, and took him with me into the dark.

CHAPTER THIRTY-SIX

After a few minutes of lazy, emotional afterglow and the world's quickest shower, Varro and I headed to the cargo bay to see Anna, Nick, and Siarvez off. We were met with a host of knowing grins from the rest of the crew.

"Yeah, yeah, go ahead and get it out of your systems," I said, but I couldn't help my own smile, especially when Varro wrapped an arm around my waist.

The crew ribbed us for a few minutes while *Starlight* connected with *Loddat,* and I let them because I loved them and hated good-byes. I knew we couldn't take everyone we met with us, but I kind of wished we could.

I slipped away from Varro and held out the bundle I'd brought for Anna. "These belong to you," I told her. "They're from the exhibition. The dress will need to be cleaned but the crown should be okay."

She shook her head. "You keep them. You deserve them

after all this." She waved her fingers around in a sort of noncommittal gesture that encompassed everything at once. "And I'll make sure Alina sends you the compensation I promised."

"You don't nee—" At her glare, I swallowed the denial and said, "Thank you."

"If you ever want to model for me in the future, you have my card. Hopefully next time won't be quite so explosive."

"It's too bad the attack overshadowed the clothes," I said. "They were amazing."

"Are you kidding?" Siarvez interjected. "You couldn't *pay* for this kind of publicity. Photos and videos from the event have been all over the news for days, and not just the fashion news."

Anna nodded. "All's well that ends well, and this should give the new line a nice little boost."

Nick rolled their eyes but looked at Anna with fond exasperation. When Anna turned to speak to Tavi, I grinned at Nick and mouthed, "Good luck."

Nick's chin dipped in wry acknowledgment, then they raised a hand in farewell.

"Thanks for your help," I said, echoing the gesture. "I hope your next job isn't as exciting."

Nick's expression softened as they watched Anna talk to Tavi. "I don't know," they murmured. "This wasn't so bad."

I suppressed my smile. Someone here had it bad, all right.

Siarvez stepped in front of me and bowed with his left arm across his chest. "It was a pleasure to meet you, Ms. Ildez."

"You, too. I hope you have a safe trip home."

Siarvez bent closer. "Watch out for Liang," he murmured. "He's more upset than he lets on."

"I will," I assured him.

"And take care of yourself. If you ever need anything, I remain in your debt."

I shook a warning finger at him. "I'm done with debts. Unless you ever have any designer clothes that need a new home, then I wouldn't say no to a loan or two."

Siarvez's eyes sparkled. "A woman after my own heart. Come and find me after your next adventure. Bring your crew."

"I will."

"Then I'll look forward to it. Farewell." He bowed, and I nodded to him.

Liang and Siarvez spoke for a few minutes, then everyone said their final farewells. Tears misted my eyes as Anna, Nick, and Siarvez crossed the airlock tunnel to *Loddat.* Varro pulled me into his arms. "They're okay because of you," he murmured.

"Because of *us,* and the whole crew."

I blinked away the tears as Tavi closed the hatch and disconnected us from the other ship. "Have you heard back from the admiral?" I asked her.

"She upped the contract price to a million five."

I whistled. "Damn. Someone wants Morten caught."

Tavi's face clouded as she nodded. "He might be a traitor, but he also knows something the FHP doesn't want to get to Empress Nepru."

"You think Ohashi is double-crossing us?" Eli asked.

"No," Tavi said, "but I think her superiors might not be as on board with the traitor removal as she is. But she swears she has support, and I believe her, to a certain extent."

"I'll start digging," I said.

Tavi looked over my shoulder at Varro. "Are you sure? Maybe you should take some time—"

"I understand Kee still has duties to the crew, and I would never interfere with them," Varro said.

I smiled at him over my shoulder. "What he said. Don't worry about us. We'll make it work."

Tavi pulled me into a hug. "I'm glad," she whispered. "And don't think I'm not going to corner you later with a bottle of wine for all the details. You're *glowing*."

I laughed and squeezed her tight. "You would be, too, if you'd just spent the last thirty minutes getting your mind blown completely out of your body in record time. In fact, I remember a certain captain sporting a very similar look just recently."

Tavi flushed as she let me go, but she couldn't hide the satisfied gleam in her eyes. "Let me know what you find on Ohashi. I'm going to get us heading toward the wormhole."

I nodded, and the rest of the crew cleared out, leaving Varro and me alone. I snuggled into his arms. "Thank you for understanding."

"Of course. We're both still part of the crew, and there will be times when that takes precedence." He brushed a tiny, light kiss over the corner of my mouth. "So we'll just have to make it up later."

"I have plans for later. Would you like to see?" When he nodded, I clearly pictured myself on my knees in front of him while he stood with his head thrown back, his body arched in ecstasy.

Varro's hands clenched against my back. "I like your plans."

"I thought you might."

He reluctantly let me go. "Find everything you can about Ohashi, then come find me. You owe me a fantasy."

I kissed him and retreated to my engineering control room.

I HAD TO GIVE OHASHI CREDIT: SHE'D GOTTEN BASTION UP AND running in record time after she'd received the encryption key.

By the time I sat down at my terminal, the station was already directing traffic again. I used my access, which thankfully still worked, to pull down some of the most pertinent surveillance vids of the attack just in case they were inconveniently "lost" in the chaos.

Then I started digging into Ohashi herself, along with her command chain. I spent hours tracking down details on her, and the deeper I dug, the more I thought she was genuine. Her communications, both public and private, backed up her position, and she'd removed more than one questionable officer under her command.

Her command chain was more of a mixed bag, but Ohashi, at least, really wanted the traitors removed and she had the ear of a few powerful people high in FHP Command. All of what she'd told us was true.

I searched until I couldn't keep my eyes open anymore, then sent a summary to Tavi to review before deciding if we should cross into Valovian space or not.

Then I dragged myself to my bunk. I was halfway across the room before I realized that my bed wasn't empty.

Varro was sprawled across half the mattress, his head on a second pillow that definitely hadn't been there before.

I stripped out of my clothes as warmth filled my chest. We hadn't talked about it, but I was glad he was here.

I got ready for bed, then eased in next to him, trying not to wake him. I failed, and he blinked at me, his gaze fuzzy with fatigue. "Did you find what you needed?"

"Yes, go back to sleep."

He curled around me, tucking me against his chest. "I hope you don't mind that I'm here, but if you do, I'll leave."

"I like you here," I whispered.

He nuzzled my shoulder. "Good, because I like being here."

A SHIP-WIDE ALARM WOKE ME AFTER A NIGHT THAT WAS FAR TOO short. I listened as the alarm repeated. Tavi wanted us on the bridge in thirty minutes. I tried to sit up, but a heavy weight across my waist kept me pinned in place. I blinked at the tan arm for a second before I remembered that Varro had been waiting in bed for me.

Heat flushed through me as I remembered what we'd used the bed for before that.

Varro pressed a kiss against the back of my shoulder. "Good morning."

"Good morning to you, too. I'm glad you're not a dream."

Varro's hand slid up to cup my breast, and he pinched my nipple gently. "Could a dream do this?"

I gasped and arched. "Maybe a very good one."

He hummed deep in his chest and pulled me over on my back. "What about this?" His mouth latched onto my breast and each tug of his lips against my nipple sent sparks fizzing along my nerves.

"Ah . . . maybe?" I smiled. "I think I had a dream like this once."

He hummed again and I shut my eyes against the flood of pleasure. He pressed kisses from my sternum down across my belly, and lower still, until pleasure threatened to blot out everything.

"Wait," I gasped, tugging on his hair. "Come with me."

"Flip over."

I nearly kicked him in my haste and we both laughed. The laughter turned to a moan as Varro pulled me up on my knees, then his thick length pressed home, his big hands clenched around my waist.

Fuck me, but that felt good. He could wake me up like this every day for the rest of our lives.

Varro groaned as he caught the thought, but rather than being alarmed that I was already thinking long-term, I could feel his control unraveling, which pushed my own desire higher. He accepted me for who I was, impulsiveness and all. He rocked against me, gently at first, then harder, until every stroke caused fireworks to race across my nerves.

"Touch yourself," he ordered, his voice tight with tension.

The order itself was nearly enough to get me there, but I dropped my shoulders to the bed, which made him feel even better. My fingers glided through slick heat, building the pleasure until the world disappeared in an explosion of bliss.

Varro groaned from deep in his chest as he felt me clench around him, then he followed me into pleasure.

WE WERE ONLY *SLIGHTLY* LATE TO THE MEETING. TAVI RAISED HER eyebrows, but she didn't call us on it—especially because Torran arrived even later than us, his hair wet from the shower. I shot Tavi a significant glance, but she merely gave me a satisfied grin and said nothing.

Once everyone had arrived, Tavi stood with Luna in her arms. The little burbu didn't like wormholes, and neither did the Valoffs on the crew. Wormholes made them antsy, and since Varro and I were connected, I felt a ghostly echo of the low-level hum in the air. I shivered. No wonder they hated being around them.

"Kee researched Ohashi last night," Tavi said, "and the admiral is legit. Her command chain is more questionable, but that's to be expected. Morten knows something that the Feds are desperate to keep from Empress Nepru, and at this point, we're the best chance of catching him. *Victory* traversed the wormhole approximately six hours ago."

"Any idea what's awaiting us on the other side?" Eli asked.

Tavi deferred to Torran. "If Fev sent a message to the empress that we're in pursuit, then we might have an escort waiting for us," he said. "If not, we have a writ of safe passage, so we *should* be allowed through without issue."

"And in a bit of good news, I heard back from Lexi. She's going to meet us on Valovia, mostly because she's already there as we speak."

A shocked murmur ran through the room. "Did she say why?" I asked.

Tavi shook her head. "I have to assume it's for a job."

"Or for a certain green-eyed teleporter," Eli grumbled.

My eyebrows rose. Lexi and Nilo had gotten along as well as oil and water. They were exactly alike, which meant they knew exactly how to get under each other's skin.

Tavi slashed a hand through the air to cut off the speculation. "Whatever the reason, we'll have a little extra backup. But that doesn't change the decision you need to make now. If you've changed your mind or thought of a reason we shouldn't go, now is your chance to speak," Tavi said. "There is a Fed ship standing by that Ohashi assures me is loyal to her. They will return you to Bastion, no questions asked. You can choose not to go for any reason." Her gaze cut to Varro and me. "You don't need to explain yourself."

Varro slipped his hand into mine, and I clutched it. In truth, going back into Valovian space scared the shit out of me, but I would hate myself if we didn't at least try.

Tavi waited, but no one said anything aloud and the comm stayed quiet, too. She blew out a heavy breath and gave us a grim smile. "Let's go catch a traitor."

Varro pulled me into his side, love and worry echoing across our connection. I felt the same. But no matter what happened, we'd face it together, with the rest of our crew.

Morten and Fev wouldn't know what hit them.

Want to go on another adventure with the Starlight's Shadow crew? Catch up with the gang in *Capture the Sun*, as mysterious Lexi Bowen and sexy Nilo Shoren get their love story.

Coming out early 2023

ABOUT THE AUTHOR

Jessie Mihalik has a degree in computer science and a love of all things geeky. A software engineer by trade, Jessie now writes full-time from her home in Texas. When she's not writing, she can be found playing co-op video games with her husband, trying out new board games, or reading books pulled from her overflowing bookshelves.